THE
UNIVERSE
VERSUS
ALEX WOODS

GAVIN EXTENCE

HODDER

First published in Great Britain in 2013 by Hodder & Stoughton
An Hachette UK Company

First published in paperback in Great Britain in 2013
1

A CIP catalogue record for this title is available from the British Library.

B-format paperback ISBN 9781444765892
A-format paperback ISBN 9781444768923

Printed and bound by Clays Ltd, St Ives plc ——

Hodder & Stoughton policy is to use papers that are natural, renewable and
recyclable products and made from wood grown in sustainable forests.
The logging and manufacturing processes are expected to conform to the
environmental regulations of the country of origin.

Hodder & Stoughton Ltd
338 Euston Road
London NW1 3BH

www.hodder.co.uk

'AN EXT...   ...E BOOKBAG

'THIS IS A STORY THAT WILL HAVE YOU SMILING
   ...OUGH YOUR TEARS ... UNFORGETTABLE'
                                                          RED

...NE OF THE FUNNIEST AND MOST
...EARTBREAKING DOUBLE ACTS IN
...GES ... AN EXCEPTIONALLY GOOD
...EBUT NOVEL 5*'
                                                          HEAT

...ALLY LOVELY DEBUT. VERY INTERESTING, SLIGHTLY
...IRKY STORY ... HANDS TO MY FACE CRYING'
                                                GRAHAM NORTON

...EX'S STORY TREADS THE FINE LINE BETWEEN
...GHT AND DARK, LAUGHTER AND TEARS'
                                                           GQ

...TH WRITING THAT IS LOGICAL YET LYRICAL, COMIC
...T COMPASSIONATE, GAVIN EXTENCE HAS REVEALED
...E SIMPLE BEAUTY OF LAUGHTER, FRIENDSHIP, LOVE
...D REASON'
                                                         LITRO

...UNNY, TOUCHING ... EXTENCE UNFOLDS
...S OFFBEAT TALE WITH SKILL BUT HIS
...AL TRIUMPH LIES IN PROVIDING SUCH
...A MEMORABLE VOICE'
                                              THE SUNDAY TIMES

For Alix, without whom this book would not exist.

ENTENDER

They finally stopped me at Dover as I was trying to get back into the country. I was half expecting it, but it still came as kind of a shock when the barrier stayed down. It's funny how some things can be so mixed up like that. Having come this far, I'd started to think that I might make it the whole way home after all. It would have been nice to have been able to explain things to my mother. You know: before anyone else had to get involved.

It was 1 a.m., and it was raining. I'd rolled Mr Peterson's car up to the booth in the 'Nothing to Declare' lane, where a single customs officer was on duty. His weight rested on his elbows, his chin was cupped in his hands, and, but for this crude arrangement of scaffolding, his whole body looked ready to fall like a sack of potatoes to the floor. The graveyard shift – dreary dull from dusk till dawn – and for a few heartbeats it seemed that the customs officer lacked the willpower necessary to rotate his eyeballs and check my credentials. But then the moment collapsed. His gaze shifted; his eyes widened. He signalled for me to wait and spoke into his walkie-talkie, rapidly and with obvious agitation. That was the instant I knew for sure. I found out later that my picture had been circulated in every major port from Aberdeen to Plymouth. With that and the TV appeals, I never stood a chance.

What I remember next is kind of muddled and strange, but I'll try to describe it for you as best I can.

The side door of the booth was swinging open and at the same moment there washed over me the scent of a field full of lilacs. It came on just like that, from nowhere, and I knew straight away that I'd have to concentrate extra hard to stay in the present. In hindsight, an episode like this had been on the cards for a while. You have to bear in mind that I hadn't slept properly for several days, and Bad Sleeping Habits has always been one of my triggers. Stress is another.

I looked straight ahead and I focussed. I focussed on the windscreen wipers moving back and forth and tried to count my breaths, but by the time I'd got to five, it was pretty clear that this wasn't going to be enough. Everything was becoming slow and blurry. I had no choice but to turn the stereo up to maximum. Handel's *Messiah* flooded the car – the 'Hallelujah' chorus, loud enough to rattle the exhaust. I hadn't planned it or anything. I mean, if I'd had time to prepare for this, I'd have chosen something simpler and calmer and quieter: Chopin's nocturnes or one of Bach's cello suites, perhaps. But I'd been working my way through Mr Peterson's music collection since Zurich, and it just so happened that at that precise moment I was listening to *that* precise section of Handel's *Messiah* – like it was Fate's funny joke. Of course, this did me no favours later on: the customs officer gave a full report to the police in which he said that for a long time I'd resisted detention, that I'd just sat there 'staring into the night and listening to religious music at full volume, like he was the Angel of Death or something'. You've probably heard that quote already. It was in all the papers – they have a real boner for details like that. But you should understand that at the time I didn't have a choice. I could see the customs officer in my peripheral vision, hunchbacked at my window in his bright yellow jacket, but I forced myself to ignore him. He shone his torch in my eyes, and I ignored that too. I just kept staring straight ahead and focussing on the music. That was my anchor. The lilacs were still there, trying their best to distract me. The Alps were starting to intrude – jagged, frosted memories, as sharp as needles. I swaddled them in the music. I kept telling myself that there was nothing *but* the music. There was nothing but the strings and the drums and the trumpets, and all those countless voices singing out God's praises. I know in retrospect that I must have looked pretty suspicious, just sitting there like that with my eyes glazed and the music loud enough to wake the dead. It must have sounded like I had the entire London Symphony Orchestra performing on the back seat. But what could I do? When you get an aura that powerful, there's no chance of it passing of its own accord: to be honest with you, there were several moments when I was right on the precipice. I was just a hair's breadth from convulsions.

But after a while, the crisis abated. Something slipped back into gear. I was dimly aware that the torch beam had moved on. It was now frozen on the space two feet to my left, though I was too frazzled to figure out why at the time. It was only later that I remembered Mr Peterson was still in the passenger seat. I hadn't thought to move him.

* * *

The moments ticked on, and eventually the torchlight swung away. I managed to turn my head forty-five degrees and saw that the customs officer was again speaking into his walkie-talkie, palpably excited. Then he tapped the torch against the window and made an urgent downwards gesture. I don't remember pushing the button, but I do remember the rush of cold, damp air as the glass rolled down. The customs officer mouthed something, but I couldn't make it out. The next thing I knew, he'd reached through the open window and flipped off the ignition. The engine stopped, and a second later, the last hallelujah died on the night air. I could hear the hiss of drizzle on tarmac, fading in slowly, like reality resolving itself. The customs officer was speaking too, and waving his arms in all these weird, wobbly gestures, but my brain wasn't able to decode any of that yet. Right then, there was something else going on – a thought that was fumbling its way towards the light. It took me for ever to organize my ideas into words, but when I finally got there, this is what I said: 'Sir, I should tell you that I'm no longer in a fit state to drive. I'm afraid you'll have to find someone else to move the car for me.'

For some reason, that seemed to choke him. His face went through a whole series of strange contortions, and then for a very long time he just stood there with his mouth open. If it had been me standing there with my mouth open, it would have been considered pretty rude, but I don't think it's worth getting too uptight about things like that. So I just waited. I'd said what I needed to say, and it had taken considerable effort. I didn't mind being patient now.

When he'd cleared his airways, the customs officer told me that I had to get out of the car and come with him straight away. But the funny thing was, as soon as he said it, I realized that I wasn't quite ready to move yet. My hands were still locked white on the steering wheel, and they showed no signs of relinquishing their grip. I asked if I could possibly have a minute.

'Son,' the customs officer said, 'I need you to come *now*.'

I glanced across at Mr Peterson. Being called 'son' was not a good omen. I thought I was probably in a Whole Heap of Shit.

My hands unlocked.

I managed to get out of the car, reeled and then leaned up against the side for a few seconds. The customs officer tried to get me to move, but I told him that unless he wanted to carry me, he'd have to give me a moment to find my feet. The drizzle was prickling the exposed skin on my neck and face, and small tears of rain were beginning to bead on my clothing. I could feel all my sensations regrouping. I asked how long it had been raining. The customs officer looked at me but didn't reply. The look said that he wasn't interested in small talk.

A police car came and took me away to a room called Interview Room C in Dover Police Station, but first I had to wait in a small Portakabin back in the main part of the port. I had to wait for a long time. I saw a lot of different officers from the Port Authority, but no one really talked to me. They just kept giving me all these very simple two-word instructions, like 'wait here' and 'don't move', and telling me what was going to happen to me next, like they were the chorus in one of those Ancient Greek plays. And after every utterance, they'd immediately ask me if I understood, like I was some kind of imbecile or something. To be honest with you, I might have given them that impression. I don't know. I still hadn't recovered from my seizure. I was tired, my co-ordination was shot, and on the whole I felt pretty disconnected, like my head had been packed with cotton wool. I was thirsty too, but I didn't want to ask if there was a vending machine I might use in case they thought I was trying to be clever with them. As you probably know, when you're in trouble already, you can ask a simple, legitimate question like that and end up in even more trouble. I don't know why. It's like you cross this invisible line and suddenly people don't want to acknowledge that everyday things like vending machines or Diet Coke exist any more. I guess some situations are supposed to be so grave that people don't want to trivialize them with carbonated drinks.

Anyway, eventually a police car came and took me away to Interview Room C, where my situation was in no way improved. Interview Room C was not much larger than a cupboard and had been designed with minimum comfort in mind. The walls and floor were bare. There was a rectangular table with four plastic chairs, and a tiny window that didn't look like it opened, high up on the back wall. There was a smoke alarm and a CCTV camera in one corner, close to the ceiling. But that was it as far as furnishings were concerned. There wasn't even a clock.

I was seated and then left alone for what seemed like a very long time. I think maybe that was deliberate, to try to make me feel restless or uncomfortable, but really I've got no definite grounds for thinking that. It's just a hypothesis. Luckily, I'm very happy in my own company, and pretty adept at keeping my mind occupied. I have about a million different exercises to help me stay calm and focussed.

When you're tired but need to stay alert, you really need

something a bit tricky to keep your mind ticking over. So I started to conjugate my irregular Spanish verbs, starting in the simple present and then gradually working my way through to the more complicated tenses. I didn't say them aloud, because of the CCTV camera, but I voiced them in my head, still taking care with the accent and stresses. I was on *entiendas*, the informal second-person present subjunctive of *entender* (to understand), when the door opened and two policemen walked in. One was the policeman who had driven me from the port, and he was carrying a clipboard with some papers attached to it. The other policeman I hadn't seen before. They both looked pissed off.

'Good morning, Alex,' said the police officer whom I didn't know. 'I'm Chief Inspector Hearse. You've already met Deputy Inspector Cunningham.'

'Yes,' I said. 'Hello.'

I'm not going to bother describing Chief Inspector Hearse or Deputy Inspector Cunningham for you at any great length. Mr Treadstone, my old English teacher, used to say that when you're writing about a person, you don't need to describe every last thing about him or her. Instead, you should try to give just one telling detail to help the reader picture the character. Chief Inspector Hearse had a mole the size of a five-pence piece on his right cheek. Deputy Inspector Cunningham had the shiniest shoes I've ever seen.

They sat down opposite, and gestured that I should sit down too. That was when I realized that I'd stood up when they walked in the room. That's one of the things they taught you at my school – to stand up whenever an adult enters the room. It's meant to demonstrate respect, I guess, but after a while, you just do it without thinking.

They looked at me for quite a long time without saying anything. I wanted to look away, but I thought that might seem rude, so I just kept looking straight back and waited.

'You know, Alex,' Chief Inspector Hearse said finally, 'you've created quite a stir over the past week or so. You've become quite the celebrity . . .'

Straight away, I didn't like the way this was going. I had no idea what he expected me to say. Some things there's no sensible response to, so I just kept my mouth shut. Then I shrugged, which wasn't the cleverest thing to do, but it's very difficult to do nothing in situations like that.

Chief Inspector Hearse scratched his mole. Then he said: 'You realize that you're in a lot of trouble?'

It might have been a question; it might have been a statement. I nodded anyway, just in case.

'And you know *why* you're in trouble?'

'Yes. I suppose so.'

'You understand that this is serious?'

'Yes.'

Chief Inspector Hearse looked across at Deputy Inspector Cunningham, who hadn't said anything yet. Then he looked at me again. 'You know, Alex, some of your actions over the past hour suggest otherwise. I think if you realized how serious this was, you'd be a lot more worried than you appear to be. Let me tell you, if I was sitting where you are now, I think I'd be a lot more worried than you appear to be.'

He should have said 'if I *were* sitting where you are now' – I noticed because I already had the subjunctive on my mind – but I didn't correct him. People don't like to be corrected about things like that. That was one of the things Mr Peterson always told me. He said that correcting people's grammar in the middle of a conversation made me sound like a Major Prick.

'Tell me, Alex,' Chief Inspector Hearse went on, '*are* you worried? You seem a little too calm – a little too casual – all things considered.'

'I can't really afford to let myself get too stressed out,' I said. 'It's not very good for my health.'

Chief Inspector Hearse exhaled at length. Then he looked at Deputy Inspector Cunningham and nodded. Deputy Inspector Cunningham handed him a sheet of paper from the clipboard.

'Alex, we've been through your car. I think you'll agree that there are several things we need to discuss.'

I nodded. I could think of one thing in particular. But then Chief Inspector Hearse surprised me: he didn't ask what I thought he was going to ask. Instead, he asked me to confirm, as a matter of record, my full name and date of birth. That threw me for about a second. All things considered, it seemed like a waste of time. They already knew who I was: they had my passport. There was no reason not to cut to the chase. But, really, I didn't have much choice but to go along with whatever game they were playing.

'Alexander Morgan Woods,' I said. 'Twenty-third of the ninth, 1993.'

I'm not too enamoured with my full name, to be honest with you, especially the middle part. But most people just call me Alex, like the policemen did. When you're called Alexander, hardly anyone bothers with your full name. My mother doesn't bother. She goes one syllable further than everyone else and just calls me Lex, as in Lex Luthor – and you should know that she was calling me that long before I lost my hair. After that, I think she started to regard my name as prophetic; before, she just thought it was sweet.

Chief Inspector Hearse frowned and then looked at Deputy Inspector Cunningham again and nodded. He kept doing that, like he was the magician and Deputy Inspector Cunningham was his assistant with all the props.

Deputy Inspector Cunningham took from the back of his clipboard a clear plastic bag, which he then tossed into the centre of the table, where it landed with a quiet slap. It was extremely dramatic, it really was. And you could tell that they *wanted* it to be dramatic. The police have all sorts of psychological tricks like that. You probably know that already if you ever watch TV.

'Approximately one hundred and thirteen grams of marijuana,' Chief Inspector Hearse intoned, 'retrieved from your glove compartment.'

I'm going to level with you: I'd completely forgotten about the marijuana. The fact is, I hadn't even opened the glove compartment since Switzerland. I'd had no reason to. But you try telling the police something like that at around 2 a.m. when you've just been stopped at customs.

'That's a lot of pot, Alex. Is it *all* for personal use?'

'No . . .' I changed my mind. 'Actually, yes. I mean, it was for personal use, but not for *my* personal use.'

Chief Inspector Hearse raised his eyebrows about a foot. 'You're saying that this one hundred and thirteen grams of marijuana *isn't* for you?'

'No. It was Mr Peterson's.'

'I see,' said Chief Inspector Hearse. Then he scratched his mole again and shook his head. 'You should know that we also found quite a bit of money in your car.' He looked down at the inventory sheet. 'Six hundred and forty-five Swiss francs, eighty-two euros and a further three hundred and eighteen pounds sterling. Found in an envelope in the driver's side-compartment, next to your passport. That's quite a lot of cash for a seventeen-year-old to be carrying, wouldn't you say?'

I didn't say anything.

'Alex, this is very important. What *exactly* were you planning to do with this one hundred and thirteen grams of marijuana?'

I thought about this for quite a long time. 'I don't know. I wasn't planning anything. I guess I probably would've thrown it away. Or maybe I would have given it away. I don't know.'

'You might have *given* it away?'

I shrugged. I thought it would have made quite a good gift for Ellie. She would've probably appreciated it. But I kept this to myself. 'I've got no personal interest in it,' I affirmed. 'I mean, I enjoyed growing it, but that was all. I certainly wouldn't have kept it.'

Deputy Inspector Cunningham started coughing very loudly. It was the first sound that had come from him and it made me jump a bit. I'd thought perhaps he was a mute or something.

'You grew it?'

'I grew it on Mr Peterson's behalf,' I clarified.

'I see. You grew it, then gave it away. It was basically a charitable enterprise?'

'No. I mean, I never really owned it in the first place. It always belonged to Mr Peterson, so I was in no position to give it away. Like I said, I just grew it.'

'Yes. You grew it but you have no *personal* interest in the substance itself?'

'Only a pharmacological one.'

Chief Inspector Hearse looked at Deputy Inspector Cunningham, then tapped his fingers on the tabletop for about a minute. 'Alex, I'm going to ask you one more time,' he said. 'Do you take drugs? Are you on drugs right now?'

'No.'

'Have you *ever* taken drugs?'

'No.'

'Right. Then there's something you'll have to clear up for me.' Deputy Inspector Cunningham handed him another sheet of paper. 'We talked to the gentleman who stopped you at customs. He says that you were acting very strangely. He says that when he tried to detain you, you refused to co-operate. In fact, he says, and I quote, "The suspect turned up the music in his car until it was so loud that they probably heard it in France. Then he proceeded to ignore me for the next few minutes. He was staring straight ahead and his eyes looked glazed. When I eventually managed to get him to leave his vehicle, he told me that he was not in a fit state to drive."'

Chief Inspector Hearse put the sheet of paper down and looked at me. 'You want to explain that for us, Alex?'

'I have temporal lobe epilepsy,' I explained. 'I was having a partial seizure.'

Chief Inspector Hearse raised his eyebrows again and then frowned very deeply, like this was the last thing he wanted to hear. 'You have epilepsy?'

'Yes.'

'No one told me anything about that.'

'I've had it since I was ten. It started right after my accident.'

I touched my scar. 'When I was ten years old, I was—'

Chief Inspector Hearse nodded impatiently. 'Yes. I know about your accident. *Everyone* knows about your accident. But no one mentioned epilepsy to me.'

I shrugged. 'I've been seizure-free for almost two years.'

'But you're saying that you had a seizure earlier, in the car?'

'Yes. That's why I'm no longer in a fit state to drive.'

Chief Inspector Hearse looked at me for a very long time and then shook his head. 'You know, Mr Knowles gave us quite a detailed report, and he never once mentioned that you'd had a seizure. And I think that's the kind of thing he would have mentioned, don't you? He said that you sat perfectly still and didn't look at all agitated. He said you looked a little too calm, given the circumstances.'

Chief Inspector Hearse had a real thing about me being too calm.

'It was a *partial* seizure,' I said. 'I didn't lose consciousness and I didn't have any convulsions. I managed to stop it before it spread too far.'

'And that's the full explanation?' Chief Inspector Hearse asked. 'If I run a blood test right now, it will come back clean? You haven't been taking drugs?'

'Only carbamazepine.'

'Which is?'

'It's an anti-epileptic,' I said.

Chief Inspector Hearse looked ready to spit. He thought I was being funny. He told me that even if I was telling the truth, even if I *did* have temporal lobe epilepsy and I *had* had a complex partial seizure, that still didn't go nearly far enough to explaining my behaviour, not to his mind. They'd found one hundred and thirteen grams of marijuana in my glove compartment and I wasn't taking that fact nearly seriously enough.

'I don't think it's that serious,' I admitted. 'Not in the grand scheme of things.'

Chief Inspector Hearse shook his head for about ten minutes and then said that possession of a controlled substance with probable intent to supply was a Very Big Deal indeed, and if I told him otherwise, then either I was trying to be funny or I was, without question, the most naïve seventeen-year-old he'd ever met in his life.

'I'm not being naïve,' I said. 'You think one way; I think another. It's a genuine difference of opinion.'

Needless to say, they wouldn't let the drugs thing go for ages. It was a strange situation where the more open and honest I tried to be, the more convinced they became that I was lying. Eventually, I told them that I *wanted* to take a blood test: I figured they could argue with me until Judgment Day, but they couldn't argue with science. But by the time I was demanding my right to a blood test, I think they had pretty much decided to move on anyway. The fact is, we still had one more thing to discuss. It should have been the very first item on the agenda, but like I've said, the police can be pretty dramatic if they think it'll get results.

'The final item on the inventory . . .' Chief Inspector Hearse began. Then he rested his elbows on the table and put his head in his hands. He looked down and didn't say anything for a very long time.

I waited.

'The final item,' Chief Inspector Hearse began again, 'is one small silver urn – retrieved from the passenger seat. Weight approximately four point eight kilograms.'

To be honest with you, I'm not sure why they bothered weighing it.

'Alex, I have to ask: the contents of that urn . . .'

Chief Inspector Hearse looked straight in my eyes and didn't say anything. It was pretty clear that he *wasn't* going to ask, despite what he'd said, but I knew what the question was, obviously. And really I'd had enough of all these psychological games. I was tired and thirsty. So I didn't wait to see if Chief Inspector Hearse was ever going to finish his question. I just nodded my head and told him what he wanted to know.

'Yes,' I said. 'That was Mr Peterson.'

After that, they had about a million more questions, as you might imagine. Obviously, the main thing they wanted to know was exactly what had happened over the last week, but, to tell you the truth, I'm not ready to talk about that yet. I don't think there would be much point – and there was even less point at the time. Chief Inspector Hearse told me that he wanted a 'clear, concise and full explanation' of all the relevant circumstances that had led to my being stopped at customs with one hundred and thirteen grams of marijuana and Mr Peterson's remains; but that was a lost cause from the word go. Sometimes when people ask you for a full explanation, you know damn well that's the last thing they want. Really, they want you to give them a paragraph that confirms what they already think they know. They want something that will fit neatly in a box on a police statement form. And that can never be a full explanation. Full explanations are much messier. They can't be conveyed in five unprepared, stop-start minutes. You have to give them time and space to unfold.

That's why I want to start back at the beginning, where the police wouldn't let me start. I'm going to tell you my story, the full story, in the manner I think it should be told. I'm afraid it's not going to be brief.

IRIDIUM-193

I could start by telling you about my conception. My mother was always extremely forthcoming about this aspect of my existence – possibly because there was so little she could tell me about my father and it was her way of compensating. It's kind of an interesting story, in a weird, slightly unpleasant way, but for all that, I'm not sure that's the best place to begin. It's not the most relevant place to begin, anyway. Maybe I'll get to it later.

For now, there's a more obvious place to begin: with the accident that befell me when I was ten years old. Of course, you probably know at least a little about this already. It was planetary news for several weeks. Still, that was more than seven years ago. Memories are short, and since it was so pivotal in determining the direction my life was to take, I can't very well ignore it.

I'm calling it an accident for want of a better term, but really, this isn't the apposite word. I'm not sure there *is* an apposite word for what happened. The press mostly called it a 'freak accident', or occasionally an 'accident unprecedented in recorded human history' – even though this second claim turned out to be not quite the case. There must have been hundreds of thousands of words written about it during the two weeks I was unconscious, and, for me, this is one of the strangest things to get to grips with. Because my own memory of what happened is entirely non-existent. The last thing I remember with any certainty is a school trip to Bristol Zoo where I was reprimanded for trying to feed a Mars bar to a spider monkey, and that was at least two weeks before I was taken into hospital. So a fair amount of what I'm going to tell you next I've had to reconstruct from other people's accounts: from all the newspaper articles I read afterwards, from the doctors and scientists who talked to me while I was recovering, and from all the thousands of different eyewitnesses who saw what was to strike me in the moments before it did. A lot of those eyewitnesses wrote to me, or to my mother, when it became clear that I was going to pull through, and we kept every letter. Along with the hundreds of saved newspaper cuttings, these form the basis of a scrapbook three inches thick, which I must've read through a dozen times. It's funny, because by now I must know as much about what happened to me as anyone else, but it all comes from reading and listening. As far as my personal awareness of the incident goes, there's nothing there. I was probably the last person on the planet to find out what had befallen me. The first I knew of it was when I woke up in Yeovil District Hospital on Saturday, 3 July 2004, having just lost a whole month of my life.

When I came to, my first assumption was that I was in heaven. I thought it had to be heaven because everything was painfully white. Some experimentation revealed that I still had eyes and working eyelids, despite being deceased, and I could squint in cautious, half-second bursts, which seemed the best option until my eyes had had a chance to adjust to the afterlife's billion-watt glare.

They'd taught us a little bit about heaven in school, and we used to sing about it a lot in assembly, but I wasn't quite sure that I believed in it until I awoke there. I hadn't had what most would term a conventional religious upbringing. My mother didn't believe in heaven. She believed instead in an invisible spirit world that we passed over to when we died, but that wasn't completely separate from the world of the living. It was just another plane of existence, and even though we couldn't see or smell or touch it, there were messages coming through from there all the time. My mother made a good part of her living from interpreting these messages. She was 'receptive' to the other world in a way that most were not. I always imagined that it worked kind of like the radio or something, with most of us being tuned to static.

Anyway, I was fairly sure that I'd ended up in heaven and not just another plane of existence. I could see further evidence for this hypothesis through my squinting eyes, in the form of two angels – one fair, one dark, both clad in turquoise – who were hovering either side of me, though I couldn't figure out quite what they were doing. Deciding that further investigation was required, I ignored the pain and forced my eyes wide open. Immediately, the fair angel hopped backwards and let out a tremendous, high-pitched yelp. Then I felt a sharp, tugging sensation, but I had no idea where it was coming from. I shut my eyes tight.

'Oh, shit!' said the fair angel. 'Shit, shit, shit!'

19

It was then that I realized I had a left hand, because the fair angel had taken hold of it.

'Jesus! What the hell happened?' the dark angel asked.

'He's awake! Didn't you see?'

'He's *awake*? Shit, is that blood?'

'His cannula came out!'

'It came *out*?'

'He scared the hell out of me! It was an accident!'

'It's all over his sheets!'

'I know, I know! It looks worse than it is. Just find Patel – quick! I need to stay here and keep pressure on his hand.'

I heard quick footsteps, and a few moments later, a man's voice was talking to me. It was deep and calm and authoritative.

'Alex?' he said.

'God?' I responded.

'Not quite,' the voice said. 'I'm Dr Patel. Can you hear me okay?'

'Yes.'

'Can you try to open your eyes for me?'

'They hurt,' I told him.

'Okay,' said Dr Patel. 'Don't worry about that now.' He rested his hand on my forehead. 'Can you tell me how you're feeling?'

'I don't know,' I replied.

'Okay. There's nothing for you to worry about. Nurse Jackson has gone to find your mother. She'll be here very soon.'

'My mother?' I was starting to think that this might not be heaven after all. 'Where am I?' I asked.

'You're in the hospital. You've been with us for thirteen days now.'

'That's almost two weeks,' I pointed out.

'That's correct,' Dr Patel confirmed.

'Why am I here?'

'You had an accident,' Dr Patel said. 'Don't worry about that now.'

I fumbled in the darkness for a few moments. 'Did something happen at the zoo?'

There was a long pause. 'The zoo?'

'The zoo.'

'Alex, you're a little confused right now. It might take some time for your memory to come back. I'd just like you to answer a few quick questions and then you need to rest. Can you tell me your full name?'

'Yes,' I said.

I thought that was a strange question.

'Can you tell me *now*, please?'

'My name is Alexander Morgan Woods.'

'Excellent. And how about your mother's name?'

'Rowena Woods.'

'Good. Very good,' Dr Patel said solemnly.

'She's a cartomancer,' I added.

'When's your birthday, Alex?'

'Not until September,' I said. 'Am I going to die?'

Dr Patel laughed. Nurse Angel squeezed my hand. 'No, Alex, you're not going to die!'

At that point, I heard more loud, quick footsteps, followed by a strange scream and lots of sobs. I didn't need my eyes open to know that that was my mother. Nurse Angel let go of my hand, and a second later I felt my neck pulled to one side and lots of soft, frizzy hair fell across my face.

'Mrs Woods, please!' Dr Patel warned.

My mother kept on sobbing. I could feel warm tears wetting my face.

'Mrs Woods, you have to be careful of his stitches!'

But my mother had decided that she wasn't going to let me go for at least the next twenty-four hours. She was still holding me when I fell asleep.

I soon discovered by touch that my head had been bandaged all the way round, ear to ear. Above and below this, my scalp had the texture of Fuzzy Felt. What hair I'd had was mostly gone.

'We had to shave your head so that we could operate,' Dr Patel told me. 'It's standard procedure.'

'You had to operate?' I was very impressed by this.

'Oh, yes,' said Dr Patel cheerily. 'You had to be taken into theatre the moment you arrived. It took a team of surgeons four hours to patch you up. Your skull was fractured just above your right ear – split clean open, like an eggshell.'

My jaw hit the floor. 'Like an *eggshell*?'

'Like an eggshell,' Dr Patel repeated.

'Dr Patel, please!' said my mother. 'That's not a pleasant image. Lex, close your mouth.'

'Could they see my brain?' I asked.

'Yes, I believe they could,' Dr Patel said gravely. 'But only after they'd drained away the excess fluid and removed all the grit and dust that had accumulated in the wound.'

'Grit and dust from the Rock?' (The Rock had been capitalized in my imagination from the first moment I'd heard about it.)

'Actually, most of it was ceiling plaster.'

'Oh.' Needless to say, this was a little disappointing. 'Are you sure it was just plaster?'

Dr Patel glanced across at my mother, who had her arms folded and her eyebrows up. 'We'll know more soon,' he told me. 'I believe some swabs were sent away for analysis.'

'Swabs?'

'Some little rubbed-off samples,' Dr Patel explained.

'They took swabs from my brain?'

'No. They took swabs from your scalp and skull. When there's grit in your brain, it's best not to rub it.'

'Dr Patel, really!' said my mother. 'Lex, stop touching that.'

I took my hand away from my bandages. Everyone was quiet for a few seconds.

'Dr Patel?' I asked.

'Yes, Alex.'

'If they weren't allowed to touch it, how did they manage to get all the grit out?'

Dr Patel smiled. My mother shook her head. 'They used suction.'

'Like with a *Hoover*?'

'Yes. Exactly like that.'

I wrinkled my nose. 'That doesn't sound all that safe either.'

'It's a very small and precise Hoover.'

'Oh.' I looked across at my mother. She'd unfolded her arms and was pretending to read her book. 'Then what?' I asked. 'You know, after they'd taken the swabs and drained the fluid and Hoovered up the grit?'

'After that, it was really quite simple,' said Dr Patel. 'They cleaned the wound with salt water, attached a special plate to your skull to cover the fracture, took a small skin graft from your thigh to patch up your scalp and then sewed you up good as new.'

'Wow!' That explained the bandage on my leg. 'Does that mean that underneath all these bandages I'm like a Frankenstein? With all those stitches holding my head together and a great big metal plate bolted to my skull?'

'Yes, exactly so,' said Dr Patel. Then he paused briefly. 'Except the plate isn't metal. It's made from a special absorbable material that gradually breaks down over a period of months while your skull repairs itself underneath. Eventually, the whole plate will be gone, the stitches will dissolve, and you'll be just like a normal boy again.'

'But I'll at least have a scar?'

'You *might* have a scar.'

I frowned and tapped my head.

'Lex!' warned my mother without looking up from her book.

I stopped tapping my head. 'Dr Patel, where do they go after they dissolve?' I asked. 'You know, the stitches and the special skull plate?'

'Well,' he replied, 'any material that the body can use is recycled and turned into other useful things, like muscle and fat. And the rest is simply broken down and excreted.'

I thought about this for a few moments. 'You mean it comes out in your stools?'

'Lex!' barked my mother.

'That's what they call them in the hospital,' I pointed out. 'It's the proper medical term.'

'Actually, most of it leaves the body in the urine,' said Dr Patel.

'Okay, I think that's more than enough information for one day,' said my mother.

After that, Dr Patel wouldn't tell me anything interesting

about my wounds unless my mother was out of the room, and that didn't happen very often.

Even though my head was patched up and healing itself underneath the special absorbable bone plates, I still had to stay in hospital for another week so that they could keep an eye on me and make sure that I was getting the proper amount of rest and protein. I saw about a million different doctors, and twice as many nurses, and I had to go for X-rays so that they could check how my skull was doing, and then I had to answer questions and perform all these strange little tasks that had been designed to make sure that my brain was functioning correctly.

It seemed that it was.

My five senses were all in good working order. I could still read and write, and I still knew my times tables, one to twelve. My ability to manipulate oddly shaped blocks was unimpaired, and after a few days of solid food and increasing exercise, my movements and co-ordination were pretty much back to normal. The only thing that showed any signs of damage was my memory, and this damage was so specific that it hardly seemed to be a problem. I could still memorize lists of words or numbers, and I performed well on spot-the-difference and missing-object puzzles. I could remember what I'd had for breakfast and what happened yesterday and my first day at school and the time I sat on a wasp at Weston-super-Mare. I could still name almost every animal I'd seen at Bristol Zoo: the spider monkey, the ring-tailed lemur, the golden tamarin and so on and so forth. And based on these facts, there was no general problem with my episodic or semantic memory. There was simply a missing month, four weeks of my personal history that had fallen into a deep dark hole. Despite all Dr Patel's reassurances, I couldn't help wondering if that month hadn't somehow ended up in the dust bag of the brain surgeon's very small, very precise Hoover.

It was my mother who had found me, of course. She had heard both explosions from the kitchen, separated by at least a minute of quiet. The first, she said, sounded like a very distant gunshot, or maybe a car backfiring. The second sounded like the roof collapsing. The upstairs landing was carnage – a minefield of fallen pictures, smashed glass and displaced ornaments from the dresser that stood opposite the stairs. Pewter candelabra, a sacramental chalice – that kind of thing. The bathroom door was closed but not locked. I was lying on the floor in a pool of blood and shattered porcelain. My mother said that she screamed so loudly that it was probably this, and not the explosion itself, that brought Mr and Mrs Stapleton, our elderly neighbours, running. It was really a good job they turned up. I suspect my mother was way too hysterical to call an ambulance.

Apparently, she hardly left my side for the next two weeks. She insisted on sleeping at the hospital. The nurses had to wheel a special bed into my room once she'd made it clear that if they weren't able to accommodate her, she'd simply sleep on the floor. From the way she described it, it sounded kind of embarrassing. Luckily, I was deep in my coma at this point. In fact, I was aware of absolutely nothing – but this was one medical reality my mother was quick to dismiss.

'I talked to you every day,' she told me. 'I knew that there had to be a part of you that could still hear me.'

'I don't think I could hear you,' I said – for the thousandth time.

'There was a *part* of you that could hear me,' my mother insisted.

'I don't *remember* hearing you,' I said.

My mother chortled carelessly. 'Well, of course you don't remember it! You were fast asleep. And we don't remember things when we're fast asleep, do we? That doesn't mean you couldn't hear *at the time.*'

I frowned. I wasn't sure that this made sense, but then, there was a lot from the past month that didn't make sense.

Highest on the list was the accident itself. Of course, I knew the basic facts about what had happened to me – from my mother, and from Mr and Mrs Stapleton and the ambulance men who had been up to visit me after I woke up – but this actually didn't amount to very much. They'd found the Rock straight away – apparently you couldn't miss it – but no one could be sure that it had actually hit me. One of the ambulance men told me that it seemed more likely that I'd been struck by a piece of shrapnel or falling masonry from the ceiling. 'If you'd been hit by the Rock itself,' he said, 'I don't think we'd be having this conversation right now.'

To my disappointment, Mr Stapleton, who'd been the first to pick up the Rock, supported this theory. He said that it was only the size of an orange but, in his estimation, it must have weighed at least four or five pounds, which is as much as a two-litre bottle of Diet Coke. 'IT FELT LIKE A LEAD WEIGHT,' he shouted. (Mr Stapleton always shouted because he was extremely deaf.) When I asked him what it looked like, he told me that it was 'BLACK AND PECULIAR-LOOKING, LIKE IT HAD BEEN CAST IN A MOULD'. But I didn't find this description even close to adequate.

'What do you mean?' I asked. 'What kind of mould?'

'FREEZING!' Mr Stapleton assured me.

'WHAT KIND OF MOULD?' I repeated.

'A PECULIAR ONE. LIKE IT WAS MADE BY ALIENS!'

I was desperate to see it, of course, but when I asked my mother, she said that someone had taken it away weeks ago.

'Who?' I demanded.

My mother shrugged. 'Actually, I'm not sure who she was. She said she was a scientist. Dr Monica Somethingorother. I was much too upset to take it all in. She caught me while I was right in the middle of packing a suitcase to bring back to the hospital.'

'But who was she? Where did she come from? Where did she take my Rock?'

'Lex, I've told you – I don't know! She said that she needed to take it away to do some important tests. At the time, I couldn't have cared less.'

'Is she coming back?'

'She didn't say.'

'You didn't ask?'

'Lex! I'm not going to repeat myself.'

I felt dismal. I was sure that because of my mother's short-sightedness I'd never get to see my Rock and no one would ever be able to tell me the things I wanted to know about it. For the time being, I could only console myself by reading and re-reading the articles that the Stapletons and various doctors and nurses had collected. It was from these sources that I started to patch over the hole in my memory, which would have otherwise remained obstinately unfilled.

The fireball, it transpired, was first seen over the northeast tip of Northern Ireland at around 3.27 in the afternoon on Sunday, 20 June 2004. Anyone who was outside at the time, or looking out of a window facing in the right direction, would have seen it. Apparently it was three times brighter than the full moon and shot across the sky like a bullet. After being witnessed by about a hundred thousand people in the Belfast region, it took just a few seconds to cross the Irish Sea, rocketed over Anglesey and then disappeared behind thick cloud cover over North Wales. It re-emerged just north of the Severn estuary, startled half of Bristol and then ended its journey somewhere over Somerset. At the time, no one knew exactly where that somewhere was, but there was a lot of speculation. Several hundred people swore blind that they saw it explode directly over Wells Cathedral, and for a while, this was reported as fact in the local and national papers. Then, after a couple of days, a scientist from the University of Oxford appeared on the news saying that, in actual fact, because the impactor struck the Earth at an extremely acute angle and exploded high in the atmosphere, 'it would have been very difficult for any single eyewitness to identify accurately the precise point of detonation.' In response, Graham Alcock, a writer for the *Wells Herald*, pointed out that this wasn't the testimony of a 'single eyewitness', but rather 'two policemen, three busloads of tourists and an entire pilgrimage of nuns'. This prompted (two days later) a letter from Professor Miriam Hanson, a psychologist from Bristol, who wanted 'to clarify that the issue of reliability is not, in this case, bound up with the number of people who witnessed the phenomenon, much less their good character. The fact is that the *apparent* explosion of the meteor over Wells Cathedral was in all probability an optical illusion created by the height and expanse of the building relative to the position of the observers. In a scenario like this, eyewitness testimony has to be taken with a large pinch of salt.' Her letter, published under the title '28 Nuns *Can* Be Wrong', did nothing to quell the debate, which went on in the same vein for most of the next week, drawing in such luminaries as the Archbishop of Canterbury and *The Sky at Night*'s Chris Lintott.

I found all these arguments extremely interesting when I was finally able to read about them – which is one of the reasons I mention them now – but I should point out that, for most, the 'Wells Controversy' was nothing more than a sideline. Most people weren't interested in knowing about the precise point of detonation or the attempt to reconstruct the meteoroid's original orbit round the Sun. They were only interested in the 'human cost' of recent events, and on that topic, the consensus was absolute. The archbishop, the scientists, the journalists, the letter-writers – they all said the same thing: that given the mass and composition of *my* meteorite fragment, which was quickly established, and given the speed at which it must have burst through our bathroom roof, which was considerable, it was really nothing short of a miracle that I had survived.

It was five days later, the day before I was discharged from Yeovil District Hospital, that I finally got the answers I'd been looking for. This was the day that Dr Monica Somethingorother rematerialized, appearing like an out-of-breath vision at my bedside. She'd arrived unannounced and brought with her a scruffy sports bag and enough data about meteors, meteorites and meteoroids to make my head spin for the next week.

Her real name turned out to be Dr Monica Weir, although I misheard it at first, naturally. She wasn't a medical doctor, but a doctor of astrophysics, specializing in planetary science, at the Imperial College in London. And she wasn't much like any other adult I'd ever met. For a start, it seemed to me that she could answer any question you put to her – and, more surprisingly, she *would* answer any question you put to her. With most adults (with my mother, in particular) there came a point, after the third or fourth question in a row, when they stopped answering; or, more often, the answer they gave would be no answer at all – 'because it just is!' or some equally frustrating variant. But with Dr Weir, there was no cut-off point. She seemed quite capable of explaining everything, right down to the smallest detail. And the more questions you asked, the more willing she seemed to bombard you with information; she couldn't utter a ten-word sentence without making it sound like an excerpt from a Royal Institution Christmas Lecture. She also dressed kind of funny. Not funny like my mother, who dressed 'alternatively', but more old-fashioned and mismatched, as if she'd selected all her clothes at random from a 1950s jumble sale. I suppose, really, she dressed like her mind was on Higher Things, which was fine by me – although I'll admit that I wasn't sure of her at first, mainly because I still felt like she'd stolen my Rock. And I was not alone in this sentiment.

It turned out that quite a few people – quite a few other astrophysicists – felt this way too. Once they learned that she'd swooped across to Somerset to claim possession of the meteorite, mere hours after the news had broken, there was quite a backlash. The words 'insensitive' and 'unethical' came up quite a lot. Then there were several stroppy emails written by various scientists at the universities of Bristol and Bath, who were furious that such an important local fall had been whisked away to London before the dust had even settled. But Dr Weir didn't seem particularly bothered by any of this. She would later tell *New Scientist* magazine that 'the most important thing was that the fall was recovered promptly, undamaged and uncontaminated. If I'd left it any longer, there was a real chance that it could have been taken by a private collector. After all, this wasn't a normal situation. Everyone in the country knew precisely where this fragment had landed. And you have to remember that within twenty-four hours the whole county was swarming with meteorite hounds. I felt it my duty to claim it at once in the name of Science!'

Once she'd explained her actions to me, I was very pleased that Dr Weir had arrived so promptly to claim my meteorite in the name of Science. In the two weeks she'd had it, she'd managed to find out an incredible amount about my Rock. And the first thing she was eager to point out was that it was *not* a rock in any ordinary sense of the word.

'You see, Alex,' she said excitedly, 'your meteorite is largely composed of metal. It's actually a member of the iron–nickel subgroup. They're much rarer than the common chondrites and achondrites – the rocky meteorites. They're much denser too. That's one of the reasons it was able to pass through your roof so easily, without fragmenting. Your meteorite weighs just over two point three kilograms and would have been travelling at a terminal velocity of almost two hundred miles per hour when it struck the top of your house. You know, Alex, it's an absolute miracle that you're still here.'

'Yes,' I agreed, rolling my body weight across my knuckles. I was sitting on my hands because I felt very fidgety, and I had my eyes fixed on that scruffy sports bag. I know that it's rude not to look at someone when they're talking to you, but I couldn't help it. I was mesmerized. I was staring at that bag so hard it was in serious danger of bursting into flames.

'Dr Weird—' I began.

'Actually, Alex, it's Dr *Weir*.'

'Oh.'

'Call me Monica if you like.'

'Dr *Weir*,' I said, 'have you got my iron–nickel meteor in that bag?'

Dr Weir smiled patiently. 'What I have in this bag, Alex, is your iron–nickel meteo*rite*. That's what we call it once it has dropped to Earth. It's only called a meteor while it's burning in the Earth's atmosphere. And before that, while it's still in space, it's called a meteoroid. Would you like to hold your meteorite?'

'More than anything.'

It was the size of an orange but a very funny shape – kind of pointy on one side, where it had split from the original impactor, and curved on the other, where it had been super-heated by friction with the Earth's atmosphere. And on the jagged side, it was covered in small fissures and at least a dozen little craters, like tiny alien thumbprints. Dr Weir held it very gently, in both hands and close to her chest, as if it were some kind of fragile woodland creature. 'Be careful, Alex,' she said. 'Remember that it's much heavier than it looks.'

I held my hands out like a shallow bowl. I was prepared for its weight, but I wasn't prepared for how cold it was. My hands were still warm from being under my bottom and the iron–nickel meteorite felt like it had been pulled straight from the fridge.

'It's freezing!' I gasped. 'Is that because it's from outer space?'

Dr Weir smiled again. 'Actually, Alex, it's at room temperature. It just *feels* cold because it's extremely conductive. It's drawing a lot of heat from your hands. As to where it's from, well, that's one of the things we can be fairly certain about. It probably originated in the molten core of a large asteroid that was destroyed through collision billions of years ago. Do you know what an asteroid is?'

'Asteroids are great big boulders in space,' I said. 'The *Millennium Falcon* had to fly through a whole field of them to get away from Darth Vader's *Star Destroyer*.'

Dr Weir nodded enthusiastically. 'Yes, that's right. But that was in a galaxy far, far away. In our solar system, most of the asteroids – and there are millions and millions of them – orbit the Sun in a wide belt between Mars and Jupiter.'

At this point, Dr Weir drew me a detailed diagram showing the Sun, the planets and the Asteroid Belt. It wasn't to scale, she said, but it was accurate enough for our purposes.

'Now, Alex. Usually these asteroids don't get anywhere near the Earth, as you can see. But occasionally, they get thrown out of their regular, stable orbits. Sometimes they collide like snooker balls, and sometimes they get captured by Jupiter's enormous gravity and then launched on a whole new path round the Sun. As you probably know, Jupiter is extremely massive and has a very powerful gravitational field. Some of these captured asteroids will eventually impact with Jupiter, and some are thrown so far that they leave the solar system entirely. And some – a tiny, tiny percentage – become meteoroids. That is, they're hurled onto an orbit that puts them on a direct collision course with the Earth.'

Dr Weir drew on her diagram a little dotted line representing the hypothetical path of a disrupted asteroid crossing the Earth's orbit. I thought that this was something my mother would have enjoyed looking at. She often talked about how the movements of the planets could affect events on Earth, but she'd never really explained how that worked. Dr Weir explained it much better.

'Anyway,' Dr Weir continued, 'most of the asteroids that collide with the Earth are very tiny and are vaporized high in the upper atmosphere. But a few – like yours – are big enough and dense enough to make it all the way to the ground without vaporizing. And an even smaller number are so big and heavy that they're hardly even slowed down by the atmosphere. They leave craters and create huge, incredibly destructive explosions. Most scientists agree that it was probably a meteor originating in the Asteroid Belt that killed all the dinosaurs.'

I looked at the orange-sized meteorite in my hands. 'I'm not sure that one meteor could have killed *all* the dinosaurs,' I said sceptically.

Then Dr Weir talked for a very long time about how the meteor that probably killed all the dinosaurs was much, much bigger than mine – probably at least ten miles wide – and how a meteor that big would have caused waves as high as mountains and then acid rain and forest fires and a cloud of dust that would have circled the entire planet and blocked out most of the sunlight for the next several years. There wasn't any meteorite left from that meteor because it had exploded with the force of one hundred billion megatons of TNT, but there *was* a huge sixty-five-million-year-old impact crater under the sea near Mexico. There was also a suspiciously high amount of iridium-193 in the sixty-five-million-year-old rock samples. Iridium-193 was one of the two stable isotopes of iridium, and it was extremely rare on Earth but much more abundant in meteoroids. An isotope was something to do with atomic mass and extremely tiny particles called neutrons, but that was somewhat harder to grasp, and Dr Weir told me that it wasn't necessary for me to understand all the subtleties right there and then. The main point, she said, was that finding all that iridium-193 in the sixty-five-million-year-old rocks was like finding a smoking gun.

I thought about all this information for a long, long time.

'Dr Weir?' I asked. 'Did they find any iridium-193 in my head? You know, after they took the swabs? Because that would be a smoking gun too, wouldn't it?'

Dr Weir was delighted with this question. She told me it was exactly the sort of question a scientist would ask. And the answer was yes: the swabs had been analysed using all sorts of special chemical tests, and this had confirmed the presence of a number of meteorite metals, including iron, nickel, cobalt and *lots* of iridium-193. Not enough to build a spark plug, she said, but still lots by normal, earthly standards. And this meant that it was 99.999 per cent certain that my skull had been struck directly by the meteorite fragment, and not merely by falling masonry, as the ambulance man had suggested. That made me only the second person in recorded history to have been significantly injured by a direct meteorite hit.

I felt very triumphant at this point, but also slightly nervous. Because there was one question I still needed to ask.

'Dr Weir,' I said, 'what's going to happen to my iron–nickel meteorite now? Do you have to take it away again?'

Dr Weir smiled and stayed quiet for a few moments. 'Well, Alex, I think really that should be up to you. I don't need it any more. I've got enough data and samples from that meteorite to keep me busy for the next six months at least. Usually I'd say that a specimen that beautiful should be put on display in a museum, because I'm sure that there are a lot of people who'd love to see it. But, really, it's your call. If you want to keep it, you should keep it. Don't let anyone tell you that you can't.'

I hugged the meteorite close to my chest. 'I think I'd really like to keep it,' I said. 'At least for now.'

And I did. I kept my meteorite on a special shelf in my bedroom for the next five years. Then, on 20 June 2009, I decided to let other people enjoy it too. It felt like the right time, but I'll get to that later on. I think, for now, I've said enough about my meteorite. If you want to go and see it, you can. It's in a glass cabinet on the first floor of the Natural History Museum in London, in a section called the Vault – about a hundred metres from the dinosaurs.

THE QUEEN OF CUPS

Once all the doctors had agreed that my brain was okay and my skull was healing itself beneath its degradable bone plates, I was discharged from hospital and into a series of media scrums. The first occurred six feet outside the main entrance, the second at my mother's car, the third at our front gate, the fourth in the same place the following morning, the fifth just outside my mother's shop, the sixth as we were closing up that evening and so on and so forth for the next two days. Rather surprisingly, my thirteen-day coma had helped to sell a lot of newspapers. It didn't matter that twelve of those days had been completely uneventful. A whole universe of speculation had been created from just a few unpromising particles. According to reliable and never-named sources in the hospital, my situation was critical, then desperate, then critical but stable, then just stable, then uncertain, then (for twelve hours) improving, then uncertain again and then steadily bleaker with each passing day until everyone agreed that there was very little chance of my ever waking up. At that point, I woke up, escaping the cul-de-sac into which I'd been written.

Of course, journalists were not tolerated within the hospital walls – not unless they had broken bones or terrible diseases – but that didn't stop several dozen well-wishers ('friends of the family' and 'distant relations') turning up on the ward during visiting hours (and I should tell you that our 'family' had about three friends and precisely zero known relatives). My mother left instructions at reception that no one should be allowed through without her explicit agreement and all incursions were quickly repelled. The articles written about my recovery were, therefore, just as speculative and non-eventful as those that had documented the various phases of my unconsciousness. But during the week that I was awake, the media did at least have plenty of time to work out all the best ambush points for when I was finally set free.

Progress across the hospital car park was glacial, and by the time we'd made it out and were waiting at the roundabout, my mother had resolved that I was not going to answer any more questions or stand still for any more photographs. She couldn't stop the reporters from lurking around her car or inspecting the inside of our wheelie bin, but she was not going to put me on parade; and the only time she came close to breaking this resolve was during the final stage of the ongoing bathroom-roof saga, which is another thing I should probably tell you about.

Upon arriving home, I discovered to my horror that the bathroom roof had been repaired and was now completely back to normal. It was only in the newspaper cuttings that I would ever get to see the devastation wrought upon our house by 2.3

kilograms of metal travelling at two hundred miles per hour. It transpired that the roof had actually been fixed weeks ago, by a local builder who had offered his services for free. He had tried to contact my mother shortly after the accident, but she was away at the hospital, and in no state to think about roof repairs. Luckily, the Stapletons, who were collecting our mail and looking after Lucy, had been able to accept this kind offer on our behalf. But then I woke up and my mother could think again and she was overwhelmed with gratitude and immediately told the builder that she wouldn't dream of letting his generosity go unrewarded. After all, his was a small, family-run operation, and our bathroom had been a bomb site. It wasn't just the metre-square hole that had been punched in the roof – there was also the floor, which needed retiling, and the shattered sink, which needed replacing. The cost in terms of labour and materials must have been substantial. And because we had comprehensive insurance, it seemed silly that the builder should be left out of pocket.

It was this last piece of information, of course, that had finally swayed him. He sent my mother the invoice, she sent the invoice to the insurance company, and, two days later, the insurance company sent her a very long, very wordy letter saying that regrettably they were unable and unwilling to foot the bill. In a strange oversight, our house was covered against fire, flood, subsidence, earthquakes, vandalism, terrorism and every extreme of weather – including blizzards, tornadoes and hurricanes – but *not* against meteors, which fell into the category 'Acts of God'. As a large corporation of international repute, with shareholders and premiums to consider, they didn't feel it would be ethically responsible if they agreed to pay my mother's claim – not when our builder had previously been so willing to work for nothing (a detail that had made the local papers and which had not escaped their notice).

'An *act of God*!' my mother fumed, scrunching the letter to the density of a neutron star.

'Dr Weir said it was probably an act of Jupiter,' I told her.

My mother looked at me for a long time with a strange crooked expression. Then she said, rather mysteriously: 'I think, Lex, it was an act of Mars.'

My mother often said mysterious things, and usually there wasn't much point asking for an explanation, which would in turn need explaining. Sometimes you'd find out what she meant, and sometimes you wouldn't. In this case, I *did* eventually find out what she was talking about – it was to do with tarot and the Tower, and a truly bizarre act of prophecy – but you'll have to wait a while to hear about that. First, I have to conclude the roof saga.

My mother isn't usually quick to anger – she tends to kind of float around in this weird insulated bubble, like the ones they use to contain children without immune systems – but the day she received that letter from her insurance company, she was filled with righteous fury. She felt herself to be left with three equally unpleasant options: 1) tell the builder that he wasn't going to get paid after all (this was never going to happen; my mother has never broken a promise in her life); 2) take out a second mortgage; 3) sell me and my exclusive interview to the highest bidder – and, as I've said, for a few hours, this third option was looking like the lesser of the three evils. People from magazines and production companies had been leaving messages on my mother's answering machine for at least a month at that point. We both knew that she only had to give the word and *Richard and Judy* would happily pay to have our entire roof retiled in meteorite-proof armoured plating. But, for my mother, the issue was not primarily a financial one. She felt that even if the insurance company hadn't broken the literal terms of the contract they shared, they had certainly broken the spirit of that contract, and this was just as serious a matter. She was not going to be happy until they'd been made to see the error of their ways.

She spent the rest of the evening deep in her own counsel, and the following morning, I knew from her changed demeanour at breakfast that she'd hit upon a solution. As it turned out, this solution was basically a form of blackmail or extortion, but for the reasons outlined above, I don't think my mother ever considered it in this light. She saw it as the only way to balance the moral books.

She phoned the insurance company at nine o'clock on the dot and told them the following: if they (the insurance company) genuinely believed that they shouldn't have to pay for our roof because it was some form of divine judgment on our family – and as such not covered in our policy – then perhaps they'd like to contact the press to make this opinion known? If not, she'd be more than willing to do it for them.

The next day, we received a second letter from the insurance company saying that while they accepted no liability for the damage to the roof, they would be happy to pay the bill as a gesture of goodwill. My mother wrote back saying that while she had serious doubts about the sincerity of their 'goodwill', she was nevertheless prepared to accept it at face value – although she also suggested that they rethink the wording of their documents in the future. She was still upset about the 'Acts of God' clause, and would remain so for some time.

By the time I'd woken up and been discharged from hospital and escaped the media and seen the satisfactory conclusion to the story of the broken roof – by then, it was pretty much time for the summer holidays, and my mother didn't know quite what to do with me. Since she worked in the shop full time six days a week, and had done so for as long as I could remember, this wasn't exactly a new problem. But that summer, the need for me to be fully and properly supervised at all times seemed especially high on my mother's agenda. I could understand that she didn't want me to be on my own, but to my mind, the best solution was also the simplest. In fact, this solution seemed so obvious to me that I was amazed my mother had not even considered it.

'I don't see why I can't just stay in the house with Lucy,' I said. 'She's in most of the day, near enough, so I won't be alone – not really.'

'Lex, that's just about the silliest thing you've said all morning,' said my mother.

'It's not *that* silly,' I snarled.

'I hardly think that Lucy counts as adequate supervision.'

'She can keep an eye on me and I can keep an eye on her. You know, in case she's got any ideas about getting pregnant again.'

Upon hearing this, Lucy turned her head and shot me an extremely withering look. My mother snorted. 'Lex, we both know that if Lucy decides to get pregnant again, then there's very little either you or I can do about it.'

'Yeah, but maybe if she had a bit more company—'

'Lex!'

And my mother gave me the look that meant *this conversation is over!* Lucy, meanwhile, rose from her chair and left the room, with her nose pointedly in the air. A few seconds later, I heard the cat-flap slam. This was typical Lucy behaviour. She never acted much like a cat – I never once saw her climb a tree or chase a bird – and, since I could remember, I'd always thought of her more as an older sister. I'm aware this may sound odd, but you have to bear in mind that our family was very small. I didn't have any human siblings, nor a father, that I knew of. I also had no living grandparents and no aunts and uncles, and hence no cousins either. I had my mother, and she had me, and we both had the cat, and growing up in a situation like that, it always seemed obvious that Lucy was an integral part of our family unit, which I was loath, even in my imagination, to deplete. Furthermore, it was quite apparent, as has already been indicated, that Lucy shared my concerns that our family was a little on the small side. By the time I was ten, she'd already borne four litters, and at the time of writing, this number has risen to nine. This might seem improbable, but you have to bear in mind that cats remain fertile throughout their lives and are capable of reproducing several times every year. The world record for the number of kittens born to a single mother across her lifespan is four hundred and twenty.

Unfortunately, if Lucy had notions of increasing the size of our family, she was fighting a losing battle. My mother refused to have her spayed because she thought this was against the natural order of things, but neither was she willing to keep any of Lucy's kittens – whether long- or short-furred, male or female, black, white or any combination in between. Each new litter was of unknown paternity and this threw up some pretty weird and wonderful genetic variations. These variations tended to affect how long each new kitten ended up being advertised in my mother's shop window. Generally, the long-furred kittens were snapped up much more quickly than the short-furred kittens, because these were seen as having *pedigree*, although, in my opinion, the short-furred, scraggly ones were usually friendlier and more fun. The ones that inherited their mother's long white fur also tended to inherit much of her aloofness, suggesting that there was a direct connection between these two characteristics. But, obviously, this is just speculation. I'm not a cat geneticist.

The main point is this: for whatever reason, my mother didn't agree that Lucy was a suitable babysitter for me during the summer holidays. In fact, after the coma and everything, she seemed reluctant to let me out of her sight for even ten minutes, which I didn't think was very fair *or* very rational. Later, after Dr Weir had sent me a big book all about meteoroids, meteors and meteorites, I was able to explain to my mother that the chance of me getting struck by another meteor – that is, two meteors in one lifetime – was about one in four quintillion (which is a four with eighteen zeroes after it), and that these odds would be unaffected by whether she was watching over me or not. If she was serious about protecting me, then she should keep me locked up in a metal box in the basement. I rehearsed this speech at least ten times before I aired it, so, let me tell you, it was pretty well honed. I don't think the wording or delivery could've been bettered. But this made no difference to my mother. She didn't care *how* many zeroes there were, I still had to go to work with her every day. It was that or spend the day at the Stapletons', and, between you and me, this wasn't such a great alternative. So I ended up spending most of the summer in my mother's shop.

Sometimes I was allowed to help with little jobs like restocking the shelves or counting out change, and when my mother was doing a reading, I was in charge of lighting and maintaining the candles, but for the rest of the time I just had to sit quietly and read – either behind the counter or, if I was lucky, upstairs in Justine and Sam's flat. Justine worked in the shop as well. I'm not sure what Sam did. She was quite a few years younger than Justine and seemed to spend a lot of time in the flat. Sam was short for Samantha. Sam and Justine were lesbians. As my mother explained to me when I was six, this meant that they preferred each other's company to the company of men (though fortunately, at that age, I didn't count as a man, so they were always quite tolerant of me). When I asked my mother if she was a lesbian too – as she also seemed to prefer Justine and Sam's company to the company of men – she almost had a fit laughing. Then, when she'd picked herself up off the floor, she told me that these days she didn't worry too much about the company of men *or* women because she was celibate. But this was another of those things that she wouldn't explain any further, and when I tried to look up 'celibate' in the dictionary, I couldn't find it. It certainly wasn't where I expected it to be – in between 'seller' and 'Sellotape'.

Rest assured: by the time I was ten, I had managed to find out what my mother meant. She meant that as far as our family was concerned, only the cat had a sex life.

* * *

My mother's shop was down an alleyway just off Glastonbury High Street and was called the Queen of Cups. The Queen of Cups is a tarot card, as you may already know – especially if you've seen the James Bond film *Live and Let Die*. *Live and Let Die* was one of the few subjects on which my mother and I were always in agreement. We both thought it was the best Bond film. My mother liked all the tarot and the voodoo. I liked the bit where the main bad guy swallows a compressed-air bullet and explodes over the shark tank. But that was before I became a pacifist.

Anyway, if you've seen the film, you might remember that the Queen of Cups in an upside-down (or 'ill-dignified') position signifies a deceitful, treacherous or unreliable woman. But upright, as it was displayed on my mother's shop front, it basically means the opposite: a woman blessed with wisdom and sensitivity – intuition, special vision and so on. It was this set of meanings my mother was trying to convey when she chose the name.

On the ground floor, there were four rooms: the large front room, a smaller back room, a stockroom and a toilet. In the front room we sold lots of different books about Wicca and astrology and numerology and divination and runes and, of course, tarot. We also sold lots of different decks of tarot cards and tarot accessories, as well as candles and crystals and incense and oils and potions. My mother mixed a lot of the potions and oils herself, but not in a cauldron. She used a seven-litre stockpot.

The back room, which wasn't much bigger than the stockroom, was where she did her readings, and it was always very dim back there. The single window was permanently shuttered, the walls were painted dried-blood red, and, as I've already mentioned, my mother tended to prefer candlelight to electricity, which helped with the psychic vibrations. It also helped to create an appropriate atmosphere. Without all those candles, and of course the tarot table with its black silk covering cloth, the room would have looked too much like what it was: a modestly sized red closet.

Because of my role as keeper of the candles, I was allowed to sit in on most of my mother's readings, but I should tell you that that is *not* normal tarot procedure. Tarot requires a lot of focus, and, usually, having a third person present during a reading is regarded as an unwanted distraction, for both the reader and the querent. When it came to me, however, no one seemed to worry too much. This may be because most people don't regard a child as a whole other person. I sat quietly in the far corner and was easily overlooked, and when I had to perform my candle-lighting duties, I tried to keep my movements slow and solemn and silent, like my mother had taught me. In this way, I wouldn't disrupt the delicate atmosphere of the reading. If anything, I probably *added* to the atmosphere, like some strange, mute goblin that would emerge now and then from the gloom to tend to the various flickering fires. As long as I didn't touch the cards, there was really no chance of my presence affecting the smooth running of the reading. Touching the cards, at any time, was Absolutely Forbidden.

My mother always had at least three or four readings every week, even before my accident. And afterwards – or more specifically, after the interview she did for the *Psychic News* – she started to get many, many more. For a while, people actually came from quite a long way away to have a forty-minute reading with my mother.

In case you're wondering, the *Psychic News* wasn't a paper that told you the news for next week. It was a monthly magazine that told you what was new in the world of clairvoyance. My mother agreed to an interview a couple of months after I'd awoken from my coma, long after the general press interest in my accident had fizzled out.

I probably don't need to tell you that of all the strange articles that were written about my accident, the one in the *Psychic News* was the strangest. This was the article in which my mother revealed that she'd foreseen the entire catastrophe. Of course, she didn't realize that she'd foreseen the entire catastrophe until after it had happened. This was one of the reasons that she could not have taken measures to avert it. The other was that it was unavertable.

Although I was present at the reading in question, which occurred eight days before the meteor, it's one of those memories that I assume ended up in the hospital Hoover. So you'll have to bear in mind that the following account is based solely on what my mother has told me. In other words, you should take it with a pinch of salt.

The querent's name was Mrs Coulson, and she was a regular. She came for a reading once every couple of months, usually for help with specific problems. Tarot isn't all about predicting the distant future. Lots of people come with particular questions they want answered – about their careers, or relationships, or even their finances. On this occasion, though, Mrs Coulson didn't have a specific problem or question in mind. She was going through an unusually calm period and just wanted a broad overview of the forces operating in her life at that moment, along with some clues as to what this might mean for the weeks to come. Mrs Coulson was a woman not keen on surprises.

As an experienced reader of the cards, my mother was used to delivering a certain amount of bad news in a non-threatening manner. But in Mrs Coulson's reading, there was *only* bad news, and minimizing its impact was no mean feat. In her retrospective interview, my mother went so far as to say that not only was this the worst spread she'd ever encountered, but it was pretty much the worst spread imaginable. Some years later, I worked out the odds of drawing at random any particular seven-card spread (such as my mother was using that day), which turned out to be a little over a million billion to one; and based on this knowledge, I can go further and tell you that, if my mother is to be believed, then the spread she uncovered that day was the worst ever drawn, and will remain so for the rest of human history.

It's a common misconception that Death is the worst card in the tarot pack. This is not true, although it's easy to see where the confusion comes from. Most traditional tarot decks, those with pictures derived from medieval illuminations, show Death in his familiar guise – bony and cloaked, passing through a barren landscape and wielding his scythe to sweep away the skulls of the departed. But if you look more closely, you'll see something else. You'll see that in Death's wake, small shoots are beginning to grow again. Because in most tarot spreads, Death is not as scary as he seems. Death simply means change – and often a release or rebirth: the end of one thing and the start of something else.

In contrast, all the *really* bad cards in the tarot pack tend to have pretty innocuous names – like the Tower, for example, which always spells calamity. Its picture depicts the eponymous tower being struck by a bolt of lightning from the clear blue sky, often accompanied by two figures plummeting headlong from the windows. Needless to say, Mrs Coulson drew it in her spread. It was preceded by the ill-dignified Chariot, signifying a sudden and terrible loss of control, and the Moon, portent of fear, delusion and evil astrological influences.

'You're a Cancer, aren't you?' my mother asked Mrs Coulson, keeping her voice admirably steady.

Mrs Coulson answered in the affirmative.

'Hmm,' said my mother. 'That's . . . interesting.'

'It is?' Mrs Coulson rejoined, twitching nervously.

'Mars is in your sign at present,' my mother clarified. 'It's also associated with the Tower, just as the Chariot is tradition-ally ruled by Cancer. I fear these things are no coincidence. This may be a trying month for you, though things should come to a head by the twenty-third, when Mars moves into Leo. After that, things may start to improve.'

Having thrown Mrs Coulson this scant reassurance, my mother flipped the next card, and immediately went several shades paler.

'The Nine of Swords,' she announced, again controlling her voice.

'That's not good, is it?' Mrs Coulson gulped.

'It's not a particularly welcome card,' my mother equivocated, 'but neither is it the worst card in the deck. We should proceed to the resolution before rushing to any judgment.'

Upon saying this, my mother hastily flipped the final card,

which was the ill-dignified Ten of Swords. *This* was the worst card in the deck. The inverted Ten of Swords is another sign of impending catastrophe, with the added twist that this card, unlike the Death card, often signifies a literal death. By the time my mother had registered this final jigsaw piece, her mind was doing somersaults trying to turn the abomination before her into the kind of five-minute summary that would not induce a heart attack. The only consolation she could find was that the cards had offered up little in the way of specifics. This was extremely unusual for a tarot reading. There were several clear omens of doom, but the combination of cards left this doom unnamed. Furthermore, the card in the present position – which was supposed to provide precise information about the nature of the querent's enquiry – was the most baffling in the spread. This was the Page of Coins, which usually denoted a serious and studious young man, perhaps a close friend or relative. But Mrs Coulson was forty-five and single, with no immediate family and ovaries that were surely borderline extinct. She had no significant young men in her life, and this seemed unlikely to change.

So at the end of their allotted time, after a lot of questioning and fruitless head-scratching, all that my mother could really tell Mrs Coulson was the following.

In the near future, there was going to be some kind of mishap. This would be unexpected in nature and completely outside of her control. It might be connected to a young man, or it might follow on from some *apparently* good news – Mrs Coulson would be wise to trust neither. It might also be connected to some kind of poor decision in the distant past. In the longer term, Mrs Coulson would have to prepare herself for testing times, and perhaps a certain amount of uncertainty.

Privately, of course, my mother feared the worst. She embraced Mrs Coulson at length before she left the shop, and felt awful that she had to accept payment for the reading. But there was no way out. To refuse payment would have looked ominous in the extreme. And the gesture would have been futile. By my mother's best estimation, Mrs Coulson had less than eleven days left to live.

In hindsight – barring one or two minor details – it was a prediction of stunning accuracy. The only significant problem was that it had been misdirected. Several times afterwards, my mother wanted to know if there was any chance – any chance at all – that I'd been playing with her cards before she and Mrs Coulson had entered the room, at the time when I was supposed to be preparing the candles. Obviously, because of my amnesia, this was not a question I could answer to her complete satisfaction. I could only reassert my awareness that touching the cards was, in all circumstances, Absolutely Forbidden.

As to the wider significance of this episode, I'd rather not venture an opinion. In summary, I'll simply reiterate the facts, such as they are.

My mother uncovered a terrible tarot spread – easily the worst she'd ever seen. Shortly afterwards, I was hit by a calamity from the clear blue sky. Meanwhile, Mrs Coulson had a rather uneventful week.

Some months later, after much soul-searching, my mother was still turning over her recollections of *that* incident, and was fast coming to the conclusion that my presence at her readings might no longer be viable. It wasn't just that my mind was maturing and my own psychic vibrations were becoming louder and more intrusive. There was something else too – something she was close to intuiting. There were several instances, during quiet times at the shop, when I caught her looking at me with a pensive pout and furrowed brow. Then, one day, she came straight out and asked me if there was anything she should know. This was the kind of worrying question that my mother liked to ask me from time to time, and usually I'd have been happier just to reply in the negative and leave it at that. But these were not usual circumstances, and I knew that this matter would not be dropped until I'd at least given it its due consideration.

So, after some moments of creasing my own brow, I decided to tell her that I'd been having some pretty funny dreams recently.

'What sort of dreams?' my mother asked eagerly.

'Like daydreams,' I said, 'but peculiar ones.'

I could tell from my mother's expression that this was not precisely what she had in mind. I tried again.

'There was also a bit of a strange incident the other day,' I said, after a short hesitation.

My mother nodded that I should continue.

'When I was going to the stockroom,' I explained, 'I thought that I could smell the candles burning next door. But then when I went in to investigate, all the candles were out.'

I knew that I hadn't done my story its full justice, but took some consolation in the fact that this made it less likely that my mother would persist in her enquiries.

'It's probably nothing,' I concluded.

'Oh, no,' my mother disagreed, her furrows deepening. 'It's definitely something.'

'What kind of something?' I asked, rather cautiously.

'*Something*,' my mother repeated.

Once more, my mother's intuition proved itself a powerful force; because approximately six months after my accident, aged eleven and one quarter, I had my first epileptic fit.

4

ELECTRICAL STORMS

It happened at around nine o'clock one weekday evening, not long after Christmas. My mother heard me fall in the kitchen. It was like the meteor all over again, just on a much smaller scale. Having checked the roof, my mother knelt beside me and held my head while I shook and jerked and frothed at the mouth, my eyes wide open but rolled back in their sockets so that only the whites were visible. I was oblivious to all this, of course; I'd lost consciousness by then. I wasn't aware of anything until several minutes after the convulsions had stopped, and the last thing I remembered from before was walking into the kitchen to get a glass of milk. I had a headache like a hammer in my skull. I was very cold, and my pyjama bottoms were wet. I'd lost control of my bladder at some point while I was unconscious. I should tell you that having a generalized seizure is not a very dignified experience.

Dr Dawson, who lived just across the street, came over to examine me about ten minutes later. He gave me some diazepam, which is a sedative that makes you very sleepy and also helps to prevent fits. Then he made us an appointment to see him at the surgery the next morning. He suspected straight away that I'd had an epileptic seizure, but said that I'd have to be referred to the hospital for further tests.

I wasn't referred to Yeovil District Hospital this time. I had to go to Bristol Royal Infirmary because they had better equipment and lots of specialist doctors. The doctor who talked to me and my mother, before and after the tests, was called Dr Enderby, and he was actually a *triple* specialist. He was a neurologist who specialized in epilepsy, with a particular focus on childhood epilepsy. I think that it was very fortunate that I fell into Dr Enderby's care. There weren't many other doctors in the country who knew as much about childhood epilepsy as he did.

At this point, I should definitely take a bit of time to say some more about Dr Enderby, as he was to become an important figure in my life over the next few years.

I liked Dr Enderby a lot. But having said that, I liked most of the doctors and scientists I met; and I met quite a few between the ages of ten and eleven. For a time, it seemed as if I collected doctors and scientists the way normal kids collected football stickers. But what I mean to say is that from the beginning I felt Dr Enderby and I had quite a lot in common – despite the fact that he was a prominent neurologist and I was still in primary school.

Like me, Dr Enderby was quite bald. I was quite bald because after my accident my hair never grew back properly above my right ear. I had this peculiar missing clump. My mother said that it was hardly noticeable and that I should just give my hair a chance to grow back to its former glory – after a few months, the thin patch would be completely covered. (My mother wasn't keen on short hair.) But the fact was that after my accident I never felt comfortable once my hair started to get past a certain length – grade four, or thereabouts. I felt less self-conscious about my visible scar than I did about the uneven way in which my hair tried to grow. So ever since the accident, I've kept my hair in a permanent crew-cut. I own some clippers and never go more than three weeks without shaving my head.

Of course, my baldness wasn't exactly the same as Dr Enderby's. While I could have grown hair if I'd chosen to do so, Dr Enderby no longer had this option. He'd started to go bald at the age of eighteen, and was completely hairless by the time he finished medical school. And while my hairlessness was (like Lex Luthor's) the result of a terrible accident, Dr Enderby was bald because of genetics. He didn't need to examine his DNA to know this. He had two bald brothers, who were also doctors at Bristol Royal Infirmary. Dr Enderby (the neurologist – Dr Enderby Number One, as I thought of him, even though he was actually the youngest brother) told me that he and his two brothers made a point of never meeting up within the hospital grounds. This was because most patients found hospitalization to be an unsettling experience, and seeing three bald doctors with identical name badges could only make this worse. Dr Enderby was a pretty funny man when he wanted to be.

He was also quite a strange man. In his own way, he was probably as weird as Dr Weir. As well as being a neurologist, he was also a committed Buddhist. This meant that he didn't believe in God or heaven but he still thought that we should all be nice to each other because this was the most skilful way to get through life. He also believed that regular meditation made you a better, wiser person (though this was not the primary reason he suggested it for me). He said that meditation helped you to rely on your own inner resources to cultivate happiness and guide you through life's various stresses, and in the godless Buddhist universe, being able to rely on your own inner resources was particularly important.

Dr Enderby's views on God and meditation were definitely linked to his views about the brain. On his office wall, he had a funny little plaque with spidery black writing on it – like old, joined-up handwriting. And this is what it said:

> *The Brain is just the weight of God –*
> *For – Heft them – Pound for Pound –*
> *And they will differ – if they do –*
> *As Syllable from Sound –*

The first time I saw that plaque, I had very little idea what it meant, and absolutely no idea why there were all those dashes and random capital letters scattered all over the place. (Mr Treadstone, my then future English teacher, would have red-penned each and every one of those.) But I loved the way it sounded nevertheless.

When I eventually got round to asking Dr Enderby about the plaque, a few years later, he told me that it was the last stanza from a poem by a very old, very dead American poet called Emily Dickinson. When I asked him what it meant, he wouldn't tell me. Instead he asked what *I* thought it meant.

'I don't know,' I said after a few seconds of scratching my crew-cut. 'I know what the words mean, but I can't make sense of them all together.'

'Hmm,' said Dr Enderby. Then he scratched *his* head for a bit. 'Well, what do you think the difference between a syllable and a sound is?'

'There isn't all that much difference,' I said. 'A sound is a sound, and a syllable's kind of a sound too. A syllable's a chunk of sound in a word. Or sometimes it's the whole word. Like the word "sound" is a sound made of one syllable.'

I wasn't too satisfied with the way I'd explained this, but Dr Enderby seemed to understand. 'So maybe that's the point,' he said. 'Maybe they *aren't* all that different. Just like God and the brain aren't all that different.'

'How can God and the brain not be different?' I asked, frowning.

Dr Enderby smiled and adjusted his glasses. 'Well, for each of us the brain creates a whole, unique universe. It contains everything we know. Everything we see or touch. Everything we feel and remember. In a sense, our brains create all of reality for us. Without the brain, there's nothing. Some people find this idea scary, but I think it's rather beautiful. That's the reason I like to keep that plaque on my wall, where I can see it every day.'

I told Dr Enderby that I was still a little confused at this point – what with him being a Buddhist.

'When I look at that poem, God's just a metaphor,' Dr Enderby explained.

'So you don't think that God created the brain?' I asked.

'No, I don't think that,' Dr Enderby replied. 'I think that the brain created God. Because the human brain, however wonderful, is still quite fallible – as both you and I know. It's always searching for answers, but even when it's working as it should, its explanations are rarely perfect – especially when it comes to very big, complicated questions. That's why we have to nurture it. We have to give it plenty of space to develop.'

That was the gist of what Dr Enderby told me. His brain had spent a tremendous amount of time thinking about the brain.

The first time we met, he said that my 'first fit' was probably *not* my first fit. It was more likely my sixth or seventh or thirteenth or twenty-third – but no one could tell me for sure. As I've mentioned, in the months preceding my collapse in the kitchen, I'd been having lots of strange, out-of-place thoughts – thoughts involving weird pictures and sounds, and often weird smells. I'd dismissed them as daydreams, even though they felt more like night dreams – short, peculiar night dreams that would start without warning and then, just as quickly, dissolve back into the present. Furthermore, they'd been bad enough, and frequent enough, to draw comment at school, where I'd been diagnosed with 'concentration issues'.

After I told Dr Enderby this, he said that mine were 'classic' symptoms of partial epileptic seizures originating in the temporal lobes, and usually, at this point, he'd be asking me if I'd suffered any significant head injuries in the past eighteen months. But in my case, this was unnecessary. Dr Enderby could see my scar with his own eyes, and he already knew about the meteor. *Everybody* knew about the meteor.

Nevertheless, I still had to go through a lot of physical tests before Dr Enderby's final diagnosis could be made. He shone a torch in my eyes and prodded and pinched me in various places to test my sensations and reflexes. Then I had to have blood tests, and then an electroencephalography, where they attach wires to your scalp to measure the electrical activity in your brain. In case you didn't know, epilepsy is all to do with excess electrical activity in the brain. It works as follows.

Everybody's brain is a hive of electrical activity, and usually all the electrical signals behave as they should – they start, spread and stop as required. But in an epileptic fit, something abnormal happens. The neurons start sparking erratically, more or less at random, and instead of a narrow, regulated current, you get a chaotic flood of electricity pulsing through the brain. And the specific symptoms you experience tell you where the electricity has gone haywire. So jerks or twitches or convulsions indicate electrical activity in the motor cortex, the area of the brain responsible for controlling movement, and hallucinations indicate problems with one of the perceptual centres. And in a generalized epileptic seizure, there's a complete loss of consciousness, which indicates that the malfunction has spread through the whole cortex to the brainstem. This is what I experienced in the kitchen and what most people would recognize as an archetypal fit. Dr Enderby said that an epileptic seizure was like a thunderstorm taking place in the brain – a storm that temporarily knocks out all the communication links so that any messages from the outside world get either lost or scrambled. All that's left is your brain talking to itself.

Needless to say, my electroencephalography showed lots of abnormal spikes. Along with all the other evidence, this pretty much confirmed the provisional diagnosis of epilepsy, but it couldn't give any insight into the underlying cause – for this, I had to have an MRI scan, which uses giant magnets and radio waves to create a 3-D map of your brain's structure. Dr Enderby warned me that in more than half of all cases, no physiological cause for epilepsy is ever found. But in my case, there was good reason to suspect that a physiological cause *would* soon be discovered – as indeed it was.

The MRI scan showed subtle damage to my right temporal lobe, which was exactly where Dr Enderby expected to find it. But discovering a physiological cause for my epilepsy was not necessarily a good thing. Structural brain damage made it highly unlikely that my symptoms would clear up of their own accord. I'd probably suffer further seizures, which would have to be controlled with anti-epileptic drugs.

Two weeks later, this is exactly what happened. I had another generalized seizure and was put on anti-epileptic drugs. I've been on them ever since.

BRAINBOUND

Here's what came next, condensed.

My fits got worse. I could no longer go to school. We had to house-swap with Sam and Justine so that I could stay home while my mother continued to work. My world shrank down to five small rooms. I had strange visions. I read a lot. I continued my correspondence with Dr Weir. I got used to managing my condition. I gradually got better. And one day, about a year down the line, I was well enough to return to school. We got our house back.

Now here's the expanded version.

Things got much worse before they started to get better. Shortly after my original diagnosis, I was having generalized seizures every week and complex partial seizures most days. My epilepsy was severe and poorly controlled, and seemed, at first, completely unpredictable, which is what made it so debilitating. I couldn't go to the supermarket with my mother for fear of collapsing in the cereal aisle. Of course, during a full seizure, I'd be happily oblivious to all the drama. It was only in the woozy aftermath that I could take stock of my humiliation. Often there'd be tears and dribble. Often there'd be a fair amount of urine. Often there'd be a small circle of gawking onlookers. People are always drawn to scary and embarrassing public displays, and they don't come much more scary or embarrassing than watching an eleven-year-old boy convulsing in a puddle of pee.

Soon, going outside became one of my main triggers. Or more specifically, as Dr Enderby told me, it was the heightened stress of worrying about public seizures that was triggering my public seizures. I had to learn to manage my anxiety.

This was not something I had much chance of managing. Every time my mother tried to take me anywhere, I'd immediately start to panic, which would trigger a fit. The only places I felt safe were at our house, at the shop, in the car and at the hospital. It doesn't matter if you have a fit in the hospital, because everybody expects that kind of behaviour in hospitals and there are hundreds of people ready to take care of you. I wasn't even *slightly* worried about having a fit in the hospital; and, for this reason, I never had a fit in the hospital. My condition was cruel and stupid.

But in those early days, it wasn't just the frequency of my epileptic fits that kept me at home. It was also the side effects of the anti-epileptic drugs. For the first couple of months, before my system had properly adjusted to the carbamazepine, I was all over the place. My mind felt dull and foggy. I was constantly tired. I often felt sick and dizzy. My head hurt. My vision wobbled. My legs wobbled. I started to acquire what my mother generously called 'puppy fat'. Eventually, I was prescribed more drugs – strong painkillers and anti-sickness pills – to counterbalance the effects of my other drugs. This helped for a while, but the fits still showed no sign of improvement. So my dose of carbamazepine was increased and the side effects, having begun to die down, enjoyed a new lease of life. Dr Enderby said that we shouldn't be worried. Each patient was an individual, and often it took many months to get a prescription just right.

In the meantime, my mother said that she wanted to start me on a complementary therapy – something homeopathic. Dr Enderby was reluctant to support this decision. He said that while there were some alternative therapies that had been proven helpful in treating epilepsy, homeopathy was not one of them. From a scientific standpoint, homeopathy had never been proven helpful in treating *anything*. And often it could be a distraction (an expensive distraction) from those treatments that *had* been proven effective.

My mother calmly pointed out that she knew several people who had benefited enormously from homeopathic medicine.

Dr Enderby calmly pointed out that he knew of lots of people who hadn't. Then he started talking about placebos.

A long, patient and fruitless argument followed.

Eventually, Dr Enderby conceded that it would be okay for my mother to try me on a homeopathic treatment as long as I also continued to take my prescribed medications. To be more specific, this is what he said: at worst, a homeopathic treatment certainly couldn't harm me.

After consulting a homeopath, my mother put me on *cuprum metallicum* and *belladonna* – copper and deadly nightshade. I started on a 12X concentration of each, which meant that the active ingredient had been diluted down to one part in a trillion. Later, when this had no noticeable effect, the dose was increased to 24X – one part per trillion trillion. Later still, I was put on a 100X deadly nightshade pill. This dosage was even more diluted and potent. In fact, it was so diluted that its very existence was like a raised middle finger to four hundred years of scientific progress. Specifically (and I'm not making this up), if you took a single molecule of the active ingredient in deadly nightshade and dropped it into a glass of water the size of the known universe – well, the *belladonna* pill I was taking was approximately one hundred million trillion times more diluted than that.

This was probably why Dr Enderby didn't think a homeopathic remedy would do me any harm. In that concentration, deadly nightshade is no longer deadly. But I only realized all this much later on. At the time, aged eleven and a half, the homeopathic pills were just two more pills on the daily pill pile. I was taking at least six a day at one point, and asking zero questions.

Because I could no longer leave the house, I could no longer go to school; and because I could no longer go to school, my mother had a problem on her hands. She could not afford to stop working, but I was much too young and much too ill to be left on my own. A full-time babysitter was also out of the question. My mother wanted me close by so that she could be there the second I had my next fit, and home and work were separated by a ten-minute drive.

Our house was (and is) located in the village of Lower Godley, about six miles northeast of Glastonbury. You may not have heard of it, but that's okay. Lower Godley is a very small village.

It's basically just a long, straight road with houses on either side, fields beyond the houses, and a little bulge in the middle where there's a shop and a church and a post office. It has a population of about four hundred and twelve and a very infrequent bus service. About the only interesting thing I can think of to tell you about Lower Godley is the following: Lower Godley implies the existence of an Upper Godley, but (for some reason no one in the village knows) there is no Upper Godley. If it ever existed, it doesn't any more. It's also possible that whoever named our village thought that Godley on its own was a stupid name for a village, and so added the 'Lower' more or less on a whim. I don't know. But for whatever reason, the village ended up with a somewhat misleading prefix, and this is by far its most interesting feature.

Anyway, to return to the point, our house in Lower Godley was too far away from my mother's work for me to stay there in the daytime without her worrying, and this is why we ended up swapping homes with Justine and Sam. My mother, I should tell you, owned the flat above the shop as well as the shop itself. She had bought both with her inheritance money, which she had come into when my grandfather (her father) died from a heart attack, soon after he discovered she was pregnant with me.

Sam and Justine didn't mind swapping houses for several reasons: first, our house in Lower Godley was much bigger and nicer than the flat above the shop; second, it had a garden filled with interesting wildlife; third, they were happy to help. They also didn't mind looking after Lucy. Lucy couldn't come with us because the flat was too small and was surrounded by unfamiliar roads and alleys, so it wouldn't have been safe to install a cat-flap. And since Lucy had always been an outdoors cat, my mother didn't think she'd like being confined.

'At least it would stop her from procreating,' I told her, very sullenly.

I was upset because I wasn't crazy about being confined either. But after we'd moved, I realized that the flat really wasn't big enough to accommodate the cat. It was barely big enough for my mother and me. Apparently, we'd managed to live there before, up until I was about three years old, but I didn't really remember this. And I was much smaller then, so it probably didn't feel quite so cramped.

The five rooms in the flat varied in size from small to extremely small, in a gradually descending hierarchy, like a set of those Russian dolls. My mother's bedroom was the only room approaching normal size. After that, the kitchen was a little smaller, and the living room smaller still. The bathroom was so pokey that you could use the sink, the shower and the toilet all at the same time, though not without consequences. And finally – bottom of the heap, smallest doll in the set – there was the 'box' room. Sam had managed to squeeze a desk and chair in there so she could use it as an office for whatever it was she did. I, however, managed to squeeze an entire bed in there. This left a foot-wide corridor of floor space and a door that could not be fully opened. Originally, my mother had insisted that it wasn't possible to fit a bed in the box room and said we'd have to share, but she had underestimated the extent to which I valued my privacy. Possible or not, I was determined that my bed was going into that room, and after I'd removed the wheels from its base and taken the finish off the doorframe, it slid in like a Tetris block. Then, after a great deal of soul-searching, I decided to sacrifice the strip of room in which I could walk to a very thin bookcase. On the bookcase I put a lamp and my meteorite. This left just one corner of my room in which I could stand up – a space considerably smaller than the inside of a phone box.

All of my clothes had to live in a chest in the living room, but most of the time, I just stayed in my pyjamas.

My world had become very small, and it stayed like that for a long, long time.

After a while, anything can become routine – even fits. I got used to them, and eventually, my mother did too. As Dr Enderby explained to us at a very early stage, epileptic fits look a lot scarier than they are. They can't really hurt you unless you happen to fall and hit your head or bite your tongue while you're unconscious. Serious injuries are rare, especially in short-lived episodes, and my fits never lasted more than a few minutes.

I learned how to recognize the early stages of my seizures many months before I learned how to halt their progression. The early warning that some people get before a seizure is called an 'aura', and it usually manifests itself as a very specific sensation or emotion – a ringing in the ears, a loss of balance, a sudden feeling of déjà vu. In my case, the aura was always the same – a sudden, powerful smell. This might sound strange, but it isn't. Dr Enderby told me that lots of people with temporal lobe epilepsy experience strong olfactory – smell-related – hallucinations. The aura I experienced told him that my seizures were originating in my olfactory cortex before spreading to the other parts of my temporal lobe – the parts responsible for memory and emotion and so on.

Once I became able to recognize my aura and understand the progression of my seizures, they became much less disorientating. Sometimes when I experienced partial seizures without losing consciousness, it wasn't that different to falling asleep – at the stage when you're still half awake and tiny pictures just kind of pop in and out of your head like scraps of film. These visions were still strange, but once I knew what was happening, they were rarely disturbing.

My mother bought me a book about epilepsy that Dr Enderby had recommended, and in this book it said that people suffering from temporal lobe seizures often experience deeply religious visions. The nature of these visions depended on the religious background and upbringing of the patient, and people had reported seeing all kinds of curious hallucinations: angels, demons, dazzling white lights, pearly gates, bearded men, many-armed elephants, the Virgin Mary, Jesus playing a trumpet – that kind of thing.

In my most frequent recurring vision, I saw a scrawny, dirty, naked peasant hanging by his feet from a tree.

'That's the Hanged Man,' my mother whispered when I told her.

'I know it's the Hanged Man!' I snapped. And I realized straight away that I shouldn't have told her. Now she'd want to make a big deal out of it.

'It often signifies inertia – a life held in suspension,' my mother pointed out.

'I know what the Hanged Man signifies,' I assured her.

'You'll tell me if you see anything else, won't you?' she asked.

I decided at that point that I probably *shouldn't* tell her if I saw anything else. I knew what she was thinking. I could see the cogs turning. Despite everything that Dr Enderby had told us, she was still thinking that I'd inherited 'the family gift'. She was thinking that my brain had started to predict the future, or at the very least, the present.

The period of my confinement was also the period in which I developed my insatiable appetite for reading. Reading, it turned out, was one of the only things I *could* do. I couldn't go anywhere, and I didn't really like watching TV unless there was a James Bond film on. About the only programme I liked to watch regularly was *The Simpsons*. Sometimes my mother watched it with me after she'd closed the shop. But most of the time, watching TV in my pyjamas made me feel like an invalid.

Reading, on the other hand, never made me feel like an invalid. And I found that the quiet concentration required actually helped to reduce the number of daily seizures. It put me in a state of mind that was good for me.

After I'd read through my book on epilepsy a few times, I had my mother order some more of the same from the mobile library, along with an introductory guide to the brain and neurology, called *The Brain for Dummies*. I also read and re-read the book on meteors and meteorites that Dr Weir had sent me. It was by a man called Martin Beech who lived in Wiltshire, right next door to Somerset. My favourite chapter was the one in which Mr Beech discussed the probability of getting directly struck by a meteor heavier than one gram, which, if you lived for one hundred years, was about one in two billion. Mr Beech (who had written his book before the Woods Impactor) said that although there had been several near misses, there was only one well-documented case of a person being seriously injured by a meteor strike. The person in question was Mrs Annie Hodges of Sylacauga, Alabama, USA, who was struck in the stomach by a four-kilogram meteor on 28 November 1954. She was reposing on her couch at the time. Her meteor, like mine, burst through the roof, but she wasn't so badly injured on account of the fact that the stomach can take a blow better than the head.

Martin Beech included a photo of Mrs Hodges in his book. The photo showed her standing below the hole in her ceiling with the Mayor of Sylacauga and the Chief of Police. The mayor and the Chief of Police are smiling at the camera, but Mrs Hodges is not. She's looking very intensely at her four-kilogram stony meteorite, which she's holding in both her hands. She looks kind of pissed off.

This is what Martin Beech wrote about Mrs Hodges and her meteor injury: 'This story reminds us that even very low-probability events can, and indeed do, occur.'

I liked that sentence a lot. I underlined it in black biro.

I didn't just read about brains and meteors, though – my interests were slightly wider than that. I also read *Alice in Wonderland* and *Through the Looking Glass*. (My epilepsy book said that Lewis Carroll also had temporal lobe epilepsy, which was probably one of the reasons he had such a strange imagination.) Then, after I'd finished with Lewis Carroll, I started to read a lot more fantasy books, most of which Sam lent me. I read *The Hobbit* twice. Then I read *The Lord of the Rings* twice. Then I read *His Dark Materials* twice. I read all these books twice because I liked them so much that as soon as I'd finished them, I immediately wanted to go back to the beginning and start again. When I look back at the year I spent in the box room, I think these were the books that stopped me from feeling sorry for myself and got me to thinking that, on the whole, my life wasn't so terrible. When I read these books, I no longer felt like I was confined to a very tiny world. I no longer felt house-bound and bedbound. Really, I told myself, I was just *brain*bound, and this was not such a sorry state of affairs. My brain, with a little help from other people's brains, could take me to some pretty interesting places, and create all kinds of wonderful things. Despite its faults, my brain, I decided, was not the worst place in the world to be.

My correspondence with Dr Weir started after I was released from hospital and has continued through to the present day. I enclose now carbon copies of the letter I sent from the box room (2005) and the reply I received.

Dear Dr Weir,

Thank you for my Christmas card. Jupiter is a very pretty planet, but not quite as pretty as Earth. I was very surprised to hear that the Great Red Spot is three times bigger than the whole Earth. That must be a very impressive storm. Jupiter is even more massive than I thought. If you have any more photos of the planets, I'd like to see them very much. Usually I'd Google them, but unfortunately I don't have access to the internet at the moment.

I'm sorry I haven't written to thank you sooner, but I have been suffering from quite a lot of epileptic fits. In case you don't know, an epileptic fit is where the electricity in your brain gets overactive and causes convulsions and hallucinations, et cetera. I was diagnosed with temporal lobe epilepsy (TLE) just after Christmas when I fell unconscious in the kitchen. I think I'm starting to get better now, though. Dr Enderby, my neurologist, is very nice. He prescribed me some carbamazepine, which is an anti-epileptic drug. It used to make me feel very tired and sick, but now that I've got used to it, it's not so bad.

Unfortunately, I've not been able to go to school for many months because my fits have been too frequent and severe. Dr Enderby says that stress is one of my main triggers at the moment, but there are things I can learn to help with this. The good thing about being off school is that at least I've been able to do lots of reading. I've read Martin Beech's meteorite book at least five times, and also lots of books about the brain. Dr Enderby says that it's good for me to know about my condition and I've enjoyed learning about my temporal lobes and neurons and synapses, et cetera. I never realized the brain was so complicated. Dr Enderby told me it's the most complicated collection of atoms in the known universe. That blew me away!!! I think when I grow up, I might like to be a neurologist, unless I decide to be an astrophysicist instead. ☺

Anyway, despite all the learning I've been doing by

myself, the Local Education Authority still wrote to my mother saying that if I couldn't go to school, they might have to send a private tutor round to give me lessons. But luckily we don't have to pay any extra for this. It's all included in my mother's taxes.

Thank you again for my card and for Martin Beech's meteorite book. I hope you are well and your research is going well and the other astrophysicists have forgiven you for being the first to examine my iron-nickel meteorite. I still plan to donate it to a museum one day, but for now I still like to look at it on quite a regular basis. It's on my bookcase next to my bed, so it's usually the first thing I see when I wake up, which is nice.

Yours sincerely,

Alex Woods

Dear Alex, [Dr Weir replied]

It's lovely to hear from you again, although I'm very sorry to hear that you've been so ill. I know that epilepsy can be a very difficult condition to deal with, but I've Googled Dr Enderby and, I must say, it sounds like you're in very capable hands. Stay positive and I'm sure you'll continue to get better.

I'm thrilled that you're taking such an interest in science! You sound as if you already know a great deal about the brain, so I'm sure you'll make a wonderful neurologist (and if you decide to become an astronomer, so much the better!).

Since you enjoyed Martin Beech's meteorite book so much, I think you'll also enjoy *The Universe: A Beginner's Guide* [enclosed]. Think of it as a 'get well soon' present! It has lots of information about the stars and the planets and the Asteroid Belt, as well as some superb photos from the Hubble Space Telescope.

Do make sure you write again soon. I'll be very eager to hear how you're getting on – especially with all the reading!

All my best wishes,

(Dr) Monica Weir

P.S. Please send my warm regards to your mother as well.

Over the next months, I became more and more used to managing my condition. Dr Enderby taught me several exercises designed to help me stop seizures in their earliest stages – as soon as I became aware of my aura. These exercises were all based on staying calm and alert and focussed – on switching my attention away from unwanted thoughts and feelings and towards some kind of anchor.

I watched my breath. I counted to fifty. I named each of the planets and major moons in turn, starting at the Sun and working my way out to the Kuiper Belt. I listed every character from *The Simpsons* I could think of. I remained calm and alert and banished any distractions to a separate corner of my mind and focussed my attention like a laser. It was a very strange experience. I told Dr Enderby that it felt like Jedi training. Dr Enderby replied that it *was* like Jedi training. It was a form of meditation – a way of helping my brain to stay poised and peaceful.

Music was another anchor that I tried. Dr Enderby said that research had shown that, for many people, listening to music could help to slow or stop the progression of a seizure. But you had to *really* listen, and some types of music tended to work better than others. Ideally, the music should be calm and have a reasonably intricate structure. Instrumental classical music had been shown to work the best in most cases. Unfortunately, my mother didn't own any instrumental classical music. There were only five CDs in the flat. Four were 'relaxation music' – whales and dolphins and panpipes and so on – and the other was a weird compilation album from the 1980s. The first track on it was 'Enola Gay', an ancient song about the atomic bombing of Hiroshima by Orchestral Manoeuvres in the Dark. The second was '*Neunundneunzig Luftballons*' by Nena, which also had something to do with nuclear annihilation. This was a popular theme of the 1980s because Ronald Reagan was President of the United States and everyone feared the worst – but that was something I would only come to understand later on, after talking at length with Mr Peterson.

After some experimentation, I found that the dolphins did nothing, the panpipes worked okay, and 'Enola Gay' made my seizures considerably worse.

The private tutor sent by the Local Education Authority was called Mrs Sullivan. She was nice enough, but she was only paid to come for three hours a week and most of that was spent going over all the things I already knew. Mrs Sullivan said that the most important thing at that moment was to make sure that I was up to date with everything that would come up in the Key Stage 2 SATs, which I should have taken several months earlier. She wouldn't teach me anything new – any of the secondary-school stuff I *should* have been learning at that age.

'One thing at a time, Alex,' she insisted.

This, unfortunately, made our lessons rather tedious. My attention wandered a lot. I'd decided that I liked learning better when I could do it in my pyjamas in the privacy of the box room.

When I was eventually allowed to sit my SATs, I passed them with no problems at all. But by that time, I was a whole year behind everyone else my age, and the Local Education Authority decreed that when I started secondary school, I'd be starting in the year below. I didn't know enough to skip a year.

I would have liked to have pointed out to whoever made the final decision that actually I knew quite a lot of things – things that some twelve-year-olds *didn't* know. I knew a surprising amount about the anatomy and physiology of the brain. I knew the difference between meteoroids, meteors and meteorites. I knew words like achondrite and olfactory and cerebellum. But I don't suppose this would have made much difference. My self-education had been scattergun, at best, and most of the knowledge in my head was the wrong sort of knowledge. I didn't know half the things I was *supposed* to know at twelve years old.

I knew that iridium-193 was one of two stable isotopes of iridium, a very rare, very dense metal, but I didn't know that the periodic table even existed.

I knew how many zeroes there were in a quintillion, but I thought that algebra lived in ponds.

I'd picked up a few Latin words, and a smattering of Elvish, but my French was non-existent.

I'd read more than one book of more than one thousand pages (more than once), but I wouldn't have been able to identify a metaphor if it poked me in the eye.

By secondary-school standards, I was quite a dunce.

WELCOME TO THE MONKEY HOUSE

In case you didn't know, in secondary school – especially in the early years of secondary school – diversity is not celebrated. In secondary school, being different is the worst crime you can commit. Actually, in secondary school, being different is pretty much the *only* crime you can commit. Most of the things the UN considers crimes are not considered crimes at secondary school. Being cruel is fine. Being brutal is fine. Being obnoxious is fine. Being superficial is especially fine. Explosive acts of violence are fine. Taking pleasure in the humiliation of others is fine. Holding someone's head down the toilet is fine (and the weaker the someone, and the dirtier the toilet, the finer it is). None of these things will hurt your social standing. But being different – that's unforgivable. Being different is the fast-track to Pariah Town. A pariah is someone who's excluded from mainstream society. And if you know that at twelve years of age, you're probably an inhabitant of Pariah Town.

Being different sounds like a simple concept, but actually, it's quite complex. For a start, there are a few types of difference

– a selected few – that are acceptable and won't result in you getting mud and stones hurled at you. For example, if you're different because your family is unusually rich (as long as it's the right kind of rich) and has three cars (the right kind of cars), then you'll probably be okay. Secondly, there are some combinations of difference that can cancel each other out. For example, if you're abnormally stupid in almost every area but also happen to have abnormally good hand–eye or foot–eye co-ordination – that is, if you're abnormally good at sports – then you'll definitely be okay.

The crime of being different is really the crime of being *offensively* different, and this can be broken down into several sub-crimes.

1) **Being poor**. This is the worst crime you can commit, but, again, it's not as simple as it sounds. Being 'poor' really means not having the right stuff – Nike trainers, an appropriate amount of pocket money, a PlayStation or Xbox, a mobile phone, a flatscreen TV and computer in your bedroom and so on and so forth. It doesn't matter if you don't have these things for reasons other than poverty. You're still poor.

2) **Being physically different** – too small, too gangly, too spotty, buck teeth, braces (to prevent buck teeth), too skinny, too fat (equals *very* fat), too hairy, not hairy enough, excessively ugly, tendency to stutter or stammer, unacceptable pitch of voice, unacceptable accent, unacceptable odour, disproportionate limbs or features, cross-eyed, bug-eyed, lazy-eyed, poor vision/ crap glasses, lumps, bumps or humps, excessive freckling, large visible moles, unacceptable skin colour or tone, sickly, disabled, unacceptable bone structure, ginger hair.

3) **Being mentally different** – too clever, too stupid, too swotty, bookish, nerdy, weird hobbies and interests, just weird, incorrect sense of humour.

4) **Having unacceptable friends or relatives**. Associating with people who commit the crimes listed above and below is also a crime – even if you live in their house and have little choice in the matter. Having a parent who won't let you do all of the things you should be allowed to do – the things everybody else is apparently doing – is also unacceptable.

5) **Being gay**. This has surprisingly little to do with what you do with your private parts (or, more accurately, what you'd *like* to do with your private parts). Being gay is more a state of mind, or sometimes, less often, a state of body. You could almost include it as a sub-crime in 2) and 3), but really, it goes beyond both of these categories. And because of the number of times it crops up as a specific accusation, it definitely deserves its own special category. But the best way to explain what 'being gay' means is to tell you some of the things that are gay.

If you're a boy, any display of sensitivity is gay. Compassion is gay. Crying is supergay. Reading is usually gay. Certain songs and types of music are gay. 'Enola Gay' would certainly be thought gay. Love songs are gay. Love itself is *incredibly* gay, as are any other heartfelt emotions. Singing is gay, but chanting is not gay. Wanking contests are not gay. Neither is all-male cuddling during specially designated periods in football matches, or communal bathing thereafter. (I didn't invent the rules of gay – I'm just telling you what they are.)

Girls can be gay too, but it's much harder for them. And

girls don't tend to call each other gay as much as boys do. When a girl is gay, she's called a dyke. Reasons for being a dyke include having thick limbs, bad hair or flat shoes.

Usually you have to commit quite a few of these crimes (or one very serious sub-crime) to earn yourself a permanent residence in Pariah Town. But as you've probably worked out, I committed crimes in every category.

1) I was poor – despite my mother owning a successful business, a house, a flat and a car. Compared to many single parents, my mother was a tycoon; but as I've explained, poorness and poverty aren't the same in secondary school. I could have taken in photocopies of my mother's bank statements and this wouldn't have swayed a single mind. The evidence against me was too damning. I didn't have the right stuff, therefore I was poor.

2) and 3) My epilepsy meant that I was both physically and mentally different in a very obvious way – I was sick in the body *and* in the mind. I was also quite short and a late developer, but this was just about compensated for by my being kept back a year – although, in most ways, being kept back a year was definitely *not* an advantage. This circumstance presented further evidence that I was probably retarded – even though I knew a lot of strange things (not the right things) and was also a swot. I may well have been unique in that I was the only person who seemed simultaneously too clever *and* too stupid.

4) You know about my mother already.

5) Most of my traits and all the things I liked were super-supergay.

Needless to say, the early years of secondary school were not a happy time for me.

My secondary school was called the Asquith Academy. My mother chose it for me because it had good exam results and excellent resources and promoted 'timeless' values. (This was how the Asquith Academy described itself in its brochure and on its website: 'The modern school with timeless values.') It was the kind of school *she* would have hated if she'd been forced to go there. But as I've already mentioned, there were different rules concerning what was right for her and what was right for me. The most important thing for her was that she be free to express herself and free to follow her own fantastic beliefs wherever they happened to lead her, disregarding any logical holes along the way. The most important thing for me was that I got excellent exam results so that I'd have the opportunity to do whatever I decided to do *later on*. This was especially important now that I had epilepsy. My mother was determined that I should not get left behind, and she was adamant that no school in the county could refuse me. It didn't matter how limited spaces were: it would have been discrimination had they turned me away.

The Asquith Academy was named after Robert Asquith, the man who paid to have it built and continued to pay for a significant proportion of its running costs. Robert Asquith, as we all learned in the first year, was a self-made multimillionaire, which is one of the best things you can possibly be. His company started out making roller-balls for mice (computers, not rodents), and, for a long time, these were the best roller-balls on the planet. Then when a new company started making better roller-balls, Robert Asquith used some of his millions to acquire and gut his younger rival. This was called the free market. Then he moved his operations to China, where most of the people were peasants and happy to work for much lower wages than people in the UK. This was called globalization. Eventually, because of lasers, many mice no longer needed roller-balls, so the factories in China had to close, and I guess all the Chinese peasants lost their poorly paid jobs, just like all the English workers had lost their jobs when operations moved to China. But by this time, Robert Asquith had his millions invested in software and electronics and e-solution consultancies and so on.

This meant that although Robert Asquith's story incorporated many trials and tribulations, it was ultimately uplifting. The moral was work hard and never give up.

The Asquith Academy was modelled on some ancient grammar school near Shepton Mallet that Robert Asquith had attended from the ages of eleven to eighteen and which had been blown into a million pieces in the 1980s by a catastrophic explosion in the boiler room. Luckily, the explosion had happened very early in the morning, so no one was killed but the caretaker.

There was little chance of the Asquith Academy exploding, as it had state-of-the-art under-floor central heating. It also had a Latin motto, which appeared in a little banner on all its signs and letterheads. This was the same motto that had belonged to Robert Asquith's exploded grammar school: *Ex Veritas Vires*.

In English, this means: 'Welcome to the Monkey House.'

I'm joking. That's what the school motto *should* have been.

Ex Veritas Vires really means: 'From Truth, Strength!'

These were noble sentiments, but I'm not sure how well they applied to our school's overall ethos.

At the Asquith Academy, learning was 'outcome-orientated'. This meant that you learned how to do well in exams, and this was why the exam results were always so good. It all made perfect sense. If it wasn't likely to come up in an exam, it wasn't worth knowing – that was the Asquith policy. If we needed any additional inspiration, that's what the legend of our super-rich founding father was all about. Education didn't have to be its own reward. Education brought rewards in later life. If we worked hard, passed our exams and never gave up, one day we too could be as rich as Robert Asquith.

'Outcome-orientated' learning also meant that lessons were often very didactic, which meant that you had to learn lots of facts and you had to learn what you should think about those facts. Of course, I didn't mind learning facts – I *liked* learning facts – but it would have been nice to have had a context too. For example, in physics, they taught us all about gravity and that f = ma and about Newton's Laws of Motion – which we had to learn word for word – but they taught us nothing about Newton himself. When I looked him up on the internet, I discovered that Newton was a pretty weird and interesting guy. It turned out that he had come up with gravity and his Laws of Motion while he had nothing else to do because he was locked away at home, hiding from the plague – brainbound. *That* was pretty interesting. It also turned out that he invented a new type of telescope and spent a lot of his spare time trying to turn base metal into gold. These things were pretty interesting too. And then I found out that he had wild, staring eyes, crazy silver hair, and an arch-enemy called Robert Hooke, who may have been a hunchback. All this was *really* interesting. It turned out that Science had some great stories and characters, but you never got to hear about them in science lessons. I'm not saying that we should have spent hours and hours learning Newton's biography, but five minutes would have been nice. Knowing a bit about Newton makes $f = ma$ all the more inspiring. But unfortunately, knowing about Newton was not in the exams – it was irrelevant.

As you may have guessed, the official ethos of the Asquith Academy was kind of stuffy. All the male teachers had to be addressed as 'Sir', and all the female teachers as 'Miss', and whenever an adult walked into the room, everyone had to stand up as a sign of respect. And there was a correct way of doing everything, and everything had to be done correctly. There was a correct way to stand and a correct way to sit and a correct way to shake hands and a correct way to knot your tie and a correct way to speak. Correct speaking was particularly important.

Mr Treadstone, my years seven-through-eleven English teacher, who was also the deputy head, was the main policeman in charge of ensuring that the English language was never violated – not in writing and not in casual conversation. Mr Treadstone wanted you to pronounce everything correctly, and preferably with no accent – no 'West Country twang'. He also insisted that you use the full and correct term rather than second-class derivations: 'hello' instead of 'hi'; 'yes' instead of 'yeah', 'yep', 'yup' or '(y)uh huh'. In my case, Mr Treadstone quickly identified a specific problem area, which was my tendency to use vague and redundant colloquialisms, especially when I was trying to explain something. I said 'like' too much, and seldom in the appropriate context. I said 'pretty' when I meant 'rather'. I said 'y'know' as a kind of pointless, mid-sentence percussion. (He *didn't* know – that was why I was telling him.) And worst of all was my apparent inability to utter a three-sentence paragraph without using 'kind of' as a modifier. This phrase had no place in the English language. If I needed a modifier, he referred me back to rather – or slightly, or quite, or largely, or mostly. Any one of these would be preferable to my unfortunate verbal tic.

Although I don't use it nearly so much any more, I've decided, five years down the line, that Mr Treadstone's verdict on 'kind of' was kind of unjust. Obviously, this phrase can be redundant or reductive, or just plain stupid in some sentences, but not in *all* sentences. I wouldn't, for example, use a sentence like 'Antarctica is kind of cold', or 'Hitler was kind of evil'. But sometimes things aren't black and white. And sometimes 'kind of' expresses this better than any other phrase. For example, when I tell you that my mother was kind of peculiar, I can think of no better way of putting this.

However, for Mr Treadstone, 'kind of' – the undesirability of the phrase itself – was simply the most annoying part of a broader problem. Ideally, he said, I should try to address my reliance on modifiers at a more fundamental level. Mr Treadstone believed that there was *always* an apposite word. The English language, after all, was the richest in the world. If you couldn't find the apposite word, if you found your language slipping into the mire of vagueness and obscurity, this meant that you needed to work on your vocabulary. Because the apposite word certainly existed – and it was very eager to make your acquaintance.

In the early years at Asquith, I was constantly working on improving my vocabulary, and since I read so much – especially in the way of obscure medical and scientific tracts – I was often encountering words that no one else knew. But I still found that when I spoke – when I tried to explain things in real time – I struggled to find the apposite word. Later, whenever I was struggling to find the apposite word or phrase, I developed the habit of trying to imagine what Mr Peterson might say in that situation. Mr Peterson had a way of getting right to the point. He would have called this 'cutting through the crap'.

As for Mr Treadstone, this is what I think Mr Peterson would have said about him: Mr Treadstone had a Serious Bug up his Ass.

The Asquith Academy was really a school full of weird contradictions. It was an ultramodern building – only five or six years old when I started there – but it had an ancient Latin motto. It had quadrangles built out of steel and glass. In lessons, you learned how to pass exams, and outside of lessons, you learned about correct language, behaviour and posture. The Asquith Academy was constantly trying to elevate its pupils in terms of their morals and values, but in many cases, it was fighting an unwinnable war. As I've already implied, many of the pupils who went to Asquith weren't exactly enlightened. Some of them were barely *evolved*. They were just extremely two-faced. They learned how to behave correctly in supervised society, and behaved like gorillas everywhere else.

In my year, most of the gorillas had telling nicknames. There was Jamie Ascot, whom everybody – friends and enemies alike – called 'Jamie Asbo', because of what he'd been caught doing in his next-door neighbour's pond. Then there was Ryan Goodwin, known to all as 'Studwin' or 'Studdo' – not because of his success with the ladies, or the quality of his genome (which was questionable), but after a late sliding tackle that had hospitalized Peter Dove. And then there was Declan Mackenzie, whom most people called 'Decker'. This was a simple abbreviation. The fact that he liked to beat people up was a happy coincidence. Asbo, Studwin and Decker formed a formidable bullying alliance. There were also various other bullies within the school, but I mention these three in particular because they all happened to live near me. We caught the same school bus, they were my most frequent tormentors, and they play a pivotal role in my story.

Decker Mackenzie was the leader. It wasn't that he was the strongest – Studwin, whose shoulders were half as wide again as anybody else's, could have annihilated him in a fight. And he wasn't exactly the wittiest guy on the planet – Jamie Asbo had a much sharper, crueller wit. Decker Mackenzie was simply the loudest and most aggressive of the three. I'm not sure how things work in the wild, but in the playground hierarchy, Decker Mackenzie was alpha male through sheer force of will – through his unshakeable belief in his own right to dominate. Studwin and Asbo were his underlings, his loyal henchmen.

At the other end of the social ladder, the bullied also tended to acquire telling nicknames (most of them dreamed up by Jamie Asbo): Ian Stainpants (formerly Ian Stainfield), Gyppo Johnson, Brian Bin-Bag Beresford (whose mother insisted on repairing his clothes rather than buying new ones), Snotty George Friedman and so on and so forth. As for me, I found myself at the receiving end of many different nicknames. For a while, I was 'Ally Twatter' (a feeble reworking of Harry Potter, based on the fact that I had a visible scar, a witch for a mother, was prone to seizures and, presumably, was a twat). Later, I was Weirdo Woods, and then Wanker Woods – with a handful of obvious variants (Wankshaft, Wankstain, Wankface). But fortunately none of these nicknames gained popularity. Most of the time I was just Woods, and wished for nothing more than to be as plain as my surname – widespread, forgettable, ordinary.

CREOSOTE

There are two ideas I want you to think about at this point.

1) In life, there are no true beginnings or endings.

Events flow into each other, and the more you try to isolate them in a container, the more they spill over the sides, like canal-water breaching its artificial banks. A related point is that the things we label 'beginnings' and 'endings' are often, in reality, indistinguishable. They are one and the same thing. This is one of the things the Death card symbolizes in tarot – an end that is also a new beginning.

It's only in stories that we find clearly marked beginnings and endings, and these have been selected from a very deep well of possibilities. I could have started my story by telling you about my conception, or my mother's adolescence, or the formation of the solar system – the birth of the Sun and the planets and the Asteroid Belt four and a half billion years ago – and any one of these would have been a reasonable place to begin, as was the place I finally settled on.

2) The universe is at once very orderly and very disorderly.

There is large-scale mechanical determinism – Newton's Laws of Motion, gravity, snooker balls, ballistics, the orbits of heavenly bodies. There is Chaos Theory, which is still a form of determinism, just impossibly complex – systems that are very difficult to understand or predict because of their extreme sensitivity to small variations and chance occurrences (the Butterfly Effect). Then there is quantum randomness at the sub-atomic scale – uncertainty, unknowability, games of chance, probability in place of classical predictability. And there might also be free will to throw into the mix.

It's possible to find order in chaos, and it's equally possible to find chaos underlying apparent order. Order and chaos are slippery concepts. They're like a set of twins who like to swap clothing from time to time. Order and chaos frequently intermingle and overlap, the same as beginnings and endings. Things are often more complicated, or more simple, than they seem. Often it depends on your angle.

I think that telling a story is a way of trying to make life's complexity more comprehensible. It's a way of trying to separate order from chaos, patterns from pandemonium. Other ways include tarot and science.

The moment I'm about to describe is the culmination of one set of chaotic circumstances and the starting point for another. It's a moment that makes me think about how life can seem highly ordered and highly chaotic all at the same time. It's an ending and a new beginning.

It was 14 April 2007, a Saturday. It was three days after the day Kurt Vonnegut died, but I didn't know that at the time. I found out later on. I hadn't heard of Kurt Vonnegut at that point.

I'd been to the village shop to collect a couple of essential items, and was now taking the scenic route home – round the back of the churchyard, past the duck pond, over the stile, on to the bridle path, past the allotments and houses, off the bridle path at Horton Lane, through the kissing gate, up to the junction and then a short road-walk home. I was carrying my mother's hessian bag, on which was printed in green ink the phrase *Reduce, reuse, recycle*. This was not an acceptable brand of bag to be associated with, and I knew this very well; but since I was only going to the village shop and back, and since Lower Godley wasn't exactly Milan, I thought I'd probably be okay. As it turned out, I was wrong.

'Nice bag, Woods!'

It was Decker Mackenzie. He was sitting on the wall of the churchyard, which God had built approximately buttock-high, and drinking a can of Red Bull, which is an energy drink made from caffeine and taurine and lots and lots of sugar. He was flanked, as always, by Studwin and Asbo. Studwin had his Nike baseball cap pulled so low down his forehead that most of his face was invisible. He was holding a thick branch that had probably fallen from one of the oaks or sycamores, and was poking around in the dirt like some kind of Neanderthal who'd just discovered his opposable thumbs. Asbo was rolling a cigarette. Asbo was *always* rolling a cigarette. No single twelve-year-old could have smoked as many cigarettes as Asbo managed to roll. There weren't enough unsupervised hours in the day. It's possible that Asbo spent a lot of his private time *un*rolling cigarettes. I don't know. I'd walked right into their territory without noticing them. The reason I didn't notice them was that I'd been absorbed in the front cover of my magazine, which

I now dropped into my mother's unacceptable bag. This turned out to be quite a stupid action – it drew attention to the magazine, and yet more attention to the bag.

'Whatcha got there, Woods?'

I kept my eyes down and continued walking. This was the only sensible policy. A few moments and I'd be safely past them and on my way.

'What's in the bag, Woods?' Decker snarled.

'If you can call it a bag,' Asbo added.

'More like a crap sack,' Decker elaborated. 'What's in it?'

'It's nothing,' I said, quietly and rather unconvincingly.

What was actually in the bag was this: the latest edition of the *Sky at Night* magazine, which, in the days before I had my subscription, I used to have ordered in to the village shop every month; a box of cat treats for Lucy – who was again eating for several; and half a bunch of grapes, which I'd been planning to feed to the ducklings, who were only a few weeks old. There was no item in this inventory that was worth broadcasting. Especially not the grapes. Feeding the ducklings, needless to say, was one of the gayest things imaginable.

I tried to shuffle past but Studwin had raised his ogre arm to block my path.

'Come on, Woods,' jeered Jamie Asbo. 'Don't be shy.'

'It's just shopping,' I mumbled.

'Hmmm,' Decker mused. *'Just shopping.* Sounds suspicious.' He crushed the Red Bull can in his hand and then chucked it over his shoulder into the churchyard. It bounced off a gravestone before landing on the final resting place of Ernest Shuttleworth, dedicated husband and father, startling a blackbird in the process.

'My God!' Decker said, loudly and suddenly, as if struck by the thunderbolt of inspiration. 'It's not *porn*, is it, Woods?'

'Gay porn,' Asbo clarified.

'*Obviously* gay porn,' Decker agreed.

'Tut tut tut,' Studwin tutted. (And let me tell you, for Studwin this was pretty articulate stuff.)

'It's porn, isn't it?' Decker repeated.

Clearly, there was no correct answer to this question. It was designed to be unanswerable. If I said 'yes', they'd call me a pervert and then empty my bag into the street. If I said 'no', they'd tell me that I had no dick and then empty my bag into the street. I should have stuck to my policy of saying nothing. Instead, I went for ill-fated option three: trying to battle idiocy with logic.

'It can't be porn,' I pointed out, 'because they don't sell porn in the village shop. Gay or otherwise.'

This provoked many hoots and howls of laughter.

'Yeah, you'd fucking know, wouldn't you, Woods?' Declan Mackenzie asked. Studwin had started to rub his stick suggestively. I assume it was supposed to be suggestive. He may have been trying to figure out how to make fire.

'I'm going home now,' I said. And I stepped out into the road, far enough to be out of range of Studwin's stick, and started walking quickly down the lane.

Unfortunately, the bullied don't get to decide when enough is enough – and any effort to usurp this decision will inevitably be met with reprisals. I was immediately aware that they had left the wall and were now following me, a few metres behind.

'Don't go home yet, Woods. It won't be dark for hours. I'm sure your mummy won't mind.'

'His mummy's probably out on her broomstick.'

I gritted my teeth and picked up my pace. My mother's broomstick was purely ornamental.

'Woods, why don't you like us? Why won't you be our friend?'

I probably don't need to tell you that this was sarcasm, which Oscar Wilde called the lowest form of wit. But Oscar Wilde had clearly not heard of setting fire to your own farts, which was also a popular form of humour at my school.

I stayed calm and continued to walk. I watched my breath rising and falling in my chest. Something hit me on the shoulder. I felt with my fingers. Mud. (At least, I hoped it was mud.) I stayed calm. I started counting to ten, visualizing each number in golden italics. *One, two, three, four* . . . Another projectile sailed past my right ear. Where the hell were all the people? The dog-walkers? The joggers? The postman? It was a mild, sunny day. Why were all the driveways empty? I was experiencing the helplessness of nightmares, and I had no idea what I was going to do. What *could* I do? (Leap the church wall, sprint across the graves, hammer on the closed oak door and scream, 'SANCTUARY!'?)

I picked up my pace as I rounded the corner. I could see the stile ahead, but still no people. I tried to calculate if I could outrun my pursuers. It seemed unlikely. Although things had improved, I was still, to a certain extent, battling the 'puppy fat' that had resulted from the year spent in my pyjamas. In contrast, my pursuers were all on the football team. But then, they were all smokers too. Hopefully Mr Banks, our biology teacher, hadn't been lying to us and smoking really *did* diminish your lung capacity. It seemed plausible. Although that stuff about it stunting your growth was clearly a fabrication.

Another piece of something hit me in the back to a chorus of cheers.

It was at this point that calmness jumped ship. My mind skipped in a couple of frantic, useless circles; then my legs and spinal cord decided to stage a *coup d'état*. No time for the executive decision: we were running.

Like many decisions that bypass the neocortex, this turned out to be a poor one. There's a good chance that my tormentors would have grown bored soon enough – as long as I remained unresponsive. This is why hunted animals play dead. But as soon as I started to run, the predator's instinct kicked in. I was running, they were chasing, and we were, all four of us, locked into a shared fate. Furthermore, the stakes had been raised. Now, when they caught me, they'd be *obliged* to take action. They couldn't let me go. They couldn't back-pedal and let me off with just another verbal battering. I would be captured, spat on, possibly stripped and then thrown into the nearest patch of stinging nettles. The humiliation was over and now the pain was about to begin.

I ignored the turn-off to the duck pond (for now, the ducklings would have to fend for themselves; I'd be no use to the ducklings dead) and continued straight ahead, running full tilt. I had enough of a surprise head start to make it over the stile unimpeded – an obstacle that was a greater problem for my pursuers, who had to co-ordinate and proceed one at a time. But my advantage couldn't last for long. Like all prey, I had the greater incentive in the chase, but the predators, I was beginning to suspect, had more stamina. And I was also encumbered by a bag of shopping. It wasn't heavy, but it was still a hindrance. Lucy's cat treats were bouncing around with the regular rattle of a military drum. And my heart was pounding too, and the blood was surging in my ears, and my breath was coming in thick, ragged pants. And still there was not a soul to be seen.

A risky, time-consuming glance over my shoulder revealed that the gap had neither narrowed nor widened. They were still a good lorry-length behind me, but they showed no signs of slowing. This was just sport to them – no different to football practice. There was no question in my mind that some part of me – my legs, my lungs – would give out long before they got tired enough to end the pursuit. I had no chance of outrunning them in the open. I veered off the bridle path, across a muddy, barren field and towards a distant hedgerow that marked, I hoped, the boundary back to civilization.

The ground was uneven and difficult. My feet hurt, my legs hurt, my chest hurt, my head hurt. There was a drainage ditch ahead, a narrow channel of green-brown water separating me from my goal. I hardly slowed. I slid down the near bank, jumped, scrambled up the far bank and reached the hedge in a few shaky bounds. I looked round. All three of my pursuers had reached the opposite bank of the ditch, and I'd reached the point where I could no longer run. The hedge was my only option – unpromising as it now appeared. It was comprised of mature, prickly conifers, planted close together to form a darkly tangled wall – dense enough to make any sane, moderately sized creature think twice before attempting an incursion. But *this* moderately sized creature had left his sanity in the lane behind the churchyard. I held my mother's bag to my chest and launched myself at the midpoint between two burly firs. I was swallowed in musty darkness. Something tore. Branches splintered and swiped my face. Needles pricked my hands. I closed my eyes, lowered my head and pushed forward like a charging bull. And then I was free. I fell forward into dazzling sunlight. Something broke underfoot – a small plant or shrub. I could hear shouting through the conifers, and then a hail of sticks and stones and mud started raining all around me.

I quickly took in my surroundings – someone's long, narrow garden. The house was completely obscured by trees and trellises. There was a shed to my left and a greenhouse to my right, and high fences marking the perimeter beyond. I heard a rustling behind me, but my legs were beaten. Now that I'd stopped, I couldn't start running again. It was all I could do to hobble to the shed. The door wasn't locked – my first and only lucky break. Inside, my eyes darted for something I could use. Old plant pots, a length of hose, some bamboo poles, a pair of gardening gloves, a rusty rake. Then, with the last of my pitiful quota of strength, I managed to drag a heavy bag of compost behind the closed door. Then I sat on the compost bag, my back against the door and my legs braced and my whole body locked as rigid as the atoms in a carbon nanotube.

A second later, someone was trying the door. The pressure increased. A few dull thuds clattered through the wood. But it was clear that the door wasn't going to budge. There was too much force shoring up its base.

There was a lot of swearing and yelling from outside. Then I heard the sound of breaking glass, and more shouting. Then everything was quiet.

I counted to a hundred.

When I peered outside, there was no one to be seen. But from the amount of glass that glittered in the sunlight, it seemed as if half the greenhouse had been demolished. I'd later discover that only seven panes of glass had actually shattered. But at the time, I was in too much of a daze to take in details. Now that the chase was over and I was no longer focussed on the necessities of self-preservation, my mind had started to spin in a familiar, juddering dance. I knew that I had to calm myself again. I had to sit still and concentrate and wait for this to pass.

I got back in the gloomy shed, my refuge from the destruction outside, and I sat on the floor against the far wall with my head in my hands. I was, by then, extremely disorientated. I tried to focus but the whole place smelled of marzipan and creosote, and this was preventing my mind from settling. It was too late to move, though. At this point, movement would make things worse. I had to sit motionless and work through my exercises. I could see chariots and unruly horses. I tried to breathe. I started listing prime numbers. I could see blackbirds circling. I felt extremely exhausted.

I've no idea how much time passed, but when I came round from my dream, the atmosphere had changed. Something had awoken me. There was a current of air cutting through the creosote; the shed door had been pushed fully open, and in the doorway was a figure – a silhouette framed in sinking sunlight.

It was a man. There was a man looming in the doorway, and he was pointing at me with a stick – a long, cylindrical stick. It gleamed dully in the darkness. My heart jumped into my mouth.

The man was pointing a gun at me.

PENANCE

'Don't shoot!' I yelped, raising both my hands above my head. 'I'm an epileptic!' I added. I don't know why I added this second part. It may have been some delirious attempt at explanation; it may have been an appeal for leniency.

The single-cylinder gun barrel remained poised.

I felt ice crystallizing in my bowel. My eyes were watering, blurring out the details so that I could only see the dim outlines of my impending doom. Then a bright orange circle suddenly flared against the background darkness. I expected a bang and a bullet, the powdery smell of fireworks. Instead there was a faint crackle and a smell like very strong parsley. I thought another fit was coming.

'So,' my executioner asked, 'you wanna tell me what in the name of Jesus F. Christ you're doing in my shed?'

I wasn't surprised to discover that he spoke with a slow American drawl. In the fever dream my mind was spinning – which owed as much to Hollywood as it did to blind panic – it seemed reasonable enough that I was to be murdered by a cowboy. And there certainly wasn't time to clear up the mystery of Jesus's middle initial.

'Well?' the voice prompted. 'What's the matter? Cat got your tongue?'

'Resting!' I squeaked. 'I was just resting!'

This provoked a short, sharp snort, like the warning bark of an angry dog. 'Well, I guess trashin' someone's glasshouse must really take it out of you, huh?'

I didn't say anything. My brain is not to be relied on in a crisis.

'So, you done restin' now, kid? You ready to step outside so we can talk, or shall I come back later?'

I weighed my options, and decided that I'd rather die on my feet in the sunlight than curled up in the dark. But then, when I tried to rise, my legs buckled beneath me. I gave up and buried my head in my arms.

'If you're going to kill me,' I pleaded, 'I'd prefer it if you made it quick.'

'What the hell're you talkin' about, kid?' The cowboy took another drag on his parsley cigarette. 'What's the story here? You funny in the head or something?'

I nodded vigorously.

'Come on – on your feet!'

The cowboy stepped back into the sunlight to clear the doorway for my exit, and at the same moment, he lowered his gun – which resolved itself into what it had been all along. Three feet of lightweight aluminium. Grey plastic handle. A crutch.

The ice melted. Sensation rushed back to my limbs, and with

a breath that brought relief to every cell of my body, I rose and stumbled out into the light, reborn and ready to face whatever punishment awaited me.

Fear distorts the world. Fear sees demons where only shadows dwell. This was the lesson I'd eventually learn.

My captor was not the dark menace imagination had made of him. He leaned heavily on his crutch, walking with a pronounced limp in his right leg. He was thin and wiry. His face was pale and drawn and grizzled with silvery stubble. He had some sparse patches of hair at his temples, but little left on top. He was old. The only things about him that retained the kind of brisk authority I'd projected into the darkness were his eyes, which were a sharp, flinty grey, and his voice, which was hard and cutting.

'You're not gonna bolt on me, are you, kid?' he asked.

I shook my head.

'You promise?'

I nodded, still tongue-tied.

He pointed at me with his crutch. 'You got anything that doesn't belong to you in there?'

I gawked blankly.

'The bag, kid. What's in the bag?'

I dropped my eyes. I was still holding my mother's bag. I was clutching it protectively to my chest. My tongue untied itself. 'Cat biscuits!' I blurted. 'Cat biscuits and a magazine and half a bunch of grapes. It's all mine. You can check. I'm not a thief!'

'Just a vandal, huh?'

The old man looked at me very keenly, and then shook his

head and dropped his cigarette to the ground. He crushed it out with his left foot.

'Y'know, I've seen some pretty dumb crimes in my time, but this is possibly the dumbest. I know that an appetite for destruction and intellect don't always walk hand in hand, but by any standard, this here's pretty goddamn mystifying.' He gestured again with his crutch, first at the greenhouse, then at the shed. 'I'm probably wastin' my time askin', but I don't suppose you've got an explanation for all this?'

'It wasn't me,' I explained.

'I see. Who was it, then?'

'Some other kids.'

'Which other kids?'

I gulped. 'Just some other kids, that's all. They were chasing me.'

'Right. And where are they now?'

'I don't know.'

'I guess they just vanished, huh?'

'I think they must have gone back through the hedge.'

We both looked in the direction of the hedge. It was an impenetrable grey-green wall.

'Your friends must be regular Houdinis,' the old man said.

'They're not my friends!' I replied.

He looked at me for a very long time, then shook his head again.

'You got a name, kid?'

'Alex,' I said, very quietly.

'Just Alex?'

'It's short for Alexander,' I elaborated.

My captor clicked his tongue and scowled. 'Who's your father, kid?'

'I don't have a father.'

'Gotcha: immaculately conceived!'

Fortunately, I knew what this remark meant. It was very sarcastic. It meant that I was like Jesus – not the result of sexual intercourse, which, in the Bible, was a terrible sin.

'That's not what I meant,' I said. 'I had a father but my mother's not exactly sure who he was. I was conceived in the normal way. Somewhere near Stonehenge,' I added.

'Your mother sounds like a hoot.'

'She's celibate now,' I said.

'Okay. This is all fascinating stuff, but let's cut the crap. Tell me who your mother is, kid. I want her name. Her *full* name.'

'Rowena Woods,' I said.

This prompted a lot of blinking, followed by another short, bark-like laugh. 'God al-fuckin'-mighty! You're *that* kid?'

I should point out that, aside from the expletive, this was not an uncommon reaction when a stranger found out who I was.

The old man had tilted his head and I could see that he was peering very closely at the white line across my right temple, where my hair still refused to grow.

I waited patiently.

The old man exhaled and shook his head again.

'Where's your mom right now?' he asked. 'Is she home?'

'She's at work,' I said.

'Okay. Tell me what time she gets home.'

I looked at the shattered glass littering the ground and bit my lip.

* * *

I should explain something at this point.

There were two things that I couldn't tell my mother about that Saturday. And unfortunately, these were the two things – the only two things – that could have saved my story from falling into senseless pieces.

First, I couldn't tell her the names of my pursuers. This would have been suicidal. I was certain that my silence – along with the sustained possibility that I could, at some point, if pushed, break this silence – was the only thing that could guarantee my safety over the coming weeks. Having got away with criminal damage, my trio of tormentors, I thought, would not be eager to press their luck. For now, and, hopefully, for many more months, they'd have to find someone else to traumatize.

Second, I couldn't mention my seizure. As things stood, I was already in grave danger of losing all my hard-won freedoms. If my mother even *half* suspected that my epilepsy was returning to its former severity, I'd be straight back into the shackles of full-time, round-the-clock supervision. I'd lose my Saturdays. I'd lose my Sundays. I'd lose my post-school afternoons. I doubted that I could persuade her that this was a one-off – that, despite evidence to the contrary, I was coping perfectly well on my stringent regime of drugs and meditation.

So my defence was in tatters from the outset. All that remained were the indisputable facts: trespass, a broken greenhouse and so little remorse – or such blithe stupidity – that I hadn't even bothered to flee the scene of the crime.

My mother was distraught.

'Lex, how *could* you?' she said.

'I've told you: I didn't!'

'I did not raise you to be the kind of boy who takes pleasure in acts of wanton destruction. I raised you to have principles! I raised you to be kind and polite and loving! And truthful!'

'I *do* have principles!'

'Your actions say otherwise.'

'But they weren't my actions!'

'Yes. So you've said. And I'd love to believe that, Lex – I truly would. But you give me no reason to believe it.'

'That's because you're not listening to me!'

'Tell me who your accomplices were. *Then* I might start to listen.'

'They weren't my accomplices. I'm not responsible for what they did.'

'If you continue to protect them, that makes you an accomplice! It makes you as guilty as they are.'

I scowled at the ground and tried to think of a way to dispute the logic of this argument.

'Tell me who they were,' my mother repeated.

'I've told you. It was just some kids from the village.'

'Names, Lex. I want names.'

'Their names aren't important. The important thing is that they were to blame, not me.'

'Lex, this is really quite simple. If you don't tell me which of your friends did this, then all the blame will rest with you.'

'They're not my friends! Which part of the story did you not understand?'

'Don't you get smart with me! Just tell me who they are.'

'Why don't you ask the cards?' I said sullenly.

My mother stayed silent and looked at me for a very long time. I couldn't stand the way she was looking at me. She didn't look angry any more. She just looked hurt.

I lowered my eyes. Somehow, after a five-minute argument with my mother, I no longer felt so innocent. I felt like an *accomplice*.

'Let me tell you something, Lex,' my mother said eventually. 'And I'm not sure right now whether or not it will mean anything to you – but I want you to listen. And I want you to think about it very carefully before you decide to say anything else.

'Isaac Peterson is not a well man. He's old and he's frail. And he's also all alone in the world. Can you imagine what that might feel like?'

I knew exactly what my mother was up to here: sending me on a guilt trip. Mr Peterson wasn't *that* frail. His limp just made him incredibly slow on his feet, not infirm. And as for his age – well, he *was* almost twice as old as my mother, but he wasn't nearly as old as Mr Stapleton, for example, who was approximately one hundred. The only indisputable fact in my mother's assessment was that he was all alone in the world, and it was this that made my supposed trashing of his greenhouse so appalling.

In case you don't happen to live in a small village, I should tell you the following information: in a small village, everyone knows at least three things about everyone else. It doesn't matter how reclusive you try to be. The three things that everyone in the village knew about Mr Peterson were as follows:

1) He'd had one of his legs torn to ribbons in the Vietnam War, which was a war fought between America, North Vietnam and South Vietnamese guerrillas in the 1960s and 1970s.

2) His wife, Rebecca Peterson, an Englishwoman, had died three years earlier after a protracted battle with pancreatic cancer.

3) Because of facts 1) and 2) he was not of sound mind.

When my mother told me the first two facts – the third I had to infer – my last thoughts of self-preservation crumbled to dust. Because of Mr Peterson's unfortunate situation, there was no chance of my escaping with just a slap on the wrist. Someone had to hang for the wanton destruction of his greenhouse, and that someone, evidently, was me.

All that was left to be resolved were the precise terms of my penance.

Mr Peterson's house was a good house for a recluse. It was tucked away down a narrow, winding lane – at least two hundred yards back from the main road – and had a long private drive flanked by fifty-year-old poplars, which stood like sentinels guarding the only entrance and exit. Inside the main compound, there were more trees and hedgerows that had been allowed to grow several feet above head-height, and next to the front door there was a large bay window that revealed nothing more than a few inches of gloomy window sill. The curtains were closed. They had been closed yesterday too. They didn't look like they were ever opened. Streaks of dirt and dust were visible in the dark folds of the fabric. I wrinkled my nose. My mother gave me a little prod in the small of my back.

'Ouch!' I protested.

'Don't drag your feet, Lex.'

'I wasn't!'

'Putting this off isn't going to make it any easier.'

'But what if he doesn't want to be disturbed?'

'Don't be a coward.'

'I'm just saying that maybe we should ring first.'

'We don't need to ring. You're doing this *now*.'

A few more steps and we were at the gabled porch.

'Go on,' my mother prompted. 'This is *your* responsibility.'

I tapped on the door, with all the power of a farting flea.

A breathless moment passed.

My mother looked at me, rolled her eyes and knocked again on my behalf – thunderously.

There was an immediate outbreak of noisy barking from inside. I jumped about a foot in the air.

'Lex, stay calm! It's just a dog!'

This did little to reassure me. I felt uncomfortable with dogs. We'd always been a cat family. Luckily, it would turn out that Mr Peterson's dog was even more of a coward than I was. He only ever barked when he was woken unexpectedly from a deep sleep, and this was a bark of abject panic – instinctual and frantic and completely devoid of aggression. But I didn't know this at the time. I didn't realize that the ten seconds of barking would inevitably be followed by a hasty retreat to the back of the closest sofa. I assumed that this was the Hound of the Baskervilles, baying for my blood.

A light came on, visible through a narrow pane of frosted glass above the door. I felt my mother's hands clamp down on my shoulders. My moral fibre was still very much in question.

The door swung open.

Mr Peterson's flinty eyes regarded me over his reading glasses, flicked briefly towards my mother and then returned to my face. He didn't look surprised. He didn't look pleased either.

I felt another poke, this one in my lower spine.

'I'm here to apologize and to offer to make amends,' I blurted. It sounded rehearsed. It *was* rehearsed, but that wasn't the point.

The point was I had to make it sound sincere. If I got the tone wrong, it wouldn't help my case.

Mr Peterson raised his eyebrows, then kind of scrunched his face up a little.

I waited.

He drummed his fingers against the doorframe.

I waited some more.

'Okay, kid,' he prompted. 'So apologize. Knock yourself out.'

I looked at my mother dubiously.

'It's a figure of speech,' my mother said. 'It means you should get on with it.'

'Oh.'

I cleared my throat. Mr Peterson shifted his weight. He looked as eager to get this over with as I was. That gave me a glimmer of hope.

'I'm very sorry about your greenhouse and for trespassing on your property,' I said. I felt another prod in the back. 'And,' I added, 'I'd like to make it up to you in any way I can. For example, I'd be very happy to volunteer for any odd jobs you might need doing.'

'Odd jobs?'

I could tell this wasn't a welcome proposition. Mr Peterson looked like he had toothache. I ploughed on regardless, delivering the rest of my speech to the doormat.

'I could clean your windows,' I said, 'or weed your garden or run any errands you might have.'

'Can you re-glaze my glasshouse?'

I thought this was probably sarcasm. I decided not to answer.

'Also,' I said instead, 'I noticed that your car hasn't been washed for a while, so mayb— Ow!'

I took this latest poke as a sign that I should stick to the script and not try to improvise.

'Anyway,' I concluded, 'because I can't repair your greenhouse, I'm offering to place myself in your service until such a time as you deem the damage to be repaid in full. It's penance,' I added, glancing up from the doormat.

Mr Peterson frowned, cleared his throat, then frowned again.

'Look, kid,' he said. 'I'm not sure that's such a great idea. What I mean is, I think maybe it's better if I just accept your apology and we call it quits.'

'Yes, that's also—'

At this point, my mother stepped in. 'Excuse me, Mr Peterson. If I may?' She didn't pause to hear if she might. 'That's very gracious of you – extremely gracious – but I hardly think a simple apology can suffice in this instance, not given the severity of the crime.'

I saw my glimmer of hope sputter and die.

Mr Peterson's face was still fixed in an uncomfortable grimace.

'You do agree that this is a serious matter?' my mother prompted. 'Because I got the impression yesterday that you were very keen to see Alex suitably punished.'

'Well, yeah, that's a given, but—'

'Can you suggest a *more* suitable punishment?'

'Maybe not. But this isn't exactly what I had in mind. I mean, to be frank, Mrs Woods, I really don't think it's my place—'

'Mr Peterson, this is a matter of principle,' my mother insisted. 'Alex has to learn a lesson here. He needs to understand that his actions have consequences.'

'Okay, agreed. And look, the last thing I want to do is screw up any lesson you're trying to teach your son, but—'

'Excellent! I'm glad that we're of the same opinion. Because I assure you: Alex and I have discussed this matter at length, and we both agree that if he's to make amends in any meaningful way, he has to repay his debt to you – not to me. It's the only way we can move on from this.'

Mr Peterson threw me a look that said: 'Help!' I threw him a look back that told him that none of this was *my* doing and that against my mother I had no help to offer.

He flapped and flailed his arms for a bit, then swore under his breath. My mother pretended she hadn't heard. I knew that the battle was already lost. It was lost the moment he'd opened the door.

'Ah, hell!' Mr Peterson rubbed his temples.

My mother waited expectantly.

'Sure, great. Why not? I'll find him some chores to do, he'll learn his lesson, and we'll all move on with our lives. Terrific.'

Sarcasm was wasted on my mother. 'Wonderful,' she said. 'So let's set a time. I thought perhaps next Saturday would be fitting?'

'Very fitting.'

'Excellent! Then it's settled.'

Mr Peterson looked at me, his eyes vaguely bemused. I gave a very small shrug – too small for my mother to notice.

'Come along, Alex,' my mother said, delivering a final poke in the ribs. 'I think you've taken up quite enough of Mr Peterson's time for one weekend.'

I suppose this last sentence must have made sense in my mother's head, but, given the arrangement she'd just brokered, its logic was lost on me.

METHANE

It was raining as I made my way down the lane and past the poplars the following Saturday. A dull, misty drizzle that felt like pins and needles. I hoped very much that I wouldn't have to weed the garden or cut the grass or clean the outside windows; and the more I looked up into the leaden sky, the more I felt sure that this, or something similarly miserable, was likely to be my fate. But, as it turned out, Mr Peterson had different plans for me.

'Can you drive?' he asked. This was the first thing he said to me after he'd unbolted the front door.

'I'm only thirteen,' I pointed out.

Mr Peterson looked at me critically, as if this were exactly the kind of can't-do attitude he'd been expecting. 'So you can't drive at *all*?'

'No.'

'I'm not talkin' a hundred-mile road trip here, kid. I just need a couple of things from the store.' He glared at the sky. 'My leg's not so great in this rain.'

'I'm only thirteen,' I repeated apologetically. For some reason,

I couldn't help feeling partly responsible for the pain in Mr Peterson's leg.

'Y'know, I'm pretty sure I was drivin' my daddy's truck by the time I was your age.'

'I don't have a daddy,' I reminded him. 'Immaculately conceived,' I added.

This was a joke. He didn't smile.

'I could *wash* your car,' I suggested.

This was met with a humourless bark. 'In this? I reckon my car's gonna get all the washing it needs today, don't you?'

'Yes, I suppose so,' I acknowledged. I felt the formidable weight of my uselessness pushing down on my shoulders.

'Anyway,' Mr Peterson continued, 'physical labour in the rain's all well and good, but I'm not sure how your mother'd feel if I returned you to her with pneumonia.'

'I'm sure she'd blame me, not you,' I said.

Mr Peterson cleared his throat the way people do when they're trying to buy some time to negotiate a tricky situation. 'Well, anyhow,' he said, 'I had something a little more instructive in mind. Your mom seemed pretty keen for you to learn something here, don't you think?'

I nodded blankly. My mother and Mr Peterson wanted me to learn that wanton destruction of a greenhouse was wrong. I knew this already. My penance was a regrettable but necessary charade, designed to make all concerned feel better about what had happened. And I told myself that, really, I had no right to be resentful about this state of affairs. But I certainly didn't expect to learn anything.

As it transpired, I was underestimating Mr Peterson's notion of moral instruction.

'Can you type?' he asked.

'Yes,' I replied.

'How's your spellin'?'

'It's okay.'

''Cos if you can't spell, then, frankly, this is gonna be a royal pain in the ass.'

'My spelling's generally adequate,' I assured him. 'And Mr Treadstone, my English teacher, says that I have a reasonable vocabulary for my age. Although there's always room for improvement. What do you want me to type?'

'We're gonna write some letters,' Mr Peterson said.

The first thing I learned that day was this: what you think you know about a person is only a fraction of the story.

As I've said, in Lower Godley, everyone thought that they knew all the things (usually no more than three) that were worth knowing about everyone else. Everyone knew that Mr Peterson was a reclusive Vietnam veteran whose wife had died of pancreatic cancer. Everyone knew that my mother was a clairvoyant and a single mother with funny opinions and funny hair. And everyone knew that I had been hit by a meteor and wasn't quite right in the head and was subject to convulsions.

These things were all true. But they were not the only truths.

Mr Peterson's house wasn't dingy and dusty as I'd expected. In the back, everything was neat and tidy, and although it was a very grey day, the living room was still filled with daylight from the window that overlooked the garden. There were also two standard lamps and tall bookcases and art prints on the wall. And there was a large floor cushion where Mr Peterson's dog was dozing. He looked up and sniffed curiously when I walked in, then closed his eyes and went back to sleep. He was very old, so he spent a lot of his time sleeping. I would later discover that he had been rescued from an animal shelter a couple of years earlier – which was why he had part of his right ear missing – and he was called Kurt, which was short for Kurt Vonnegut Jnr, which was the name of Mr Peterson's favourite author, who had died ten days previously. Mr Peterson didn't mind rescuing a very old dog, because old dogs don't need much exercise and are happy just to have a warm place to sleep. When I asked what kind of dog Kurt was, Mr Peterson told me that he was some kind of mongrel.

A few feet away from Kurt was the thing that surprised me the most, which was a very new, very shiny computer sitting on a desk next to a large, flatscreen monitor. For some reason, I'd assumed that I'd be using one of those ancient typewriting machines that they used to have years ago. But sometimes people have homes and possessions you don't expect, and hobbies you can't even imagine.

It turned out that Mr Peterson's hobby was writing letters to politicians and, occasionally, prisoners. He was in a special letter-writing club. You had to pay a monthly membership fee and then you got sent the club magazine, which was full of the names and addresses of people all over the world whom you might like to write to, even though most of them would never write back. The politicians were generally too busy or didn't care for personal correspondence, and the prisoners weren't often allowed to answer their mail. They were quite lucky that they were allowed to *receive* mail. Mr Peterson's letter-writing club was called 'Amnesty International'.

At first, I was dubious that my mother would agree that

writing letters to prisoners was morally instructive, but Mr Peterson, who was extremely crazy, insisted that it was. He told me that most of the prisoners we'd be writing to shouldn't have been put in prison in the first place. They were good people who'd been locked away and denied their most basic human rights. They weren't allowed to act according to their consciences or even to express their opinions without fear of persecution and physical reprisals – although Mr Peterson doubted very much that I could imagine what that was like. I told Mr Peterson that since I went to secondary school, I thought that I could imagine it fairly well. And as for the fact that most of the prisoners had been wrongly imprisoned – on spurious charges, without fair trial, or for crimes they probably didn't commit – well, this was another thing I could sympathize with.

I typed while Mr Peterson dictated, spelling out the names and places that were causing me trouble. But after a while, he told me that my typing sounded like a horse clattering over cobblestones, so he put on some music, which he said was a sherbet quintet. I didn't know what this meant, and I didn't ask. But the music was quite pleasant, and it didn't have any singing, so it didn't affect my concentration.

We must have written five or six letters that afternoon. It turned out that there were a lot of people in the world who were being denied their basic human rights. We wrote to our local MP asking if he could raise in parliament the issue of British prisoners who were being held without trial in an American prison in Cuba, which was a large island in the Caribbean run by communists. We wrote to a judge in China asking for the immediate release of five men and women who'd been put in jail for protesting about their homes being destroyed to clear space for an Olympic stadium. And we wrote to the Governor of Nebraska to ask if he'd consider not executing one of the state's prisoners, who'd been convicted of killing a police officer when he was eighteen years old. He was now thirty-two and there was no physical evidence linking him to the crime, just the testimony of two witnesses who'd later changed their stories. The state was planning to kill him by passing electricity through his body until his heart stopped beating. This was a very dramatic, if slightly messy, way of ending someone's life. Most other states – even Texas – had now stopped using the electric chair as the default method of execution, but Nebraska still held on to its quaint, old-time values.

Mr Peterson, it turned out, was against the possibly innocent being killed by the state. And he was also against the definitely guilty being killed by the state. He was a pacifist, which meant that he was against violence *period*. This information (which would have been extremely useful a week earlier) raised several questions in my head.

'But what if you have to kill someone to stop him from killing other people?' I asked. 'What if it's self-defence?'

'I hardly think killing a man behind bars counts as self-defence, do you?'

'No, but in general – what if it was real self-defence? What if someone was trying to kill *you*?'

'I guess I'd have to die with the moral high ground.'

I thought this was probably a joke, but I wasn't certain.

'I'd like to think I'm not capable of violence any more,' Mr Peterson clarified, 'no matter what the circumstances.'

'Is that because of what happened to you in Vietnam?' I asked. 'You know, with your leg and everything?'

121

'Hell, kid! You ask a lot of questions.'

'You did want me to learn some things,' I pointed out.

'Didn't your mother ever tell you that there're some questions it's not polite to ask?'

'Yes,' I admitted, 'she has told me that.'

'Well, I'd say that *this* is one of those questions, wouldn't you?'

'Yes, I suppose so.'

All the interesting questions seemed to fall into this category.

'Mr Peterson,' I said after a while, 'I think I might probably be a pacifist too. I mean, I don't think that people should fight – not in ninety-nine point nine per cent of circumstances, anyway.'

'Good for you, kid. It's important to have principles.'

'It's also because I don't think I'm very good at fighting,' I confessed.

'Well, that's okay too. It's no crime *not* to be able to fight.'

'Oh.'

This was big news to me. In school, being good at fighting was generally seen as a positive attribute, like being good at sport.

'But I think I might fight if there was absolutely no other choice,' I added. 'You know, like if someone was attacking Lucy.'

'I don't know who that is.'

'Lucy's our cat.'

'Cute name.'

'It's short for Lucifer.'

'Of course it is. Why would anyone want to attack your cat?'

'It's hypothetical. That means it's just an example.'

'I know what hypothetical means, kid.'

'Oh. Well, anyway, Lucy's pregnant at the moment, so she couldn't run very fast if she had to escape from an enemy. And she's not very good at hiding because she's all white. She's kind of luminous, even at night. That's how she got her name. Lucifer means "the bringer of light".'

'I know. It's also the name of the devil – you realize that, right?'

'Yes, I realize that. But my mother has quite a lot of sympathy for the devil. She thinks he's misunderstood. She says that there's a certain balance in the cosmic order and that creation and destruction are really just two sides of the same coin.'

'I'll be honest, kid: your mother's general outlook is a real head-fuck. I'm not sure I want to spend a whole lot of time trying to figure it out.'

Mr Peterson, I'd noticed, wasn't really one for monitoring his language.

'She also says that *sometimes* it's okay to be a rebel,' I said. 'She doesn't think that God sounds like such a great boss. Not the way he's presented in the Bible, anyway. She thinks that if she'd been an angel, she'd probably have quit too.'

'Better to rule in hell than serve in heaven.'

'Yes,' I said, 'that's actually a very good way of putting it, although my mother's not too fussed about ruling either. She doesn't like hierarchies – except in our family, where things are different. But, anyway, my point is that Lucy's not evil. She's just a cat. And if, *hypothetically*, someone were to attack her, then I'd probably have to step in. I think it's probably okay to fight if you're defending someone who's in danger and can't defend herself, don't you?'

'There's an exception to any rule.'

'So you'd stop being a pacifist if it was a last resort?'

Mr Peterson knotted his brow for a while. 'Listen, kid, morality's not all black and white. There're some very big grey areas. I think, from what you've been telling me, maybe your mom'd agree with that too.'

'I see,' I said.

And, in truth, I may be guilty of mashing together several different conversations here. It's difficult to remember when and how everything was said. But, really, that's not so important. The important thing is that in the course of the day, against all my expectations, my penance had stopped feeling like penance. Even though he was crazy, talking to Mr Peterson seemed to make a whole lot more sense than talking to my mother.

Later on, after we'd finished writing our correspondence and Mr Peterson had gone outside for a herbal cigarette, I spent some time looking through the archive of letters on his computer, which was very large. This wasn't snooping, because Mr Peterson had said that I should save and file the letters we'd written and had directed me to the relevant folder, and I figured that if he didn't want me to look, then he obviously wouldn't have done this. Also, I thought it would be morally instructive.

Anyway, I checked to see how many letters there were in total – there were hundreds, all sorted into separate folders by year and month – read a handful with interesting-sounding titles and then closed the documents folder and switched off the monitor. Then I checked the bottom of the mouse, as was my habit whenever I used a new computer. It was a recent model with a red laser beam instead of a roller-ball, so there was no chance that it had been made by Robert Asquith's Chinese peasants.

Then I swivelled in the swivel chair for a bit.

Halfway through a spin, I noticed a photograph on the wall near one of the tall bookcases. It was the only photo in the room. As far as I could work out, it might have been the only photo in the whole house. I went over for a closer look. This wasn't snooping either. I was just curious.

The photo showed a woman who looked a few years younger than my mother – maybe thirty at the very most. Her hair was cut short and she was wearing a black beret. She had her head tilted and was smiling impishly at the camera.

'Is that your daughter?' I asked politely when Mr Peterson came back into the room. At least, I *thought* I was being polite. But it turned out that this was not a good question to ask. I could tell that straight away. There was an atmosphere.

I should explain here that although my mother had told me that Mr Peterson was 'all alone in the world', I thought she was referring only to his living arrangements and the recent death of his wife. I didn't know that he literally had no other family anywhere. I was always very conscious of the fact that it was normal for people (other people) to have several generations of relatives scattered all over the county and country, and often abroad too. And the reason I didn't associate the woman in the photograph with *Mrs* Peterson was that it was a million miles away from my mental picture of what Mrs Peterson should be like. It hadn't occurred to me at this point that Mr and Mrs Peterson had probably been young once. Added to this, the photo really didn't look like an old photo to me. With her short hair and tilted head, Mrs Peterson had a weirdly modern look about her.

As it turned out, the photo had been taken in 1970 at an antiwar demonstration in Washington DC. This was a couple of years after Mr Peterson had returned from Vietnam with his crippled leg and Purple Heart, which was the medal awarded to American soldiers who injured themselves at work, and which Mr Peterson no longer had in his possession, since he'd thrown it into the Pacific Ocean from a cliff top in Oregon. Mrs Peterson, who wasn't actually Mrs Peterson at the time, had been in the United States of America on a student visa. She was deported in 1971, and Mr Peterson decided to leave with her. He'd had enough of his country by then.

The reason he chose to keep that photo – and *only* that photo – on display was this: that image was the exact opposite of his last memory of his wife – when she had lost all her hair and half her body weight and was dying in hospital. That photo was how he preferred to remember her.

Also, while I'm explaining this background, I should add that Mrs Peterson couldn't have children due to a problem with her fallopian tubes, which was another of the many reasons why my original question about the photograph had been such a bad one. But, of course, these were all things I found out much later on. At the time, Mr Peterson only told me that the photograph was of his wife, and then there was a kind of awkward silence during which I shuffled my feet and didn't know what to say.

This is the reason I ended up pulling a book from the bookcase. I felt like I needed something to occupy my hands and eyes.

Unfortunately, my hands and eyes found themselves confronted by three sets of breasts on three nearly naked women. They were wearing very flimsy white gowns, mostly transparent. I went the approximate colour of a beetroot. My mother always told me that when it came to the naked human form, there was nothing to be scared or embarrassed about. But I wasn't so sure. You could see their *nipples*.

I averted my eyes a modest three inches to the north. The book was called *The Sirens of Titan*. It was one of Mr Peterson's Kurt Vonnegut books, pulled from the third shelf of the bookcase, where there were at least fifteen or twenty others, all lined up in a neat, orderly row.

'That's a funny name for a book,' I said with a gulp. 'Are those women going to get arrested?'

Mr Peterson didn't know what the hell I was talking about.

'They're not wearing many clothes,' I pointed out.

'What's your point?' he asked.

'So I thought maybe the sirens might be for them.'

Mr Peterson frowned.

'I think the police are allowed to arrest you for wearing too few clothes,' I explained.

Comprehension dawned on Mr Peterson's face. 'No, kid. Not sirens as in police sirens. Sirens as in Homer.'

I frowned. 'Simpson?'

'*The Odyssey*!'

I looked at him blankly. At some point in the last thirty seconds, we'd stopped speaking the same language.

Mr Peterson sighed and rubbed his wrinkled forehead. '*The Odyssey*'s a very old Greek story by a very old Greek man called Homer. And in *The Odyssey* there are these very beautiful women called sirens who live on an island in the Mediterranean and cause shipwrecks. They sing an enchanting song which lures sailors to their doom.'

'Oh,' I said. 'So the women *are* the sirens? And that's why they're not wearing very many clothes?'

'Right. Except in Kurt Vonnegut's book the sirens don't live in the Mediterranean. They live on Titan, which is one of Saturn's moons.'

'Yes, I know *that*,' I said. (I didn't want Mr Peterson to think I was an idiot.) 'It's the second largest moon in the solar system, after Ganymede, Jupiter's largest moon. It's actually larger than Mercury, though not nearly so dense.'

Mr Peterson frowned again and shook his head. 'I guess these days school puts a big emphasis on the sciences instead of the arts, huh?'

'No, not really. School puts a big emphasis on exam questions. Do sirens breathe methane?'

'Methane . . . What in hell're you talkin' about, kid?'

'Do they breathe methane – the sirens? It's just that Titan's lower atmosphere is mostly a mixture of nitrogen and methane, so some scientists think that if there's life on Titan, it would have to run on methane rather than oxygen – or, more specifically, on the hydrogen in the methane. It couldn't run on nitrogen because nitrogen's inert.'

'I don't think the nature of the air's ever discussed.'

'Oh.' I checked the inside cover. 'It says that it was first published in 1959, and the *Pioneer* and *Voyager* missions didn't reach Saturn until the late seventies and early eighties, so I suppose it's likely that Kurt Vonnegut didn't know all that much about the methane.'

'The methane's not important. That's not what the book's about. It's a story, for Christ's sake!'

'Okay.' I waited a few seconds. 'So what's the story about?'

Mr Peterson exhaled slowly through his teeth. 'It's about a very rich man who goes to Mars and Mercury and Titan.'

'I see. Is he an explorer?'

'No, he's the victim of a series of accidents.'

My frown of concentration deepened. 'That sounds a bit far-fetched. I don't think you could accidentally visit all those planets.'

'He accidentally joins the Martian army and then he gets shipwrecked – twice. First on Mercury, then on Titan.'

'How does he *accidentally* join the Martian army? That sounds a bit far-fetched too.'

'It doesn't matter if it's far-fetched. That's beside the point. It's satirical. Please tell me you understand what satire is?'

'Is it like sarcasm but cleverer?'

'No, not really. Look: this conversation could last for ever. Maybe you should just read the damn book?'

'You'll let me borrow it?'

'That depends. Can you take care of it?'

'I take care of all my books,' I assured him.

'Then you can borrow it. Hell, it'll be a damn sight easier than standing here answerin' questions all day!'

'I *am* quite interested in space,' I acknowledged.

'No shit! Just don't get your balls in a knot over the chemistry.'

I glanced south.

'Suspend your disbelief for a couple of hours. You understand what that means?'

I thought for a few seconds. 'Forget about the methane?'

'Right. Forget about the methane!'

And that's how I ended up borrowing my first Kurt Vonnegut book. It was more or less an accident.

Although my mother was very comfortable with the naked human form, I still wasn't sure that she'd approve of Kurt Vonnegut's book cover. Something told me that this was likely to be one of those instances where I *thought* I understood her rules, but they turned out to be more complicated than they first appeared. Two nipples might have passed her scrutiny without comment, but I wasn't so sure about six. At the very least, I knew that any book flaunting that much mammary was bound to lead to some form of embarrassing conversation. You probably understand why I decided not to mention it. Instead, I holed up in my room and spent much of that evening and the following day reading.

I now find myself confronted with the same problem that had probably confronted Mr Peterson a little earlier: any synopsis of the book's plot is bound to sound insane. Nevertheless, here goes . . .

While flying their spaceship to Mars, Winston Niles Rumfoord and his dog, Kazak, get sucked into a chrono-synclastic infundibulum, which spatters them halfway across the galaxy in a long, spiralling energy wave that stretches from the Sun all the way to Betelgeuse, the red supergiant that sits on Orion's right shoulder (assuming he's facing us). Although Rumfoord's mass has apparently been converted into pure energy, he rematerializes periodically – on Earth and Mercury and Titan – to discuss the nature of God (indifferent) and make predictions about the near future of mankind. One of these predictions is that Earth's richest man, Malachi Constant, will go to Mars then Mercury then Titan, where he will impregnate Rumfoord's semi-widowed ex-wife. These things duly happen. There are also subplots concerning a tiny alien robot, giant bluebirds and the sirens themselves, who turn out to be not all they promise. In the end, Malachi Constant dies while enjoying a pleasant hallucination, and Winston Niles Rumfoord and his dog get blasted in different directions across the cosmos.

About halfway through, I thought I probably understood what satire was. I thought that it was when you talked about important things in a kind of disguised funny way. But rather than obscuring this importance, satire made it clearer somehow – more pure and easier to understand. So, for instance, in *The Sirens of Titan*, the soldiers in the Martian army all have tiny radio antennas implanted in their heads so the generals can control their thoughts and issue commands from a very long distance away. When I returned the book, the following Saturday, I asked Mr Peterson if I was right in thinking that this was an example of satire.

'Bingo,' Mr Peterson said.

'It's a pretty funny image,' I noted.

'It's a pretty *accurate* image,' Mr Peterson replied. 'It's pretty much the essence of being a grunt in the army – being turned into a remotely controlled weapon for your country.'

'Don't you think it's good to serve your country?' I asked.

'No, I don't,' Mr Peterson said. 'I think it's good to serve your principles. And in the army you don't get to pick and choose your fights according to your conscience. You kill on command. Don't ever surrender your right to make your own moral decisions, kid.'

'I'll try not to,' I said.

I enjoyed talking to Mr Peterson a lot, and, oddly enough, he seemed to enjoy talking to me. I mean, he was always moaning about it and saying that I asked too many questions – many of them idiotic – and telling me that I was 'too weird for words', but despite all this, he still let me come over every Saturday and some Sundays to help out with the letter-writing and walking the dog and so on. Officially, this was still part of my penance, which, as we'd agreed, would not be over until such a time as Mr Peterson decided that the destruction of his greenhouse had been paid for in full. But this time never came. After a few weeks, there was no longer any discussion regarding my ongoing 'servitude'; I just turned up every Saturday at ten and found the door already unlocked.

Of course, the other justification for my coming over each week was that having enjoyed *The Sirens of Titan* so much, I'd decided that I wanted to work my way through the rest of Mr Peterson's Kurt Vonnegut library. Between the two of us, we'd agreed that this would be good for my ongoing moral education.

So, having conquered *Sirens* and satire, I moved on to *Cat's Cradle*, which is about some weaponized ice that destroys the world. After that, I read *Slaughterhouse-Five*, which is about time travel and the burning of one hundred thousand Germans in Dresden, which was a real-life event that Kurt Vonnegut had witnessed during World War II. And after that, I started reading *Breakfast of Champions*, which was probably the most valued book in Mr Peterson's library. It was a first edition and an early present from his wife. On the inside cover there was an inscription that read: *I think you'll enjoy this story; you'll definitely enjoy the pictures. With all my love, R.*

'I probably don't need to tell you to take special care of this one, do I?' Mr Peterson asked.

'No, you don't,' I agreed.

I understood straight away the significance of Mr Peterson lending me that book. Although he never said anything, I knew that he'd now forgiven me for his greenhouse.

Later, when I packed the book into my bag, I handled it as carefully as if it were one of Lucy's newly born kittens.

SARS

Since my mother worked, and my father was a phantom, I relied on the school bus to get me home each day. The school bus was not specifically a *school* bus; it was a public bus operated by Somerset and Avon Rural Stagecoach, the company that ran most of the local buses. But because it was timetabled to pass the Asquith Academy at 3.45 each afternoon, most of its passengers were schoolchildren. It was also, undoubtedly, the worst vehicle in the SARS fleet. This may have been a coincidence, but it seemed infinitely more likely that someone, somewhere, had a very rational fear of sending a properly upholstered vehicle out on the school run. The 3.45 from Asquith was not properly upholstered. Nor was it (or its regular driver) particularly stable. It was a rusting, rickety affair that, like the space shuttle, had served many more missions than its original engineers could ever have foreseen or condoned. At the traffic lights, it would wheeze and shudder like a giant asthmatic cyborg. When accelerating or braking, its entire frame would groan and rattle ominously. These death rattles were at their worst at the back of the lower deck, close to the engine, but they could be felt throughout the structure, no matter where you chose to sit. This was one of the two reasons that attempting to read on the school bus was ill advised. The other was that reading for pleasure, as I may have mentioned, was stupendously gay and, as such, was best kept a private vice.

Four days out of five, I wouldn't have *dreamed* of trying to read on the school bus. My usual strategy for the school bus was to try to find a seat on the lower deck among the general public – who never ventured upstairs – and as close as possible to the driver, who looked the kind of man liable to explode the second his dubious authority was put to the test. When this strategy failed – for the lower deck was often filled by civilians with pushchairs and shopping, leaving the raucous anarchy of the upper deck the only option – it was best to find a seat as close to the front as possible and spend the whole journey looking at the floor, saying nothing and making no sudden movements. I spent most of my journeys on the school bus in this manner, staring quietly at my feet. When I was feeling exceptionally brave, I stared out of the window instead.

Wednesday afternoons provided the only respite – the island of calm in a noisy, turbulent sea. And I had sport to thank for this. In line with traditions that had been upheld, though apparently not invented, by Robert Asquith's old grammar school, Wednesday afternoons were always given over to sport. Wednesday afternoons meant football practice, and football practice meant a much quieter, happier bus.

This was the reason my guard was down that day.

At 3.40, the upper deck was half empty. I had a seat at the

very front, as far away from the juddering engine and all other passengers as physically possible, and I didn't plan to spend the next twenty minutes contemplating the floor. I planned to do some reading.

At the time, I was about two-thirds of the way through *Breakfast of Champions*, which was about an arts fair in Ohio, an old, impoverished science-fiction writer called Kilgore Trout and a rich car dealer called Dwayne Hoover who goes nuts and decides that everyone else on planet Earth is a robot – convincingly designed but lacking feelings and imagination and free will and all the other ingredients that make a soul. Dwayne Hoover gets this idea from reading one of Mr Trout's science-fiction stories. Then he goes on a violent rampage.

As with many of Kurt Vonnegut's books, the plot was kind of insane and kind of irrelevant. You could, I thought, chop up the book, shuffle the pages and then reassemble them at random without doing too much harm to your reading experience. The book would still work. This was because every page – almost every paragraph – was a weirdly brilliant self-contained unit.

What I really liked about *Breakfast of Champions* was this: unlike most books, it didn't assume that the reader knew very much about anything – neither about human beings nor their customs nor the planet they inhabited. It was written as if its reader were, most likely, an alien from a distant galaxy, which is to say that it explained *everything*, from peas to beavers – often in rather eccentric detail, often with accompanying pictures and diagrams. It explained all those things that every other book seemed to think were too obvious to need explaining. And the more I read, the more I realized that most of these things *weren't* obvious after all. Most of them were decidedly odd.

I suppose I must have been very deeply absorbed in Mr Vonnegut's writing that day, because it took me a long time to notice that something was afoot. As it chugged away from the school gates, the bus was much noisier, much fuller, than it should have been. A dim, nagging irritation began to pull into focus. Then something clipped my ear. A piece of screwed-up paper. Of course, this made no sense. It was Wednesday, the day of reprieve – Alex Woods's day off. I turned round in my seat, still more baffled than alarmed at this point.

I was confronted by the extremely unwelcome sight of Decker, Studwin and Asbo. They were sitting a few rows back, with a couple of other members of the first eleven, even though it was a Wednesday. I was so bewildered by this cruel and unreasonable turn of events that I accidentally initiated a conversation. This really was *asking* for trouble.

'You're supposed to be at football practice,' I pointed out.

'Mr Hale has the shits,' said Declan Mackenzie.

Mr Hale has the shits. It sounded like the title of a play. A play of dubious merit. Either that or one of those coded sentences that spies use to confirm their identities. It was neither, obviously. Decker was trying to tell me something literal and profound.

'Mr Hale's *ill*?' I asked.

'The shits,' Decker repeated. 'Went home after lunch.'

Mr Hale was the football coach. Without him, there could be no football practice. Things were beginning to click into place. As to the accuracy of Declan Mackenzie's medical diagnosis, I can't vouch for it, but neither was I going to question it. Although he was a straight-talker, not given to prettying up his language with pointless ornamentation, it seemed unlikely that Mr Hale would choose to broadcast the nature of his complaint with such unflinching candour. But then, such news did have a tendency to travel, whatever the intentions of its subject. And it would have come as no great shock to find my darkest suspicions concerning the school cafeteria so emphatically confirmed.

'I'm sorry to hear that,' I said, after a short pause for thought.

Declan Mackenzie looked at me with utter disdain, as if he held me personally accountable for the state of Mr Hale's bowels. He was feeling belligerent, I could tell. Deprived of football, his combative instincts required an alternative outlet. 'You *reading* something, Woods?'

'I was trying to,' I said. It was a stupid thing to say, but unexpected changes to my routine always throw me off balance.

Decker Mackenzie spat on the floor.

I turned back in my seat, as calmly and casually as possible.

This was the point at which I should have returned the book – the book that Mr Peterson's dead wife had given him – to the relative safety of my bag. But hindsight makes geniuses of us all. At the time, I was fearful of provoking any further interest. They'd all already seen the book, and I thought that any attempt to conceal it now would be met with anger and suspicion. So instead, I stared resolutely at the opened pages, not taking anything in, simply willing my aggressors to lose interest.

And, miraculously, it seemed to work. No further insults or missiles were forthcoming. I felt my muscles relax. I counted to sixty to reassure myself that the danger had passed. I counted to one hundred and twenty to be doubly sure. Then I started reading again, very slowly, concentrating hard to calm my mind.

Five minutes later, I felt my heart leap into my mouth. Quick and quiet as a cockroach, Declan Mackenzie had sneaked up behind me and snatched the book from my hands.

I cried out in dismay. Studwin and Asbo cheered appreciatively.

'Give it back!' I yelped. There was no authority in my voice. It came out as what it was: a terrified mouse-squeak.

'Share and share alike,' Declan Mackenzie intoned moronically.

'Please!' I pleaded. 'It's not my book!'

'If it's not your book,' said Decker, 'then I don't have to give it back.' A bully's unassailable logic. He'd opened the first page, his thumb braced forcefully against the spine, his hands grubby and clumsy.

'Please! You're going to damage it.'

Mackenzie's eyes widened in evil joy. He'd found the dedication. '*I think you'll enjoy this story*,' he recited in a whining falsetto; '*you'll definitely enjoy the pictures. With all my love, R.*'

Story, pictures, love – each word reverberated over the juddering engine, each word more damning than the last.

Studwin snickered. Asbo howled with delight. There were little ripples of laughter all the way to the back of the bus. This, apparently, was the type of verbal lynching that everyone could enjoy.

I found myself on my feet, my face red with public ridicule. But my humiliation was now a secondary concern. The priority, I knew, had to be the rescue of Mr Peterson's book. I made a lunge for it; Declan Mackenzie pushed me back as easily as he might have plucked the legs from a crane fly.

'Please!' I implored (for what would turn out to be the final time).

Decker had opened the book somewhere in the middle, hunting for more ammunition. He wasn't disappointed. He opened the book on the page containing a large hand-drawn picture of a stegosaurus, and read aloud the accompanying caption: '"A dinosaur was a reptile as big as a choo-choo train."'

There was more laughter. It was a funny sentence, but I doubt this was the reason.

'Fucking hell, Woods!' squealed Decker. 'You really *are* retarded!' Or he squealed something similar. I was no longer listening. He now held the book aloft and was waving it around like the monkey with the bone at the beginning of *2001: A Space Odyssey.*

It was at this point that I decided I didn't want to be a pacifist any more. I decided that if ever there were a just war, this was it.

As I've already mentioned, I'd held for some time the untested suspicion that I wouldn't be much to shout about in a fight. This turned out to be the case. The little I knew about fighting I'd gleaned from James Bond films and from watching the occasional altercation between Lucy and one of the neighbourhood toms – whose advances were not *always* welcomed. Neither of these sources provided a good grounding in the realities of hand-to-hand combat.

What I did have on my side was the element of surprise and a complete disregard for the rules of 'fair' fighting – that and a decent grasp of the physics of moving bodies. Borrowing a little kinetic energy from the accelerating bus, I sprang at Declan Mackenzie and raked my claws across his face, opening up several deep gashes, the best of which stretched all the way from the outer corner of his left eye to his downturned lower lip. There was a yowl of mingled disbelief and pain, vibrant blood, and a single arm raised defensively, and rather too late, to his mutilated cheek. That, I thought, was my opening. I abandoned my wild, unsustainable attack and made a grab for the book. Unfortunately, my plan – insofar as there had been a plan – had failed to account for the reflexive tightening of my enemy's grip in response to sudden, unexpected pain. My fingers closed, pulled and slipped. Then my arm went dead from the shoulder. I fell forward into one of those strange boxers' cuddles. There were lots of screams and shouts, and the general clamour of people shifting up and down the bus to make space for the fight or secure a seat closer to the ringside. I grabbed again at my opponent's face, but instead found myself holding, then pulling, a handful of hair. There was a general tutting and groaning, even from the girls; my tactics were not endearing me to the crowd. Then all the air left my lungs. There was less pain than I'd been expecting – Declan Mackenzie hadn't had the room to deliver a knockout blow – but I still found myself stumbling backwards into the metal frame of the nearest seat. I was quite proud that I didn't *fall* to the floor; although the floor, inevitably, was where I ended up. Still unable to breathe correctly, I backed away to the very front of the bus and then, with a quiet dignity, lowered myself into a sitting position in the aisle. Declan Mackenzie was soon looming over me again, his foot poised curiously in midair, as if he couldn't quite decide whether to kick me or stamp on me. I didn't much care which option he plumped for – my defensive strategy was unaltered. I raised my knees as high as they'd go, held my legs with both arms and tucked my head in, like a turtle retreating into its shell. A half-hearted boot struck my outer thigh, but it didn't really hurt too much. In the warm, musty darkness of my almost foetal position, I sensed that I was no longer such an appealing target for physical violence. It would take a sustained, purposeful attack to cause me any significant damage, and if this hadn't happened yet, it wasn't *going* to happen.

It turned out that Declan Mackenzie had a better conclusion in mind. He stepped back, slid open the top panel of the nearest window and flung Mr Peterson's book from the top deck of the speeding bus. Then he spat on me and returned to his seat.

No one moved to stop or help me as I pulled my bag across my shoulder and then half crawled, half fell down the stairs to the lower deck. My body was battered, but my mind was surprising clear. I would not experience my inevitable seizure until several hours later, in the privacy of my own bedroom, clutching my iron–nickel meteorite to my chest.

'You have to stop the bus!' I told the bus driver.

This was the first time I had ever spoken to the bus driver, who did not present himself as the kind of man who'd appreciate the effort. Even under normal, stationary circumstances, the bus driver bubbled with barely suppressed rage. His characteristic facial expression suggested a furious impatience for retirement or death – whichever came quicker. He had what my mother would have identified as a pitch-black aura, and it was a diagnosis no sceptic would have disputed.

Upon my addressing him, the bus driver had started grunting incomprehensibly.

'I'm sorry,' I interrupted, 'you're not speaking clearly and I don't have any time to waste. This is an emergency. Stop the bus.'

'I don't see a bus stop, do you?'

'It's an emergency! You have to stop the bus!'

'I don't *have* to do anything,' the bus driver growled.

I could see there was no reasoning with him. No words of mine were going to persuade him to make an unscheduled stop in the middle of the B3136. It was drizzling outside; prompt action was essential. Without thinking too much about the likely consequences, I turned to the door and pulled the emergency release lever. There were several gasps, simultaneous with the screeching hiss of airbrakes and a sudden jolt forward. My arm was wrenched from the vertical support pole. Something hit my shoulder; something bruised my buttocks. But, miraculously, I stayed on my feet.

I was out the door the second the bus halted. I later found out that the bus driver spent the next five minutes flapping his arms at the roadside, incandescent with rage and completely at a loss as to what he should do next; there was no protocol or precedent for an incident such as this. But at the time, I was more or less oblivious to this exterior drama. I didn't bother looking back. I ran like a maniac, my pace never slackening. My mind was fully focussed on its goal. I was determined, somehow, to turn back the clock.

Every problem, I told myself, has its mathematical solution. My problem was that I had no idea at which point along the B3136 Mr Peterson's book had exited the school bus. I had been on the floor at the time.

So what *did* I know?

I knew that the B3136 was a windy country road, and I knew that the school bus was old, heavy and cumbersome. It seemed unlikely, therefore, that the bus had been travelling very quickly.

A mean velocity of thirty miles per hour was my estimate – and, really, this was being generous. Thirty miles per hour, I thought, was probably close to the upper limit of which the school bus was capable.

So how much time had passed between the book exiting the window and the bus coming to a stop? Since I hadn't had the presence of mind to check my watch, this was harder to estimate. I had to rely on woolly subjectivity. How long had it taken to regain my breath, grab my bag, fall down the stairs, argue with the driver and force the bus to a standstill? I decided that all of that must have taken at least two minutes, but no more than three.

Thirty miles per hour equals half a mile per minute. Distance equals velocity multiplied by time. I deduced that Mr Peterson's book was between one and one and a half miles away.

So how fast could I run? I knew that running a mile in four minutes was considered to be an impressive athletic achievement. I was pumped full of adrenaline, but I was certainly no athlete. I allowed myself another six minutes of running time. Then I started searching.

I searched the wet grasses and hedgerows for over an hour. I found enough drinks cans and crisp packets and chocolate-bar wrappers to fill a couple of bin liners. I found toilet roll and broken glass and fast-food packaging and a cereal box. I found all sorts of items lost or thrown from cars: a soft toy rabbit, a wing mirror, a windscreen-wiper blade. I found a few inexplicable oddities: a trowel, a pair of tartan slippers, a tennis racket, underpants. Near a lay-by, I found a prophylactic – a *used* prophylactic. It was laid out rather neatly on a small grey stone. At that point, I started to cry. I sat down on the verge – a safe five metres from the soiled condom – and I stared at my wet, muddy shoes and I cried. I was feeling pretty disgusted with the state of the universe. It wasn't simply that people were having intercourse at the side of the B3136. I supposed that was okay in the grand scheme of things, since they were at least taking precautions not to bring any more babies into the world. I'd decided that the world was not a fit place for babies. But, still, these people obviously didn't care much about anybody else. They obviously didn't care about the countryside. No one did. The more time you spend rooting around at the roadside, the more you have to accept that fact. That condom wasn't biodegradable – obviously. It would probably lie there for an aeon. It would probably outlive the trees and the birds, and all of the books in existence.

As for *Breakfast of Champions*, that was already a lost cause. My maths had been ridiculous from the outset. There were too many guesses, and too many variables, and I knew nothing about the likely trajectory of a book thrown from the upper deck of a moving bus. It could have ended up anywhere. It could have sailed over a hedge and ended up in the field beyond, out of sight and out of reach. And even if I'd found it, the book would have been ruined. An hour of light rain had soaked all the foliage. I was soaked too. I had my cagoule in my bag, but I hadn't bothered to put it on. I hadn't noticed that I was getting wet until I abandoned my search.

After a while, I stopped crying and stood up and headed back down the road. I thought it would probably take me about an hour and a half to walk home. With any luck, I might be able to get back before my mother. I didn't want my mother to know what had happened. At that point, I still thought I could keep it from her.

I'd walked about half an hour beyond the point where the bus had stopped (which I'd recognized from the beech trees and the tyre marks) when another car pulled over. People had been pulling over every five minutes for the last hour to check if I was okay. I guess I didn't *look* okay. There was no good reason to be walking down the B3136 in the rain.

This time, it was someone I knew. It was Mrs Griffith, who worked at the post office and spoke fluent Elvish. Mrs Griffith knew that I liked *The Lord of the Rings*, so whenever I went into the post office she'd greet me in Quenya, the language of the High Elves. Mrs Griffith liked languages a lot. She wasn't so keen on working in the post office, but unfortunately, speaking fluent Elvish was not a marketable skill.

She didn't greet me in Elvish that day. As the electric window slid down, I could see that her lips were pursed in a concerned pout.

'Hello, Alex,' she said.

'Hello,' I replied.

'Are you okay?' she asked.

'Yes, I'm okay,' I said.

'Why are you walking in the road?'

'I missed the bus,' I lied. I didn't like lying, especially not to someone like Mrs Griffith, but I thought, in this case, it was probably for the best.

Mrs Griffith frowned and shook her head. 'You're *walking* home?'

'Yes. I thought it would be quicker than waiting for the next bus.' (This lie was just about plausible. SARS ran a very irregular bus service.)

'It's an awfully long way,' Mrs Griffith pointed out.

'Yes, I know,' I said.

'And it's raining,' she added.

'Yes, it is,' I agreed.

'I'm not sure your mother would want you walking so far in the rain.'

'No, maybe not. It might be better if you don't mention it. I don't expect I'll do it again. It's too far.'

'Can I give you a lift?'

'Yes, that would be very helpful. Thank you.'

'Hop in, then.'

I wetted my hand on my cagoule and rubbed away the boot mark that Declan Mackenzie had left on my trouser leg. Then I hopped in.

I got home twenty minutes before my mother, which gave me enough time to feed Lucy and change out of my wet clothes.

THE APPOSITE WORD

I was summoned to Mr Treadstone's office at ten o'clock the following morning. The bus driver had reported me, of course, as had several passengers on the lower deck. When you live in a village (and have been hit by a meteor), most people know your face and name. In hindsight, I never stood a chance.

When it came to discipline – when it came to most things – Mr Treadstone had a meticulous attention to detail. By ten o'clock, one hour into the formal investigation, he had already amassed a wealth of information concerning the previous day's 'incident'. He'd spoken to the bus driver (a short, frustrating conversation, I imagine) and gathered statements from two of the civilians who'd phoned the school to register their complaints. Two of my more pliable peers had also been called in for questioning: Amy Jones, whose father was a school governor, and Paul Hart, whose mother taught art. From these interviews, Mr Treadstone knew all about the fight. He knew that I had tried to claw Declan Mackenzie's face off, and he knew that in the ensuing struggle some property of mine had been thrown overboard. The plain facts of the conflict were easy to establish. Only the motives remained unknown, and these would be uncovered soon enough. Mr Treadstone was very big on uncovering motives. He always said that the only way to kill the weed was to kill the root.

The weed was a metaphor for deviance.

As with every trial that had ever taken place in Mr Treadstone's office, ours was to be a swift, no-nonsense affair. Since the legwork had already been done, and the verdict was already known, there was little that could delay the keen sword of justice. Charges would be levelled, statements read, explanations demanded and rejected, and punishments meted out. These accelerated proceedings would be bookended by the rather lengthier pre- and post-trial lectures, which Mr Treadstone believed to be the most crucial part of any disciplinary hearing. These lectures provided the opportunity to make sure that everyone understood the nature of the weed, and was fully committed to stopping its spread.

Strangely enough, Mr Treadstone's views on crime and punishment were not unlike my mother's – though in all other ways, they were as different as two people could be. Criminality, impropriety, scruffiness, poor diction – Mr Treadstone treated all these things as if they caused a kind of cosmic disorder, a general untidiness, that *had* to be rectified. And punishment by numbers was never enough. The books had to be balanced in the appropriate manner. Mr Treadstone, too, was a great believer in fitting punishments and public displays of remorse. When, for example, it was discovered that Scott Sizewell had been making an obscene gesture in the school photograph (this was an exceptionally dumb crime), Mr Treadstone hauled him up in assembly to make a dramatic apology before all six hundred of his fellow pupils. And this was no simple 'sorry'. Scott Sizewell's speech – prepared under strict supervision – lasted four minutes and was more akin to the statements made by disgraced politicians.

When it came to fistfights, Mr Treadstone believed that there was only one satisfactory resolution to such an infringement. Each party had to apologize – first to Mr Treadstone, then to each other – with what was deemed to be an adequate degree of sincerity, and then they had to shake hands (firmly, with eye contact; this was *always* the correct way to shake someone's hand). It was a solemn ritual, which was supposed to signify a definitive end to hostilities – a return to civility and the rule of law.

Civility was also to be the major theme of our pre-trial lecture, which began promptly at 10.02.

'We live in a civilized society,' said Mr Treadstone, 'and in a civilized society we resolve our differences in a civilized manner. We do *not* solve our problems with violence.'

Mr Treadstone was speaking hypothetically, of course – about ideals rather than reality. Or I supposed he was talking hypothetically. Otherwise, this would have been, as Mr Peterson would say, Grade A Horse Shit. At that very moment, we, the civilized world, were mired in two major wars in the desert, and from what I'd seen on TV, the men fighting these wars were widely regarded as heroes. We had nuclear submarines armed with bombs that could flatten cities, and many extremely civilized people agreed that this was only prudent – given how *un*civilized many other countries (and all of their inhabitants) were known to be.

I should probably tell you that I had a lot of pent-up hysteria that morning. I had spent most of the previous night awake. By daybreak, I had suffered three seizures – two partial, one convulsive; all three kept secret from my mother – and felt physically and psychologically frazzled. Without wishing to be overly dramatic, my mind felt like a saucepan full of writhing snakes, and the only way I could keep the lid on was through unwavering, single-minded vigilance. All my well-honed meditation and distraction techniques came into play. There was no hope of cultivating my usual sense of calm, so I aimed instead for a kind of detached numbness – layer upon layer of thick insulation to protect me from further injury. And for a while, this worked reasonably well. There were only one or two moments when I felt like laughing or crying or both.

'You are ambassadors for the school,' Mr Treadstone intoned. 'When you are out in the local community, when you are travelling to and from the school grounds, you are still carrying the school flag – and you *will* behave accordingly.'

I stared solemnly at the floor and counted to fifty in Roman numerals. This was an acceptable posture given the circumstances. Mr Treadstone only expected eye contact when he was addressing you directly, by name or through a non-rhetorical question; and by the time Mr Treadstone addressed us that day, my mind was somewhere else entirely. (I was thinking about Kurt Vonnegut in his meat locker while Dresden burned above him.) His demand for a response seemed to come from nowhere.

'Well?' he prompted. 'What do you have to say for yourselves?'

My numbed mind fumbled for thought. Declan Mackenzie reacted with the pin-sharp reflexes of a cornered weasel. 'Sir,' he said, 'I know that fighting's wrong. And usually no one dislikes violence more than me—'

'More than *I*,' Mr Treadstone corrected.

'No one dislikes violence more than I,' Declan Mackenzie agreed, 'but this was self-defence. Ask anyone. *He* attacked *me*.'

He touched his hand to his left cheek at this point. Exhibit A: three or four angry-looking wounds. The scratches were now a reddish-yellow colour, and his left eye was puffy and purple. The wounds did look reasonably impressive, but I suspected they were actually quite superficial. In contrast, though much of my bruising was severe, it was all on places like my hips and buttocks – places I didn't care to make public. And I suppose under questioning I would have been forced to admit that most of these injuries were *technically* self-inflicted, having been accumulated while I was falling down the stairs or rattling around in the doorway as the bus performed its emergency stop. Visually, Declan Mackenzie held a major advantage. He also had going for him the fact that his phoney-baloney ungrammatical speech at least *sounded* sincere. When I tried to riposte, mine was the hollow monotone of the clinically depressed.

'Yes,' I admitted, 'I attacked first. But that's pretty irrelevant.' Mr Treadstone's lip curled, perhaps because of my choice of modifier, perhaps because of my presumption in telling him what was or wasn't relevant. I wasn't sure which. 'It's not relevant,' I continued drearily, 'because he started it. He provoked me. This was his doing, not mine.'

'It takes two to create a conflict,' Mr Treadstone noted.

It was one of those statements that sounds true but doesn't feel true. I was surprised to discover a small flicker of dissent somewhere in my gut. But my gut, sadly, was no public speaker.

Whatever I wanted to express slipped from my grasp. I only managed to repeat myself, an atom less robotically. 'This is his fault. He started it.'

'I did not!' Declan Mackenzie wheedled. 'I was only messing around. It's not my fault he can't take a joke!'

'Theft is no joke,' I said.

I felt sure Mr Treadstone would support me in this sentiment. He did not. By then, he'd lost his patience. 'That's quite enough,' he said, raising his hands. 'This is disappointing, very disappointing . . . I can see that neither of you is willing to accept your share of the responsibility for yesterday's disgraceful display. But I *am* going to get to the root of this matter.'

Mr Treadstone took a seat in his high-backed chair to show that he was prepared to wait for as long as it took.

'I'm not interested in excuses,' he said. 'I want answers. Straightforward answers. Woods!' His index finger swung dramatically in my direction. 'Why did you assault Mr Mackenzie?'

'He stole my book. He threw it out of the window.'

'Mackenzie?'

'I was upset. He attacked me!' He touched his cheek again, close to his puffy eye socket. 'He could have blinded me!'

'It's actually pretty difficult to blind someone,' I pointed out.

'He came at me with his *nails*!'

Mr Treadstone frowned, which was the only possible response to a disclosure such as this.

'That was after you'd stolen my book,' I pointed out.

'Woods: you'll address your answers to me, and speak only when I ask you to, not before. Mackenzie: why did you take Mr Woods's book?'

Declan Mackenzie stared sullenly at the floor.

Mr Treadstone clicked his tongue. 'Woods: why did Mackenzie take your book?'

'I think you'll have to ask *him*,' I said.

'I've asked him. Now I'm asking you.'

I stayed silent, but it was soon clear that Mr Treadstone was not going to let this matter lie. He was still determined to uncover motives. 'Well?' he asked. 'I expect an answer, Woods. Why did Mr Mackenzie take your book?'

In my defence, this was a very stupid question to ask; and it was certainly the wrong question to ask *me*. I was no psychologist. Declan Mackenzie's motives had always been a perfect mystery to me. How was I supposed to give a reasonable answer when I doubted that such a thing even existed? Who knew *what* went on in Declan Mackenzie's mind? He wasn't exactly the most rational member of the species. My vaguest intuition was that if he'd had a motive, it had probably been something to do with humiliation – with some kind of urge to make other people feel like something the cat had dragged in. But the more I thought about *that*, the more incomprehensible it seemed.

I spent what seemed like many minutes struggling with this mental block, my pent-up hysteria rising and falling in the background. Mr Treadstone raised his eyebrows and tapped the desk with his fingertips.

'You want to know why he did it?' I asked. 'Why he took my book?'

'Yes, Mr Woods. As we've established, some time ago. I'm not going to repeat myself. I want you to answer the question in plain English.'

The apposite word had by now found its way to the very tip

of my tongue, and once it was there, I had little notion of calling it back.

'It's because he's a cunt,' I said.

The word kind of hung there in the air for a while, as if I'd somehow managed to render it in a cartoon speech bubble. No one reacted. No one had been expecting it, least of all me.

Then the bubble burst.

Mr Treadstone went the colour of a blood blister. Declan Mackenzie went the colour of mint ice-cream. And I think I probably managed to stay my regular colour. But on the inside – on the inside, something had shifted.

Let me tell you: there's this state of mind that doctors call 'euphoria'. Some temporal lobe epileptics can experience it during a seizure, when the brain's emotional centres are suddenly overloaded with electricity and start to malfunction. Normal people can sometimes get it too, when they feel like they've achieved something magnificent or are on drugs. Well, anyway: I'm fairly sure that euphoria was what I was experiencing at that moment, and for a while, I thought that convulsions were imminent. There was the same sense of unreality, the same lifting feeling – almost of weightlessness. But at the same time, my aura was absent. There were no distractions, no hallucinations. It felt more like I was rising, as if from a dense fog, into clear skies and golden sunlight. My vision was sharp, and my head was clear, and I felt a calm that went far beyond normal calm.

'What?' asked Mr Treadstone. Not 'Pardon?' or 'Excuse me?' or any of the other polite alternatives that he drummed into us daily; and I knew from his colouring that he'd heard well enough the first time. But for some reason, he was giving me the chance to reconsider.

I did not want to reconsider.

My words now struck me as the only meaningful words that had been uttered all morning. I would not have taken them back for all the money in Robert Asquith's bank account. Declan Mackenzie was precisely what I'd said he was, and I felt no reservations about having pointed this out. It wasn't as if anything bad could happen to me now – or nothing worse than what had gone before. Mr Treadstone could expel me, I supposed – but that wouldn't be so terrible a consequence. (I would be home-schooled again, which was a more efficient way to learn.) Declan Mackenzie could beat me up again – but that would hardly make my words *less* true. I realized at that point that I had no fear of Declan Mackenzie any more. Sitting there with his green face and his puffy eye and his cowardly evasions, he struck me now as a pretty insignificant figure. So, presented with the chance, I decided to repeat my assertion, adding nothing but the school motto, *Ex Veritas Vires*, which I thought made an interesting coda.

Declan Mackenzie's jaw hit the floor. Mr Treadstone leapt from his chair like a firework.

'Mackenzie: out! NOW! Woods: not another word! Not another BREATH!'

The lecture that followed was extremely animated, but also far too long and repetitious to report here. Once it was over, Mr Treadstone phoned my mother at work, and my mother pleaded for clemency based on the mitigating circumstances of my illness and previous good record. They eventually agreed that a week of detention – in conjunction with the additional discipline I'd be facing at home – would be the minimum punishment for the terrible thing I'd said. Declan Mackenzie, in contrast, received a single day's detention. My crime in using *that* word was deemed to be five times worse than anything he could possibly have done to me.

By the evening, any sense of euphoria was nothing more than a memory. I felt exhausted and miserable, and once more at a loss for words.

I hadn't had enough time to rehearse what I was going to say to Mr Peterson. I had only a two-hour window before my mother got home – at which point, I was sure to be grounded for the next month (two months, as it turned out). And, anyway, the more I thought about it, the more I realized that there was little I *could* say. I could lay out all the facts, make my excuses, give a detailed, eloquent account of all the torment I'd suffered since – and none of this would change a damn thing. The final result was just as hideous.

By the time I was passing the poplar sentinels, my heart was in my mouth. And by the time the door swung open, any dream of eloquence had gone the way of the dodo.

'I'm afraid I lost your book,' I blurted. And it was such an awful, inadequate sentence. But what else could I say? I didn't have my mother's knack for delivering bad news. I just wanted to get the words out before my courage left me entirely.

Mr Peterson looked stricken. 'You lost it?'

I nodded. My voice was paralysed.

'You *lost* it?'

'Yes, I'm—'

'You *knew* what that book meant to me!' Mr Peterson was holding his head like he had a migraine.

'It wasn't my fault!' I pleaded. 'I was on the school bus and—'

'The school bus! You took it on the school bus?'

I could see straight away how irresponsible this was. I gave up trying to pretend that this was anyone's fault but my own.

'I'm extremely sorry,' I said. 'And I know that's not good enough. I know I can't replace it—'

'No, you can't! Jesus! I must be an *idiot*!'

I didn't know what to say.

'Go home, kid,' Mr Peterson said eventually. 'I don't want to look at you right now.'

I had no thought of staying – of trying to explain things properly. I turned and I ran. And I didn't stop running until I was home.

PIERCING

For the next eight weeks, right up to the summer holidays, I found myself once more under the worst kind of house arrest – the kind masterminded by my mother. Having received three strikes in quick succession (vandalism, fighting, swearing), I was no longer trusted to take responsibility for my own punishment. I was barely allowed out of my mother's sight. Every morning she drove me to the school gates, and every afternoon I was collected from the same spot. Usually it was my mother who did the collecting too, but sometimes Justine was sent in her place, and, once or twice, even Sam was roped in to cover the school run. It was very inconvenient for all concerned. Not that Justine or Sam ever complained – they were always very patient with me – but I could tell that they were keen to see me back 'on the rails' as quickly as possible. And when it came to the subject of my various crimes and misdemeanours, I faced a united front.

'You know that fighting rarely solves anything,' Justine said. 'It usually makes matters worse.'

'Yes, I know,' I said.

'And that word you used,' Justine added, wrinkling her nose, 'that word really is *extremely* offensive. Especially to women.' (And from the vehemence in her voice, I knew that what was true of women in general was doubly true of lesbians – although the logic of this was light-years beyond my grasp.)

My mother, of course, had already lectured me at length on the appallingness of *that* word. So had Sam, who was usually more moderate when it came to such things.

'It's a vulgar, obnoxious, *male* word,' Sam said, which confused me for quite some time.

'Why's it a *male* word?' I asked.

Sam looked at me for a few moments to gauge whether or not I was being deliberately stupid, then said: 'You do know what that word means, don't you?'

'Of course I know what it means!' I searched my mental thesaurus, ruled out every alternative, then said: 'It refers to the part of the woman where babies come out.'

'Exactly! And you can see why that's demeaning, can't you? You can see why it's *so* offensive?'

I thought about this for a while. 'No, not really,' I concluded. 'I mean, I wasn't actually using it in that context. Also, surely what's so offensive is that the word's so offensive, rather than the word itself?'

Sam made me repeat this sentence, then told me I was being pedantic and perpetuating a sexist mindset. I felt quite aggrieved by this.

'*I* didn't make it the worst word in the world,' I said.

* * *

After I was picked up from school I was not allowed home unsupervised. Instead, I had to spend two hours every afternoon (and another nine on Saturdays) at the shop, which was a further inconvenience for all concerned. This was at the time when Justine and Sam were first having their 'problems', the nature of which was none of my business. All my mother would tell me was that they were going through a 'rocky patch', and this was why Justine often appeared so out of sorts – a fact that had not escaped my notice. A lot of the time, Justine seemed so far away that I was sure she had passed over to one of my mother's other planes of existence; and often, when she came back from a break, her eyes would be all raw and bloodshot. Really, it was the worst possible time for me to be underfoot – a truth that I was quick to point out to my mother.

'Yes, it is,' she agreed. And then she said no more on the matter.

So Justine was in a bad mood, my mother was in a bad mood, Sam was in a bad mood, and of course, I, too, was in a bad mood. For the first several days I was extremely sullen, and after that, merely bored. My mother tried to find small jobs to occupy me – stock checks and the like – but more often than not, there was little I could do to pass the time. Mostly, I sat in the far corner behind the counter – as far into the far corner as I could skulk – and spied on the comings and goings of the customers.

I probably don't need to tell you that my mother's shop was frequented by a *lot* of odd people. I'd estimate that less than a third of her clientele could be classified in any other way – just the tourists, really, and the occasional group of school girls, my age or a little older. Some of them I recognized from Asquith, but if any of them ever recognized me, none went so far as to acknowledge my existence. This was not particularly awkward; I was used to not having my existence acknowledged by girls. What *was* awkward, however, was that my mother had decided that groups of school girls were the only demographic that posed a serious shoplifting risk, and as such required 'special monitoring' from the moment they entered to the moment they left.

'Keep an eye on those girls,' she'd tell me.

'Why me?' I'd plead. '*You* keep an eye on them!'

'Don't be silly!' she'd say in an infuriating whisper. 'I'm sure it's not *that* much of an ordeal for you.'

'They'll think I'm staring!'

'So what? That doesn't seem to bother you most of the time.'

'This is different. It's embarrassing! What if they catch me? What if they look up and find me watching them?'

This would provoke a delighted tinkle of muted laughter. 'Well, you could try smiling, Lex. You'll probably find they're not quite so scary as you imagine!'

This annoyed me a lot. For a start, I didn't think that my mother was ideally placed to set herself up as a relationship coach. Furthermore, the truth of the matter was that on a one-to-one basis I was actually much more comfortable with girls than I was with boys – I always had been. It was only groups of girls I struggled with. Because in groups girls *were* scary. They were always whispering and giggling and exchanging coded glances. It was unfair to expect me to try to deal with that. But, as always, there was no arguing with my mother. It fell to me to watch and squirm and blush, and later to report any activities that could be construed as 'suspicious'.

This task was close to impossible for two main reasons. First, groups of girls *always* look suspicious. Second, most of my mother's other customers looked just as suspicious. In my mother's shop, suspiciousness was such a relative concept that the term was basically meaningless. I remember, for example, one man dressed in a leather trench coat and a broad-brimmed leather hat who spent an awfully long time looking at the pickled animals – maybe as long as forty-five minutes. Then he turned and left without saying a word. And behaviour like this was not uncommon. The only reason I remember that man in particular was that I always paid extra attention to men of his type – loners of a certain age who lurked with an apparent lack of purpose. This harked back to a recurrent fantasy from my earlier childhood, in which one of these anonymous men would suddenly announce himself as my phantom father. In some versions of the fantasy, the man in question had come purposefully to observe me in secret before choosing to unveil himself. In other versions, he would be there by pure coincidence; it was only when he looked up from his contemplated purchase that he would notice *me*, or sometimes my mother – or she would notice him, all of a sudden, always with a dramatic intake of breath.

It was only when I got a little older that I became aware of the various problems and improbabilities bound up with this daydream. For a start, it seemed extremely unlikely that my father knew of my existence, or even suspected it. I also had reason to doubt that after so many years, my parents would be capable of recognizing one another. When I asked my mother for information regarding their relationship, she tended to respond with words like 'brief' and 'functional'. More specifically, I'd managed to ascertain that their affair had not outlasted the daylight hours of the winter solstice, and from my mother's perspective, it had been about procreation and nothing more. All she could tell me about my father was that he was healthy (or so he appeared) and sexually competent (evidently) – and, once she had established these facts, anything else seemed rather extraneous. She hadn't paid a great deal of attention to anything so abstract as his appearance and general character, and nothing had stuck in her memory. Without wishing to sound overly critical of my mother, by the time I was born, I don't think she would have been able to pick my father out of a three-man line-up.

Nevertheless, even after my childhood fantasies had lost much of their lustre, the *idea* of my father still retained some grip on my imagination. I still had an image, based on next to nothing, of how my father might look and act. I imagined him as some kind of Tom Bombadil type – all boots and beard, with a deep love of the woodlands and no employment history. Most of the vaguely suspicious lone men who came into my mother's shop seemed to fit this profile, but, even so, the arrival of such specimens was a relative rarity. I'd be lucky to observe more than two a week, and after they'd left, boredom was quick to return.

Unfortunately, there was no chance of my negotiating a reduction in the length of my jail term – not without an admission of guilt followed by a suitably convincing, and elaborate, display of remorse. My mother wanted me to write letters of apology to Mr Treadstone and Declan Mackenzie (and probably to the cantankerous bus driver too) – even *after* I'd given her a (nearly) full account of the circumstances that led to me acting and speaking as I did. We had the same circular argument again and again. I told my mother that I didn't feel guilty because my words and actions (however unpleasant) were justified by circumstance – and for this reason I was not prepared to apologize to *anyone*. I'd rather die. My mother maintained that if I was able to comprehend the appalling gravity of what I'd done, then I'd apologize in a heartbeat. I'd have to. In the meantime, I was just being obstinate, and wilfully ignorant.

'I don't think you can possibly understand how offensive that word is,' my mother told me one afternoon, elaborating on a familiar theme. 'If you did, you never would have used it.'

'I know how offensive it is,' I assured her.

'No, you don't! You obviously don't. Honestly, Lex, I don't know what's worse: that you said it in the first place or that you refuse to realize how horrible it is!'

'I know how horrible it is! It's the worst word in the English language – everyone knows that. That's why I chose it. I didn't just pick it at random!'

'You shouldn't call anyone that – ever. I don't care how much you *think* you were provoked.'

'He deserved it!'

'No, he didn't – no one deserves that kind of abuse.'

'No one?'

'Yes – no one!'

I waited for a few moments. 'What about Hitler?' I asked. I'd been thinking of playing the Hitler card for a while, even though I knew it was unlikely to strengthen my argument – my mother's counter-attack was too obvious.

'Oh, Lex, really.' She planted her hands on her hips. 'I can't believe what I'm hearing! Are you seriously comparing the Mackenzie child to *Hitler*?'

'Well . . . I don't know. I suppose not. But then, Declan

Mackenzie hasn't had as much time to develop his evil. He hasn't had access to the same resources. I'm sure when Hitler was a child no one realized how bad *he* was either.'

'Lex, this is beyond ridiculous! It's offensively idiotic!'

'All I'm saying is that it's a bit early to tell. But I'm sure that if you put Declan Mackenzie in charge of a country, then things would start to go downhill pretty quickly.'

'Lex, listen to me: Declan Mackenzie is *not* evil. He may be obnoxious and immature and angry and unpleasant and all the other things you say he is, but that doesn't mean you should demonize him. You don't know everything about him. You certainly don't have the right to say what you said. Otherwise, how are you any better than he is? Well?'

'He deserved it! He's not just unpleasant – he's cruel. He takes pleasure in humiliating other people!'

'Oh, really?'

'Yes – really!'

'And what exactly do you think *you* were doing when you called him what you did?'

I stayed silent.

'No, really, Lex: I'd like to know. You certainly humiliated him. How did that make *you* feel?'

'That was different,' I mumbled. 'He deserved it.'

'We're not talking about whether he deserved it any more. We're talking about how it made you feel.'

'That's not relevant,' I said. 'It's completely different.'

Somehow, despite all my resolutions, my mother had found a way to taint whatever brief victory I'd had. Any sense of triumph I'd had regarding the Declan Mackenzie incident was now on the wane.

'I'm still not going to take it back,' I said petulantly.

My mother shrugged. 'I can't make you.'

But what she really meant was that she no longer felt she had to. She'd brought at least one aspect of my rebellion into disrepute, and in so doing, she'd stripped away the purity of the whole. It was a minor victory, but a victory nonetheless. Even though I stuck to my guns and served out the rest of my sentence in surly silence, we both knew she'd won.

I'd taken to walking two full circuits of the school field every lunchtime – a walk that filled an hour and took me as far away from other people as I could hope to get. Needless to say, this was not the most inspiring walk in Somerset, but during this period, with my evenings and weekends forfeit, it was the best that was available to me; and in some places it was not altogether dull. Since the lone groundsman employed by the school had his work cut out in maintaining the quadrangles and the central football fields and all those anterior zones that were visible to visitors and passers-by, the perimeter of the school field, bordered by tall fences and hedges, was always a neglected area, and in summer, it became particularly unkempt. In summer, the grass around the perimeter was thick and tangled and fresh-smelling, and there were patches of weeds and wildflowers that attracted bees and various types of butterfly. Occasionally, if you were lucky, you might also see a fieldmouse scampering through the undergrowth, or a squirrel darting for the nearest tree; and as a general rule the further you got away from the school buildings, the wilder the wildlife grew, and the fewer the people liable to spoil it. Towards the furthest reaches of the playing field, you were several times more likely to see a magpie or a family of finches than another human being (discounting Mrs Matthews, the music teacher, who was a keen ornithologist).

I walked the same two circuits every day for several weeks – whatever the weather, varying nothing but the direction – and in all this time, I never had to speak a single word to anyone. Left alone with my thoughts, this was by far the most fulfilling hour of the day, and I hoped – and expected – to preserve it as such. But then, one unremarkable, overcast afternoon, everything changed. That was the afternoon I first encountered Ellie. She hunted me down quite purposefully, at a time when everybody else was happy to ignore me – but, in hindsight, that was pretty typical of Ellie. She was an extremely contrary girl.

I already knew her vaguely – or I knew *of* her – even though she was fourteen months and three whole school years older than me. Her full name was Elizabeth Fitzmaurice and she was notorious for getting into trouble. More often than not, it was to do with her flagrant contempt for the school dress code. She preferred to dress herself somewhere between emo and goth. You probably know about goths already, and you might know about emos too, but just in case you don't, I'll elaborate a little, since both are familiar from my mother's shop.

Goths like to wear dramatic black makeup and dramatic black clothes (long studded boots and corsets and chains and collars and so on). Emos have a similar fondness for black, but tend to be less theatrical and more geek-chic in appearance (which is very different to just plain geek). Their clothes are usually quite smart but also exceedingly tight – especially their trousers. Goths are into vampires, Satanism, loud music and very public displays of personality, whereas emos, in general, have a deeper, inner despair and are more into things like irony and self-harm.

Ellie mangled the two categories together: she had a lot of despair but she was not coy about expressing it, and I think on those occasions when she harmed herself, this was largely a matter of misjudgement. She wore a *lot* of eyeliner and eyeshadow, and her hair was as black as a raven's wing. Her fringe was long to the point of complete impracticality, and was typically swept across the left side of her face, where it typically rendered her a Cyclops.

'Woods!' she gasped from some ten metres away. 'Wait!'

Up to this point, I'd been making every effort to ignore her, but once she hailed me, I was out of appealing options. I could either run or stop. I stopped.

'Jesus!' Ellie said, and stood for a while, breathing heavily. 'Jesus in fucking heaven, Woods! How fast do you walk?'

This question did not require an answer.

'Hello, Elizabeth,' I said, and immediately saw her lip curl.

It turned out that Ellie was extremely touchy about her name. She would later tell me that she had been named after 'John the fucking Baptist's mother'. John the fucking Baptist and his mother were characters in the Bible.

'It's Ellie or nothing!' Ellie told me.

'I didn't want to seem over-familiar,' I explained.

Ellie looked at me blankly.

'I was trying to be polite.'

This provoked a short snort of laughter. 'Polite!'

'Yes.'

'Fuck, Woods, you of all people! Since when have you bothered with *polite*? Everyone knows you've got the foulest mouth in the entire school!'

'That was a one-off,' I told her. 'And I had extremely good reasons for saying what I did.'

Ellie flicked her fringe back from her eyes, folded her arms beneath her small but intimidating breasts, then regarded me for some time – and I was sure that every stage of this routine was designed to make me feel uncomfortable.

'Okay then, Mr Polite,' she said. 'So why *did* you say it?'

I thought about this for a while, trying to figure out how best to phrase it, and eventually, this is what I came up with: 'Because naming something takes away its power.'

Ellie looked at me, then rolled her eyes. Ellie was always rolling her eyes. From the number of times she did it in the average conversation, you'd have thought that she'd invented and patented the manoeuvre. 'God, you're weird!' she said.

'Yes, I know,' I conceded.

'It's not an insult,' she added. 'It's just . . . well, there are certainly worse things to be.'

'Thank you.' To me, not being insulted was as good as a compliment. 'Now can I ask *you* a question?' I asked.

'As long as it's *polite*,' Ellie said.

'Well, no . . . not exactly. It's about what we've been talking about. You know: the C-word.'

'Ask away.'

'Well,' I began, clearing my throat. 'Ever since I said it, people have basically been queuing up to tell me how terrible it is – you know: how it's the worst word in existence, and how it's *especially* offensive to women. And, well, I suppose it's that last point that I wanted to ask you about . . .'

'You want my opinion?'

'Yes.'

'As a *woman*?'

'Yes.'

Ellie rolled her eyes again. 'What's the big deal? It's just a word.'

'Right.'

'Cunt, cunt, cunt, cunt, cunt, cunt, cunt!' Ellie added, to make her point. (Ellie liked to make her points unambiguously.)

On the whole, I felt pretty vindicated by her response. 'Thank you,' I said. 'This has been very interesting.'

I started walking again. She grabbed my arm.

'Hang on!' Ellie said. 'Stop being weird for a second. There's something else I need to ask you. Unless of course there's somewhere you need to be?' she added, quite sarcastically.

'Well, I *was* hoping to do another lap of the field,' I said.

Ellie winced. 'What for? Oh, never mind! I'll walk with you. Just give me a second.'

She removed a pack of cigarettes from her shoulder bag and lit one. I looked around nervously.

'Oh, relax!' Ellie admonished. 'No one's looking.'

'Aren't we a bit . . . out in the open?' I asked.

'Trust me,' Ellie said, 'out in the open's the best place to smoke. No one expects it. All those places where people usually smoke – you know, behind the pavilion and down the side of the art block –' I didn't know, but I let her continue – 'well, all those places are completely retarded. Those are the places people get caught. You'd have to be a moron to smoke in any of those places. But out here – well, there's zero chance of getting caught out here. You can see anyone approaching a mile away.'

'And they can see you,' I said.

'Yes, but they'd need a fucking telescope to see what you're doing.'

'Mrs Matthews has binoculars,' I pointed out.

'Mrs Matthews is a mouse!' said Ellie. 'She's the kind of woman who'd turn and wet herself before she'd risk any kind of confrontation.'

'I see.'

'I don't suppose I should offer you one?'

'No, you shouldn't.'

After that, she fell into step beside me and spoke at length about her piercing. It transpired that as an early fifteenth birthday present to herself, Ellie had decided to get her eyebrow pierced. This explained the mysterious plaster above her right eye, which I'd been trying not to look at. Less well explained was her presumption that she could get away with her facial piercing in the long term.

'I thought it would be like with my hair,' she told me. 'You know: I went out and I got my hair dyed, and it's permanent – so, really, my parents had no choice but to accept it. What else could they do? I mean, they ranted and raved for weeks, but it was totally worth it.

'Anyway, I thought this would be the same. But when I got home on Saturday, they both went completely insane. Honestly, you'd have thought I was *pregnant* or something.'

I kept quiet. I didn't think there was much I could say to this.

'Well,' Ellie continued, 'it turns out that I'm not even allowed to come to school with my eyebrow pierced. Can you believe that?'

'Yes,' I said.

'It's against the dress code! Un-fucking-believable!' She took an angry drag on her cigarette. 'Anyway, so after my parents had shouted at me for about a gazillion years, eventually they forced me to take it out, and now I have to wear this stupid plaster until the hole's healed itself.'

'Oh,' I said. 'Yes, that's unfortunate.'

An uncomfortable silence passed. Ellie glanced furtively to her left and right. 'It's still in,' she whispered.

I felt something close to an involuntary shiver. 'The eyebrow?'

'Yes, that's right. My mum confiscated the ring they put in, but I bought a little bar too. She didn't know about that. I figured you can't see it under the plaster anyway, so what's the difference?'

This scheme, I thought, had a rather obvious flaw.

'Yes, I know what you're thinking,' Ellie said. 'But I've got a plan. I figured I'd make a huge fuss about having to wear this stupid plaster for the next few days, then I'll redo my hair so that it's parted at the left and swept over like so.' She gestured vaguely with her non-smoking hand. 'That's a bit of a pain because my right's my better side – obviously – but it won't seem that suspicious because I'll have spent so much time moaning about how everyone keeps staring at my plaster. Then when it's time for it to come off in a few weeks' time, I'll simply keep my new hairstyle, and hey presto! Problem solved.'

'That's your plan?' I asked. 'To comb your hair over your piercing and keep it there for ever?'

'No, not *for ever*. Just for the next year or so. I'll have to buy a lot of hairspray, I suppose. Would you like to see it? My eyebrow?'

She didn't wait for an answer. She stamped out her cigarette. Then she carefully removed her plaster and flicked it away into the hedge.

'You know, you really shouldn't litter,' I pointed out.

'Jesus, Woods,' said Ellie. 'You're quite the comedian.'

'I was being serious.'

'Yes, I know. That's what's funny.'

Ellie's 'bar' was visible as two tiny blue spheres – like ball bearings that had been glued to her face, one above the other on either side of the fine black hairs that constituted the outer extremity of her eyebrow. The surrounding skin was red and inflamed. 'Pretty cool, huh?' asked Ellie. Then, again not waiting for an answer, she removed another plaster from her bag and re-patched herself.

We continued to walk and Ellie lit another cigarette and eventually got to the main point that had brought her to me.

'I want you to ask your mother if she'll give me a job,' Ellie told me.

I didn't know what I'd been expecting, but this was not it. 'A job?' I repeated dumbly.

'Yes, a job. Weekends, evenings, summer holidays – whatever. I need the money. My allowance has been stopped, and I don't think it'll be coming back for a while.'

I didn't think so either.

'I think if I *have* to get a job, then working for your mother might be fun,' Ellie said.

I frowned. I couldn't imagine *anyone* thinking that working for my mother would be fun. Also, I couldn't imagine Ellie's parents consenting to this arrangement, and I felt obliged to point this out.

Ellie rolled her eyes. 'I'm not going to tell them – obviously! I'll tell them I'm working in fucking Topshop or something.'

'Oh,' I said. Then I thought for a bit. 'I'm not sure it's fully legal for my mother to employ you,' I continued. 'Not without your parents agreeing to it.'

Ellie shrugged. 'Would your mother actually care about something like that?'

'No, maybe not,' I confessed. I had no choice. I'm not much of a liar, especially under pressure.

'So you can at least *ask*? Maybe put in a good word for me?'

'Yes, I suppose I could,' I said.

To tell you the truth, it wasn't an idea that thrilled me. But with the summer being the tourist season, and Justine slipping to another plane of existence, I thought that my mother might well be looking for additional staff. And I suspected that Ellie was *exactly* the kind of girl she would choose to employ. I also suspected that being around Ellie for more than ten minutes at a time would prove to be a real headache. But I could see that I'd at least have to ask – there was little hope of getting out of it now.

'Woods, this has been thrilling,' Ellie said, crushing out her second cigarette. 'Really – we should do it again sometime.'

This was sarcasm, or irony, or *something*. I ignored it.

'You'll talk to your mother for me?' she asked again, fixing me with a stare that made me feel it would be unwise to refuse.

'Yes, I'll ask her,' I promised.

'Wonderful.'

Ellie removed some kind of body spray from her bag, closed her eyes and sprayed herself from head to toe. Then she saluted me, turned on her heels and cut a direct path back towards the school buildings.

I did not enjoy the rest of my walk.

* * *

175

It was a couple of days later that the parcel arrived. My mother was parking the car in the garage (which often took a while due to her poor spatial awareness) so, as usual, I was the first through the front door and the first to pick up the post. But it was some moments before I noticed that the parcel was addressed to me. I was not used to receiving post, and, in fact, only one person had ever sent me parcels. That person was Dr Weir. She, as you may recollect, had sent me Martin Beech's meteor book and, later, *The Universe: A Beginner's Guide*. I thought that this package was also the right size and shape to be a book, but the writing on the front was certainly *not* Dr Weir's. Dr Weir wrote like a doctor: hers was an elegant, almost illegible scrawl – full of loops and squiggles and elaborate flourishes. The writing on the front of this parcel was angular block capitals. I put some food down for Lucy, then took the parcel up to my room and opened it.

What fell out on my desk was a new paperback edition of *Breakfast of Champions*. There was no note, but when I opened the front cover, I found this inscription:

I figured you'd want to find out how it ends. Come over and tell me what you think when you've finished.

After looking at this for some minutes, I put pen to paper and wrote the following reply, which I posted the next day:

Dear Mr Peterson,

Thank you for the book. It was very unexpected. I thought you'd probably be angry at me for ever, given what happened, and given that I did a pretty appalling job at explaining what happened. I'll try to explain now, as best I can, but there might be bits

that don't make much sense to you, since I'm
sure school was very different in your day and
people probably acted more decently and less like
chimpanzees.

[Here followed a concise account of all the events that had
led up to my losing the original copy of Mr Peterson's book.]

I'm very sorry that I didn't tell you all this sooner,
but I was very traumatized by what had happened,
and also I didn't want you to think I was making
excuses or shirking my responsibility. I do feel
responsible for what happened because it happened
on my watch and in hindsight I think my actions were
very reckless. I've decided to become a pacifist again,
not only because I'm very poor at fighting and don't
care for it one little bit, but also because I now
realize that even as a last resort fighting gets
pretty lousy results.

Anyway, despite the fact that my actions may
have made a bad situation worse, I hope you can see
that I am not entirely to blame. I may have acted
stupidly, but I acted with good intentions, and I
think you'll agree that this counts for something.

Unfortunately, I won't be able to come over and
tell you what I think about *Breakfast of Champions*
in the immediate future because I am currently under
house arrest - for the fighting incident described
above, and also for a later incident where I used the
worst word in the English language in front of the

deputy headmaster. (You probably know which word I mean, so I won't spell it out.) However, I shall certainly stop by when (or if) my mother decides that I've learned my lesson and my liberty is restored to me.

Thank you again.

Yours sincerely,

Alex Woods

I should probably tell you that having written this letter, I was baffled that I'd not thought to write sooner. Explaining things in writing, when I had time and space to think, and to say what I really meant, was so much better than trying to communicate in real time.

I wished I could *always* communicate in writing. That, I thought, would make my life a whole lot easier.

Eventually, of course, my house arrest did end, and I went unannounced to Mr Peterson's the following Saturday and met him in the driveway. He was just on his way out, taking Kurt for a 'short' walk – which, I should clarify, meant short in terms of distance, not time. What with Kurt's age and Mr Peterson's leg, all their walks were 'short', but none was brief. Still, it was now high summer, and the day was dry and bright, and as you know, I was now accustomed to at least an hour's walk each day, five days a week. I was happy to tag along, no matter how long the short walk ended up taking.

Since my letter, I'd had several more weeks to work on the full, proper apology that I still felt was owed, but having written, rewritten, memorized and rehearsed this speech, I found that

Mr Peterson wouldn't let me get past the first (elaborate) sentence. For some reason I couldn't yet grasp, he seemed to think that he was more at fault in the matter than I was, and to be honest, this was kind of awkward. I felt compelled to point out, for at least the third time, that the rare first-edition copy of *Breakfast of Champions* inscribed by Mrs Peterson had been destroyed in my care – and as a result of *my* actions.

'Do you know what Mrs Peterson would've said about that?' Mr Peterson asked me.

I thought about this for a while. 'I suppose she might have said that you should never have lent me the book in the first place – you know, that it was asking for trouble.' In actual fact, I thought this was more like something my mother would have said, but, really, I had no other point of comparison.

Mr Peterson screwed his face up slightly, in what I'd come to interpret as his version of a smile. 'No, she wouldn't have said that. That's the last thing she would've said. She would've said that a book's a great way of sharin' ideas, but beyond that, it's just pulped trees. She would've told me that I've been actin' like a goddamn moron. Do you understand what I'm saying?'

I thought about this for a long time too. 'I'm not sure,' I said eventually. 'I think you're saying that the book's not important, because it's the ideas inside that are important. Except I know the book *was* important, because it was a present, and it can't be rep—'

'I'm not sayin' that the book wasn't important. I'm sayin' there are things that are *more* important. I'm sayin' that all the things that were important about the book . . . well, they weren't really anything to do with the book itself. They're more up here –' at this point, Mr Peterson tapped his head, close to the

179

temple – 'and they haven't gone anywhere. *Now* do you understand?'

'I think so,' I said.

'Okay. So please – no more apologies.'

'Okay.'

'From what you've told me, it's not so much your fault anyway. Some of those guys at your school sound like prize assholes.'

'Yes,' I agreed. 'I can imagine quite a few of them winning prizes in that department.'

I then spent some time trying to explain to Mr Peterson about all the complicated rules and laws that govern appropriate behaviour in the playground – about how everyone was expected to think and act the same way and if you didn't, you were generally treated as some kind of leper. My mother always told me that things would get easier with time, that people would get more tolerant and all these 'problems' would suddenly seem quite trivial, but Mr Peterson said that this was only half true.

'Your mom's not exactly normal,' he told me.

'No,' I agreed.

'And she might find it very easy to be that way, but for most people it isn't. It's always easier to go along with what everyone else thinks. But having principles means doing what's right, not what's easy. It means having some integrity – and that's something that *you* control. No one else can touch it.'

Integrity. I tried the word out in my head and made a special note of it for future reference. Because as soon as Mr Peterson said it, I thought that that really *was* the apposite word. It occurred to me that this was an idea I'd been thinking about, or trying to think about, for the past several weeks.

'Mr Peterson,' I said, 'I think in a way, I was trying to say something with integrity when I used that word I used. You know which word I mean?'

'Yeah, I know which word you mean,' Mr Peterson confirmed.

'Well, I've not really been able to explain this to anyone, because everyone agrees that that word's forbidden, and can't be used in any circumstances – but really, I think that it needed saying. And when I said it, I didn't feel like I was doing anything wrong. I felt like I was doing something, you know, *principled*. That's when I felt like I had the most integrity. Does that sound stupid to you?'

'No, it doesn't. I think that integrity can show itself in all sorts of ways, and sometimes you can break the rules and still act with integrity. Sometimes you have to. Just don't expect too many people to accept that.'

'I won't,' I said. 'Although, under normal circumstances, I'm not really one for breaking the rules – or for discourtesy. I've always been very good at school. Actually, that's one of the reasons my peers don't like me much. You're not supposed to be enthusiastic about learning. It's the wrong thing to be interested in. People get very suspicious if you're too into things like reading and maths and so on. But I expect that seems a little strange to you. I'm sure it was very different when you were at school.'

Mr Peterson snorted. 'Kid, I'm American. We've been suspicious of intellectuals for hundreds of years. When I was your age, it was the early 1950s – thinking too much was seen as unpatriotic, and things haven't changed a whole lot since. Just look at some of the morons we've made president. Bush! Fuckin' Ray Gun!'

I knew who Bush was, of course. He was on television a lot because of Iraq and so forth. He was having a special relationship with Tony Blair, the Prime Minister, and looked a bit like a monkey. From what I'd gathered, most people didn't much care for him; Mr Peterson said he was barely bipedal. But as for 'Ray Gun', I had no idea what that meant. I suspected it was probably some kind of nickname, but I thought I'd better check.

'Rea-gan!' Mr Peterson enunciated. 'He was the fortieth American president. Before that he was Governor of California, and before that he was a B-movie actor – a pretty lousy B-movie actor. Honestly, if you'd seen him in those godawful movies in the fifties, you'd have sworn there wasn't a job on the planet he'd be worse at. Not until he became president. He was president for most of the eighties.'

'I wasn't alive in the eighties,' I pointed out.

'Count yourself lucky. It was pretty much Satan's decade whichever side of the Pond you found yourself on.'

'Oh.' I made a mental note to verify these facts on Wikipedia later, and also to Google 'B-movie' and 'the Pond'.

Sometimes our conversations demanded a lot of further research, but I was very glad that Mr Peterson and I were friends again.

DEATH

A year passed. It was a time of strengthening and consolidation. At school, I had no further trouble – or little worth speaking of. There was still the odd insult thrown my way by Declan Mackenzie and his brotherhood of baboons, but on the whole, their powers were much depleted, and no match for my newfound integrity, which swaddled me like a protective cloak. In lessons, I reverted to my natural behaviour. I worked unashamedly hard. I raised my hand and answered questions. I spent a lot of time researching and polishing my homework – more time, I imagine, than any other fourteen-year-old on the planet. I got into the habit of spending two hours every weekday evening in Glastonbury Library, and often several more at the weekend, and I got to know all of the librarians very well. I liked the librarians because they were extremely calm and orderly and quiet – and helpful too. I soon discovered that if you wanted a book they didn't have, they'd gladly order in a copy – free of charge. The council paid because the council thought that reading was good for the soul, and wanted to encourage it in any way they could. I thought it must be very satisfying to work for an institution with such lofty ideals, and decided that after being a neurologist or an astronomer, being a librarian would probably be my third choice of job.

While I buried myself in quiet study, Ellie, in contrast, continued to get into trouble at least three or four times every single week. First, of course, there was her ill-fated eyebrow scheme. As I'd foreseen, no amount of hairspray could conceal the truth indefinitely. In actual fact, I think it was within a few days of our first speaking that Ellie's eyebrow bar was found, seized and consigned to landfill. Ellie's mother then visited every jeweller and tattooist in a ten-mile radius, handing out A4-sized photographs of her daughter. Above the photo was Ellie's date of birth and home phone number, and below – in case anyone missed the point – there was the following caption: *Do NOT pierce this child!!* In addition to the capitals and double exclamation mark, Mrs Fitzmaurice also used red ink. Mrs Fitzmaurice didn't trust the jewellers and tattooists of Glastonbury one little bit.

Then there was a second (equally humiliating) cataclysm a few months later, when Ellie's parents finally discovered that their daughter was not working at Topshop as they'd been led to believe. I had the misfortune to witness the altercation that followed. Mr Fitzmaurice came round to our house to make it quite clear that he did *not* approve of my mother's shop and would not allow his daughter to work in such an environment. This led to my mother delivering a rather long and extremely tedious doorstep lecture on the fundamentals of witchcraft: spiritual growth, communing with nature, the harmony of the inner and outer elements, astral projection, the seven realms of knowing and being . . . 'Black magic', she pointed out, was just a small piece of the overall picture, and much misunderstood by the layman. For the most part, it was no scarier than the miracles attributed to Jesus: walking on water and coming back from the dead and so on. At this point, Mr Fitzmaurice threatened to call his lawyer, and eventually, my mother conceded that she couldn't continue to employ Ellie in the face of such obstinate opposition.

Sadly, this was only a temporary setback. Ellie returned to my mother's employment as soon as she turned sixteen, shortly after her GCSE results (which were never to be spoken of in polite conversation); and soon after that (having decided that life with her parents was unbearable), she moved into the flat above the shop. By that time, of course, Sam had moved out and Justine had gone to India to 'find herself'.

As I'd predicted, being around Ellie – in those early days – was rarely stress-free. Not only did you have to contend with the thick cloud of world-weariness that characteristically enveloped her, but beyond this there was also the gentle or not-so-gentle teasing, the perpetual eye-rolling, the overbearing sarcasm and mascara. And then, every so often, and completely out of the blue, she'd get all sweet and sisterly – with soft little smiles and playful pokes and punches. That was even worse. At least with the sarcastic, scowling Ellie I had a clear picture of where I stood. Smiley Ellie confused me. Several times it was only patient meditation in the stockroom that saved me from a seizure.

It was around this time that I started to get a much better handle on my condition. I was still having biannual appointments with Dr Enderby, and after I turned fourteen, my mother reluctantly agreed that I should be allowed to attend these appointments alone. It was, after all, somewhat awkward having to take time off work on a Saturday to drive me to Bristol, and Dr Enderby had said that there was no reason I shouldn't be allowed to come to the hospital on my own. He thought it was a very positive decision because it meant that I was 'taking charge' of the situation. I caught the 376 bus, which ran hourly from Glastonbury High Street and took me all the way to Bristol Central, which was only five minutes' walk from the hospital.

When I first started attending my appointments alone, I was averaging one or two generalized seizures a month, and Dr Enderby doubted that increasing my medication would lower this base rate to any significant degree. Since we'd already established that my seizures tended to have clear and predict-able triggers – stress, anxiety and sleep deprivation – we agreed that it would make more sense if I continued to work on my strategies for 'coping with adversity', cognitive behavioural therapy and so forth. In particular, Dr Enderby was concerned that I was applying my meditation exercises too irregularly and too late – that I was relying on these techniques as 'crisis control' when ideally they should be seen as long-term preventative exercises. He gave me an analogy to explain what was going wrong.

'It's like you're trying to bail water out of a leaky boat in the middle of a storm,' Dr Enderby informed me. 'There's water coming in from every direction – from the leaks and the waves and the rain – and at the same time, you're having to contend with half a dozen other distractions: the thunder, the wind, the floor rocking beneath you. In these circumstances, staying afloat is almost impossible. What you need to do is ensure that your boat's always in a good state of repair: then when the storm hits, you'll be ready for it. Do you understand what I mean?'

'Yes, I think so,' I told him. 'My brain's the unseaworthy boat, and the storm's stress or adversity. And I guess my meditation exercises are the hammer and nails and planks and tar, et cetera, that I'm going to use to fix all the leaks before I go sailing.'

Dr Enderby smiled. 'Yes, that's right – although I wouldn't describe your brain as unseaworthy. Not exactly. But you get the general idea: you need to practise your exercises regularly – every day if you can – to give yourself the best possible chance of staying afloat.'

So that's when my meditation regime really began in earnest – and it's a regime that's continued ever since; in the past four years, there have only been one or two occasions when I haven't started the day with a half-hour meditation. It was apparent from the outset that early mornings worked best, as this was the time when my head was clear and free from distractions. Generally, I'd rise between half six and seven and begin my practice as soon as I was fully awake. On Dr Enderby's advice, I built a small 'shrine' in the corner of my room. This contained a soft mat and cushions, a table lamp with three brightness settings, and a small space reserved for books and CDs. I never listened to music during my meditation as this was much too distracting, but afterwards, I often liked to spend fifteen minutes listening to one of the classical albums that I'd borrowed from the library or Mr Peterson. In terms of relaxation, I found that Chopin's nocturnes took some beating.

In the privacy of my own head, for reasons that will now be obvious, I labelled my new regime 'working on my boat', and this metaphor proved so compelling that I'd soon found a way to incorporate it into my meditations in the form of a visualization exercise. I'd start by picturing my boat in its idealized form – a small but sturdy vessel with a shallow draught and its name (*Serenity*) painted on the side in turquoise lettering – and I'd imagine it floating high on a flat sea under an overcast sky. Slowly, I'd introduce some small waves into the scene, then wind and rain and lightning, increasing the power of each until a full, howling thunderstorm was in progress. My boat would rise and fall amidst this tempest, being rocked and whipped and battered by the waves, but nevertheless enduring – its integrity unbreachable. Then, eventually, the sea would become silent. The wind would drop, the waves would settle, the clouds would disperse, and at last everything would be blue and tranquil. I'd see my boat at the centre of a sparkling, sunlit ocean, a perfectly flat horizon stretching out in every direction.

This was the image I'd return to whenever my serenity was threatened (by my mother, by Ellie), and soon I found that I was coping much better with day-to-day stresses. I was sleeping better. I was having fewer seizures. My mind felt generally clearer. But I had yet to face any serious test.

Until the day I'm now going to describe to you, I had no way of knowing how much stronger my boat had become.

It happened not far from the post office. I forget the precise date, but it must have been early summer 2008. It was a Saturday, shortly after lunch – maybe two or three o'clock.

We'd just rejoined the main road from a bridle path, which was why Kurt wasn't on his lead. Another minute, another thirty seconds, and I'm sure he would have been safely restrained once more. As with all accidents, it was the chance confluence of any number of circumstances, and if any of these had been just a little bit different, it would never have happened.

I dimly recall Mrs Griffith's Golf approaching as Mr Peterson and I passed the tall privet hedge that bordered Mr Lloyd's front garden. She couldn't have been driving very quickly – certainly no more than thirty miles per hour – but at the time I was slow to recognize her. Mr Peterson saw her first, and was first to raise his hand as her car drew closer. Mrs Griffith, I should tell you, was one of the few people in the village to whom Mr Peterson spoke on a semi-regular basis (on account of all the stamps he had to buy each month). Nevertheless, I think that both of our waves were mostly mechanical that day. I suppose we were talking at the time, and so were partially distracted from our surroundings. Not that this would have made much difference. There was no time to react – it was all over in the same instant it registered.

The noise, we later found out, was the firing to life of a chainsaw. Mr Lloyd had chosen that afternoon to straighten out his hedge. But at the time, since he was concealed from view, there was no way of knowing this, and no chance to prepare. There was simply an explosion of sound a little to our right, and in the same moment Kurt bolted instinctively in the opposite direction – onto the road and straight into the path of Mrs Griffith's oncoming car. She had no time to react, and by the time she'd hit the brakes, the impact had already happened. There was a dull thud, a metallic screech, the smell of burnt rubber. Mrs Griffith's car came to a halt about twenty metres or so down the road, and a second later, everything was still and silent. The chainsaw, evidently, had been shut off at the sound of the accident.

Kurt was lying motionless a metre from the far kerb, and blood was already beginning to pool at his hind legs. It was only when we got to him that it was apparent he was still breathing.

When Mrs Griffith joined us in the street she was shaking and her face was white as chalk. She had her fingertips held to her lips and just kept stammering the same two sentences again and again: 'I didn't s-s-see him! He just ran out in front of me!'

Mr Lloyd, by this time, was standing at the end of his driveway with his mouth agape, still in a thick pair of gardening gloves and looking as helpless and incongruous as a freshly landed fish; and for some long moments, I was about as much use as he was. I didn't know what to do or say. My mind had turned to solid ice. Mr Peterson, meanwhile, was trying to tend to Kurt and comfort Mrs Griffith at the same time.

'It's not your fault,' he told her, 'but we need to get him to a vet – right now. Can you drive us?'

Mrs Griffith didn't appear to understand the question. Mr Peterson had to repeat himself twice before she started nodding, and then once more to get her moving. He turned to me as she was reversing the car parallel to us. 'I'm gonna need some help liftin' him, kid. Can you help me?'

I tried to speak but no words came. The bleeding from Kurt's injured leg seemed to be getting worse, and the haunch was twitching every few seconds. I hadn't ever seen that much blood before. But Mr Peterson, I suppose, had seen injuries far worse. He stayed completely calm and focussed.

'It's okay, kid,' he said. 'You'll be okay. We just have to get him to the car. We'll do it together.'

He took off his jacket and wrapped it round Kurt's

hindquarters. Then he gestured to me. 'All I need you to do is support his head and front legs. We'll lift on three.'

'I don't think I can,' I blurted.

'Yes, you can. You'll be okay. It'll all be over in a half-minute. I just need you to be with me for that time. Okay?'

I closed my eyes and took several ragged breaths.

'Alex? Open your eyes. Stay with me.'

I opened my eyes.

'You're gonna be okay. Just hold it together for a couple more minutes. On three . . .'

Kurt whimpered loudly as we lifted him, and for a second, my blood ran cold. But then he was silent, and the worst was over. He was awkward to manoeuvre, but he didn't weigh much, and within a minute, we had him laid across the back seat of Mrs Griffith's Golf. Mr Peterson got in the back with him, and I got into the front passenger seat, and fifteen minutes later, we had arrived at the vet's surgery.

After Kurt had been sedated and one of his back legs had been bandaged, the vet called us back into the treatment room. Kurt was still stretched out on the stainless-steel table in the centre of the room. He looked very peaceful, like he was in a deep, dreamless sleep.

'The bleeding's not as serious as it first appeared,' the vet told us solemnly, 'but the leg's broken in two places. I'm afraid when the sedative wears off he's going to be in quite a lot of pain.'

'But he's going to be okay?' I asked. 'I mean, he's going to live?'

The vet looked at Mr Peterson and something seemed to

pass between them. 'All his injuries are treatable,' she said. 'But you have to understand that Kurt's a very old dog. The chances of him making a *full* recovery are slim. Even in the best scenario, it's doubtful that he'll ever be able to walk on that leg again – not without considerable pain.'

Mr Peterson nodded but didn't say anything.

'But he's going to live?' I persisted.

The vet looked at me, then glanced back at Mr Peterson. 'Would you like me to give you a few minutes?'

'Yes, if you would,' said Mr Peterson.

'A few minutes for what?' I asked, and at that point, I genuinely didn't know the answer. I'd never been exposed to circumstances like these before. Outside of the rather unusual environment of my mother's shop, I had no experience of how people spoke – or didn't speak – about death.

Mrs Griffith had taken a tissue from her bag and was dabbing her eyes again. Mr Peterson looked very grim and determined. 'Kid, I'm sorry. The vet's going to put Kurt to sleep. There's nothing else we can do.'

My stomach reeled. 'The vet said it's just his leg! She said it's treatable!'

Mrs Griffith put a hand on my shoulder. 'Alex,' she said softly, 'I don't think you understand what the vet meant. She said that the injuries are treatable – not that they *should* be treated.'

'But if they're treatable, then of course they should be treated. She didn't *have* to say it. It's obvious!'

'It wouldn't be kind,' Mr Peterson said. 'You have to understand that.'

'The vet can save him!'

'It wouldn't be saving him – not really. I know it's difficult, but you have to try to understand. Once he wakes up, he'll be in a lot of pain – and it's not the sort of pain that's gonna go away. He'll have to live with it all the time, for however long he's got left. That's what we have to save him from.'

'We can't just let him die!'

Mrs Griffith squeezed my shoulder.

Mr Peterson looked at me for a while, then said: 'I'm sorry, kid. But we *are* going to let him die.'

At this point, I started to cry. Mr Peterson's expression never wavered.

'He's not going to suffer,' he told me. 'He'll just drift off peacefully. It's the only kind thing we can do for him now. You know that, don't you?'

We were all silent for a while.

'What will happen afterwards?' I asked finally. 'After he's put to sleep?'

'I'm not sure what you mean,' Mr Peterson said.

'Can we bury him?'

'Do you think that's something that might help you?'

'Yes.'

'Okay. Then we can bury him.'

The spot we chose was pretty much the only spot available – a large flowerbed close to the west hedge at the back of the garden, just past the shed and the greenhouse. The previous inhabitants had been a couple of rosebushes who'd succumbed to disease a year or so earlier. Mr Peterson had been meaning to replace them ever since, but it was only after the burial that he finally got round to it.

It took a long time to dig the hole. It ended up being about five feet long, two feet wide and three feet deep. That's thirty cubic feet of dirt I had to excavate – more or less alone. Mr Peterson helped for a bit, but I could soon see he was struggling, and, really, I knew that this project was my responsibility, not his. I'd insisted on it, after all. So after a few minutes, I told him that I didn't mind doing all the digging on my own. There wasn't really enough space for two people to manoeuvre in, anyway. He smoked one of his marijuana cigarettes and watched me for a while. Then he went back inside. I think he understood that digging this grave was something I had to do by myself.

As I've already indicated, this was the first time I'd ever encountered death as something more than an abstract concept on a tarot card, and this, perhaps, explains the strength of my reaction. In hindsight, I suspect I must have looked increasingly absurd as I dug out that hole in Mr Peterson's former rose garden. By the time I'd finished, I was waist-deep in the ground, bone-tired and covered in dirt. All I can say is that at the time it didn't feel absurd in the slightest. It felt necessary. I knew that my endeavour wasn't going to change anything, and it certainly wasn't going to make any difference to Kurt, but then, I suppose that's always the way with funerals. Funerals aren't for the dead. They're for the living.

I didn't really take any breaks. I just kept soldiering on with my spade. A foot down, things became much tougher. The soil was more compacted, there were more stones and old roots to contend with, and, of course, the further down I got, the further I had to shift the soil. By the time I'd finished, the muscles in my arms and legs and back were very tender, and I had blisters on both my hands. But this physical discomfort made me feel better somehow.

My hole was very impressive to look at, and very neat, with all its planes flattened out at right angles, or as close to right angles as I could make them. I thought that Mr Peterson would be pleased that I'd been able to dig such a regular grave. I felt like I'd achieved something important.

Back inside, I phoned my mother to let her know what had happened and that I'd be home late, and then I phoned Mrs Griffith and asked her if she'd like to come over for the burial. This seemed like an appropriate thing to do. After all, she'd been through a lot that day as well. I thought being there for the burial might help her, and she agreed. She said she'd come over presently.

At that point, it occurred to me that since I'd now taken charge of organizing a sort of funeral, it might also be my responsibility to say a few words before we put Kurt in the ground. Of course, I hadn't ever attended a funeral before, and I hadn't exactly had a conventional religious upbringing, but I'd seen enough television to know the approximate format that a funeral was supposed to follow. There are words you're supposed to say: 'Ashes to ashes, dust to dust' and so on. But I thought it wouldn't really be appropriate for me to say anything like that. It would sound much too grand, and I wasn't even a hundred per cent certain that you were allowed to perform that kind of formal funeral unless you were a clergyman, which I wasn't. In the end, I decided that it would be better if I stuck to a short reading. Something from Kurt's namesake seemed the most appropriate, so I dug out Mr Peterson's copy of *Sirens*, where I seemed to remember there being several pertinent passages about dogs and death.

The extract I'd had in mind I found on page 206, but it was much bleaker than I remembered:

An explosion on the sun had separated man and dog. A universe schemed in mercy would have kept man and dog together.

The universe inhabited by Winston Niles Rumfoord and his dog was not schemed in mercy. Kazak had been sent ahead of his master on the great mission to nowhere and nothing.

Kazak had left howling in a puff of ozone and sick light, in a hum like swarming bees.

Rumfoord let the empty choke chain slip from his fingers. The chain expressed deadness, made formless sound and a formless heap, was a soulless slave of gravity, born with a broken spine.

Apt and poetic though this was, it was simply *too* bleak to read at a funeral. Instead, I settled on Rumfoord's farewell speech on page 207, which starts: 'I am not dying. I am merely taking my leave of the solar system,' and ends: 'I shall always be here. I shall always be wherever I've been.'

It was about eight o'clock by the time we buried him, but there was still plenty of sunlight in the back garden, so doing my reading was no problem. Afterwards, Mr Peterson helped me to fill in the hole. There were only two spades, so Mrs Griffith couldn't help, but I think she was happy just to watch, and getting earth back into a hole's much easier than getting it out. Within a few minutes, the flowerbed was pretty much back to its former state.

A little later, while Mr Peterson was smoking another of his cigarettes, Mrs Griffith told me that she'd liked my reading very much.

'It was Kurt Vonnegut,' I said. 'That's who Kurt was named after.'

'I see,' said Mrs Griffith. 'Well, it really was a lovely reading.'

Later still, after Mrs Griffith had left, when the sun had dipped behind the hedge and the sky had turned pastel violet, Mr Peterson came back out from the house and said that he thought I'd better be getting home soon, before my mother started to worry.

'Okay,' I said. 'Can I have a few more moments, first?'

'Okay. You want me to wait?'

'Yes, please. I won't be very long.'

I'd been wrapped up in my thoughts, and had quite lost track of the time, but I should tell you that I wasn't feeling sad any more – not really. Neither was I feeling agitated. There was none of the tumult I'd come to expect in the quiet aftermath of a stressful event. It was very peaceful out there in the garden, with the sky darkening and no sound but the wind in the trees. If I closed my eyes, it felt like I'd drifted into the final scene from my meditation, with nothing around me but soft sunlight and the deep blue sea.

'Mr Peterson?' I asked after a while. 'What do you think happens when we die?'

He looked at me for a few seconds, as if trying to gauge something in me. Then he said: 'I don't think anything happens when we die.'

I thought about this for a few moments. 'Neither do I,' I said.

It was the first time I'd told anyone that. It was probably the first time I'd acknowledged it to myself. It felt like a big admission to make, but, still, I was glad I'd said it. It was an important thing to say.

After that, we turned away from the flowerbed and walked back to the house.

HALF A MONTH OF SUNDAYS

In the weeks that followed, I grew increasingly concerned about Mr Peterson's mental well-being. As I hope I've made clear, I think that I handled Kurt's death as well as could be expected – all things considered. After the initial shock, I grieved, I dug my hole, and I came out a little stronger on the other side. But as for Mr Peterson, well, with him there was just a kind of blank wall, a silent muddling through. I wasn't sure his response was healthy.

One thing I noticed was that he seemed to be smoking a lot more marijuana, and although I now knew that he grew it in his loft under two rows of high-pressure sodium lamps, which had allayed my initial concerns that his drug use might be funding terrorism, I still had my worries about the physiological effects of his habit. It elevated his mood, I suppose, but only temporarily. Afterwards it made him sluggish and introspective. It slowed him down. Several times, I told him that I thought he might be smoking too much. This was his reply:

'Jesus, kid – you're not like any other fifteen-year-old on the planet!'

I wouldn't be fifteen for a few more months, but I let this detail slide. Mr Peterson never seemed sure how old I was from one minute to the next, and by his standards, this was an excellent estimate.

'I'm worried about what it might be doing to your brain,' I told him, very reasonably. 'I don't know if you're aware of this, but brain cells aren't like skin cells or liver cells. They don't regenerate. People with perfectly healthy brains are always finding ways to mess them up; and, to tell you the truth, it annoys the hell out of me.'

'Kid, I've been smokin' this stuff for forty years,' Mr Peterson pointed out. 'I'm not gonna quit now just because you've got it in your head that it's some kind of terrible vice.'

'I didn't say it was a vice,' I countered. 'I said I don't think it's good for you.'

'Jesus! Nothing fun's good for you! Not in the sense you mean, anyway. For someone who knows so much about brains, you sure know squat about minds.'

'I *do* know about minds,' I insisted. 'And I know that a healthy mind requires a healthy brain.'

'Well, your view of a healthy brain's pretty damn narrow,' Mr Peterson objected. 'We all need our crutches.'

I wasn't going to try to convert Mr Peterson to the wonders of meditation. I'd tried before, and failed. He didn't seem to get the boat analogy at all. But it was obvious to me that he needed something other than marijuana to fill the hole that Kurt's passing had left.

The few times I raised the idea, he was adamant that he wasn't going to get another dog – not in the foreseeable future, anyway – and I suppose it was this, as much as anything, that made me worry. I thought perhaps Kurt's death had hit him quite a lot harder than he was letting on. After all, Kurt had been more or less the *only* company he'd had for the best part of three years. It looks very bleak set out in print like that, but this fact was true and unavoidable. Without Kurt, I couldn't imagine him leaving the house nearly so often. He'd just revert to being a hermit.

Although it might not be obvious to an outside observer, dog-walking in the countryside is quite a sociable activity. In a one- to two-hour walk, you'll probably meet a couple of dozen people, and the presence of an animal or two tends to grease the wheels of friendly conversation like little else. At the very least, people will smile and say, 'Hello,' or, 'What a friendly dog!' And those people whom you see more than once will usually stop for a chat and say things like 'How are you?' or 'I can't remember the last time we had an August this wet!' and so on. I thought that Mr Peterson was bound to miss all these little interactions, even if he didn't realize it.

He'd still have all the correspondence he carried out for Amnesty International, I supposed – and sometimes people even wrote back – but that wasn't the same as interacting with people face to face. It wasn't the same as having a community.

There were several occasions when I found myself thinking it was a shame we were both atheists. Otherwise we could have gone to church, which I imagined must be quite a sociable activity too, and would have provided a regular outing for Sundays, when the shop and the post office – the only other attractions in Lower Godley – were closed. Of course, I didn't really know for sure what went on in church, but I had the vague idea they spent a lot of time talking about morality and the state of the universe, which appealed to me quite a lot. The only thing that didn't appeal to me was the supernaturalism – that and the fact that they only read the Bible, which, from the little I'd seen, wasn't exactly a page-turner.

I thought that if you could address these issues, you'd have the kind of community it would be nice to be a part of. And it was from this thought that the Secular Church was born.

By the time I first mentioned it to Mr Peterson, the idea had been bubbling away for a while. It seemed like the solution to a lot of problems.

Ever since I'd finished reading *A Man Without a Country*, some months earlier, I'd been thinking that I'd like to re-read all the Kurt Vonnegut books. I imagined I'd probably get more out of them a second time round, now that I was approximately ten per cent older than when I'd first picked one up. Furthermore, I realized this did not have to be a solitary pursuit.

Further enquiries in Glastonbury Library were encouraging. Fiona Fitton, the head librarian, told me that she thought setting up a reading group was a very good idea. They had a special noticeboard in the entranceway where things like that were advertised.

'Would *you* be interested in joining?' I asked.

'Yes, Alex,' she said, 'I'm sure I would.'

'I don't mean hypothetically,' I clarified. 'I mean, when I've worked out all the details, shall I sign you up?'

This sentence seemed to amuse her – it made quite a lot of smile lines appear at the corners of her eyes. 'Smile lines' was a term Fiona Fitton had coined to refer to her many transient wrinkles. She often used it to express how much something she'd read or heard had pleased her. 'It made all my smile lines come out!' she'd say. She was a few years older than my mother – maybe forty or so – and her hair was strawberry blonde, getting more and more strawberry towards the roots. I'd been telling her for some time that she should *definitely* read some Kurt Vonnegut. I thought that plenty of his sentences would bring out her smile lines.

'Alex, you can sign me up!' she said. 'Non-hypothetically. Just pick a day when I'm not working.'

'I thought Sundays would probably be convenient for most people,' I said.

'Yes, Sundays would be perfect,' she agreed.

With this first foundation stone laid, I started thinking about the other readers I knew who might be interested in joining my Kurt Vonnegut book club.

There was Mrs Griffith, for a start. Ever since the funeral, when she'd said that she'd enjoyed my reading, I'd been meaning to drop a copy of *Sirens* off at the post office. (It wasn't exactly *The Lord of the Rings*, but from personal experience, I knew it was perfectly possible to enjoy both.) Then there was Dr Enderby. He already knew a bit about Kurt Vonnegut because we'd talked about him at some of my appointments. Dr Enderby had read *Slaughterhouse-Five* at university, three decades ago, and he said that he remembered it being very funny and very sad. But he hadn't read any more Kurt Vonnegut since then. Dr Enderby said that these days it was difficult to find the time for reading – or for reading anything other than medical journals (which were essential) or Emily Dickinson poems (which were very short).

Personally, I thought that Dr Enderby needed to *make* time

for reading, which is what I told him at our next appointment. I also told him that he should view it the same way he viewed his meditation. Regular reading made you a calmer, wiser person. It was good for one's boat.

Needless to say, this proved a compelling pitch.

'A book club?' Mr Peterson asked.

'Yes, that's right. But only with Kurt Vonnegut books. We'll read all of them, start to finish. Nothing else.'

I couldn't look over to see his expression, but I got the feeling that Mr Peterson was frowning. The reason I couldn't look over was that I was driving at the time and I had to keep both eyes on the road. The only reason you should *ever* take your eyes off the road when you're driving is to check your mirrors, which you should do briskly and often, especially when turning or pulling out at a junction. Of course, since I was not quite fifteen at the time, my driving was restricted to Mr Peterson's lane (which was usually empty) and his private drive (which was always empty), but it was still best to be vigilant at all times. Technically, I shouldn't have been driving at all. Not only was I two and a bit years too young, I was also too epileptic to hold a licence. You're only allowed to drive if you've been seizure-free for a full year. My seizures were increasingly infrequent, but they hadn't ceased entirely.

'But you *know* when you're gonna have a fit,' Mr Peterson had pointed out (at the onset of our lessons). 'You've got that weird sixth sense, right?'

'Yes,' I acknowledged. 'I always know. I get a very strong aura prior to any major seizure.'

'Great. So if you're gonna have a fit, just tell me and stop the car. Hell, you're not gonna be travellin' at more than twenty, twenty-five miles per hour anyway. I don't think we'll be in any imminent danger.'

Mr Peterson thought it would be better for me to learn to drive sooner rather than later, not only because it would be useful, but also because he thought it would be good for my confidence; and, in hindsight, I suppose he was right. I was surprised to discover that driving came quite naturally to me. I was a cautious driver, but never a nervous one, and I never felt in danger of a seizure while at the wheel. In fact, I found the quiet concentration that driving required kept me extremely calm and composed.

After a few half-hour lessons, I knew how to stop and start the car, how to check my blind spot, and mirror-signal-manoeuvre. Soon after that I mastered the clutch: I could pull away without stalling, and change between first, second and third. (There was never any call for fourth.) And after only a few more lessons, I felt that my reverse- and parallel-parking were really rather elegant. Mr Peterson didn't have a garage, but we used two lines of plant pots to construct a standard-sized parking bay. None of these plant pots ever got damaged.

Anyway, since I was having another driving lesson at the time of our conversation, I couldn't look over to verify that Mr Peterson was frowning, but there was certainly a lot of scepticism evident in his voice.

'A book club that *only* reads Kurt Vonnegut?' he asked.

'Yes, that's right.'

'I'm not sure you're gonna get an overwhelming response to that idea,' Mr Peterson predicted.

I was prepared for this, of course. 'Actually,' I said, 'I've already found a few people who've said they might be interested: Mrs Griffith, Dr Enderby – my neurologist – and Fiona Fitton, who works at Glastonbury Library. She even said we might be able to order in multiple copies of the books we need, just in case there are people who'd like to join but can't afford it. The council will pay because the council thinks reading's good for the soul.'

'I see.'

'So, anyway, I'm happy to organize it all. But we'll need somewhere to host it, obviously.'

'Right. And where did you have in mind?'

'Well, your house seems the obvious choice. I guess we can probably squeeze a fair few people in the front room before things get too tight. And then there's all this space for parking.' I gestured with my left hand. We were just pulling up to the house at that point.

'Keep both hands on the wheel, kid,' Mr Peterson warned.

I returned my hands to ten to two and brought the car to a gentle halt in front of the bay window. 'I've already thought of a snappy name,' I said. 'I think a reading group should have a snappy name to attract members, don't you?'

Mr Peterson didn't ask about my snappy name, but I could tell his curiosity was piqued.

'"The Secular Church of Kurt Vonnegut,"' I said.

'Jesus F Christ,' said Mr Peterson.

'It'd be like a regular church but with no singing or praying, and better stories. We can meet every Sunday.'

'*Every* Sunday?'

'Right. A book a week.'

'Kid, most people don't read that quick.'

'It's only twenty to forty pages per day. They're not long books.'

'Trust me. A book a month is more realistic. Most people have busy lives.'

'Oh.' I frowned. 'Well, I suppose one Sunday a month would be okay. That means it'll take a bit more than a year if we just stick to the fourteen novels, or about eighteen months if we include the short stories and essays and journalism as well.'

Mr Peterson was definitely scowling at this point. 'Kid, you've lost the plot. What exactly are we gonna do in this *church*?'

'I figured we'd discuss morality and so on.'

'Morality?'

'Well, yeah. After all, it *is* quite a large theme of the books. But there are lots of other things too. You know: satire, time travel, war, genocide, jokes, extraterrestrials. What do you think?'

'I think I'm gonna end up with a bunch of nuts in my house.'

'Does that mean you're willing to host it?' I asked.

Mr Peterson chewed his lip for a bit. 'Okay, kid,' he said eventually. 'Find enough people and I'll let you hold it here.'

'How many people's "enough" people?' I asked.

'A half-dozen, excluding us. Of course, there's no chance in hell you *will* find that many people. Not in a month of Sundays. That's the only reason I'm agreeing.'

'Understood,' I said.

That evening, buoyed by our conversation, I designed and printed my poster for Glastonbury Library, which looked like this:

EVER WONDERED WHY WE'RE HERE?

WHERE WE'RE GOING?

WHAT THE POINT IS?

CONCERNED ABOUT THE STATE OF THE UNIVERSE IN GENERAL??

THE SECULAR CHURCH OF KURT VONNEGUT

A book club for people interested in
all or some of the following:

morality, ecology, time travel, extraterrestrial life,
twentieth-century history, humanism, humour, et cetera

Phone Alex Woods: ***** *** ***

The stars, as you've probably worked out, were the digits of my home phone number, which I'm not going to reveal in case of nuisance calls.

A week later, I got my first response – or pair of responses – from John and Barbara Blessed. Their surname was pronounced Bless-ed, in two syllables, as in 'Blessed are the meek . . .' Considering the name of my reading group, this was a curiously apt surname, as Barbara Blessed, whom I spoke to on the phone, was quick to point out.

John and Barbara Blessed were both teachers, but not at Asquith. John Blessed turned out to be a compact, soft-spoken man who taught physics at a sixth-form college in Wells. Barbara

Blessed was two inches taller than her husband, taught maths, suffered from chronic insomnia and knew π to one hundred decimal places. As you probably know, π is the number equal to a circle's circumference divided by its diameter, which is approximately 3.14159. It's a number that you can't write in full because it goes on literally for ever. Most people count sheep when they can't sleep, but Barbara Blessed recited π.

John and Barbara Blessed were both interested in time travel. John Blessed collected research papers on the subject and would later explain to me that on a sub-atomic scale, time travel was in fact a rather common phenomenon. But when it came to macroscopic objects, such as human beings and spaceships, most physicists agreed that the laws of nature probably conspired to make time travel a practical, if not physical, impossibility. Personally, John Blessed was of the opinion that 'whatever time is, it's not what we think it is.' It was an opinion he shared with not only Kurt Vonnegut but also Stephen Hawking. John Blessed said that when physicists worked out a Theory of Everything (ToE), concepts such as space and time might no longer be tenable on a fundamental level, though they'd still be useful for day-to-day purposes such as arranging appointments and going to the supermarket.

Of course, most of this did not come up during that first phone conversation, in which I spoke to John Blessed only indirectly, via his wife. This is what she said: 'Forgive me, Mr Woods, but my husband's been on about this ever since we first saw your advert, and I really think I need to put him out of his misery. He wants to know if you're *the* Alex Woods.'

This foxed me for only a few seconds.

'I think there's a good chance I might be *the* Alex Woods,' I admitted, cautiously. 'But obviously it depends on which Alex Woods your husband has in mind.'

Barbara Blessed cleared her throat. 'It's preposterous, really, but my husband has it in his head that Alex Woods was the name of the young boy who was hit by a fragment of the Wells meteor. You probably remember the story: it was in the papers for weeks. Anyway, I told him that even if he *has* remembered the name correctly—'

'Yes, that was me,' I confirmed.

The phone was quiet for a bit. I could hear the Blesseds conferring in the background. Then Mrs Blessed came back on the line. 'I hope you don't think it's rude of me to ask, but how old are you, Alex?'

'I'm almost fifteen,' I said, 'but my reading age is higher.'

This was not a joke, but it made Barbara Blessed laugh like a drain nonetheless.

After that, I took down Barbara Blessed's email address and told her that I'd contact her once I'd finalized the date for our inaugural meeting. I also promised to bring along my iron–nickel meteor fragment.

In Glastonbury Library, a few days later, I recruited my second librarian. This was Sophie Haynes. She was fifty-five years old and the serenest of all the Glastonbury librarians. Her hair was the colour of graphite, and she always wore floaty ankle-length skirts or dresses rather than trousers, which rendered her walk more of a glide. She liked cryptic crosswords and William Blake, which I had discovered one afternoon while she was on a tea break and I was sitting in one of the soft chairs in the reading area, researching Emily Dickinson. William Blake was also a deceased poet, and artist, who had written a very famous poem about tigers:

> Tyger! Tyger! burning bright
> In the forests of the night,
> What immortal hand or eye
> Could frame thy fearful symmetry?

The fact that he couldn't spell notwithstanding, I liked William Blake's poem very much. When Sophie Haynes showed it to me, I told her that although I didn't get all of the imagery straight away, reading it still made my heart beat a little bit faster, and she said that this probably meant I'd understood it well enough. The tiger had claws and jaws that could rip through human flesh as easily as I might skin a banana, and, for William Blake, it was difficult to reconcile the existence of such a creation with a benevolent creator. Sophie Haynes directed my attention to the penultimate stanza:

> When the stars threw down their spears,
> And watered heaven with their tears,
> Did he smile his work to see?
> Did he who made the Lamb make thee?

This I got. In return, I directed Sophie Haynes to page 159 of *Breakfast of Champions*, where Kurt Vonnegut had expressed similar concerns vis-à-vis the rattlesnake: 'The Creator of the Universe had put a rattle on its tail. The Creator had also given it front teeth which were hypodermic syringes filled with deadly poison . . . Sometimes I wonder about the Creator of the Universe.'

Because of this earlier exchange, I knew it was the 'secular' part of my reading group that would appeal in particular to Sophie Haynes. Sophie Haynes, in fact, was a secular humanist, which meant that she thought God and the devil and heaven and hell were all figments, but this didn't matter because it was possible (and preferable) to have a system of ethics based on shared human values and rational enquiry instead of supernatural scripture. Kurt Vonnegut was also a secular humanist, and so am I, although I didn't fully realize this until I buried Mr Peterson's dog. Before that, I didn't know what I was. In contrast, Sophie Haynes was a convert. She'd been raised a Christian but lost her faith after her appendix burst on her twenty-first birthday. The human appendix was another thing that no sane, kind and competent designer would have designed.

With the ball now gaining momentum, it occurred to me that there were many finer details I was going to have to address. For example, I knew that we were going to read all the Kurt Vonnegut novels, fourteen books in fourteen months, but I didn't know what order we were going to read them in. It was a simple problem that gave me some difficulty.

Originally, I'd assumed we'd just go through them in chronological order, starting with *Player Piano* and ending with *Timequake*. But the more I thought about it, the more I realized this might not be the most interesting way to set about matters. *Timequake* was a good book to finish on, but *Player Piano* was not the best place to start. It was far too conventional, with too much plot and description and not enough humour and digression. As Kurt Vonnegut books go, it was very atypical.

In the end, I decided that the best thing would be to meander through our bibliography more or less at random, jumping back and forth in time as necessary. This seemed like the approach Kurt Vonnegut would most approve of. But then, having thought about it some more, I realized that there was no reason a non-chronological order had to be a *random* order. It should still have some kind of logical flow. So I sat down with fourteen small strips of card on which I wrote the names of the fourteen Kurt Vonnegut novels and then spent half an hour juggling them into the perfect non-chronological sequence, taking into account things such as theme, form and character.

Mr Peterson said that it seemed like I was planning a doctoral thesis, not a book club. But, beyond that, he refused to offer any constructive advice. He said that this was *my* project, and I'd have to figure out how best to make it fly.

This was a worrying thought.

It probably sounds stupid, but before then, even with all the planning and recruiting I'd already done, it hadn't really occurred to me that this was *my* project, or that I had to 'make it fly'. Before, I'd just kind of assumed that it could fly on its own – that once I'd set things in motion, they'd have their own life and trajectory. But now I could see that this might not be the case. It was possible that once I'd assembled my book club, it would still require planning and structure to keep it airborne. I'd need a strategy to make things work.

My breakthrough came one morning after I'd emptied my head with an especially long and peaceful meditation. It was a simple idea that popped into existence almost of its own accord and which I included as an instruction in my first group email: while reading that month's book, everyone should make a note of any sentences or paragraphs that they found especially pleasing, pick a favourite and bring it along to our first meeting.

This, I thought, was an extremely practical plan, what with Kurt Vonnegut being so quotable. It was also extremely democratic, and would provide nine separate springboards with which to launch ideas.

Nine was the number of people my book club eventually ended up with.

My final recruit was Gregory Adelmann, who also saw my poster in the library. He'd been reading another notice at first – an advert for a pudding club, which is a club where a bunch of people get together periodically to try new puddings – but said that my poster had stolen his attention because of its large number of question marks and unconventional lengthening of etc.

Gregory Adelmann was thirty-two years old and a freelance food writer. This meant that most of his work involved eating in restaurants and then saying what he thought of his meal. He ate in restaurants all over the west of England – sometimes as far away as Exeter. Unfortunately, though, Greg Adelmann suffered from a major handicap for a food critic: he found it very difficult to write bad reviews. This was because his mother had always taught him that if you don't have anything nice to say, it's better to say nothing at all. She'd also taught him that it wasn't good to be a fussy eater – not when so many people in the world were malnourished. So, in some respects, Gregory Adelmann had made an odd choice of career.

You could always tell when Gregory Adelmann had really disliked a meal because he'd spend most of his word count talking about the restaurant's décor or its location or parking facilities. He'd also devised an alternative rating system to get around his dislike of saying unpleasant things. This used a ten-point scale where five out of ten was the lowest possible score. Five out of ten on the Greg Adelmann scale was equivalent to one out of ten on anyone else's. Four out of ten was equivalent to food poisoning.

Gregory Adelmann was neat, well mannered, slightly round and, according to Mr Peterson, as gay as the Venusian night is long (one thousand four hundred and one hours). But I only had his word to go on. As you'll probably understand, because of all the misinformation I'd been bombarded with at school, I didn't have a very good gaydar.

Let me tell you: it's a very strange experience watching something you've created – something you've conjured from air, born of your brain – take form as a living, breathing, interacting entity. And it was with what I imagined to be an inventor's sense of achievement that I watched events unfolding on that first Sunday in October, in the low morning sun of Mr Peterson's front room. Two sofas and four smaller chairs were set out in a pair of semicircles, one against the bay window, the other on the facing wall. There was coffee and tea and Diet Coke laid out on the unfolded dining table (which I'd had to dust – I don't think it had been unfolded for some years). Everyone seemed to be getting on with everyone else. Dr Enderby was deep in conversation with Sophie Haynes. Fiona Fitton was laughing at something Barbara Blessed had said, her smile lines out in force. Mrs Griffith had made flapjacks and was dispensing them from a foil platter.

I was standing a couple of paces back, holding on to my iron–nickel meteorite. As always, holding on to that very cold, very dense, four-and-a-half-billion-year-old piece of asteroid made me feel secure, anchored to something considerably greater than myself. Mr Peterson was standing beside me. The look of vague bafflement that had adorned his face for much of the previous half-hour had, by then, faded back into his characteristic grimace. I don't think he'd actually believed that anyone was going to turn up until we'd heard the first knock on the front door. Later, he'd tell me that he had almost no idea how I'd managed to persuade so many people to sign up for such an esoteric book club, but he thought it must have something to do with naïvety. It took a *lot* of naïvety to enthuse so many people. For a long time, I didn't have a clue what he meant by that.

The Secular Church of Kurt Vonnegut ran successfully for the next thirteen months, but regarding that first meeting, and the twelve that followed, there's little to tell. The only meeting I really need to tell you about is the last one, for reasons that will become extremely obvious. But I'll get to that in due course. For now, all you need know is that things got off to an auspicious start. Within a few minutes of the last person arriving, Mr Peterson banged his crutch three times on the floor, all other noise dispersed like smoke in a fume cupboard, and I began by thanking everyone for coming. I'd never had to make a speech before, but I was surprised to find I didn't feel nervous in the slightest. I felt at home.

MICROFRACTURES

To: m.z.weir@imperial.ac.uk
From: a.m.woods.193@gmail.com
Date: Fri, 15 May 2009 5:07 PM
Subject: Meteorite

Dear Dr Weir,

I hope that this email finds you well and that your recent paper on the concentration of rare earth elements in the Omolon pallasite was well received. I myself am now in much better health. I have not had a major seizure for many months. Dr Enderby is very pleased with my progress and says that eventually it might even be possible for me to come off my carbamazepine – although this hypothetical time is still a way off yet. To tell you the truth, I'm not too worried either way. Taking my pill each morning has become such a routine that it's like brushing my teeth. If I didn't have to do it, it would be one less thing to bother with, but really it's not too much of a chore. As for my daily meditation, I don't plan to stop that whatever happens re my epilepsy. I'm much more serene these days.

The main reason I'm writing to you today is as follows. As I'm sure you're aware, in just over one month's time – on Saturday, 20 June – it will be five years to the day since the meteor hit. And on Sunday, 21 June, it will be five years to the day since you came to recover the fragment that broke through our bathroom roof and put me in a coma for two weeks.

For some time now I've been thinking that I've probably held on to that fragment for long enough. When you visited me in hospital, I remember you telling me that you thought there were lots of people who'd like to see my meteorite for themselves, and I'm sure you were right. It's difficult to explain why precisely, but this feels like the right time for me to say goodbye. I guess I don't feel like I really *need* to keep my meteorite for myself any more. Perhaps it's because I'm feeling so much better.

Anyway, I thought you'd probably be the best person to ask how I should proceed with this matter. I'd be happy to hand my meteorite over to your custody at Imperial College if it would help your research or if there's a suitable home for it there, but as I've said, really I'd like to donate it to some kind of museum or gallery where as many people as possible can see and enjoy it. If you could suggest somewhere, I'd be very grateful.

Yours sincerely,

Alex Woods

To: a.m.woods.193@gmail.com
From: m.z.weir@imperial.ac.uk
Date: Sat, 16 May 2009 10:32 AM
Subject: RE: Meteorite

Dear Alex,

I'm very well (thank you for asking), and I'm delighted to hear that you're feeling so much better.

With regard to your meteorite, this is an extremely generous offer (and a very welcome one!) but I need to be sure that it's definitely what you want. You shouldn't feel compelled or obliged to do this. No one would dispute your right to hold on to your meteorite, and certainly no one would think less of you for doing so.

Having said this, it is a marvellous specimen, and given its unique historical significance, I know that there are many thousands of people who would love the opportunity to see it 'in the flesh' (as it were). Either way, this is your decision, and you should be one hundred per cent certain before you choose.

If you do wish to proceed, then I would suggest that there could be no better home for your meteorite than the Natural History Museum. They already have a wonderful assortment of meteorites from all around the world, and I know they would be absolutely thrilled to add yours to the collection. I should warn you, though, that the museum will wish to publicize your donation, and it's likely to attract some media attention too. At the very least, I'm sure that they'll want you to deliver your meteorite to the museum in person, so that they can meet you and hear your story firsthand.

Although I shall be awaiting your reply very eagerly, I advise that you take a few more days to think about this before you make up your mind. This isn't something you should rush into. Furthermore, I feel it would be remiss of me to allow you to proceed without first making sure you understand the monetary value of your meteorite, which is considerable. As you may be aware, metal meteorite usually sells for £1 per gram on the open market, but large specimens, and those prized for their historical or scientific significance, often go for much, much more. Given the significance of *your* meteorite, I would think you could easily add a zero to the end of its normal market value. So, please, take some more time to think about this! If you still wish to proceed later on, I'll be happy to get in touch with the museum on your behalf and make all the necessary arrangements. And if you have any questions in the meantime, please email or phone me at work and I'll get back to you asap.

Warmest regards,

Monica Weir

To: m.z.weir@imperial.ac.uk
From: a.m.woods.193@gmail.com
Date: Sat, 16 May 2009 3:15 PM
Subject: RE: RE: Meteorite

Dear Dr Weir,

Thank you for your suggestions. You can call the Natural History Museum straight away and make whatever arrangements are necessary. I appreciate why you think I should take a few days to think things over, but, as I've said, I've already thought matters through very carefully over the past few months, and I'm quite certain that this is what I want to do. It's the right time for me.

As for how much my meteorite might be worth, this doesn't really matter too much as I know I could never bring myself to sell it. It would feel like a betrayal, if that makes sense. The best analogy I can draw is that I'd never, ever sell my cat either – but I could let her go free to a good home if that was the best thing for her, especially if I could still visit every once in a while. I hope this clears things up to your satisfaction.

Regarding coming to London to deliver the meteorite 'in person' – I'd very much like to visit the museum because I've never been before. (I went on the website after your email, of course, and it looks like a fascinating place.) However, I'd rather there wasn't any publicity or media – at least, not during my visit. If the museum wants to put something on their website, then that's okay, but perhaps this can be delayed until after I've been and gone?

As I mentioned, the date I had in mind was 20 June. It seems fitting. And since it's a Saturday, I won't need to take any time off school. Could you ask the museum if this date is okay for them? And, of course, I'd like it if you could be there too – so long as it's convenient.

The only problem I can foresee for myself is that it's very unlikely that my mother will be able to bring me to London. Saturday is always an extremely busy day for her – espe-cially in the summer. Also, she has to get up before dawn the next day for the solstice. However, I'm sure that someone will be able to give me a lift to Bristol Temple Meads, and from there it's only one hour forty-five minutes to London Paddington. But I think someone might have to meet me there as I've never been to London and I don't know my way around. I've been looking at maps of the Underground, but I'm not one hundred per cent sure I understand how it works. Perhaps you could send me directions? The forums I've been on haven't been very helpful.

I look forward to hearing from you soon.

Yours sincerely,

Alex Woods

Following Dr Weir's directions, I took a series of escalators down into Paddington Tube Station – which really *was* shaped like a tube – and then caught a train southbound on the Circle line and got off at South Kensington. As she'd promised the museums – the Science Museum and the Natural History Museum – were clearly signposted along the underpass, and once I was back above ground, I swiftly identified the NHM as the building to my right. It was a very large, sandy-coloured oblong – approximately the same hue as a hen's egg – with many windows and decorative arches, and two turrets rearing in the distance. It looked very grand and austere in the grey morning light, quite unlike any museum I'd ever encountered. To tell you the truth, the building it most reminded me of was Wells Cathedral, and this impression was not diminished when I went inside. There was something similarly solemn and reverent in the atmosphere of the broad halls and corridors – especially when I was first admitted, when the museum was still and silent and empty.

Dr Weir had arranged for me to be admitted half an hour before the official opening time so that I could meet the museum's Director of Science and see the gallery where my meteorite was to be exhibited. As promised, she was waiting for me at nine twenty at the bottom of the wide stone steps that led up to the main entrance on Cromwell Road. I hadn't seen her for five years, but I recognized her at once. She still dressed like her mind was on Higher Things. Today, she was wearing a knee-length tweed overcoat, smart black trousers and hiking boots. I was wearing jeans, fairly traded trainers and my latest cagoule.

Dr Weir smiled solemnly and extended her hand as I approached. I felt the weight of the meteorite shift in my backpack as I took her hand.

'Hello, Alex,' she said. 'How nice to see you again.'

'Hello, Dr Weir,' I said.

'You've grown!'

'Yes,' I acknowledged.

'I'm sorry – that's a moronic thing to say, I know.'

'That's okay. I suppose I *am* fifty per cent older than the last time you saw me. I probably look a bit different.'

'Yes, you do.'

'Except for my scar, of course.'

'Yes. That's quite remarkable.'

'The impact site.'

Dr Weir nodded thoughtfully.

'I was told that it would probably fade with time, but of course, it hasn't – not yet. And for some reason my hair doesn't want to grow there any more. I end up with this fine white line.'

'Yes, I see. Still, not all scars are bad, Alex. Some are worth hanging on to, if you understand what I mean.'

'Yes, I think so. Or, at least, I think I'd miss it if it wasn't there.'

'Yes, precisely. Well, shall we go inside? The director's very keen to meet you.'

'I'm keen to meet the director,' I replied.

The Director of Science turned out to be a tall, grey-haired gentleman with a tie-less suit and the voice of a 1950s BBC newsreader – the type to be found narrating in the archive footage of Yuri Gagarin's post-orbit visit to Britain, for example. He was another doctor, of course – Dr Marcus Lean. I'd made a point of researching him online a couple of days earlier. He'd once been an eminent biologist in Cambridge, where he'd spent many years studying extremophiles, which are tiny organisms that live and thrive in extremely hostile environments – around the vents of underwater volcanoes, or in concentrated acid solutions, or under ten metres of ice at the South Pole and so on. His research had proven of great interest to astrobiologists, who believed that if extraterrestrial life were to be discovered in the solar system, it would most likely be of a similar form – microbes that could eke out an existence in the sunless seas of Europa or the frigid methane lakes of Titan.

Given Dr Lean's eminence as a scientist, I was keen to make a good first impression, but, sadly, this was not to be. The moment I met him my attention was diverted by the diplodocus skeleton visible over his left shoulder, which was as big as a bus and mounted on a huge rectangular plinth. While my jaw didn't quite hit the floor, my mouth was certainly agape, and with my attention elsewhere, my handshake was rather limp and lifeless, and unaccompanied by any serious attempt at eye contact. It's a shame, as usually my handshake is one of my particular strengths. Luckily, though, Dr Lean was forgiving of my faux pas. He said that he'd be very happy to show me around the main exhibits once we'd been up to the Vault, which was the name of the gallery where all the meteorites and other precious stones were on display.

'If you'd like to follow me,' Dr Lean said, 'it's on the mezzanine. Up the main staircase and right at Darwin.'

Darwin, of course, was Charles Darwin. He was sitting at the central summit of the grand staircase in the form of a two-ton marble statue, from where he appeared to be watching over the entrance hall with his grave, clever eyes. He looked the way he usually looks, like a doctor about to deliver some bad news, awkwardly posed in his rumpled Victorian suit, and with no great fondness for the limelight. To tell you the truth, he looked like he'd rather be digging up earthworms in his back garden – though I supposed it would be harder to sculpt a statue like that.

The Vault, at the far end of the minerals gallery, was a mesmerizing space – all stone columns and arches and low oak cabinets filled with glaring jewels: gold and sapphires and emeralds, and a diamond as large as a golf ball. Set among this company, the meteorites were, at first, easily overlooked. They were all kinds of irregular shapes and sizes, and varied in colour from coal-black to mottled caramel. Perhaps the most innocuous of all was the Nakhla Meteorite, which looked like a misshapen lump of scorched clay. Dr Lean told me that this was actually a piece of Mars. The original meteoroid had probably been blown into space by a large impact on the Red Planet's surface.

It had fallen to Earth in 1911, burning high in the skies above Egypt, from where the surviving fragments had later been recovered. Most of the other meteorites, those that hadn't been observed as Falls, had been found in places like Antarctica and the Australian outback – uniform landscapes, untouched by human development, where they stood out as geological aberrations, even to the untrained eye. Of course, since the Earth had been the victim of about four and a half billion years of steady bombardment, there were actually meteorites scattered across every corner of the globe – it was just that in most environments they lay unnoticed.

'It's not every day they come crashing through one's ceiling,' Dr Lean concluded.

My meteorite was to be displayed in a cubic half-metre of space that had been cleared at the far right of one of the wall-mounted cabinets. The museum research team, Dr Lean explained, had also selected a newspaper article to include as part of the exhibit, which was necessary to inform or remind the general public of the meteorite's 'historical significance'. The article, which I also had in my scrapbook, was from the front page of *The Times* and showed a rather dramatic helicopter shot of the hole that had been punched in our bathroom roof. The headline read: 'SOMERSET SCHOOL BOY HIT BY METEOR.'

'It was the least sensationalized article we could find,' Dr Lean told me.

By this point, I didn't think I could delay any longer. I took my iron–nickel meteorite from my backpack, where it was safely swaddled in two layers of bubble-wrap, and handed the package across for Dr Lean to unwrap.

'My word,' he said. He immediately looked about twenty

years younger, I thought, as he stood running his eyes over that scorched and pitted surface. I followed his gaze across all those familiar rises and fissures and valleys, across the microfractures running through the partially exposed cross-section. And I should tell you that I didn't feel a sense of loss as those seconds unfolded. Having seen the Vault, with its priceless collection of gems and minerals, I knew that this would be a better home for my meteorite than the top of my bookcase, which was where it had resided for the last five years. What I felt in place of loss was the strangest sense of time folding back on itself, a feeling of significance, almost akin to déjà vu. It's hard to explain, but I think what really struck me in that stretched-out moment was the impression of what might have been, had the meteorite never come to me. A kind of shadowy parallel universe.

Without the meteorite, I would have been an entirely different person. I'd have a different brain – different connections, different function. And I wouldn't be telling you this story now. I wouldn't have a story to tell.

My mother would say that everything happens for a reason, but I don't agree with that – not in the sense she'd mean it, anyway. Most of what happens is pure chance. Nevertheless, I have to admit that there are certain moments that, in retrospect, seem to shape the course of our lives to a remarkable degree. There are pinpoint events that change everything; and it is a strange curiosity, if nothing else, that the day I'm describing now, the five-year anniversary of the meteor strike, was destined to spawn another.

At lunchtime, Dr Lean led us to the museum's delicatessen near the Exhibition Road entrance and advised the woman working the till that she should allow Dr Weir and me to order whatever we wanted from the menu free of charge. Then he shook my hand again and told me that it had been a pleasure and that he'd be sure to save me a spot on the guest list for all the museum's forthcoming exhibitions and special events. I only had to email him to let him know I was coming and he'd make all the necessary arrangements.

'Thank you, Dr Lean,' I said. And this time, when I shook his hand, I made sure that my grip was solid. Perhaps a little too solid – but I thought it better to err on the side of caution. I wanted to make sure he knew that the morning's handshake had been an anomaly.

For lunch, I had a spinach and ricotta tartlet with a mixed leaf salad and three Diet Cokes. Dr Weir had a steak sandwich and a glass of red wine, and then a coffee to follow, which she sipped slowly while I told her my thoughts on the museum so far.

'I think, in a way I prefer the smaller exhibits,' I said. 'The meteorites, of course, but also the other minerals and the small insects. I mean, the dinosaurs are extremely impressive, but they're very busy too. There's too much to take in, and too many distractions. The less spectacular exhibits are a bit more . . .' Dr Weir waited patiently while I struggled for the word. I wanted to say 'intimate' but I wasn't sure this was the correct context. I thought it would be a minor disaster if I misused the word, so in the end I plumped for a lengthier explanation. 'I suppose what I mean is that the smaller exhibits give you more space to think. You can kind of lose yourself in them. You can hear the sounds that your footsteps make in the corridors and imagine exactly how the museum must have been a hundred years ago.'

Dr Weir nodded. 'I like the butterflies for similar reasons.'

A small silence passed.

'How are you getting on at school now?' Dr Weir asked.

'Better,' I said. 'Although I don't think I'm ever going to fit in very well. But I've kind of accepted that now. I like the school part, anyway – you know: the lessons themselves.'

Dr Weir nodded and sipped her coffee again.

'I think if I could just spend the whole six hours of the school day solving algebra problems, then I'd be extremely happy. But, of course, that's not exactly normal. That's the part everybody else hates. Most of the other boys can't wait for the break so they can go outside and play football. And to me, that really *is* baffling. It seems like such a waste of time and energy. It doesn't tell you anything about the world. It doesn't add or change anything. I don't get the appeal.'

Dr Weir traced a couple of orbits of her coffee cup with her right index finger, then said: 'Well, from an evolutionary stand-point, it probably owes a lot to ancient hunting rituals. Like most sport, it's about hitting targets, perfecting one's hand–eye or foot–eye co-ordination, outwitting an opponent and so forth. And, of course, there's a high degree of tribalism too. That's true of all team sports. An enjoyment of these sorts of activities is probably very deeply ingrained in the human psyche – and the male psyche especially, though to varying extents, of course.'

'I'm not a big fan of hunting rituals full stop,' I said.

Dr Weir smiled. 'No. But these things manifest themselves in many different forms. For example, many scientists believe that some of our mathematical abilities have their roots in the kind of spatial skills our ancestors needed to hunt prey and elude predators – understanding trajectories and forces, acceleration and deceleration, general mechanics. Our brains have evolved excellent software for comprehending natural laws. So maybe when you sit down and solve mathematical problems for six hours, the satisfaction you experience isn't *entirely* different to the pleasure others find in sports. They may have a common source. It's an interesting thought.'

'I don't think the football team would buy it,' I said.

'No, maybe not. But really, Alex, there's nothing wrong with being cerebral. I think you'll find that in a few years things will get much easier for you.'

'Yes, I expect so.'

'Are you still hoping to become a neurologist?'

I liked the way Dr Weir asked this question. I'd been telling people that I probably wanted to be a neurologist since I was about eleven years old, and for some reason, this was seldom taken seriously. People seemed to find it either funny or peculiar or baffling. But Dr Weir took the idea very seriously – although these days I had started to have second thoughts, as I explained.

'I think I'm leaning back towards being a physicist again,' I said.

Dr Weir smiled.

'I'm still very interested in neurology,' I clarified, 'but . . . well, I think I'm more drawn to the simplicity of physics. I like the idea that you can explain all these incredibly complicated phenomena using incredibly simple laws. Like $e = mc^2$. To tell you the truth, I don't think there's anything quite as wonderful as that. You can write it on a postage stamp but it tells you how the stars work. You don't really get that kind of perfection anywhere else in life. I seriously doubt that neurology could ever be *that* perfect. I think you could probably spend a thousand years studying the brain and it still wouldn't make people that much easier to understand.'

'Perhaps not,' Dr Weir said with a little laugh. 'But whatever you end up doing, I hope you'll consider coming to Imperial. You know, in this country there's really nowhere better to study science.'

'Yes, I think I might like that,' I said. 'Although I'm not sure about London itself yet. I mean, it's extremely crowded. I'm not sure how I'd feel about living in a city this big.'

'Yes, I can understand that too,' Dr Weir said. 'You know, I wasn't born in London, Alex. I grew up in the countryside, like you. In Cornwall, actually. But I don't think I could live anywhere so remote any more. I like having everything around me – all the museums and libraries. The only downside is the light pollution. Most nights in London you can barely make out Polaris, and anything above magnitude two is near impossible.'

I thought about this for a while. I tried to picture myself studying science in London, but for some reason, the image wouldn't quite crystallize.

'Dr Weir?' I asked. 'What grades would I need to get into Imperial?'

'You'll need three As, Alex, and at least two of them in science or maths.'

I thought some more. 'I think I'll try to get four,' I said. 'The three sciences *and* maths. You know, just to be certain.'

Mr Peterson collected me from Bristol Temple Meads just after eight thirty and then I spent the next half-hour telling him about London. There was no chronology. I told him about how insanely busy the tube had been on the way home, how incredibly large and full of people London was in general (I estimated you could fit at least fifteen Bristols inside it), how Dr Weir had said that I could probably get into Imperial if I continued to get top grades at school, how I'd come to the conclusion that I probably wanted to be a physicist rather than a neurologist because I wanted to help figure out a ToE – a Theory of Everything – which was the highest aim of modern cosmology and would finally crack the problem of how the universe *works*. Mr Peterson said this was a good goal to shoot for. But that was about all he said. Being out of practice, he found city driving – even off-peak city driving – extremely stressful, and he wasn't much of a multitasker at the best of times. In hindsight, I probably should have kept quiet and let him concentrate. (I was over-stimulated: I'd drunk too much Diet Coke that day.) But as it happened, getting out of the city was not the problem. We made it to the undulating A-road leading back to Glastonbury and Wells without mishap. Mr Peterson relaxed, and eventually I talked myself to a standstill and fell back to daydreaming about my future scientific endeavours.

The car was warm, and the road was quiet. The sun was sinking like a distress flare in the rear-view mirror, and I found myself crashing into a comfortable, flickering doze.

The next thing I was conscious of was the white van bearing down on us. Even half asleep, I saw it plain as day. Mr Peterson did not. He pulled out onto the roundabout quite calmly, as if he were manoeuvring into an empty parking bay. The van was maybe five metres away, heading straight for us.

'Van! Brakes!' I shouted. It was all I had time to shout. I felt the glancing impact as a small detonation that sent a shockwave coursing through my upper body. The world shifted forty-five degrees to the right, then juddered to a halt. We were left facing off the roundabout at an oblique angle. The van had stopped a few metres away, in the roundabout's inner lane.

'Goddamnit!' said Mr Peterson. 'You all right, kid?'

I nodded. My heart was racing at about a hundred and eighty beats per minute, but I was surprised to find that my head was perfectly clear. I felt like I'd been plunged into ice water.

When we stepped out of the car to inspect the damage, everything seemed unusually bright and well defined. There were two metres of tyre tracks on the road, and a little glass and plastic from our driver's-side headlight, and the bonnet had buckled slightly, and the panels adjoining the bumper and wheel arch were badly cracked and indented, but there was no *serious* damage to Mr Peterson's car. As for the van, it would transpire that it had suffered nothing worse than a small depression between its bumper and its front left wheel, but this was not discernible from our angle. I could only see that it was a white transit van, evidently a business vehicle. The sign on its side read: THE LONE DRAINER. I surmised that the driver was some kind of plumber. I could see him through the passenger-side window. He was making angry thrusting gestures towards the small B-road leading off the roundabout immediately to our left. Mr Peterson and I both nodded. Then the Drainer started his engine, indicated, pulled sharply off the roundabout and parked up about ten metres down the road. Mr Peterson and I got back in the car and followed.

The Lone Drainer slammed his door, pointedly, and, after several failed attempts, lit a cigarette. I suspected he was too furious to work his lighter effectively, even though the accident had not been serious, and the damage to his vehicle even less so. He was a short, mostly bald man with the red face of a cooked lobster. He was wearing a red and black checked shirt, huge black safety boots and filthy jeans. I had a lot of time to weigh him up because he wasn't making eye contact. He was squinting at his bumper and muttering to himself. He didn't look quite the ticket. Mr Peterson was of the same opinion.

'Jesus MF Christ!' he said to me under his breath. 'This is gonna be a *royal* pain in the ass.'

'Should we call the police?' I asked.

Mr Peterson snorted.

'Don't you have to call the police when there's an accident?' I persisted.

'Not an accident like this, kid,' Mr Peterson told me. 'This hardly even qualifies as an accident. We just have to swap numbers. Then my insurance can deal with it.'

'Your insurance?'

'Yes, my insurance.'

'Because it was your fault?'

Mr Peterson ground his teeth. 'Yes, it was my fault. Obviously. I didn't see him.'

'You didn't *see* him?' The improbability of this was already looming large in my mind. 'How didn't you see him?'

'I don't know how. I just didn't.'

'But he was there plain as day.'

'Kid, I didn't see him! If I'd seen him, I wouldn't have pulled out!'

'You have to pay extra attention at junctions,' I said.

'I *was* paying attention,' Mr Peterson said. 'I just didn't see him. I can't explain any better than that. I'm not infallible.'

'You're not high, are you?'

'Jesus, kid! What kind of question is that? Of course I'm not high! Do I look high to you?'

'I don't think so,' I said. I thought that if Mr Peterson were high, he wouldn't have come to collect me. He'd probably have forgotten.

'The Lone Drainer looks pissed off,' I pointed out.

'Kid, will you please shut the hell up for a second and pass me my stick? I'm sure the Drainer'll calm down soon enough. Just let me do the talking.'

I took Mr Peterson's crutch from the back seat and passed it to him. By the time we reached the van, the Lone Drainer had stopped squinting over his bumper and was staring straight at us. He was still muttering and shaking his head. Mr Peterson extended his hand.

'Isaac Peterson,' he said.

The Drainer blew out a steady stream of smoke.

Mr Peterson cleared his throat. 'Listen, I'm sorry. I'm not sure what happened back there. Is your van okay?'

The Lone Drainer spat on the ground. 'You know I could've *killed* you,' he said. It came out more as a regret than an observation. 'What the hell were you thinking? You pulled out right in front of me! Are you fucking *blind*?'

Mr Peterson exhaled through his teeth and waited for a count of three. Then he said: 'Okay. It was my fault. I'm not disputing that. But I think we should all just be thankful it wasn't serious. No one was hurt. There's no major damage. It could've been a lot worse.'

'It's a fucking miracle it wasn't worse.' The Lone Drainer punctuated this sentiment by flicking his cigarette onto the verge.

'You know, that's a bit of a fire hazard,' I pointed out.

'Let me do the talking,' Mr Peterson said.

'Your granddad shouldn't be on the fucking road,' the Drainer told me.

'My grandfather's dead,' I told the Drainer. 'The one I know about,' I added.

The Drainer decided I was no longer worth talking to. 'You're obviously not fit to drive,' he told Mr Peterson. 'It looks like you can barely fucking walk.'

'Jeez!' said Mr Peterson. 'What d'you clean those drains with, your *mouth*?' This went straight over the Drainer's head, which I thought was probably for the best. 'Look, buddy, I've apologized once. I'm not gonna apologize again. You can stand here hollerin' all you want. In the meantime, I'm gonna go write you the number of my insurer and when you get that pea-sized dint taken out of your fender, you can send them the bill. Come on, kid. I think we're done here.'

Mr Peterson started walking away. I followed. 'You need to get your fucking eyes tested!' the Lone Drainer shouted after us.

'It's no wonder he works alone,' Mr Peterson said to me.

'Are you okay?' I asked.

'Of course I'm okay. He's just some asshole. The world's full of them.'

'Yes, I know,' I agreed.

'Let's just give him the number and get the hell out of here.'

'Would you like me to give him the number?' I offered.

'We'll *both* give him the number.'

'You just watch where you're fucking going on your way home,' the Drainer warned Mr Peterson as they exchanged details. 'Try not to cause no more accidents today.'

'It's been real nice talkin' to you,' Mr Peterson said.

I didn't say anything.

The Lone Drainer spat again, got back in his van, slammed the door, performed a wobbly U-turn and then squealed away in a cloud of dust and diesel fumes. I wrinkled my nose.

'Asshole,' said Mr Peterson.

While I agreed that the Lone Drainer's interpersonal skills left a lot to be desired, he had raised at least one valid point. There was no way Mr Peterson should have missed seeing the van. It didn't seem humanly possible.

'Are you sure you don't want me to drive the rest of the way?' I asked him when we were back in the stationary car. 'I think it might be sensible, given what happened.'

'Sensible? Hell, we've had one near miss today. I'm not gonna risk anything else. You know what'll happen if the cops pull us over with the car all smashed up and you driving? I'll be the one who winds up in the Big House.'

'I was thinking about what would be safer,' I said. 'I think that should be the number-one priority, really.'

'I'm perfectly safe! I just drifted off for a second. I'm not used to driving these kinds of distances any more.'

'You didn't say you "drifted off",' I pointed out. 'You said you didn't even *see* the van. That's what's concerning me.'

'I don't know *what* happened. It was all a blur.'

'Literally or figuratively?'

'Jesus! It was a wake-up call, okay? I'll pay extra, extra attention. Is that enough to reassure you?'

'No,' I said.

Mr Peterson ignored me. He started the engine, performed a careful three-point turn and rejoined the roundabout.

After a few minutes, I said: 'Mr Peterson, we're agreed that the Lone Drainer was an asshole. That's a given. But perhaps you *should* get your eyes retested. Just to be sure.'

Mr Peterson didn't say anything. His eyes were locked on the road ahead.

A thought occurred to me. 'Mr Peterson?' I asked. 'This *is* the only time something like this has happened, isn't it? I mean, you've not had any problems like this before – with driving?'

'Of course I haven't!' Mr Peterson said. But he said it much too quickly for my liking.

I was worried.

TIMEQUAKE

The optician had, at first, been slightly baffled. After all, there was nothing wrong with Mr Peterson's eyes per se. They appeared healthy for his age. His prescription was correct. There was no sign of cataracts or glaucoma – nothing that could account for the 'blurring' and dizzy spells he'd been experiencing intermittently in the weeks since the crash. The only problem the optician could detect was that Mr Peterson seemed to be experiencing some inexplicable problem 'aiming' his eyes.

'The problem's very specific,' the optician told him. 'Focussing on stationary objects obviously isn't troubling you, and you can track horizontally. But you have a minor difficulty tracking moving objects along the vertical axis – more notably when the movement's in the downward direction, or from background to foreground. I can only conclude it's this that's causing your difficulties with driving and reading – but as to the root cause, I'm afraid there's not much else I can tell you. The problem may be muscular, but really this is just a best guess. You need to talk to your GP.'

'Maybe you could ask Dr Enderby the next time we see him,' I suggested later. Mr Peterson did not like going to the doctor's. He had been putting it off.

'I don't need to see a *neurologist*, kid,' Mr Peterson pointed out. 'The optician said it's probably just muscular. I'm not even convinced it's a real problem. Just age. All sorts of things start to pack up as you get older. This is something you've got to look forward to.'

'That's not what the optician said,' I riposted. 'He said you should see a doctor because he doesn't know exactly what the problem is. There *is* a problem, though.'

'A minor problem.'

'Do you want me to make an appointment for you tomorrow? I don't mind coming along as well – if that would help?'

'I don't need chaperoning to the doctor's! I'm capable of making my own appointments.'

'I'm not seeing much evidence of that right now,' I said. It was a tone I'd learned from my mother, and it worked.

Mr Peterson got on the phone.

The following day, the GP repeated the eye tests, then asked Mr Peterson to perform some simple tasks involving hand–eye co-ordination. She concluded that the problem wasn't muscular.

'I'm going to refer you to a neurologist,' she said.

Mr Peterson swore at length. 'I thought this was a *minor* problem. It's hardly even bothering me.'

'It's difficult to say for sure what the problem is at this stage,' the GP told him. 'But there are certain neurological conditions with symptoms similar to yours. They're mostly very rare, but it makes sense to investigate further. Just to be certain.'

'If you're going to the neurology department at Bristol, I'm definitely coming,' I told Mr Peterson later, after he'd briefed me. 'After all, I *have* been there a lot. It will make things much easier.'

'It's gonna be a waste of time,' Mr Peterson predicted. 'I've just got some weird eye-muscle thing. It's not even a real problem.'

'I think you need to leave those kinds of judgements to the doctors,' I said.

Mr Peterson snarled. But he offered no further resistance regarding my attending his appointment with him, and the following week, we met the neurologist, who was called Dr Bradshaw. He knew Dr Enderby, of course, and it also turned out that he knew of me. I found this out after I introduced myself and told him that I'd been seeing Dr Enderby for the past five years because of my TLE. Dr Bradshaw said he was familiar with my case – not the details, just the background. Everybody in the hospital knew about that.

Dr Bradshaw asked Mr Peterson lots of very detailed questions about the car accident, and after that he wanted lots of information about Mr Peterson's mobility problems. So Mr Peterson had to tell him all about his leg and how it had been shrapnelled by a Viet Cong landmine and had subsequently become gangrenous, which had caused severe and permanent damage to many of his nerve-endings, leaving him with his limp.

Dr Bradshaw absorbed these facts in five seconds of silence, then said: 'And what about more recently? Has there been any worsening of your general mobility?'

'Not so as I'd notice,' Mr Peterson replied.

'What about your balance?' Dr Bradshaw asked.

'Wonderful,' Mr Peterson said. 'I'm thinkin' of becoming a gymnast.'

'Any falls?'

'The odd stumble. Nothing major.'

'What about getting up and down the stairs?'

'That's always been a slow process. I'm used to it.'

'And how about your moods? Have you noticed any sudden mood swings? Any unusual irritability?'

'Not unusual irritability,' Mr Peterson said.

'He means he's *usually* quite irritable,' I clarified.

Dr Bradshaw didn't smile.

The tests that followed were thorough. Again, Mr Peterson had to try to follow a torch using only his eyes, and then he had to use a machine that displayed flashing lights at different points in his visual field and push a button each time he detected a flash. After that, there were tests involving focussing and pupil dilation and involuntary eye movements. Finally, he was sent for an MRI scan. Later, Dr Bradshaw would tell us that this wasn't critical for the diagnosis – which by then was already clear. It was to ascertain how far the disease had progressed, and so that the approximate rate of neurodegeneration could be charted over the coming months, and hopefully years.

Neither Mr Peterson nor I had ever heard of progressive supranuclear palsy. Dr Bradshaw told us that it was a rare degenerative disease, which affected a specific area of the brainstem, causing a deterioration in certain sensory and motor functions.

'I'm sorry, Doctor,' I said, when Dr Bradshaw had finished speaking. 'I don't want to tell you how to do your job, but from what you've said, I think you've definitely made a mistake. Mr Peterson's motor problems have nothing to do with his brainstem. That much seems quite obvious. And as for his eyes, the optician said there's hardly even a problem there. It's just a minor difficulty in one direction.'

Dr Bradshaw waited patiently for a few seconds, then said: 'I know this must be extremely hard for both of you, but there's no question about the diagnosis. It's likely that the existing mobility issues have actually masked many of the more obvious symptoms for some time. And when it comes to the visual symptoms, these are subtle but very specific. With the correct tests, they're virtually unmistakable.'

'*Virtually* unmistakable?'

'The visual tests are corroborated by the MRI scan. It shows a small but evident atrophication in the midbrain. It's an area that controls eye movements.'

'I know what the midbrain does!' I snapped. I turned to Mr Peterson, who hadn't spoken since the diagnosis. 'I think we definitely need to get a second opinion on this.'

Mr Peterson stayed silent for a few more seconds, then said: 'Alex, I want you to keep calm and quiet. I don't need a second opinion. I need facts. Doctor, this condition's gonna get worse? That's what progressive means in medical terms, right?'

'Yes. I'm afraid that's correct,' Dr Bradshaw said.

'Is there any treatment?'

'There are palliative treatments that may help to control the symptoms; physiotherapy often helps to combat some of the initial motor problems. We can also try you on a drug called levodopa.'

'And what does that do?'

'It's a dopamine precursor,' I said. 'It's used to treat Parkinson's. You don't have that either.'

Mr Peterson looked at me but didn't say anything.

'You're right,' Dr Bradshaw said patiently. 'Levodopa *is* used to treat Parkinson's, but it's also effective in some – though not all – PSP cases. Similar areas of the brain are affected in Parkinson's and PSP, and some of the symptoms overlap – though the impairment of motor function isn't so evident in the early stages of PSP.'

'But none of these things is gonna help long term?' Mr Peterson asked. 'They're not cures, right?'

'No. They're not cures.'

'How long do I have?'

'You need to understand that there's a high degree of variance among cases. There are reasons to be positive. It's not—'

'Please, Doctor. I want to know how long I've got and what I can expect in terms of future symptoms. You don't need to sugar-coat it. And leave out the jargon.'

Dr Bradshaw nodded. 'Typically, PSP sufferers live for another five to seven years after the initial onset of symptoms. But as I've said, there may be cause to think that some of your motor symptoms have been present for some time without diagnosis. Visual symptoms usually occur at a later stage. Without a clearer picture of when the symptoms first started, it's difficult to predict how quickly the disease will advance.'

'How long after the first *visual* symptoms do people typically survive?'

'Three years.'

Mr Peterson stayed quiet for a few moments. 'And what will happen to me in those three years? What usually happens? I need the facts.'

'I'm afraid your vision will continue to get worse. You'll

find it harder and harder to move your eyes, and your other motor skills are going to deteriorate as well. Eventually, you won't be able to walk any more. Your speech will become impaired, and you may have considerable difficulty swallowing. In the long term, you're going to require full-time care. I'm very sorry.'

Mr Peterson nodded. 'Thank you.'

'You need to know that there are lots of different support mechanisms that will be available to you. But I think it would be better not to talk about these in too much depth right now. I'd like to arrange a follow-up appointment, ideally for sometime next week . . .'

I stopped listening.

'I think we need to speak to Dr Enderby,' I said after we'd left the appointment. 'I'm sure that he'll be able to direct us to someone who's a bit more—'

Mr Peterson raised his hand. 'Listen, kid. I know you're very upset right now, but this isn't helping me. Please, just let me deal with this.'

'But—'

'I don't need a second opinion. What I need is some time and space to think. And so do you.'

I didn't say anything.

'Look, I know this is probably asking a lot, but right now, I need you to keep this to yourself. I don't want people knowing. I don't want to have to face a barrage of sympathy every time I go to buy milk from the store. For the next couple of months, I'm gonna need some normality – some privacy – and I'm not gonna get that if the whole goddamn village knows. If you *have* to talk to someone, then talk to your mother, but tell her the same as I've told you. I know it's gonna be difficult, but you need to respect my wishes in this.'

'Of course I'll respect your wishes,' I said. And I knew it would be easy enough. After all, there wasn't really anything to say.

When I got home, I told my mother the truth: the hospital hadn't been able to tell us anything useful. It was largely guesswork based on insufficient evidence. If there *was* a problem, it was obviously something quite trivial.

Lucy was pregnant again. We didn't need to take her to the vet to establish this. We were familiar enough with the signs, all the subtle changes in her mood and behaviour. I've no idea which litter she was on at this point – maybe her sixth or seventh. Her desire and capacity for reproduction was interminable, and for some reason, my mother seemed to grow more satisfied with each additional batch. She had an ongoing theory that Lucy always conceived on nights with a full moon, and she was certain – based on her best estimate of 'how far along' Lucy was – that this latest fertilization provided further evidence to that effect. I had to listen to all the ridiculous details of this theory twice, once at home and once at the shop, where they were recounted – at great length – for Ellie's benefit.

I was working because I wanted something mindless with which to occupy myself, and my mother's shop had seemed the best option. Additionally, I'd decided that I should start saving money for university in four years' time. I knew that living in London was not going to be cheap. I also had it at the back of my mind that if I worked all summer, I might be able to save enough money to buy a telescope, which seemed a necessary first step if I wanted to be an astrophysicist. I had a pair of 10x50 binoculars, which were okay for the moon and open star clusters and some of the brighter deep-sky objects such as Andromeda and M42 and so on, but they weren't powerful enough to split close binaries or pick out any planetary detail. At a push, I could see that Saturn was an elongated smear rather than a point of light, but I'd need a lot more magnification to resolve the rings.

Summer was really the only time when the shop was busy enough to employ three people – especially on days when my mother had to do a lot of readings. My job was always working the till. I was good with money, but I wasn't good at advising the customers about the different tarot packs, or which crystal was best for protection or stress or period pains or whatever. My standard response was that I was sure they were all equally effective. When it was very busy, the work went quickly. It was the slack periods I didn't like. Then there was no barrier between me and the incessant yabbering of my mother and Ellie, who were constantly buzzing like mosquitoes in the background. And sometimes – even worse – they seemed inexplicably determined to drag me into whatever lunacy they were discussing. The cat conversation was just a particularly bad incidence of this ongoing scenario.

'She's been an extremely productive cat,' my mother observed. 'She's been averaging . . . how many, Lex?'

'I'm trying to read,' I said. I had no desire to get drawn into another insane dialogue with my mother.

'He worked it out last time, didn't you? Something like three point seven kittens per litter, wasn't it, Lex? Although she only had two last time – both boys. But then, she's not a young cat any more. She's still doing very well, really. It'll be interesting to see how many she manages this time.'

'Maybe we should run a sweepstake?' Ellie suggested.

'You should probably get her spayed,' I said.

My mother looked at Ellie and shrugged. Ellie rolled her eyes. 'Lex, you know how I feel about that. I don't think we should be the ones who decide whether Lucy has kittens or not. She'll stop when she's ready.'

'But what's the point?' I asked. 'You never let her keep them. You seem perfectly happy to make *that* decision for her. Maybe if you let her keep her kittens, she'd stop breeding.'

My mother ignored me and directed her response to Ellie. 'Perhaps you'd like one, Ellie? I think one cat's quite enough for us right now. Taking care of kittens and young cats requires quite a time commitment. And despite what Lex says, I think Lucy tends to lose interest in the maternal role after about eight weeks. That's often the way with cats. Mostly they're very independent creatures.'

'Maybe she loses interest because she knows what's coming,' I said. 'Your whole approach to that cat's completely inconsistent. Actually, it's worse than that. It's cruel.'

My mother looked at me for a few seconds without saying anything, then turned away. 'Ellie, I think some fresh air might be a good idea. Why don't you and Lex go up to the well and get some water for the cooler. It's looking a little empty. Take both of the five-litre bottles. That should keep us going for a while.'

If I haven't mentioned it already, my mother *only* drinks Glastonbury well water. She even uses it to make herbal tea.

Ellie did not look amused. She exhaled demonstratively, to show us all and especially me how patient she was being, and what kind of effort it was costing her. 'Fine. Ten litres of well water coming up. Where are your car keys?'

'I want you to walk, Ellie,' my mother said. 'Just because you can drive now doesn't mean you have to. A bit of exercise won't do either one of you any harm.'

Ellie glared (at me, as if this absurd outing had been my idea). 'Walk? You want us to *walk* to the well? There and back?'

My mother nodded patiently. 'What did you think I meant by "fresh air"?'

'I thought it was just a figure of speech!'

'It wasn't. I want you to walk. Take your time. Enjoy yourselves. It's a nice day.'

'It won't feel so nice on the way back. You do realize how much ten litres of water weighs, don't you, Rowena? It's got to weigh about a ton!'

'For God's sake, Ellie!' I interjected. 'Ten kilograms! It's not difficult. Ten litres of water weighs ten kilograms.'

'Alex, shut up! This is *not* the time for maths! You're not helping.'

'And you're wasting your time. She's not going to change her mind.'

'No,' agreed my mother, 'she's not. You're both young and healthy. I'm sure you can manage it between you.'

Ellie glared at me again, then threw her hands in the air and thrust her jaw at the door to the stockroom. I had the feeling that I was going to be doing most of the carrying.

As soon as we were outside, Ellie lit a cigarette and exhaled an angry jet of smoke. Smoking outside was as close to fresh air as Ellie ever came. 'You know this is *your* fault,' she told me.

'You were pretty fucking rude back there. There was absolutely no need for it.'

I ignored her and subtly upped my pace. I was not prepared to be lectured to on this subject – especially not by Ellie.

'Woods, slow down! I don't want to die of a heart attack on the way to the fucking well!'

Ellie usually regressed to calling me 'Woods' when we were not in my mother's company, or when she was particularly angry. I slowed down all the same. Despite what my mother had said, it was not such a great day for walking. It was too hot and muggy. It felt like it needed to rain. I knew that I should preserve some energy for the return trek.

'Are you going to tell me what's wrong with you?' Ellie asked.

'Nothing's wrong with me,' I said. 'I just get fed up when my mother won't stop talking crap.'

'Jesus! She's entitled to her opinion, isn't she?'

'Yes. Just the same as I'm entitled to mine.'

'Exactly. Except she isn't the one getting all personal and nasty.'

'Her opinions make no sense. She's completely illogical.'

'Logic! Fuck logic, Woods! There are more important things in the world than being logical – like being *nice*, for a start. Your mum's heart's in the right place. She wasn't saying what she was saying just to piss you off. From where I was standing, she was just trying to have a reasonably pleasant conversation with you.'

'If she wants a conversation, then she shouldn't punish me for speaking my mind. It's not fair.'

'She's not punishing you, you dildo! She's giving you a chance to cool down. It's pretty fucking obvious that you're not in the best of moods today, and I suppose she's hoping that if you're not going to tell her what's going on, then you might tell me. I'm the one who's being punished here. A hike to the well is *not* my idea of a good time.'

'This has nothing to do with you. You're just collateral damage. Trust me: my mother is trying to teach me a lesson. That's the way her mind works. She's trying to force me to accept that she's right and I'm wrong. She hates it when I disagree with her.'

'Jesus, you're brain dead!' Ellie said.

I ignored her.

We'd reached the well, which was deserted except for a long row of cars that were parked up on the side of the road. Their owners had obviously headed up to the tor. I started filling the first water bottle. I knew it would take a couple of minutes, at least. The well water only gets dispensed from its wall outlet at a slow trickle, which is especially slow when it hasn't rained for a while. But I didn't mind waiting. It was past noon so the well was shaded by the embankments and the trees. Ellie had sat down on one of the benches just across the lane. She lit another cigarette.

'You know, you don't give your mother nearly enough credit,' she said. 'When has she ever told you what to think?'

'She tells me all the time.'

'When?'

'All the time!'

'As far as I can see, she'd never dream of imposing her beliefs on you. One thing you *can't* accuse her of is telling you what to think or do. She respects your independence. And that's not at all normal for parents. You don't realize how lucky you are.'

I turned back to watch the water bottle filling. I thought it was typical of Ellie to try to turn the situation around so it was somehow a commentary on her own traumatic childhood. 'You don't have the faintest idea what you're talking about,' I told her.

We walked back from the well in silence.

At my biannual check-up with Dr Enderby, I told him about Mr Peterson. I hadn't meant to say anything, but really I felt like I was left with no choice. Otherwise, this thing would just drag on and on for ever.

Dr Enderby didn't say anything while I told him about our recent trip to the hospital and the misdiagnosis. He just looked at me very calmly, allowing me to lay down the facts from start to finish. I thought it was good that he was remaining so poised and unemotional in the face of my revelations. He wasn't going to interrupt or question me until he'd had a chance to assimilate all the evidence. Then he'd know exactly how to clear up this mess. A couple of phone calls, a proper reassessment of the data and with any luck this would all be over in a matter of days – if not hours.

But when I'd finished speaking, he just continued to look at me for a few moments more, his demeanour unchanging. Then he said: 'Alex, you know that you shouldn't be telling me this, don't you? Breaking a confidence is a very serious matter.'

I felt myself reddening. 'I *am* breaking a confidence,' I admitted. 'Mr Peterson didn't want me to tell anyone. But I couldn't see what else to do. He's being ridiculously stubborn about this.'

'I can understand that you're very upset right now,' Dr Enderby said. 'And I don't doubt that you feel like you're acting for the very best of reasons. But with some things, you have to respect a person's wishes. You shouldn't force Isaac down a path he doesn't want to follow – especially at a time like this, when he probably feels like most of his choices have already been stripped away. I think you should be able to understand that as well as anybody.'

'I do understand that. Of course I do. But this is an exceptional circumstance.'

Dr Enderby continued to look at me without changing his expression. Something clicked into place.

'You already knew!' I said.

'Yes,' Dr Enderby admitted. 'I've known for some time.'

'I didn't think Dr Bradshaw was allowed to tell you.'

'He wasn't and he didn't. Isaac phoned me shortly after the diagnosis. And we've spoken a couple more times since then.'

I felt a huge flood of relief. 'So it's okay, then? I mean, I know I shouldn't have interfered, but I didn't think he was going to get this sorted out on his own. But it's okay now. You know about it and you're obviously dealing with it. Is there going to be a reassessment? Or can't you talk about that? I'll understand if you can't.'

'Alex,' Dr Enderby said softly, 'there's not going to be a reassessment. There's no need. Dr Bradshaw knows what he's talking about. He's an expert in his field.'

'Yes, of course. I'm not questioning his credentials. But misdiagnoses happen. I know they're rare, but they happen. I was looking on the internet and—'

'Alex, you have to listen to me. The diagnosis is correct. It's not going to change. I'm sorry. I wish there was a kinder way to say this, but there isn't.'

I looked at him blankly. I felt a weird, involuntary tremor in my jaw.

'What you're feeling now is perfectly normal,' Dr Enderby went on, 'but it can't be allowed to continue indefinitely. You have to accept reality. Isaac has a terminal illness. And he's going to need your support.'

I started crying. I felt Dr Enderby's hand close on my shoulder. If I'd had the co-ordination, I would have pushed it away. I didn't want it there. I felt too betrayed.

'What can we do for him?' I asked eventually. 'Dr Bradshaw said that he could go on levodopa and that might slow the neurodegeneration. Or at least help with the symptoms.'

'It might,' Dr Enderby said. 'But there's more chance that it won't. You have to be prepared for that. PSP is very difficult to treat effectively.'

'Okay. So what else is there?'

'Simple physiotherapy tends to have the best results. It won't help with the visual problems, of course, but it should counter some of the locomotive dysfunction, at least for a while.'

'But what about *real* treatments? Other drugs—'

'Alex, I'm sure that Dr Bradshaw has been through all of the treatment options with you. I'm afraid I can't tell you anything new. There aren't any miracle cures on the horizon.'

'But things are improving all the time, aren't they? I mean, neurology's advanced more in the last ten years than in the whole of the previous century. You told me that yourself.'

'Yes, that's true. And I'm sure that in another fifty years – maybe in another twenty years – the field will have changed almost beyond recognition. I've no doubt that someday all of these neurological disorders will go the same way as smallpox. But we're not there yet. I'm sorry. I know it's not what you want to hear right now.'

'But you must know *something*. What about new treatments that are still in development? Drug trials? It doesn't matter if they aren't proven yet.'

'Alex, you know what I know. If there was anything else, I'd tell you.'

I was starting to shake again. I tried to focus on my breathing. I couldn't.

'Alex?' Dr Enderby said. 'Alex, I want you to look at me.'

I looked at him.

'Do you know what's really going to help Isaac over the coming months? Just being there for him. Being his friend. Respecting and supporting his decisions. That's what's going to make a difference to him. I know it's a terrible position to be in – especially at your age – but I also know that you're going to cope with it. It might not feel like it now, but you've got a lot of strength in you. And so has Isaac. I've only got a few phone calls to go on, but in all honesty, it seems to me that he's coping as well as anyone could in these circumstances. But he still needs your friendship and your support. He doesn't need you tearing yourself in two looking for a solution that doesn't exist. He's accepted what's happening. Now you have to do the same.'

'He's seen a lot of terrible things in his life,' I said.

'Yes, I know.'

'I think that's why he's coping so well now.'

'Yes, you might be right.'

'But it's also why this is so unfair. He shouldn't have to go through this as well.'

'No, he shouldn't. No one should have to go through this. But dwelling on that thought is not going to help in the slightest. You know that, don't you?'

'Yes.'

'Because sometimes chance and circumstance can seem like the most appalling injustice, but we just have to adapt. That's all we can do.'

'Yes, I know that too.'

'I know you do,' Dr Enderby said. 'You *should* know it. Understanding and accepting that you have a permanent illness does not mean being a slave to it. It's the first step you have to take so that you can go on living your life. And I think right now that's exactly what Isaac's trying to do. He wants to make the most of whatever time he's got. We need to support him in this.'

I wiped my eyes and nodded.

'Are you going to tell him?' I asked. 'You know, that I wasn't able to keep his confidence?'

'No, Alex. I won't tell him. But I think you should. I think you should tell him as soon as possible. Just be honest. After that, you might find that things start to get a little easier.'

Dr Enderby was right. Mr Peterson was holding up remarkably well. Too well, really. And it wasn't that he was in denial or anything like that; his reaction was the polar opposite to mine. In private, he was perfectly able to acknowledge his illness and what it meant. He told me how he was feeling day to day. He kept me updated on his symptoms. These were still relatively minor at this point, but he was more able – or more willing – to spot the little signs that had been creeping into his life for some months. Standing and sitting were sometimes a bit of a trial, as were eating and picking up the post from the floor – anything that required a certain amount of balance or hand–eye co-ordination. In general, the symptoms were worse first thing in the morning and late at night. Mr Peterson said that some mornings, coming down the stairs, he was sure that God was testing him. I thought it was good that he could make jokes like that, but at this point, I couldn't bring myself to respond in kind. It felt too forced. If I managed a weak smile, I was doing well.

His visual problems were still his primary and most persistent symptom. He described his difficulty 'aiming' his eyes as being similar to having a kind of blind spot. Now that he knew it was there, he could make sure he checked it, but this took a conscious effort on his part. Scrolling his eyes up or down no longer felt like a natural, automatic response. It had become an act that required focus, planning and memory, and because of this, he was increasingly happy to let me do the driving when he needed to go to the shop or the post office. My competence behind the wheel was now beyond question – at least on these short, local trips – and it seemed highly unlikely that we'd be pulled over in the village. A police car was a rare sight in Lower Godley. Mr Peterson said that if, by any chance, the police *did* stop us, he'd claim full responsibility for the situation. I could plead ignorance or coercion. Given his condition, he no longer thought it likely that any judge would want to send him to the Big House, and we both agreed that safety should come first.

But if Mr Peterson was starting to make concessions with

his driving, he was doing no such thing with his reading. Even with his faltering vision (perhaps *because* of his faltering vision) he was still determined to see our Kurt Vonnegut book club through to its conclusion. He wouldn't hear of cancelling it. By the time we got to *Timequake*, the final novel on the itinerary I'd devised some fourteen months earlier, he could read only in short, five- to ten-minute bursts, and only at certain times of day – usually nine till twelve and three till seven. Any earlier or later was a strain. He was already having to use his finger to follow the text down the page, like a child learning to read. But he stuck with it nevertheless. It took him the best part of a month, but by the time of our final meeting, he was done. He knew it would be the last novel he'd ever read for himself.

Of course, no one else in the book club knew about his condition – no one other than myself and Dr Enderby. We were still the *only* people who knew. Even after I'd moved beyond the denial stage, I didn't see much point in telling my mother, although Mr Peterson had again said that this would be okay, and it wouldn't be breaking his confidence. He seemed to think it was important for me to talk to her, but, really, that felt like a step too far. Acknowledging reality for myself was one thing. Having to explain what was happening – and what was going to happen – to another person was something else entirely. That would make it *too* real. And I soon came to wonder if this might also be Mr Peterson's reason for keeping his illness so completely to himself.

It seemed to me that after the first couple of months, he might have brought himself to tell a few more people. He got on well with Mrs Griffith, and with Fiona Fitton. There *were* people he could have talked to, and I knew that they would have wanted to help in any way they could. I also knew that at some point – maybe not all that far in the future – this kind of support was going to be of the utmost importance. But the future was the one subject that was out of bounds. Because for all of his coping skills, Mr Peterson still refused to make any practical plans or decisions. He hadn't yet committed to any of the treatment options offered by the hospital. The information pack they had sent him, so far as I could ascertain, had remained unopened. He told me that right now he just wanted to go on living day to day. He was determined to stick to his normal routines for as long as possible. When I pointed out that things like physiotherapy and home help came with waiting lists – that you couldn't just sign up and expect immediate care – he said he simply wasn't prepared to worry about such matters at the present moment, and he didn't want me to worry either. But this was easier said than done.

I knew that there would come a point when clinging to 'normality' would no longer be possible. Sooner or later, Mr Peterson's independence was going to start to slip away from him; Dr Bradshaw had been very clear on this point. He'd *have* to start telling people eventually. He was going to require extensive medical and practical support. In the longer term, delaying – refusing point blank to make any decisions – was not going to help him. It was not a sensible strategy. At the back of my mind, in a dark, distant corner, I'd started to question if Mr Peterson was coping with his situation as well as Dr Enderby and I had first presumed.

For some time, I debated whether or not I should raise this concern with Dr Enderby when I saw him at our final book club meeting, but when it came down to it, I decided not to. (I thought I knew exactly what he'd say: that we had to go on honouring Mr Peterson's decisions and respecting his right to follow his own path.) Instead, we talked about me. Dr Enderby seemed very concerned to know how *I* was holding up. I told him the truth: that there were good days and bad days, but mostly I was trying to think positively and constructively. I was hoping for the best and prepared for the worst. Dr Enderby said this was always a sensible policy.

What I didn't tell him was exactly what my 'preparedness' meant.

I thought that if Mr Peterson had anything between two to five years left, as my research indicated, then I'd definitely have to take some time out from my education. This would probably be between school and college, or maybe between college and university, if all went well. Since he didn't have a family, it was obvious to me that no one else was going to be able to care for Mr Peterson on a full-time basis. It *had* to be me. The only problem was, I didn't know how he'd react to this proposal. I anticipated some resistance. But this was the one good thing about his refusal to make any plans. It gave me plenty of time to think things through properly, to go over all the contingencies. By the time he was ready to confront what was going to happen next, I planned to have a full arsenal of arguments ready to deploy.

While this inner drama played out, I tried at all times to maintain a neutral exterior, but this was not something that came naturally to me. There were several occasions, at that final meeting of the Secular Church, when I found myself wishing that I could be more like Dr Enderby, who, of course, was very practised at keeping all sorts of confidences (being a doctor) and never lost his composure (being a Buddhist). But to me, much of the time, a calm exterior felt like a deception; and, as I think I've mentioned, deception has never been my strongest suit.

The thing that probably saved me was that everyone was acting kind of oddly that day. I suppose it was because everything was coming to an end, and in my experience, there's often a lot of excess emotion floating around at the conclusion of long-term projects – even when that conclusion has been a successful one. It was hanging there in the air, like a thin mist, and if I appeared distant and subdued, it was probably not as noticeable as it might have been in different circumstances. Added to this, I should point out that my demeanour was certainly not the strangest that day. That accolade, as it turned out, would fall to Mr Peterson himself. In an afternoon of atypical behaviour, his stood out as *extremely* atypical. Of course, I understood the reasons for this – I thought – but I had no idea what everyone else would make of his sudden transformation.

Mr Peterson was not given to excess sentimentality. Nor was he one for long, elaborate speeches. But that day, he made it quite clear that he wanted to be the last person to speak, and that he planned to speak at some length. There were some 'philosophical' themes, close to his heart, that he wished to address in bringing matters to a close (and Mr Peterson was certainly not given to philosophizing). For a while, as he spoke, I was convinced that he was going to tell everyone about his illness. He seemed to be building up to it. But as it turned out, he said nothing directly. He stuck more or less to the point, and kept his focus on *Timequake*. Only Dr Enderby and I knew that he was also talking about himself, about his own situation; and we still managed to misinterpret what he was *really* trying to say.

'For various reasons,' Mr Peterson began, innocuously enough, 'it's taken me a very long time to read this book. Or to *re*-read it, I should say, because of course I read it when it first came out – about a decade ago, I guess. And I remember thinking at that time that it was probably the most irreverent of Vonnegut's books. A great read, of course, but not a book that took itself at all seriously.

'Well, having read it a whole lot more slowly this time round, I have to say my original impression has changed some. I guess what was driven home was something I should've already known: with Vonnegut, you can't take any kind of irreverence at face value. The funnier the joke, and the more light-hearted the approach, the more serious the implications tend to be. He said something along those lines himself, I believe – several times. Laughter, irreverence, absurdity – as often as not, these things have their roots buried deep in despair.

'The idea that time might suddenly loop back on itself, so that a whole decade of events gets replayed on autopilot, is, of course, completely absurd. It's a farce, and it plays out as a farce in the novel. It's the engine that drives the comedy, but not something to be taken seriously. Or so you might think. Because re-reading the story this time round, I found a weird thing happening. I found that I *was* taking this idea seriously. And the further I got through the book, the less farcical it seemed.

'What if you really did have to relive the last ten years of your life? Or even your whole life? Believe it or not, this idea interested me enough to do some background research – and I know that's usually more Alex's thing. But here's what I found.

'Vonnegut certainly wasn't the first one to dream up the idea of time turning back on itself. Friedrich Nietzsche, the German philosopher, actually came up with an almost identical idea in one of his books, *Thus Spoke Zarathustra*, about a hundred years earlier. Now, I've never been one for philosophy, as such. I tend to think that our morals come from our gut, and everything else is either common sense or window-dressing. A month ago, if you'd said "Zarathustra" to me, I'd have assumed you were talking Strauss. But I think I'm getting off the point. Let me tell you what Nietzsche said in his book. He said that there is no afterlife in the normal, religious sense – no heaven, no hell, no purgatory. But there isn't "nothing" either. Instead, after we die, things simply start again from scratch. We live our whole life again, exactly as it was, nothing changing from birth to death. And then the same thing happens again and again and again, on and on for ever. He called this idea the "Eternal Return".

'Well, apparently, Nietzsche may not have believed this at all – not in any literal sense. But he wrote it down in character, like he believed every word. The point of this was to set up a kind of thought experiment. He wanted the reader to take the idea seriously, to give it credence, so that he'd be forced to confront the following question: if true, is this a pleasant idea? Or, put differently: if you had to relive your life exactly as it was – same successes and failures, same happiness, same miseries, same mixture of comedy and tragedy – would you want to? Was it worth it? And it's the same thing with Vonnegut, I think.

'Anyway, if you'll bear with me a minute longer, I think there's also a second part to this thought experiment that's just as important. This concerns free will. For Nietzsche, the Eternal Return was also a way of thinking about free will from an atheist's perspective, which, of course, was still a minority perspective in those days. The Eternal Return was another way of presenting the idea that there simply *isn't* anything beyond this life. This is all there is, and if there's any purpose to be found, then it's gonna have to be found in the here and now, through our own endeavours and without any supernatural guidance. And I think for Nietzsche this idea was, frankly, a real kick up the ass. It meant that we all had a responsibility to make the best possible choices – to try our damnedest not to blow our only shot.

'Well, I think Vonnegut might've gone along with most of that too, but he also had his own ideas on free will. Because for Vonnegut, free will isn't always a given. It's something we take too much for granted – he would've agreed with Nietzsche on that – but it's also something that can quite suddenly disappear. Part of *his* thought experiment in *Timequake* involves exactly this scenario. People are forced to live on autopilot – knowing full well what's going to happen in the next ten years and powerless to change it in even the smallest way. It's treated like the most irreverent aspect of the story, but, deep down, it's the least irreverent idea. Because Vonnegut was a man who knew exactly what the loss of free will felt like. As a POW, he was forced to watch an entire city burning to the ground – and there wasn't a damn thing he or God or anybody else could do about it. All he could do was help count the corpses – all one hundred and thirty thousand of them.

'So I think Kurt Vonnegut knew the value of free will as well as anyone, but he also understood its limitations – how and where it could suddenly be taken away. And I'd like to conclude with the sentence that best sums up this position, which is Vonnegut's citation of the Serenity Prayer, in *Slaughterhouse-Five*. Of course, there were quotes from *Timequake* I could have chosen instead, but none, I think, that hits the nail so precisely on the head. And it's another one that, coming from an atheist, sounds a whole lot more facetious than it actually is:

'"God, grant me the serenity to accept the things I cannot change, the courage to change the things I can, and wisdom always to tell the difference."

'Amen.'

There was a moment of silence. I held my breath. I was waiting for the announcement that never came. Instead, Mr Peterson cleared his throat, and then said: 'On just as important a note, I'd like to thank Alex for setting this thing up. If anyone's still got the impression that I had anything to with organizing this group, rest assured, I did not. I thought the idea was completely crazy. I told him no one would come. That's the only reason I agreed to host it.'

There was a smattering of laughter. I thought Mr Peterson was probably warming to his role as speech-maker.

'Seriously, though,' he continued. 'Thank you, Alex. This has meant a lot to me, and I'm sure I'm not alone in that.'

And there may have been more as well, but if there was, I was unable to hear it. I had gone the colour of the inside of a watermelon. Then I felt my eyes starting to burn.

'I need to excuse myself for a moment,' I said.

In the bathroom, I started to cry. I washed my face thoroughly before rejoining the group.

* * *

It was an hour or so later, after everyone else had left, that Mr Peterson reiterated what he'd said earlier, as if once wasn't sufficient. 'I meant it,' he repeated gravely. 'I'm very grateful for the past fourteen months. I want you to remember that in the future.'

I knew it was the kind of sentence that required a sincere, meaningful response, but I thought if I talked at any length, I'd start crying again.

'Okay,' I said.

It was very inadequate.

And it was this, and only this, that made me return later on. As I've said, I had a general feeling that something was off-kilter that day, but nothing that would have motivated me to check up on Mr Peterson or anything like that. If anything, I had been somewhat reassured by the last part of his Kurt Vonnegut speech. It told me that he was finally prepared to face the future. He was asking for the serenity to accept the things he could not change. That was how I misinterpreted him. I focussed on the wrong part. It was pure chance that I happened to go back that evening.

I wasn't planning to stay for more than two minutes. I thought all I needed to do was turn up at the door and say the things I should have said earlier: that the past fourteen months had meant a lot to me too, and whatever happened next, he didn't have to face it alone. It wasn't the sort of thing that could wait until the next day.

But when I knocked at the front door, there was no answer. I wasn't that surprised or worried. Mr Peterson didn't always come to the door straight away, especially when he'd been smoking, as was normal at this time of the evening, and had fallen into a doze.

I knocked again, then tried the door. It was unlocked. The hallway smelled of marijuana. That *was* unusual. To my knowledge, Mr Peterson only ever smoked outside, or on the porch if it was raining. Mrs Peterson had not liked the smell of the weed, not when it got into the upholstery, anyway, and Mr Peterson always said that old habits die hard. But, really, I think it was a habit he'd chosen to stick to.

I called his name, but there was no response. I figured he'd fallen asleep in the chair, and when I entered the living room, I saw that I was right. He was slumped slightly to one side, with a blanket draped across his legs. The ashtray was next to him on the side table. Next to the ashtray was an almost empty glass of water, and next to that was an open notepad. This is what he'd written on the notepad, in large black letters: *'Please do not resuscitate.'*

I slapped his face. There was no response, but his cheek was warm, and I thought that he was still breathing. It took me only a few seconds to find the empty packaging for the pills he had taken: diazepam, paracetamol and codeine. I knew this would be important information.

I ripped his note from the notepad, shoved it in my pocket, and called 999.

17

SECTIONED

His suicide note arrived two days later, in the post. This is what it said:

> There's nothing you could have done. It was my choice and mine alone. I wanted to die peacefully and with dignity. If you don't understand that now, I hope someday you will. Please forgive me.

I had no real point of comparison, but still, I thought it was a pretty lousy note, all things considered. I filed it all the same.

It had been posted second class to ensure a sufficient delay in its arrival. He had posted another letter, marked URGENT, directly through the letterbox of the doctors' surgery, informing his GP of his intentions and asking that an ambulance be sent to recover his body asap. He also requested that my mother be informed so that she could be the one to tell me. That seemed like the best way of doing things. My mother could break it to me gently when I got home from school, by which time the ambulance would have had at least seven hours to take him to the morgue. He'd planned it so there was zero chance of my being the one who discovered his corpse. I thought that was considerate of him.

Of course, when he awoke, he was furious.

The ambulance had taken us to Yeovil Hospital. It was a repeat of the trip I'd made some five and a third years earlier, after the meteor. At that time, as you know, I was unconscious for two weeks, and when I woke up, I thought I was in heaven. Mr Peterson was only unconscious for one night, and when he woke up, he knew straight away that something had gone wrong. Even though he was extremely out of it, he had no delusion that Yeovil Hospital was the hereafter. It smelled too much of starch.

By the time he was briefly awake, I had been sent home with my mother, and the following afternoon, when we returned, he was asleep again. One of his nurses told us it was very unlikely that he'd be lucid enough to talk before visiting hours ended because they'd given him quite a lot of morphine. I'm not sure this was one hundred per cent orthodox in terms of approved medical procedure, but I could understand why they'd done it. He'd started complaining the moment he woke up. He said that this was like the worst hangover anyone anywhere had ever had to endure, which wasn't that surprising. He'd managed to poison himself quite severely before the doctors pumped his stomach. He kept buzzing the nurse to tell her that this experience was worse than Vietnam, and if they weren't going to let him die, they should at least put him to sleep for a while. Eventually, a doctor was called in, and he agreed that they couldn't just leave Mr Peterson as he was. It wasn't fair – not on the staff, and certainly not on the other patients in the ward. But unfortunately, because of the recent abuse Mr Peterson's liver and kidneys had suffered, administering any standard tranquillizer was out of the question. Instead, they shot him up, and repeated this procedure every four to six hours for the next twenty-four.

Consequently, there was little point us visiting that day.

I told my mother that if it was okay with her, I'd be taking the rest of the week off school. She agreed this was a sensible plan.

Ellie took me in the next day, and insisted on accompanying me up to the ward. I thought my mother had probably asked her to do this, but I wasn't sure. Equally, it could have been morbid curiosity. It was hard to tell with Ellie. Either way, I was glad of the lift.

Mr Peterson was thin, unshaven and scowling. He looked quite ghoulish, to be honest with you, like he'd returned from the dead – which I suppose shouldn't have been all that surprising. His expression didn't change as we seated ourselves on one side of the bed.

'Hello,' I said.

'Hello.'

His voice matched his face.

'This is Ellie. She gave me a lift in. I hope you don't mind her being here? She just wanted to stay long enough to make sure I'm okay.'

'I'm not crazy about *either* of you being here,' Mr Peterson said. 'But I doubt I'll get much say in that either.'

I ignored this.

'How are you feeling?'

'How do you *think* I'm feeling?'

'I think you're probably feeling terrible.'

'I'm feeling terrible. You know, they're not gonna let me leave this place. Not for the foreseeable future. It's official. I've been sectioned. If I try to leave, they'll forcibly detain me under the Mental Health Act of 1842, or some such horseshit. It's barbaric! I hope you're pleased.'

'I'm pleased that you're alive,' I admitted.

'Great. So that makes one of us, at least.'

I looked at Ellie. She rolled her eyes at me. For some reason, Ellie's demeanour hadn't changed one iota in the past two days. Either she'd decided that it was best to act normally with me, or she wasn't acting, and attempted suicide was just one more thing on the long list of things that didn't faze her in the slightest.

'You had no right to do what you did,' Mr Peterson continued. 'It wasn't your choice to make!'

'I see,' I said. 'And what would *you* have done if our positions had been reversed?'

'I would have respected your wishes. I would have let you die.'

I ignored this too. 'I've brought you some things from home,' I said, gesturing at the bag on the floor. 'Some clothes and books – things like that.'

'Books – great! That'll make things easier. You know I can't read worth a damn right now!'

'There's also some music. Schubert's fifth, Mendelssohn's third, Mozart's Clarinet Concerto, Mahler's fourth—'

'I would have preferred his sixth.'

'You're not well enough for his sixth.'

'What about Bach?'

'I'll bring Bach next time.'

'The cello suites?'

'Anything *but* the cello suites.'

'Jesus, kid! I don't even get to decide what I listen to?'

'There's a time and a place for Bach's cello suites, and we both know it's not while you're recovering in hospital. I'm trying to help you.'

'You want to help me?'

'Yes, of course I want to help you.'

'Fine. Then bring me something else.'

'I'll bring you whatever you want – within reason.'

'Bring me some pot.'

'I'm not bringing you pot.'

'I'm gonna go nuts in here.'

'It's ludicrous. Where are you planning on smoking it? The bathroom?'

'If I have to.'

'They're not going to release you any sooner if they catch you smoking pot.'

'They've had me on fuckin' heroin for the last twenty-four hours!'

'I'm not bringing you pot.'

Mr Peterson turned to Ellie. 'What about you, girl? Will you bring me some pot?'

Ellie regarded him frankly for a few seconds. 'I hardly think pot'll make you *less* suicidal. Do you?'

Mr Peterson snorted. 'I appreciate your concern – and your tact – but that's not something you need to worry about.'

Ellie shrugged. 'It's just my opinion. As far as I can see, you'd be better off taking some stimulants.'

Mr Peterson turned back to me. 'Jesus! Is she for real?'

'I don't know,' I said. 'Possibly.'

'She has a name!' Ellie pointed out.

'Young lady,' Mr Peterson said, 'it's too late for me to worry about learning new names. My brain's turning to mush – as I'm sure Alex has told you. It's not a pleasant thing to have to face, and the pot makes it just that little bit easier. Maybe you can appreciate that?'

'Tell me my name and I'll bring you some pot. How's that for a deal?'

'Sally.'

'*Ellie.*'

'No one's going to bring you any pot,' I said. 'Ellie's right. It's not going to help you.'

'You know, I'm gettin' pretty goddamn sick of people telling me what's *not* gonna help me.'

'Even if it did help you, the nurses are going to confiscate it within about ten seconds of you lighting up. Can't you see how ridiculous you're being?'

'This whole situation's ridiculous! And it's your fault.'

'That's not fair.'

'If you're not willing to help me, I'd like you to leave.'

'You're acting like a child.'

'Just go.'

'Fine. I'll be back later with your Bach.'

'If I were you, I wouldn't bother.'

'If you keep on like this, I might not.'

'Right now, that would suit me just fine. You've taken away the only choice I had left to me. I only hope *you* never have to find out what that feels like.'

I left without looking back.

*   *   *

Ellie caught up with me a few moments later at the Coke machine. 'Well, that wasn't exactly what I was expecting,' she said. 'You know, Woods, the deeper you delve, the weirder your life gets. Is he always like that?'

I ignored her. The Coke machine wasn't accepting one of my five-pence pieces. I kept feeding it in and it kept rolling straight back out again. I fumbled in my pocket for more change.

'Honestly, Woods, you must have the patience of a saint. You do realize he's insane, right?' I went on ignoring her. She touched my arm. 'Seriously, Alex. Are you okay?'

'No,' I said. 'I'm not okay. I'm upset and I'm angry.'

'You *should* be angry. He had no right saying what he said to you. Here – take this.' She pressed a pound coin into my hand. The vending machine ate it without giving any change. 'I don't care how ill he is,' Ellie continued. 'Some of the things he said to you were completely out of line.'

'Maybe.'

'Definitely!'

I sat down in one of the chairs opposite the Coke machine. Ellie sat beside me.

'*Are* you gonna come back later? Because I wouldn't blame you if you decided not to.'

I shrugged. 'I guess I'll come back tomorrow.'

Ellie stayed quiet for a few moments, rolling her tongue in her cheek. It seemed like she might be trying to figure out how best to phrase something. This was not usual for her. 'Okay,' she said eventually. 'But you should be prepared for the fact that it might be another wasted trip.'

'It doesn't matter if it's a wasted trip,' I said. 'I still have to come back.'

'You don't *have* to come back.'

'Yes, I do.'

'There's no point being a martyr. Seriously, I know you've got some weird ideas about morals and shit, but you can't help someone who doesn't want your help.'

'Don't be dense, Ellie. This hasn't got anything to do with morals. And I'm not expecting any miraculous overnight changes. I know that the next few days are likely to be just as bad.'

'Okay. So if you know that, then why bother? Why do you have to come back straight away tomorrow and go through the exact same thing again?'

'Because he's my friend and he needs me here – even if he doesn't realize it. Even if he spends the whole time shouting at me. If that's what he needs to do, I'll put up with it.'

Ellie rolled her eyes through a complete circuit. 'Jesus Christ, Woods! That makes no sense whatsoever! Not the part about you being friends. I mean, that's a little out there – actually, it's just plain fucking bizarre – but, still, I can see it all the same. But as far as the rest of it goes, I'm at a loss. He gets riled up, you go home feeling like shit – how's that helping anyone? Give him a few days to cool off.'

I shrugged. 'I don't expect it to make sense to you. But it makes sense to me. I know what he's like. And right now he's scared to death. He's scared and he's got no idea how to handle it.'

'So he rants at you?'

'Exactly.'

'And what – expects you to handle it just fine?'

'I *can* handle it . . . I'll have to handle it.'

'Jesus, Woods, you really *are* a fucking saint.'

'I'm not a saint. I'm just being practical.'

Ellie shook her head.

'Are you ready to leave?' I asked.

'Yes. *Please*. Let's get out of here. Hospitals do my head in.'

'I didn't make you come up,' I pointed out.

'That's not what I meant. Let's just go.'

But as soon as we were out in the car park, Ellie decided that she needed to go back and use the 'ladies' room' because she couldn't last out for the half-hour trip back to Glastonbury and apparently had only limited powers of foresight. I waited in the muggy car for what seemed like an eternity, wishing that I'd had enough change to buy another Diet Coke. I made a mental note to bring a two-litre bottle next time.

'You took an inordinate amount of time in the toilet,' I complained when Ellie returned.

'Fuck, Woods! What kind of thing is *that* to say to a girl?'

She started the car and immediately stalled.

'You left it in ge—'

'I know!'

'Also, you should remember the speed bumps on the way out, because coming in, you—'

'Just shut the fuck up and let me drive!'

As soon as we were past the roundabout, she turned the stereo up as loud as it would go. For some reason, Ellie and I could never sustain a conversation for more than a few minutes at a time.

When I returned with my mother, the next day, we were informed that Mr Peterson had been moved to more suitable, 'longer-term' accommodation. This turned out to be the psychiatric

ward – abbreviated to the 'psych ward', or simply 'psych', whenever the nurses were talking among themselves. I found this
casual shortening a little *too* casual for my taste, but my mother
seemed to think that for most people it was more likely to be
reassuring; most people, she said, were not that comfortable
with medical polysyllables. From her personal experience, she
knew that a similar shortening occurred on gynaecology, which
was always abbreviated to 'gynae' – but this was a conversation
I decided not to pursue.

Located on the second-to-top floor, 'psych' turned out to
have a surprisingly sedate atmosphere compared to the general
wards below. It immediately struck me that there was much less
bustle and pedestrian traffic. There seemed to be fewer staff
too. I'd later discover that there were also fewer patients, each
of whom tended to have fewer visitors. And, generally, the
patients could all be seen and medicated at the same set times
each day, which helped to keep things very orderly and regi-
mented. Of course, there were some 'problem patients', but
there was also an unusually large number of private rooms on
the ward, which stood ready for any person whose behaviour
was deemed 'potentially disruptive or upsetting'. These were
mostly psychotics, which meant people experiencing psychosis
– schizophrenics and so forth – not people who were just
uncommonly angry, like Mr Peterson. He was in one of the
general, four-person rooms. His bed was in the far left corner,
next to the window, from which there was a view of uninter-
rupted grey sky. I thought that unless the sun came out, the
staff would be better off closing the curtains.

My mother insisted on 'popping in to say hello' – as if this
were a social call – and proceeded to talk at some length about

Lucy's kittens, who had been born (curiously enough) on my birthday, the autumnal equinox. Since this was an unusually large and scruffy litter, my mother was still struggling to find homes for them. I doubt this was of any great interest to Mr Peterson right then, but he nodded his head every so often to show that he was listening (for some reason, he always displayed an uncharacteristic degree of patience with my mother) before politely declining her suggestion that perhaps he'd like to 'take one off our hands'. I don't know what she was thinking, but it wasn't a joke, since my mother doesn't make jokes. Either it was problem-solving on the fly, or she'd thought matters through beforehand and come to the un-fathomable conclusion that Mr Peterson's situation called for a kitten. Whatever the case, I apologized on her behalf after she'd left.

'Your mother's your mother,' Mr Peterson said. 'I'm sure her intentions are sincere.'

'Yes, probably,' I agreed. 'She's still insane, though. *She* should be on the psych ward.'

Mr Peterson shrugged.

'I brought you the *Goldberg Variations* and some more AA batteries,' I said.

'Thank you.'

'Should I ask if you're feeling any better?'

'I'm not feeling any worse.'

'That's something, I suppose.'

'They sent the shrink round yesterday. He's put me on Prozac. Prozac! He thinks I'm depressed.'

'Aren't you depressed?'

'I wasn't depressed.'

'You did try to kill yourself,' I pointed out.

'Yes. That's what he said too. Apparently that's a classic symptom. It's not thought a *sane* plan of action for someone in my situation.'

'I'm sure he knows what he's doing.'

'You've got way too much faith in doctors, kid. They ask some of the most moronic questions you've ever heard. Am I feeling hopeless or bleak about the future? You'd think they hadn't bothered to read my file.'

'I'm sure you're exaggerating.'

'Stick around and judge for yourself. One or more of them'll be back later on for the ward rounds.'

'Do you want me to stick around?'

'Why not? Later you can all get together and discuss what's best for me.'

I didn't say anything, but I didn't look away either. I just waited. I thought Mr Peterson reddened fractionally.

'You know, that girl came back to see me,' he said. 'After you'd left.'

'Which girl?'

'Don't be an idiot. You know the girl. The girl with the bangs.'

It took some time to establish that Mr Peterson was talking about Ellie's fringe.

'So are you and her—'

'No!'

'Why not? I think she likes you.'

'No, I don't think so. And certainly not like that. As far as I can tell, she only likes morons. Older morons.'

'I'm sure she'll grow out of that.'

'I'm not comfortable having this conversation.'

Mr Peterson shrugged. 'Fine. I'm just saying that for someone who doesn't like you she certainly seemed pissed when she thought I'd upset you.'

'That's just how she is. She's always pissed off.'

'She was *extremely* pissed off. She told me that I was being an asshole and right now I didn't deserve any sympathy.'

'Yes, that sounds like the kind of thing she'd say,' I acknowledged. 'She's quite direct.'

'Yes, she is. But in this case she was also right. I was being an asshole.'

'Yes.'

'I'm sorry.'

I shrugged.

'But you have to understand *what* I'm sorry about.'

'Okay. So tell me.'

'I'm sorry about what you had to go through. I know it must have been horrible.'

'Yes. It was.'

'But I'm not sorry about what I did and I'm not gonna pretend otherwise. I have to be frank about that. It just wasn't meant to turn out this way. I thought I'd planned it so it *couldn't* turn out this way. I had no way of knowing you'd come back. And I wish to God you hadn't.'

'Thanks,' I said. 'That's one hell of an apology. You know, even if I hadn't come back, there's still no guarantee that things would have turned out all that differently. Your planning was lousy. You took so many pills you were just as likely to vomit as to die. And as for the codeine, God knows what you were thinking there!'

'I was thinkin' they were the strongest painkillers I had and they'd be the easiest to overdose on.'

'It doesn't work like that. Codeine's just about the hardest painkiller to overdose on – especially if you're used to taking it.'

'I didn't know that.'

'Obviously! So you should get it out of your head that *I'm* to blame for the position you're in now. Your plan was lousy!'

'Fine, point taken! I guess next time I'll do more research.'

A thick silence descended for about a minute. I threw the *Goldberg Variations* on the bedside table and went for a walk.

Dr Bedford, Mr Peterson's psychiatrist, turned out to be a very large man with huge piano-player hands but a surprisingly soft voice. Later on, Mr Peterson told me that this was not surprising at all, since all shrinks were trained to speak like this and had to master 'the voice' before they were allowed to practise their particular brand of medicine. I decided this was almost certainly bunkum.

'How are you feeling today?' Dr Bedford asked.

'I'm feeling just fine,' Mr Peterson said.

'It's important for you to answer these questions as honestly as possible,' Dr Bedford reminded him.

'I'm sick of this place and I want out,' Mr Peterson said. It wasn't clear whether he was referring to the psychiatric ward or the universe more broadly. Dr Bedford, rather optimistically, plumped for the former.

'You know that's not possible right now,' he said softly. 'I think it would be much better if you put it out of your mind and focus on taking one day at a time. We'll discharge you the moment you're well enough, but not a moment sooner.'

Mr Peterson swore loudly. 'Doctor, have you *read* my file? You do know what's gonna happen to me in the not-too-distant future?'

Dr Bedford nodded solemnly. 'Yes. I know.'

'My eyes are gonna get a whole lot worse, and so are my legs. Eventually, I won't be able to walk at all. I'll be in a wheelchair. I won't be able to go to the bathroom unaided. I won't be able to speak or swallow solid foods. It's very possible that I'll die choking on my own vomit.'

'I understand why you feel the way you do.'

'If you understood, we wouldn't be having this conversation. Things aren't gonna get any brighter for me.'

'It might seem that way now. That doesn't—'

'Alex!' Mr Peterson spun to face me. 'Since Dr Bedford seems to have some kind of mental block when it comes to my voice, perhaps *you'd* be so good as to tell him that I'm not insane. I'm thinkin' a whole lot more rationally about this than he is.'

I felt my cheeks reddening. 'I'm sure Dr Bedford knows how to do his job,' I said.

Mr Peterson growled.

'No one thinks you're insane,' Dr Bedford continued, very calmly. 'That's not why you're here. You know that. I've told you that. You're here because you're deemed to pose a significant risk to yourself if released.'

'Yes, that's right! To *myself*.'

'Your actions have consequences for others too. I'm sure you realize that. It's not just yourself you'd be hurting.'

Dr Bedford glanced in my direction. I went a shade redder. Mr Peterson exploded.

'Oh, great! That's just fuckin' wonderful! When all else fails, there's always emotional blackmail! You think I should stay alive for other people? Spread the suffering around for as long as possible?'

Dr Bedford waited for a count of five. 'I think it would be better if I came back later. Try to get some rest.'

Then he left.

An oppressive silence dragged its feet for a few moments. Then Mr Peterson said:

'Well, kid, since you're still here, you might as well share your thoughts. What did you make of that?'

The problem was my thoughts were unclear. Too many nerves had been hit. I struggled with what I might say for some time, and then shrugged ineffectually. 'I don't think you're going to get out of here anytime soon,' I said.

Mr Peterson looked for a while like he was going to make a retort, but eventually he just nodded gloomily. We were both tired of fighting.

18

PACT

'"Yossarian was in the hospital with a pain in his liver that fell just short of being jaundice. The doctors were puzzled by the fact that it wasn't quite jaundice. If it became jaundice they could treat it. If it didn't become jaundice and went away they could discharge him. But this just being short of jaundice all the time confused them."'

I paused in my reading. 'Is jaundice the one where you go yellow?'

'That's right. From the French *jaune*.'

'Oh, yes. Of course . . . I didn't know you spoke French.'

'I've picked up a bit, here and there.'

'In Vietnam? Vietnam used to be French, right?'

'Kid, do you wanna just read the book? It'd be nice to at least get past the first page before visiting hours are through.'

I nodded, cleared my throat and resumed.

'"Each morning they came around, three brisk and serious men with efficient mouths and inefficient eyes, accompanied by Nurse Duckett, one of the ward nurses who didn't like

Yossarian. They read the chart at the foot of the bed and asked impatiently about the pain. They seemed irritated when he told them it was exactly the same.

'"'Still no movement?' the full colonel dema—"'

Mr Peterson held up his hand like he was trying to stop traffic. 'Kid, please. *Don't* try to do an American accent.'

I folded the book with my index finger still inside, saving the page. 'I thought the dialogue might sound a bit weird in British English.'

'The whole thing sounds weird. I'll just have to get used to it. It's gonna be a whole lot easier than tryin' to get used to *that*.'

'It sounded okay in my head.'

'It wasn't okay. You couldn't get away with an accent like that in Hicksville, Alabama.'

'Oh.'

'Just read it clearly, in your normal voice. And speak up a bit. I don't want to have to strain for every word.'

'I didn't want to disturb the other patients,' I confessed.

'The other patients are already disturbed,' Mr Peterson pointed out, much too loudly. 'I don't think a bit of light reading's gonna do them any harm, do you?'

I had to concede I did not. There were two other patients sharing Mr Peterson's room and it seemed unlikely that either would be making complaints. The man opposite, who looked to be around the same age as Mr Peterson, was completely catatonic. He never even moved, let alone spoke. There was a woman who may have been his wife who visited him for half an hour each day, but neither she nor the doctors nor the nurses could elicit any sort of reaction from him, not even the slightest shift in the direction of his gaze, which was frozen on the window frame. He had feeding tubes down his throat and a catheter to drain his urine. I don't know how or if he passed solids.

The other man, in the next bed along, diagonally opposite Mr Peterson, looked to be around a hundred and fifty. He never said anything either, but this was because he was constantly scribbling away in a notepad – or, more likely, a succession of notepads. The rate at which he was writing, he must have been getting through at least one a day, though it was a mystery who was replenishing his supply. He never had visitors, so I suppose it must have been the nurses or the psychiatrists. They must have thought all this writing was therapeutic.

'He must be rewriting *War and Peace*,' Mr Peterson speculated. 'You know: the extended edition.'

I hadn't read *War and Peace*, but I understood what Mr Peterson meant: *War and Peace* was extraordinarily long. This is what it was famous for. It was about twelve times longer than *Slaughterhouse-Five* and three and a bit times longer than *Catch-22*, which was also a classic, and the only book that Mr Peterson said he felt like hearing in his current state of mind.

A few pages in, once I had stopped worrying about accents and had settled into my reading, I thought I understood what he was talking about. The first chapter of *Catch-22* was not particularly complimentary when it came to the subject of medical staff, and this was another reason I felt quite self-conscious about the volume at which Mr Peterson expected me to read. He claimed that this was because his head felt 'waterlogged' – a symptom he attributed to the Prozac – but I had my growing suspicions that this was only part of the truth. I thought it might also be for the benefit of Nurse

Holloway, who was currently carrying out various routine tasks in and around the room. I felt like I'd been drawn into some kind of petulant protest against his ongoing incarceration on psych.

Still, if this was the case, Nurse Holloway wasn't taking the bait – at least not at first. She went about her business in silence while I reluctantly narrated all those details about the inefficient doctors and unfeeling nurses. It was only when I got to the part where the Texan starts talking about the 'niggers' – '"They don't allow niggers in here. They got a special place for niggers"' – that she stopped what she was doing and raised her eyebrows.

'It's okay,' I reassured her, 'it's satirical.'

'It's more that it's in character,' Mr Peterson clarified.

'Yes, that's right,' I agreed, 'but I'm forbidden from doing the accents, so it might not have been obvious.'

'I don't care *what* it's in,' Nurse Holloway said. 'I hardly think it's suitable on the ward.'

'It's highly suitable,' Mr Peterson argued.

'Not if it's likely to offend or upset the other patients,' Nurse Holloway retorted.

'Who's getting upset?' Mr Peterson asked, pointing to the other inmates. 'The Catatonic? Count Tolstoy over there?'

The Catatonic didn't move. Count Tolstoy continued to scribble. Nurse Holloway planted her hands on her hips and said: 'I'm only asking for some consideration. Can you at least keep it down a little?'

Mr Peterson shook his head. 'No dice, I'm afraid. The Prozac seems to have screwed up my hearing.'

'I'll alert Dr Bedford as soon as I can.'

'I don't want to see Dr Bedford. There's nothing Dr Bedford can do for me – nothing short of takin' me off the damn things.'

'I suppose I could censor any words that might be deemed inappropriate on the ward,' I suggested. 'You know: just say "the N-word", "the S-word", "SOB", "MOFO", et cetera.'

'There aren't any MOFOs,' Mr Peterson said angrily. 'It's too early for that.'

'It's too early for any of this,' Nurse Holloway said. 'Please: a little consideration is all I'm asking.'

So I resumed *Catch-22* in a loud British accent, now editing the swear words as I went along. Luckily, there weren't too many, so it was only a mild irritation Mr Peterson had to bear – or possibly it wasn't an irritation at all. He might have been vaguely amused. It was difficult to tell. He lay quite still, with his eyes closed, while I worked my way through chapter one. When I'd finished, he didn't say anything, so, after a gulp of Diet Coke, I thought I might as well continue.

It was only when I'd finished the third chapter that I broached the subject I'd been turning over at the back of my mind for some time. It was something Mr Peterson and I hadn't discussed for a few days – at least since the visit from Dr Bedford. I think we'd been avoiding it because the semi-truce we'd fallen into was still very fragile. I, for one, was in no hurry to get into another argument. But now, having spent a straight half-hour reading aloud while Mr Peterson rested his eyes, I thought it unlikely I'd find a more opportune moment.

'Mr Peterson,' I began cautiously. Then I trailed off. I realized there wasn't a good way to phrase what I wanted to say. I rehearsed several versions in my head, and then opted for blunt simplicity. 'Mr Peterson, you really *don't* seem very depressed to me. Not any more, anyway.'

Mr Peterson snapped his eyes open. 'I wasn't depressed to begin with. I told you that.'

'Yes, I know.'

'Depressed was never the right word for what I was – or am. It's just a label shoved on me by some shrink with too many qualifications and not enough common sense.'

'But you are . . . well, you know. If they were to let you out tomorrow, I mean, you'd still . . .'

Mr Peterson had had enough of this bumbling line of enquiry. 'For God's sake, just spit it out, kid!'

'You still want to die!' I blurted.

Mr Peterson closed his eyes again. It took him some time to reply, and when he did, his voice wasn't cold, exactly, but there was still a kind of edge to it, like he was trying to deal with two or three different impulses. 'I don't want to die, kid,' he told me eventually. 'No one *wants* to die. But you know where I'm heading a little down the line. My future's already written. If I don't want to face that, there's only one way out.'

I counted my breaths for a few moments, then said: 'But your life's not so bad at the moment. What I mean is, there are still things that you can enjoy. There's still *Catch-22*. There's still Schubert's Symphony No.5 in B flat major. Your life isn't so terrible yet, and it might not be for some time to come. You don't know how long you might still have. It might be another two or three years.'

'It might be,' Mr Peterson acknowledged, then fell silent for a while. 'You're right. I have a life worth living at the moment, and I might still have a life worth living six months from now.

Even a year from now. I don't know. But what I *do* know is that sooner or later the balance is going to tip. Sooner or later, I'm gonna have a life I can no longer bear. And by that time, chances are there won't be a damn thing I can do about it. I'll be in some kind of hospice. I won't be able to stand or speak, let alone take the necessary steps to end it all. *That's* what's unbearable.'

'But what if it didn't have to be like that?' I asked quietly.

'It is gonna be like that. That's the point.'

'I could look after you.'

'No. You couldn't.'

'I could. I've—'

'You couldn't. It would be hell for both of us. No one's gonna be able to look after me. Not the way you mean.'

'But I *want* to. Honestly, I've thought this through. By then I won't have to go to school; I mean, I can defer and—'

'Kid, please. Trust me. I know what I'm talking about here. It's not an option.'

I waited and watched my breaths again, this time for a much longer count. I was determined to keep my voice steady.

'There must be something I can say to change your mind,' I said eventually.

'There isn't.'

His voice was like iron. I knew we'd reached a standstill.

'I think I'd better go now,' I said. 'I have one or two things I need to think about on my own. I can come back tomorrow, but I don't know what's going to happen after that. My mother wants me to go back to school on Monday.'

'Your mother's right: you should go back to school.'

I shrugged. 'I suppose I'll still be able to come in for the evening visiting hours.'

Mr Peterson looked as if he was going to say something to dissuade me, but after a while, his expression changed, and in the end, he just nodded.

The following morning, I went to Ellie's flat on the pretext that I should probably thank her for intervening on my behalf with Mr Peterson. Actually, this wasn't entirely a pretext. I'd not seen her since that afternoon, and I *did* think that I should thank her. But more than this, I suppose, it was just that I needed someone else to talk to, and my options in this department were limited. Turning things over and over in isolation had led me to a certain point, but I knew that to get any further I'd have to voice some ideas aloud, just to see how they sounded. But I certainly didn't go to Ellie expecting any kind of constructive input on her part. It was more that I'd hit a wall and needed someone to talk *around* the subject with – like when you come up against a problem that's just immune to normal logic.

Anyway, I think it was a little after eleven thirty when I knocked on the external door to the flat, which was round the back and up the metal fire-escape stairs. I'd figured that this was a reasonable hour to turn up at someone's house on a Sunday, though, for me, this was mostly a matter of guesswork. Since I got up at six thirty every morning – school days and weekends – and my mother was something of a lark as well, I had only a limited idea of what might constitute normal weekend sleeping patterns. But, still, I thought that I'd erred on the extreme side of caution. Nevertheless, it took two rounds of knocking before Ellie answered the door, and when she did, it was evident that while she was awake (obviously), she wasn't exactly 'up'. She was wearing a black T-shirt and shorts that were almost briefs, and she was suffering from quite a severe case of bed-head. She'd obviously not had the chance or inclination to groom herself yet. I deduced from her angry panda eyes that her make-up was yesterday's and she was not pleased to see me. I was instantly wrong-footed.

'Fuck, Woods!' Ellie groaned. 'What time do you call this?'

I looked at my watch, then realized it was almost certainly a rhetorical question. 'I thought you'd be up,' I apologized.

'I don't get up on Sundays.'

'Oh.'

'What do you want?'

'Nothing. I was just on my way to the hospital and—'

'I can't give you a lift. I don't have the car. I'd have thought your super-size brain would've grasped that. If it's with your mother, it can't be with me.'

'Yes, I realize that. That's not what I meant. I'm getting the bus, but I thought first—'

'Woods, for God's sake! I'm freezing my arse off here!'

'Yes, I can see that. Perhaps it'd be better if I came back some other—'

'If you want to come in, come in.'

'I don't want to disturb you if you're not up.'

Before I'd got halfway through this sentence, Ellie was already heading back through the kitchen towards the living room. 'You've already disturbed me, you moron. I'd hate for it to have been for nothing. Close the door behind you. It's got to be about minus thirty out there.'

It was November. I estimated the actual temperature to be around eight or nine degrees Celsius. But I didn't think it was worth bringing this up. I came in, took off my shoes and closed the door.

Although I'd been to the flat several times since Ellie had moved in, over a year ago, this must have been the first time I'd been there without my mother, and under these new circumstances, it made quite a different impression on me. Most of the furnishings were the same, of course, but nevertheless, the general atmosphere had changed to a significant degree. Essentially, it had taken on many of the characteristics of its tenant. It was clean enough, but dark, and rather untidy in places. The curtains were closed, the washing-up was dangerously over-stacked, and there was underwear everywhere. As far as I could see, it was hanging on every radiator in every room, though Ellie assured me that this was not a permanent feature of the décor. It just happened to be 'washing day'. But as you can probably imagine, it was still disconcerting from the visitor's point of view. There was simply nowhere you could place your gaze without there being all this black bunting hovering in your peripheral vision.

As for the other changes to the flat, the main one I noticed was that the box room now appeared to be a kind of walk-in wardrobe – though the term might be a little too grand, really. I suppose 'boot closet' would be nearer the mark.

'You know, I used to *live* in that room,' I told Ellie once we were sitting in the living room, amidst a landslide of CD cases and used coffee cups. 'The box room, I mean. I lived there for a whole year.'

Ellie wrinkled her nose. 'Which room?'

'The box room,' I repeated, gesturing back through the door.

'The *cupboard*?'

'It used to be a study,' I clarified. 'Then it was my bedroom for a year when my mother and I were living here.'

'Jesus, Woods! It's a fucking cupboard!'

'I was only eleven at the time, so it wasn't that bad. My mother wasn't too crazy about the idea, but we didn't have much choice. That was when I couldn't go to school. I couldn't leave the house. My epilepsy was too severe.'

Ellie shook her head. 'Your life is like some kind of fucked-up fairy tale. You should write your biography. It'd be a hoot.'

'Autobiography,' I corrected.

'What?'

'A biography is when you write someone else's story. When you write your own, it's called an *auto*biography.'

'Fuck you. Do you want a drink?'

'Do you have any Diet Coke?'

'I have some cheap cola in the fridge. Is that good enough?'

'It depends. Does it have sugar in?'

'Yes, it has sugar in.'

'It's okay – I'll get some Diet Coke from downstairs. I can drink generic cola if I have to, but not with sugar. It sends me funny.'

'You're already funny.'

I didn't know what to say to this, so I said nothing and went downstairs to retrieve a bottle of Diet Coke from my cache in the stockroom.

When I got back, Ellie hadn't put on any more clothes, but she had cleared some space on the table for my drink and muted the television, which was tuned to one of those trashy music shows where the female performers are always bending and wriggling and the male performers are always grabbing their balls and karate-chopping the camera. Most music videos are made in such a way that even an orang-utan would understand what's going on. Anyway, I don't think Ellie was really watching it to begin with – my understanding was that this was not the kind of music she was into. She was, however, the kind of person who needed a lot of 'stuff' going on in the background in order to function properly. That's probably why she'd lowered the volume rather than turning the television off. It was another minor distraction for me to contend with, alongside the under-wear; and this, combined with the short interruption, made it difficult to dive straight into what I really wanted to talk about. I opted instead to resume the 'small talk', thinking that this would provide an easier approach.

'Interestingly,' I remarked, 'a standard two-litre bottle of cola has about seventy-five teaspoons of sugar in.'

Ellie gave me a look as if I'd just told her that I had webbed feet.

'That's about the same as an iced chocolate cake eight inches in diameter,' I added.

'Yes, Woods, that really is the most fascinating thing I've heard all day.'

'I was just trying to be conversational,' I said.

'You need a lot more practice. Let's just cut to the chase, shall we? How's your friend? Is he still crazy?'

Sometimes, in her own way, Ellie was really quite sharp.

I spent the next ten minutes explaining how Mr Peterson wasn't exactly 'crazy' – not in the normal sense – but he *was* still suicidal. And for as long as this was the case, there was no chance he'd be allowed to leave the psychiatric ward.

'So maybe it's best if he stays there,' Ellie concluded. 'Is that what you think?'

'No, not really,' I said. 'I mean, maybe for now, but not in the long term.'

'At least at the hospital he's got people looking after him.'

'He doesn't see it that way.'

Ellie shrugged. 'How do *you* see it?'

'I don't know,' I replied. 'It's all very muddled in my head. It's like things are trying to pull into focus but they're not quite able to. But I think . . . Well, I don't see things now as I did a week ago. Everything's a lot more complicated . . .'

I trailed off and had to think for some time before resuming. 'Ellie, I've never told anyone this, but you know when I was in my coma for two weeks? After the meteor?'

I thought she was bound to make some comment about this, but she didn't. She just nodded and lit a cigarette.

'Well,' I continued, 'I'm glad I woke up – obviously – but, at the same time, I've often found myself thinking that it wouldn't have mattered if I hadn't. It wouldn't have made any difference. Not to me anyway. Do you understand what I mean?'

'No,' Ellie said.

I thought some more.

'Okay,' I said. 'So what I mean is that when I was in my coma, there wasn't anything bad. Actually, there wasn't anything at all. There wasn't dreaming. There wasn't darkness. There wasn't even time. As far as I'm concerned, those two weeks simply don't exist. They didn't happen. And I think it's exactly the same thing with death. Death isn't anything either. It's not even a void – not for the person it happens to. Do you understand that?'

Ellie exhaled a long jet of smoke, then said: 'When you're dead, you're dead. I mean, it's a bit depressing for a Sunday morning, but that's what you're trying to say, right?'

'Yes, that's right. When you're dead, you're dead. That's what I believe and that's what Mr Peterson believes too. But the point is, if that's true, it *shouldn't* be depressing. And it certainly shouldn't be scary. I mean, I can see why it should be scary from an evolutionary standpoint, obviously, but not from a logical standpoint.'

'Jesus, Woods! It is scary, it isn't scary . . . I did *not* sign up for this when I opened the door. Do me a favour: spare me the mind-fuck and just tell me what you're trying to say in plain English.'

'I'm saying that death is the easiest thing in the world. It's only dying that's terrible.'

Ellie grimaced and rubbed her head.

'Okay. Forget that. The point I'm trying to make is this: for ages I just couldn't stop dwelling on the fact that Mr Peterson was going to die, but now . . . Well, now something's changed. It no longer seems like the most important thing in all this. You can die well or you can die badly, but death's just death.'

Ellie blinked at me for a few moments.

'I don't want Mr Peterson to die badly,' I concluded.

'You mean you don't want him to die in the mental ward?'

'Yes, that's part of it. I mean we don't know how long he's got left. It could be several more years. But I don't think he should have to spend more of that in hospital than is absolutely necessary.'

Ellie didn't say anything. I spent some time staring off towards the unopened curtains, then realized that it probably looked like I was staring at her underwear, which was festooned all along the radiator below. I snapped my eyes back to her face.

'He told me that you went back to see him in the hospital,' I said. 'You know, the other day, when I was waiting in the car. Well, actually, he said you went back to shout at him.'

'Yeah, about that: I know he's your friend and everything, and you probably think it was really terrible of me to act that way with a dying man, but, well, I couldn't really help it. He was just being such a *pain*.'

'Yes, I know. And I know what you were trying to do. Thank you. I think it helped.'

Ellie didn't blush exactly – Ellie *never* blushed – but I noticed that she did look away and start fidgeting with her cigarette lighter. I got the impression that if I'd been sitting within easy striking distance, she would have punched me.

'You know, Woods,' she said after a while. 'In a way – a very odd way – what with how Rowena's been with me and every-thing . . . well, you're kind of like a brother to me. A very weird, socially retarded brother, obviously, but a brother all the same. That's kind of how I have to think of you.'

I didn't say anything.

'What I mean is that you usually annoy the hell out of me, and most of the time I can't even begin to figure out what's going on in that very bizarre place you call your brain, but still, despite all that, it doesn't mean I don't feel like I shouldn't be looking out for you when stuff like this comes up.'

It took some time to sift that last sentence for compliments. I was almost certain that she'd been trying to say something nice, and that she was expecting me to say something nice in return, but before I could start to think about what that something might be, she'd already got bored and turned back to the television.

'Ellie,' I said eventually.

'Yes?'

'I like your bangs.'

This was the best I could come up with under the circumstances.

That night, I wrote down the facts, which were these:

1) Mr Peterson doesn't want to die *right now*.
2) But he does think there will come a time when he will no longer want to live.
3) The problem is that when this time comes, he might not be physically capable of acting on his wishes.
4) This is why he attempted to kill himself, and why he will continue to be a danger to himself if released from the hospital.
5) He is not depressed. He is thinking clearly.
6) He said, in his note, that he wanted to die peacefully and with dignity, which is probably true of everyone.
7) But he has already proven that this is no simple matter. Suicide is neither peaceful nor dignified. It is unreliable and messy.

I looked at these facts for some time, and eventually added an eighth:

8) He wants the right to choose for himself.

Then, after some more time, I crossed out fact eight and rewrote it as follows:

8) He should have the right to choose for himself.

That was the second hardest thing I've ever had to write.

* * *

It was another three or four days before I discussed 'the facts' with Mr Peterson. I had to accept and internalize them first, so that I could be one hundred per cent prepared for the conversation to come. I knew that there was no room for doubt any more. My arguments had to be airtight, and delivered with absolute conviction. That was the only way I could proceed.

I chose a moment when the ward was quiet, when we were least likely to be disturbed, and I kept my voice low so that neither Count Tolstoy nor the Catatonic would be able to hear what was said.

I started by telling Mr Peterson that I had a few things I needed to say, and that he should only interrupt me if anything I said seemed incorrect to him. Then I set out the facts, one to seven, pretty much as I set them out for you: same words, same order, altering only the pronouns. It was here that all my preparation paid off. I was able to speak calmly and clearly throughout, with no stumbles and no hesitation. I knew that in this instance, emotion would not be my ally. For what was to follow, I needed Mr Peterson to understand that each and every point was clear in my mind.

He didn't interrupt me once; I didn't expect him to. I knew the moment at which he'd start talking. It would be after I'd delivered point eight: *You should have the right to choose for yourself.* To which I added a coda:

'And whatever that choice is, I want to support you in it. If the time comes when you no longer want to live – when that time comes, I want to help you die.'

Now, I'd hate for you to think badly of Mr Peterson. Rest assured: he made every attempt to put this idea in the ground there and then. My suggestion horrified him – as I'd known it would. But this was a fight he was never going to win. The facts were already agreed, and incontrovertible. He needed my help. And when it came to arguing the point, I'd had time to rehearse; he had not.

He talked at me for about ten minutes straight, but it was all completely insubstantial – repetitive, incoherent ramblings about how I'd misunderstood his wishes, how I hadn't thought things through, how utterly preposterous I was being – that sort of thing.

I waited until he'd run out of steam, then said: 'I think it should be quite clear that I *have* thought this through. I've spent days and days thinking it through. If any of the facts I've laid out for you are incorrect, then please correct me. If you can't remember any of the facts, I'd be happy to repeat them for you.'

Mr Peterson said that I should forget the goddamn facts. The facts were no longer relevant. 'The only fact that matters,' he said, 'is that I can't let you help me. Not like that.'

I waited a few moments so that I could be sure he'd hear me very clearly.

'Actually, that's not your decision to make,' I said. 'You think that you should be allowed to choose your own destiny, and I agree. One hundred per cent. All I ask is that you extend me the same privilege. I've made this decision based on what I think is right – based on my conscience. To take that away from me would be unforgivable. If you respect me at all, you *have* to let me choose.'

I don't know how many minutes ticked by after that – maybe two, maybe five. Several times Mr Peterson looked like he was on the verge of saying something, but on each occasion he pulled himself back. I didn't need to say anything else. The longer the silence went on, the more secure my existing words became.

Eventually, Mr Peterson could only wave me away, pleading that he needed time to think. But I knew the conclusion was now beyond doubt. I could see tears in his eyes. It was the only time I ever saw him cry.

The next day, it was settled. Mr Peterson asked me if I understood exactly what I was agreeing to, and I confirmed that I did.

'I'm not going to change my mind,' he told me. 'At some point, I'm gonna want it to end.'

'I know,' I said. 'I just want that point to be as far away as possible.'

'I'm putting myself completely at your mercy here, you understand that?'

'That's not really how I think of it.'

'That's how you *should* think of it. That's the way it is. I can't go into this unless you're clear on that.'

'I'm clear,' I said.

From that point on, there could be no turning back. Our pact was made.

THE CANNABIS FACTORY

In the beginning, the situation was akin to a car crash. It was captivating but it was also confusing. Although something had clearly happened – something traumatic and vaguely sinister – the deeper nature of that something was difficult to define. For some time, no one was sure what had gone wrong – or where or why – and it would take a thorough sifting of the wreckage before conclusions could be drawn and guilt assigned.

Under British law, a number of crimes had been committed: that much was established early and was never in dispute. But if this was the case, then who was the victim and who the perpetrator? As I'm sure you're aware, this was the key question that preoccupied the media in the weeks following my 'arrest' at Dover, and thinking mutated through several distinct phases.

Initially, most commentators were happy to dump all the blame at Mr Peterson's feet. This option was appealing for a number of reasons. Firstly, he was dead, and therefore not in a strong position from which to defend himself. Secondly, he had no relatives to offend or enrage. Thirdly, he was an American.

Fourthly, and most importantly, he was the adult in the situation. Even those who agreed that he had the unassailable right to end his own life if he so chose were aghast at the thought that he'd somehow involved me in the process.

I was a minor – this was the plain fact that everyone kept returning to – and as such, I lacked the moral competence to make the kind of decisions that had been ascribed to me in those preliminary police statements. I think at this stage there were only one or two dissenting journalists, who pointed out that if I lacked 'moral competence', I lacked it by only a few months. But these objections were quickly shouted down, because it wasn't *just* that I was underage; it was also self-evident that I was in an extremely vulnerable position. The police had characterized me as an 'intelligent but extremely naïve, and possibly disturbed, young man'. I had no father, no friends and a mother of dubious credentials and capability. And then there was the small matter of my 'brain damage'. There could be no doubt that my ethical abilities were compromised. The fact that I'd been the one who'd driven the car to Zurich became irrelevant. If I hadn't been kidnapped in the traditional sense, then I'd certainly been manipulated – probably in all sorts of ways.

It was this last point, of course, that opened the floodgate to a further wave of speculation, now concerning the 'exact nature' of the relationship under scrutiny. It was already known that this relationship had been ongoing since I was thirteen. Given that Mr Peterson had been happily and devotedly married for almost forty years, with no history of inappropriate contact with children (or, in fact, *any* contact with children), and given also the lack of a single scrap of evidence to support the suspicion, the tabloids naturally assumed paedophilia. You can't libel the dead, and so for a couple of weeks the accusations flew – until, quite suddenly, their wings grew tired and the story's emphasis shifted once more. It wasn't that anyone became troubled by the lack of evidence. The paedophile hypothesis simply became old hat.

So the story shifted and a new villain came into the crosshairs. This time it was the clinic in Switzerland, and more specifically Herr Schäfer, its outspoken founder and director. After all, he was equally culpable in permitting me to attend the Assisted Suicide appointment. From what could be ascertained, he had even *encouraged* my active participation in 'the procedure'. After ignoring these charges for several days, he eventually issued a rebuff. If there had been any suspicion of coercion or manipulation – and this applied to my being manipulated also – the procedure would have been immediately cancelled.

But for the media, the need for further investigation was beyond doubt. My moral incompetence had already been recognized and unanimously accepted. The next step was to prove Mr Peterson had been of unsound judgement, and this battle was already ninety per cent won. As if his actions hadn't already spoken volumes, there was also the fact that he'd been hospitalized for six weeks on the psychiatric ward. He'd also been in Vietnam, a conflict that had left him permanently (if nonspecifically) 'damaged'.

Herr Schäfer's response to these conjectures was terse: the Swiss authorities had read all the documentation, seen the recordings and were satisfied that everyone involved had acted properly, responsibly and in full possession of their mental faculties. Under Swiss law no crime had been committed.

His mistake, of course, was to mention the recordings. As

you probably know by now, it's standard practice to record an assisted suicide, as this provides the safest possible evidence that it was indeed suicide. But the press had not, at that point, cottoned on to this fact, which opened up a new world of possibilities. In no time at all, the whole country seemed to be screaming for Herr Schäfer to release the 'Death Tapes'. It was undeniably in the public interest. People had a right to judge for themselves. It was the only way this matter could ever be put to rest.

Discounting the salutation and signature, Herr Schäfer's final statement on this issue – published as a letter in one of the Sunday papers – was only one line long: 'I understand that you do things differently in the United Kingdom, but in Switzerland, trial by media is not generally supported.'

This caused a minor diplomatic crisis and prompted a further week of mud-slinging in various editorials. But that really *was* Herr Schäfer's last word on the matter. He'd decided to quit while he was ahead.

And that left only me in the firing line.

It started as a trickle – the odd question raised here and there concerning my motives – and ever so slowly, perceptions started to change. I wasn't acting the way a victim should act. My emotional response just didn't ring true. And soon enough the 'revelations' began: the fact that I'd been exposed to occult ceremonies at a very young age, my history of violent and obscene conduct in school, allegations that I'd been involved from the age of fifteen in some sort of strange religious cult. What had previously been deemed social awkwardness was now full-blown sociopathy, and all those speculations about the state of my brain took on a disturbing new light. It was quite possible, some said, that I didn't even feel emotions in the same sense that regular people with regular brains did.

Of course, it would have been very difficult to re-brand Mr Peterson as a victim after all those accusations of paedophilia, but luckily there seemed to be a growing consensus that a case like this didn't necessarily require victims; or if a victim was needed, then Morality itself could take that role. In this new interpretation of events, Mr Peterson and I became co-conspirators. He'd decided to kill himself and for a fee, paid in cash and narcotics, I'd been willing to help him. And this version of events was gaining popularity even before all that stuff about the will came out. But I'm not going to talk about that now. I suppose it will probably be the last thing I talk about. I've become a little sidetracked. The point I originally intended to address was as follows.

At every stage, the media seized upon the fact that I'd helped Mr Peterson die. They called our arrangement a 'Death Pact' – but, really, that's not a phrase that tells you anything important. It's just the kind of phrase that sells newspapers. For us, it was never about death. It was about life. Knowing that there was a way out, and that his suffering was not going to become unendurable, was the one thing that allowed Mr Peterson to go on living, much longer than he would have otherwise wanted. It was the weeks leading up to our pact that were shrouded in darkness and despair; after its inception, life became a meaningful prospect once more.

Let me tell you something about time: it's not what you think it is. It's not a regular pulse beating at the same tempo for every person at every point in the universe. This was something

Einstein discovered about a hundred years ago, using his unusually large brain. He came up with some equations that showed that a person on a train travelling close to the speed of light would measure a different value for time than the person waiting for him at the railway station. Similarly, a person sitting on the surface of the Sun would find his watch subtly out of synch with a person floating weightless through interstellar space. Time has different values for different people in different circumstances. Einstein proved this idea mathematically, but, in my experience, it also holds true from a subjective standpoint.

I know, for example, that Mr Peterson did not experience the flow of time in the same way that I did during those final sixteen months. He told me often, particularly towards the end, that for him time had become a slow, peaceful drift. If I had to guess why this was the case, I'd say that maybe it was because this was time he'd never expected to have. Or maybe it was more that he was now *letting* time drift. There was a certain type of contentment in his outlook, which never strayed too far into the future. His life had become simple and uncluttered, and when you're living like that, I think time *can* seem to stretch out for ever. Matters only change when you start fretting about all the things you need to get done. The more stuff you try to force into it, the less accommodating time becomes.

Of course, Mr Peterson couldn't be completely oblivious to the future. There were still certain practicalities to be considered. There were emails and phone calls to the clinic in Switzerland, medical documents that had to be obtained, copied and posted (under the pretext of a consultation with a 'private specialist'). But once Mr Peterson's case had been assessed and a provisional green light granted, these matters could recede into the background. As long as he kept his records periodically updated, he knew that his way out had been secured. He'd be able to make his final appointment at relatively short notice, as and when the time came. But until then, it no longer had to be a daily concern. He could concentrate instead on all the other measures that were going to help him in the short and medium term.

On medical advice, he saw a physiotherapist at the hospital and was taught a regime of simple daily exercises to combat the developing problems with his gait and balance. His house was fitted with a stairlift, and sturdy railings were fixed to the walls in the bathrooms and hallways. He had Meals on Wheels visiting daily and a Lithuanian lady called Krystyn who came round twice a week to clean. In between the dusting and vacuuming and so forth, they spent a lot of time drinking coffee and talking about how peculiar the English were. Strangely, Mr Peterson's life had become a whole lot more sociable now that he found himself so physically restricted. And it wasn't just home help and the medical professionals, of course. Once people were aware of his illness, he had a small but dedicated division of weekly visitors. Mrs Griffith brought round cakes and casseroles every three or four days, regular as clockwork. Fiona Fitton and Sophie Haynes took it in turns to come over with various audio books and classical CDs ordered through Glastonbury Library. And since everyone now knew (almost) everything there was to know about Mr Peterson's situation, there wasn't much point in his being furtive any longer. He talked openly and frankly about his illness. On the subject of his suicide attempt and hospitalization, he always gave the same concise summary: 'I didn't think my life was worth living, but it turned out I was wrong.' He said that he wanted people to understand the very sane reasoning that had motivated his actions. This may have been a joke. I'm not sure. Ironically, he seemed to find it much easier to be light-hearted now that he'd acknowledged he was dying.

But if Mr Peterson's life had become a whole lot more relaxed, for me there were barely enough hours in the day. And it wasn't just that there were a lot of everyday chores that now had to be undertaken on Mr Peterson's behalf; there were also the longer-term tasks that I'd decided to complete before our trip to Switzerland.

First on the list was *learn German*. Mr Peterson told me that this would not be necessary since everyone at the clinic (and everyone in Switzerland, he suspected) spoke fluent English, but, still, I thought it was better to be safe than sorry. After all, a certain amount of comprehension was bound to be helpful. There'd be road signs and street signs and border control and hoteliers and so on. For my own peace of mind, I wanted to know at least enough to make myself understood. But unfortunately, I'd already settled on GCSEs in French and Spanish, for a mixture of practical and aesthetic reasons. So I had to use my lunch hour.

I sought out Frau Kampischler, the Asquith Academy's German teacher, and asked her if she was willing to give up her lunchtimes to act as my private tutor. She was not. But she did signpost me towards an online beginner's course and agreed to make available to me a selection of textbooks and audio resources so that I could press on alone.

I spent five solitary hours each week learning how to order *Frühstück* and ask for directions to the *Busbahnhof* and tell the immigration officer *wir werden vier Tage bleiben* and so on. Aside from the fact that it had three genders, verbs that liked to stray to the end of sentences, and monstrously long compound words like *Geschwindigkeitsbegrenzung* (speed limit), German turned out to be structurally similar to English, and although it doesn't have the world's most pleasing accent, it's at least an accent that most people know how to do – what with *The Great Escape* and *Raiders of the Lost Ark* and '*Neunundneunzig Luftballons*'. This made things much easier for me, and within six to eight months, I felt that my *Deutsch* was coming along nicely.

Unfortunately, the second goal on my Swiss checklist – passing my driving test – was not something I could so easily pursue. But if I'd been old enough, this would have been my number-one priority.

I'm not sure of the exact point when we agreed that driving to Zurich would be preferable to flying, but it must have been quite early on in our preparations. It wasn't that Mr Peterson had any particular fear of engine failure or Islamic extremists or anything like that, but he did have a definite aversion to flying. He claimed it was something to do with being shut up in a cramped space, with such a high density of other people and no means of escape. This was not an appealing scenario for his final journey, especially given that we didn't know just how bad his mobility and balance would be at that stage. We both agreed that it would be much better to drive. We could take our time and stop when and wherever we needed to and have a constant, restful view of the countryside, soundtracked by Schubert and Chopin. Mr Peterson's only reservation concerning this plan was that it entailed about twenty-four hours' worth of driving for me – the second half of which I'd have to complete alone. How was I going to cope with *that*? The truth was, I didn't know, but I felt in my gut that it was the right way to go about things. I'd never flown before, so I had no way of saying whether this would be any less stressful for me than driving. At least with driving I knew where I stood.

Anyway, while I couldn't take my test until I turned seventeen, there were still some things I could do in preparation. Because of his deteriorating eyesight, Mr Peterson could no longer instruct me properly when we took the car out, but I could still carry out familiar, low-risk routines such as driving him to the shop and back or practising my reverse-parking in his driveway. I also read the Highway Code cover to cover, so from a theoretical standpoint, I certainly knew my stuff. And then there were my other mental preparations as well.

As I mentioned, the law stipulates that an epileptic is only allowed to drive if he or she has been completely seizure-free for at least a year. Since I was certain that I wouldn't be able to lie to Dr Enderby about something like that, I knew it was imperative that I kept my boat on an even keel in the months leading up to my seventeenth birthday. This meant that despite all the extra things I now had to cram into my days, I couldn't afford to deviate too much from my well-worn routines and sleeping cycle. I still had to get to bed by ten thirty at the latest, and I still had to be up before seven for my early morning meditation and mind-calming exercises.

But, for me, this was what worked. With these adamant structures in place, I managed to stay seizure-free for close to twenty months in total. Dr Enderby was so pleased with my progress that he told me, at the biannual check-up just before my seventeenth birthday, that under normal circumstances he'd be recommending a graded reduction in my carbamazepine, with a view to weaning me entirely in the next six to twelve months. But, of course, he understood that these were *not* normal circumstances, and if I didn't feel ready – which I didn't – then there was really no reason to go tinkering with my medication for the time being.

I passed my driving theory test on the day I turned seventeen, and a week later, following a few evenings of intensive lessons and a cancellation at the test centre, I passed my practical too, with only one minor fault for undue hesitation while overtaking a horse. The examiner said that I must be a natural.

As for all the other things that filled my days to bursting point, well, you can probably imagine most of the standard chores I had to undertake on Mr Peterson's behalf. I ran errands to the post office. I tidied up on those days when Krystyn was off-duty. I took dictation for Amnesty letters. I read aloud – usually for at least an hour or two a day, usually books that Mr Peterson had read before but had never found time to revisit. He said that he found himself less and less inclined to start anything new, preferring to choose books that he thought *I* should read. After *Catch-22*, it was *One Flew Over the Cuckoo's Nest*, and after that, *A Prayer for Owen Meany*. In hindsight, he was increasingly drawn to that type of tragicomedy. But he was right to think that these books would appeal to me too. Once I'd got over my initial self-consciousness, reading aloud from these books was one of the only activities in which I found I could lose myself completely. The other was tending to the cannabis factory. But I suppose this isn't the kind of task that lends itself to a single-paragraph summary. I'll have to go into a bit more detail.

* * *

The first thing you need to know is this: my attitude to Mr Peterson's weed changed quite dramatically after his hospitalization. Let's be clear: I'm not a fan of any substance that messes with your natural brain chemistry. The idea of eating, smoking, sniffing, injecting or inserting any drug that hasn't been subjected to rigorous triple-blind testing is more or less alien to me. I can't understand why anyone would want to do that. But they do – that's the point. People also like dangerous sports like boxing and BASE jumping and big-wave surfing. I don't understand these things either. But I don't think I'd ever want to tell anyone that they *shouldn't* engage in these activities (except maybe boxing).

I suppose what I realized, at about the same time I realized that Mr Peterson should have the right to kill himself, was that in most circumstances you really shouldn't tell other people what they can or can't do to their own brains and bodies. That Mr Peterson enjoyed smoking cannabis alone, in the privacy of his own home, no longer seemed so wrong. It certainly wasn't affecting anybody else, and for him, so far as he claimed, it was a whole lot better for his personal well-being than anything a doctor had ever prescribed. Of course, it's impossible to evaluate the merits of this claim objectively, but really, that's the point. It was his choice to make. If Mr Peterson thought that smoking dried-up marijuana plants gave him a better quality of life, I felt it was my duty to support him in this. And it was apparent very early on that my role would have to be a proactive one.

Soon after he was released from psych, it became clear that the steep and narrow attic stairs were now far beyond his capabilities. This was late November, and the last time he'd been up previous to this had been right back at the end of August, when he'd harvested his crop for what he'd assumed would be the final time. After that, he hadn't replanted. Thinking that this was the end of his botanical career, he'd switched off the high-output lighting, stacked the four-gallon growing tubs neatly in the corner, swept the floor and shut up shop. But now, having decided to live a little longer, he was facing a conundrum.

Getting up the attic stairs was no longer possible, but relocating the operation was equally unthinkable. There was nothing amateurish about the set-up in Mr Peterson's loft. In thirty years as a cannabis farmer, he'd amassed a lot of heavy and high-tech equipment. There were the thousand-watt, high-pressure sodium lamps mounted in hooded brackets – kind of like the ones you find above snooker tables – that could be raised or lowered on a pulley system according to the height of the underlying plants. There was the dehumidifier and the large extractor fan, which kept the air circulating and the leaves dry and resinous. There was also the fact that the space could be made 'light-tight', and its temperature controlled with a high degree of precision, both of which were crucial in terms of optimizing growth and regulating the plants' reproductive cycles. And even if it had been possible to relocate the whole set-up to somewhere more accessible, it was clear that soon enough even simple tasks such as watering and re-potting would become impossible for Mr Peterson to carry out on his own. Someone had to take hold of the reins – and that someone had to be me. Although Mr Peterson got on well with Krystyn, we both agreed that asking her if she wouldn't mind popping up to the attic to water the cannabis might be overstepping a boundary. And anyway, as I expect you've already gathered, growing decent cannabis is *not* like taking care of houseplants. It's a surprisingly intricate enterprise.

The step-by-step manual that Mr Peterson dictated to me on the subject ran to fourteen single-spaced twelve-point Times New Roman pages, and covered every stage of the production process, from germination to drying, curing and storing. The manual (which would eventually end up in a police evidence locker) was my idea. After thirty years in the business, Mr Peterson regarded decent cannabis-growing as something of an art, but this was an outlook I could never really share. For me, cannabis-growing was always a science. It was a science, and I loved it.

It wasn't just that the attic looked and felt like a laboratory – with the lights and the pulleys and the constant hum of the extractor fan. In essence, it *was* a laboratory. It was a perfect, whitewashed environment in which every variable could be monitored and adjusted towards a single, simple outcome. There were thermometers and hygrometers, scales and tape measures. There was a cupboard full of chemicals – chemicals for de-chlorinating tap water, 'rooting hormones' for the cuttings, nitrogen- and potassium-rich plant foods, chemicals for modifying the soil acidity, which had to be kept as close to the optimum pH of 6.5 as possible. And this was just one of the many technical details that kept me enthralled. There was also the light cycle, set to simulate summer and autumn: eighteen hours of light per day during the fourteen-week vegetative stage, and then twelve per day to trigger and sustain the eight-week reproductive stage. Except, for Mr Peterson's plants, reproduction was never on the cards. As soon as they'd been sexed, all the male plants had to be culled. This was because unfertilized female plants produced several times more resin, and it was the resin that contained most of the cannabinoids – the psychoactive elements that were the whole point of the enterprise, at least as far as Mr Peterson was concerned.

For me, it was the enterprise that was the main point of the enterprise. It was the satisfaction of engineering such excellent specimens.

After a few months of me running the factory, Mr Peterson had already had more than enough of my very detailed, very technical progress reports. I think there were at least two occasions when I literally bored him to sleep – once when trying to explain the equation that describes how far the lamps should be kept from the plants, and once when espousing my hypothesis concerning why the plants utilized different wavelengths of light in the vegetative and flowering stages, which was to do with the path of the Sun and the scattering of light in the atmosphere.

Anyway, I like to think that all this scientific precision paid off in the end. I managed to oversee three abundant harvests, the quality of which Mr Peterson pronounced 'more than adequate'.

So that, in a nutshell, was my life for sixteen months. As you can see, there *were* moments of stillness amidst the general gallop – periods of respite, when I was reading aloud or tending to the plants and my mind was so absorbed that time and everything else just kind of melted into the background. But this did not stop the clock from ticking. Mr Peterson may have experienced time as a 'slow, peaceful drift', but for me, it was a swiftly accelerating blur. And it didn't take long for it to overtake us.

I suppose it was some time around the beginning of October,

shortly after I'd passed my driving test, that Mr Peterson's speech problems really started to become noticeable, though by then I'm sure they must have been developing for a while. It began with a slight slurring and slowing – similar to the way someone speaks when moderately intoxicated. Except, of course, Mr Peterson was not intoxicated (or not *that* intoxicated). He was conscious of all the little tremors that were creeping in: the difficulty in articulating certain sounds, the way that words would 'catch' in his throat, the problem he sometimes had with modulating the volume of his voice. These things started as little more than annoyances, but they continued to build and add up. Soon he was complaining that his voice no longer felt like 'his own'. It rebelled and wouldn't obey him as it should. There was no slowing of his thoughts – he could still articulate himself perfectly well in the privacy of his own head – but speaking was an increasingly laborious process.

So he adapted. More and more, he chose to communicate in writing rather than speech. I think it was a strategy born of frustration rather than self-consciousness or practicality. Writing wasn't necessarily any quicker, but it felt to him a much more reliable and satisfying means of self-expression. His writing hand never faltered the way his voice did; it seemed much truer to his intent. Nevertheless, the switch from speech to writing presented its own problems. His hands may have worked just fine, but there were still his eyes to contend with. For Mr Peterson, tracking his unfurling script across and down the page was also a very time-consuming affair. He soon declared it intolerable and started to write 'blind' – that is, without attempting to look at what he was writing. He had a pen and an un-ruled notepad that he carried with him at all times, and he tended to keep whatever he had to say short and to the point.

Is it legible? he wrote early on, when his blind-writing was still in its infancy.

'Yes, it's perfectly legible,' I assured him. 'You won't be winning any calligraphy contests, but for day-to-day communication purposes, it's fine.'

It beats the hell out of trying to talk, Mr Peterson wrote.

But the speech problems were, in the grand scheme of things, little more than an inconvenience. As long as we allowed some extra time, we could still have a strange but perfectly adequate conversation. If he'd actually lost the ability to communicate, it would have been a very different matter. But we both knew that it wasn't going to get to that stage.

It was clear by February 2011 that his restricted mobility was going to be the decisive factor for him. By this time, even using his walker, simple tasks such as boiling the kettle or going to the bathroom had become a significant trial. And one evening in early March, he conceded the inevitable. He wouldn't be able to go on living independently for very much longer; and for him, this prospect marked the cut-off point. Going into permanent, professional care had never been an option.

I think it's time, he wrote.

So that was it. I was amazed at how calm and committed I felt. But then, I'd been preparing myself for this moment for a very long time. I knew that now, more than ever, I had to be strong and unfaltering. It was a final act of friendship. That was the thought I had to cling to.

I phoned Switzerland and made an appointment for four

weeks' time, which we'd agreed would give us long enough to prepare. Mr Peterson only had to speak on the phone briefly, to confirm that these were indeed his wishes.

And in the space of that one phone call, everything was set in motion.

And neither of us expected any trouble. We didn't envisage for one minute that we'd have any problems getting away. How could we? With the exception of one or two minor details – like what the hell I was going to tell my mother – we'd planned everything out meticulously. The medical records were up to date. The car had been serviced, and was now taxed and insured in my name. The date for our departure was set. We thought we'd just slip away, quietly and unnoticed. That's what should have happened. That's what *would* have happened, were it not for the fall. It was this one initial mishap that set all the dominoes tumbling. Without that, I'm sure things would have worked out very differently.

20

ESCAPE

It was Krystyn who found him – ten o'clock on an April morning, a mere forty-eight hours before we were due to leave. He later wrote that he had no idea what had happened, but it was probably something all too simple: a mistimed step, an unseen obstacle, a dizzy spell or momentary loss of concentration. He'd tried to break his fall with his left arm, which had pretty much crumpled beneath his body weight, slowing only fractionally the impact of his head against the kitchen floor.

One attempt was enough to tell him that he couldn't tolerate any pressure on his left wrist, and he couldn't support enough of his body weight on his right arm to roll himself onto his back or side. He had no choice but to stay exactly as he was, with his left cheek pressed against the cold tiled floor, one arm bent awkwardly beneath him, and his hair matted with congealing blood.

When Krystyn arrived, she did what any sane person would have done. She called an ambulance. Mr Peterson's attempt to dissuade her was over before it began. The lines that he'd been rehearsing on the floor – that he was okay and just needed helping back to his feet, or something to that effect – came out as a series of muted groans and wheezes. This did little to counter Krystyn's initial assessment of the situation, which was conveyed in a single Lithuanian word, repeated ten or twenty times. Mr Peterson thought he could guess what the word was.

X-rays revealed a clean fracture in his left little finger, which had to be bandaged and splinted to his ring finger. He also required a dozen stitches for his head-wound. But apart from this, the doctors said, he'd had a lucky escape. Had he been in otherwise good health, he might have been sent home that same day. But as things stood, this was clearly out of the question. In normal terms, the injuries were minimal, but for Mr Peterson, they were rather more debilitating. He'd reached the point where he couldn't make do with a single crutch; he needed both hands for balance and support. But the bigger problem, of course, was the timing.

They want to keep me in for AT LEAST 2 days, Mr Peterson wrote when I made it into the hospital that evening after school.

'That's going to be cutting things a little fine,' I pointed out, as if this wasn't already implicit in the underlining. 'Is there any way they might consider letting you out a little earlier?'

They say it's too risky, Mr Peterson wrote. *They think I might have concussion because I feel giddy and can't keep their damn hospital food down.*

'You might have concussion,' I conceded.

I don't have concussion. This is how I feel all the time. It's just a pretext.

I read this and frowned. 'Why would it be a pretext?'

2 days? For concussion? That doesn't stack up. They're keeping me here because they can't send me home. That's obvious. Look at me!

I looked at him.

I can't put any weight on my left wrist. I can't even grip because of this goddamn splint. How am I going to walk out of here in the next 2 days? I'm trapped.

My mind was darting ahead. 'I'll phone Switzerland first thing tomorrow,' I said. 'I'll explain the situation and I'll get them to defer the appointment. It's not too late, right? When they discharge you, you'll still be well enough to travel.'

Mr Peterson took some time to fashion his half-page response.

Alex, they're not going to discharge me. Can't you see? No sane doctor's going to say it's OK for me to go back home. They're going to keep me here until I've lost what little mobility I've got left and then they're going to hand me over to the social workers. I'm going straight from here into a hospice. The only other way they'll let me leave is in a body bag. You must be able to see that!

I *could* see that. No matter how good his support network,

Mr Peterson couldn't go on living alone. No doctor under the sun was going to pronounce him well enough to be released into his own custody. We'd left things as late as we possibly could.

'It's now or never, isn't it?' I asked.

Yes. It's now or never. I can't miss my appointment.

'I can have the car loaded and ready to go by tomorrow night,' I said.

Mr Peterson had a small coughing fit. *That's the easy part. Have you figured out what you're going to tell your mom?*

'I'm still thinking about it,' I admitted.

Think quick! You have to tell her something. You can't just disappear for a week.

'I know.'

If she can handle the truth, tell her the truth. If she can't, tell her I want to see the Alps before I die or something like that. Anything you can get her to believe. There'll be time for proper explanations later.

I held my head and breathed deeply for a few moments.

'My mother's too unpredictable,' I said. 'I don't know if she can be trusted with the truth. But . . . well, I don't see how I can lie to her either. I'm lousy at lying at the best of times. I can't see any safe option. Every course I can imagine seems to have an equal likelihood of ending in catastrophe.'

Alex, I'm sorry – I can't help you with

this. You have to figure it out for
yourself. My gut says you should tell her
the truth, but it has to be your call.
The important thing is you have to tell
her something.

I nodded.

That just leaves the problem of how
we're going to get me out of here.

'We'll need a wheelchair, I suppose.'

They keep those fold-down ones on the
ward somewhere. You'll have to find out
where and borrow one. Say that you're
taking me to the bathroom. I don't think
any nurse is going to object to being
relieved of that duty.

'The bathroom's this side of the reception desk,' I pointed
out. 'That story's only going to get us so far.'

Getting the wheelchair's the main point.
After that we just need to pick our
moment.

I frowned and thought about this for a while. 'You know,
I'm fairly sure reception's staffed round the clock. And it's
definitely staffed during visiting hours. I don't think there's
going to be *any* moment when we can just wheel you out
unnoticed.'

Maybe not. But there are times when
we're much less likely to be detained.
If we can get past reception unseen, so
much the better. If we can't, we'll have

TO TRY subterfuge. If that fails, our best bet is speed.

'Speed?' I lowered my voice to a whisper. 'You want me to wheel you as fast as I can towards the lifts and hope for the best?'

Yes, if necessary.

'What kind of back-up plan is that?'

It's a back-up back-up plan.

'What about negotiation?' I asked. 'We explain to whoever's on reception that staying in the hospital is against your wishes and we're therefore discharging you a few days early. I know it's contrary to medical advice, but can anyone actually stop us?'

You're 17 and my brain's turning to mulch, Mr Peterson scrawled. *No one's going to think twice about stopping us. Trust me. Our wishes mean <u>squat</u>.*

I grimaced and rubbed my temples.

It's a last resort, Mr Peterson wrote, *but if we have to run, we have to run. Be prepared for that.*

'Okay,' I said.

Use my disabled badge and park as close to the front entrance as possible. As soon as we're in the car we're home free.

'Okay.'

Now go home and rest. Go to school as normal tomorrow, then come back here in the evening and we'll finalize the details. In the meantime, you think about the best time to move me and I'll do the same. And take a good look around on your way out. Check out reception and figure out where they keep the wheel-chairs.

'Okay.'

Mr Peterson scribbled a hasty note, then tore the last five or six pages out of his notebook and handed them to me.

Throw these in the trash can on your way out, his final sentence read.

The cannabis factory had been dismantled three weeks earlier, just after the final harvest. I had one and a half hand-sized pouches of dried and cured bud waiting in the glove box of Mr Peterson's car and forty-eight cans of Diet Coke loaded in the boot. I'd topped up the screenwash and inflated all the tyres to thirty-one PSI. There was a full tank of petrol and a carrier bag on the back seat filled with over thirty hours of classical music, everything from Bach to Beethoven to Bartók. The suitcases were packed and every item on the checklist had been ticked off. It was eight o'clock on a Thursday evening and I was all set to leave.

I'd told my mother that I was going to the hospital for evening visiting hours and that Mr Peterson was to be discharged at eight o'clock the following morning. I'd be back late and leaving early so that I could pick him up before school; in all likelihood, she wouldn't see much of me for the next twenty-four hours.

She asked if there was anything she could do to help – if I wanted her to phone school to explain the circumstances and say that I might be a little late the next day. She was so supportive I felt physically sick. But I knew I had to stick to the plan. There was no turning back now.

The letter I'd written her had taken a very long time – much longer than anything else I'd ever written. It went through about fifteen drafts, most of which never made it past the first half-page and ended up crumpled on Mr Peterson's living-room floor. When I'd eventually finished, I divided the final word count by the total time of composition and concluded that this was likely the most labour-intensive letter that anyone anywhere had ever written. And now I had to deliver it.

Ten minutes after I'd left Mr Peterson's driveway, I parked the car on Glastonbury High Street and crept down the darkened alleyway that led to my mother's shop. This, of course, was the only place I could leave her a letter. If I left it in my room, she might find it too soon. By leaving it on the front counter at the shop, I knew exactly when she'd read it: sometime between eight forty and eight fifty the following morning. And she wouldn't have to read it alone. Ellie would be there. Since there was a high probability of hysteria, I thought that this was an important consideration.

The light was on in the window above the shop. I could see a bright, sharply defined line bisecting the glass where the curtains hadn't quite been pulled to. Ellie was in, but that was as I'd expected. As long as I was quiet, it made little difference.

I'd already decided that the front door was unsafe. It was loaded with two sets of heavy wind chimes, which made enough of a racket to be heard through the closed door of the stockroom. It was less certain that they could be heard from upstairs, but I thought there was no sense in risking it. I tiptoed round to the back of the shop, then paused for reconnaissance just before I reached the small scrap of yard that was overlooked by the flat's kitchen window. A stealthy glance revealed that the blinds were up, but the kitchen light was out. My dark-adapted eyes could make out a faint, sallow glow, but I concluded that this must be the overspill from the light in the hallway. I knew that the security light was going to come on the moment I stepped into the yard, and that it would be highly visible through the window above, but since it was hard to imagine even Ellie sitting in the kitchen with the lights out, I had to assume that she was safely elsewhere. The yard light would be on for only a minute, and I'd have to be desperately unlucky if she came into the kitchen and spotted it in that time.

Six silent paces took me to the lower back door. I paused only long enough for my eyes to adjust to the sudden glare that was now illuminating the yard, then slipped my key into the lock. The door creaked open and clicked shut, sending a small judder up my arm. It was the kind of stiff, heavy door that couldn't be closed silently, but I thought I'd kept the noise to a minimum. I reasoned that in the muted gloom of the empty shop it probably sounded louder than it was, and unless you were listening out for it, or happened to be passing the top of the stairs at that very moment, it was the kind of dull, background noise that would pass unnoticed. Nonetheless, I was in no mood to hang about.

I took my torch from one pocket and the letter from the other and proceeded swiftly through to the front counter. I'd left the letter in an unsealed envelope in case I wanted to make any last-minute modifications before I placed it next to the cash register. But now, casting my eyes over it one last time, I concluded that there was nothing I could change or add. There'd be a time for full explanations, but this was not it. I slipped the letter back into the envelope and was just about to seal it.

The lights came on behind me.

I jumped a foot in the air, then spun to find Ellie standing in the doorway. She was holding in her raised right hand a high-heeled boot, which she'd later explain was the best weapon she could find at such short notice. When the security light had come on, and then when she'd heard the door go, she'd had very little time to react. It transpired that smoking by tea light at the kitchen table was one of the ways Ellie liked to 'unwind' in the evenings. But my incursion had put paid to that. She was once more fully wound.

'Jesus fucking hellfire Christ, Woods!' she said. 'You scared the living *crap* out of me! What the hell are you doing here? Why are all the lights out? Why the fuck didn't you come up and knock?'

I gawped and blinked like an idiot for a few faltering seconds. I didn't know what else I could say or do; I removed the letter from its still unsealed envelope and handed it to her.

Gone abroad to help Mr Peterson die, it read. Please don't worry.

From the amount of time she spent staring at it, she must have read it through at least a dozen times. Her mouth was open. Her facial expression was so frozen she might have been sculpted from ice.

'Woods, please, please tell me this is one of those jokes I'm too stupid to get.'

'It's not a joke,' I said. 'We're leaving tonight.'

I had no time to duck. Her right hand hit my cheek like a thunderclap. I sat on the floor, my ears ringing.

'You fucking moron!' Ellie yelled. 'I know the old man's as crazy as a fucking loon, but you! I thought you had at least a shred of common sense in that warped brain of yours! Good fucking God, Woods! What were you thinking? If he wants to kill himself, that's one thing, but convincing you to help him – that's just fucking sick!'

'He didn't convince me,' I said flatly. 'I had to convince him.'

Ellie raked her fingers through her hair and then started pacing back and forth like a caged animal, stopping periodically to shake her head and swear. Several times she looked like she was going to assault me again. Eventually, she stopped pacing and sat beside me on the floor, our backs pressed up against the counter.

'You need to phone your mother right this second,' she said.

'I'm not phoning my mother.'

'If you don't, I will,' she threatened.

'You're not phoning her either.'

She handed me the letter. 'Woods, this is too fucked up for words.'

'No,' I said, 'it's not. It might seem that way right now, but it really isn't. You have to trust me on this. We know what we're doing.'

'You don't know what you're doing! You don't have a *clue* what you're doing!'

I waited for a count of five and then looked her in her eye, which was barely a foot away. 'Ellie, you have to listen to me. I'm doing what I *know* is right. And nothing you or anyone else can say is going to change my mind. I've thought about this – I've spent months thinking about it – and no one's forcing me to do anything I don't agree with.'

'You're going to end up in a whole world of shit.'

'Maybe. That doesn't matter, though. I'm doing what's right.'

Ellie rolled her eyes in disbelief. 'Jesus, Woods! How can you be so sure of yourself? You shouldn't be so sure of yourself – not with something like this.'

I took several deep breaths. I knew I wasn't going to falter any more. Ellie's slap had knocked any residual hesitation straight out of my head.

'Ellie,' I began, 'I'm sure of myself because I know that from this point there are two possible futures. In one, Mr Peterson is going to die four days from now, peacefully and with no pain. In the other, he's going to die six months or maybe even a year from now, after many, many weeks of pointless suffering. He's going to die bedbound and scared and in pain, and unable even to tell anyone how terrified he is. There's a good chance that by that time he won't be able to do so much as move his eyes. Mr Peterson's not crazy and neither am I. We've chosen the way out that seems kinder to us. And if you think this decision is wrong, you don't have to support it. You don't have to do a damn thing. Just don't try to intervene. Please. I'm asking you as a friend.'

I knew that it was the most compelling argument I could deliver, and I knew that I'd delivered it well, but still, when I'd finished I was shocked to discover that Ellie was crying. She'd turned her face from me and was sobbing into her sleeve. It was a reaction I was completely unprepared for, and I didn't know what to do. I tried kind of smoothing her hair for a bit, but because her body was shaking, it was more like I was patting her on the head, the way you might a dog or a horse. I gave up and put my arm around her shoulders. She leaned her head into me, and after a few minutes, she'd stopped crying. All that was left was the occasional twitch.

'Woods, I don't know what to say any more. You're a fucking saint.'

Then she pivoted her head and kissed me. Right on the lips. I was too surprised to do much. I was far too surprised to kiss her back. To tell you the truth, I didn't really know *how* to kiss her back. In case you haven't realized yet, when it comes to certain things, I'm irremediably dense. But the odd thing – maybe the thing that surprised me the most – was that Ellie's kiss didn't feel even remotely awkward. It wasn't awkward for me, and I know it wasn't awkward for her. Afterwards, she just settled straight back into my shoulder as if nothing at all had happened. And we stayed like that for I don't know how long. My lower lip was warm and tingling. My left cheek was throbbing like I'd been stung by a wasp. And I'd lost all sense of time and urgency. I only came round when Ellie touched my left hand – the hand that was still holding the letter.

'How long did it take you to dream up that masterpiece?' she asked.

'Six and a half hours,' I admitted.

'And you're seriously planning to tell her like that?'

'I think it's the only way I *can* tell her.'

'You're putting me in one hell of a position.'

'Yes, I know,' I acknowledged. 'I didn't mean to.'

'I know you didn't.'

I thought things through for a couple of seconds. 'It might

be better if you just act surprised tomorrow morning,' I suggested.

'It might be better if you just trusted her with the truth.'

'This is the truth. I haven't lied to her.'

'Stop being a moron,' Ellie countered. 'You know what I mean.'

A few moments ticked by. I stared deep into the glass of one of the four-inch diameter crystal balls that were stationed on a shelf at the back of the room.

'I think I have to go now,' I said. 'I need to get to the hospital bef—'

'*Don't* tell me what you're doing,' Ellie interjected. 'I don't want to lie to your mother any more than I have to.'

She wriggled out from my arm, wiped her eyes and started straightening out her hair. I got up and sealed the letter, then placed it just to the left of the cash register.

'Will you at least call her tomorrow?' Ellie asked when I turned back towards the rear of the shop. 'I think you owe her that.'

I didn't say anything.

Ellie planted her hands on her hips. 'She'll want to know that you're okay.'

'Maybe I could phone you instead? Then—'

'I am *not* going to act as your go-between. Don't you dare call me unless you've called her first.'

I bit my lip. I knew that I needed to keep my head clear and focussed for the next few days, and a conversation with my mother was not going to make this project any easier.

'Well?' Ellie asked after a few more moments of silence.

'I really need to go now,' I told her.

If Ellie had still been holding the high-heeled boot at that point, I'm fairly sure she would have thrown it at me. Instead, she turned and walked back up to the flat without saying a word. I didn't pursue her. There was no time and little point.

Outside, the evening air had got noticeably colder. As I hurried back to the car, the only part of me that still felt warm was my left cheek.

Thirty minutes later, thirty minutes behind schedule, I pulled up in a disabled bay twenty metres from the front entrance of Yeovil District Hospital. The fact that it was possible to park this close to the entrance in the late evening – something that was virtually *im*possible in the daytime – had been a key factor when we'd decided on our moment of departure. At this time, the whole hospital would be quiet. The foyer wouldn't be congested with people. The lifts were more likely to be available when we needed them. There would certainly be fewer doctors on the ward. With luck, there'd be none. If it came down to it, we thought a doctor was more likely to stop us from leaving than a nurse or an orderly. Doctors were used to making swift, authoritative judgements.

Of course, our planned leaving time presented certain unavoidable problems as well. With the ward corridors empty, or close to empty, it would be much harder to slip past reception unnoticed. But Mr Peterson and I had already agreed that there was no time when this best of outcomes could be guaranteed. The overriding concern was that if we had to make a break for it, there'd be no physical barriers and no passing medical staff to halt our progress. For this reason we planned to make our exit just after 9.45, which was when the nurses did their final ward round before lights-out, leaving just one of their number to man reception. The nurses would be coming round with their charts and trolley-load of medications no later than 9.48, by which time we'd be all set to go, with Mr Peterson already loaded into the wheelchair for our fictitious trip to the lavatory. The moment the nurses moved on to the next room, we'd be on our way, with a window of at least ten minutes before they returned to reception.

It was all very clear and simple in my head, but after what had happened with Ellie, I was feeling highly alert to the potential for mishaps. Nonetheless, as I headed up to the ward, I was able to reassure myself by checking off all the accurate assumptions we'd made. Apart from a lone cleaner sweeping the floor at its far end, the foyer was dead. There was an unimpeded path from the automatic doors to the lifts, and when I reached the sixth floor, I was pleased to discover that the corridors leading to the ward were similarly deserted. There was one nurse on reception, and another in the adjoining office. The whole place was as quiet as a morgue.

Mr Peterson started scribbling the moment he saw me approaching the bed.

You're late, his note read.

'I got held up,' I explained.

Did someone hit you?

'Ellie hit me.'

That figures. What about your mom? You told her?

'It's all sorted,' I said evasively.

And?

I shrugged. 'Well, I'm here, aren't I?'

She's OK?

'She will be, I think. It's just going to take a while.'

Thankfully, Mr Peterson didn't grill me any further. There wasn't all that much time. My watch showed that we had about fifteen minutes until the evening ward round.

Put this in my overnight bag, Mr Peterson wrote. Then he passed me a second, larger note reading: *for charity*. I slipped it into the bag.

'I think you're going to be cold when we get outside,' I said.

We've been through this. I can't get dressed for a trip to the bathroom. How's that going to look? My dressing gown will have to suffice. You can throw a blanket over me when we're in the car.

'You can't wear a hospital gown all the way to Zurich,' I pointed out.

We'll find somewhere on the 303 to pull over so I can get changed. Did you get some sleep today?

'I managed a couple of hours this morning. What about you?'

I'm not driving. My lack of sleep's irrelevant. What about the ferry times?

'I've got a full print-out in the car. I think the three twenty's the one for us, but there's also one an hour later in case we miss it.'

Great. Just don't rush. Let's get there in one piece. You're not to let me die until we get to Switzerland.

'Ha ha,' I said.

Seriously. If you need to stop, we stop.

I nodded. But privately, I thought I'd like to put as much distance as possible between me and my mother by eight forty-five the next morning.

A few silent moments dragged by, then Mr Peterson slipped me another note. *I think it's time.*

I looked at my watch again. My heart had started pounding. 'I'll be back in two minutes,' I said.

I got to reception just as the ward round was beginning. As expected, neither of the fold-down wheelchairs had been left out; both were stowed in the small alcove on the near side of the reception desk. I'd already decided that I'd have to ask before taking one. The nurse left on reception hadn't yet looked up from her stack of paperwork, but there was no sense trying to sneak one of the chairs away when I had a perfectly legitimate reason for borrowing one.

I walked to the desk, clocked her name badge and said: 'Excuse me, Nurse Fletcher.'

Her eyes snapped up and straight to my left cheek. I estimated her to be around forty-five years of age. She had severe cheek-bones and a brisk, school marmish air about her, and the small bags under her eyes suggested that she'd already had quite enough of her shift. I decided to proceed with caution and extreme politeness.

'I'm sorry to trouble you,' I said. 'I was wondering if it might be possible to borrow a wheelchair? My friend, Mr Peterson in room two, needs to use the toilet and, as I'm sure you're aware, he has rather restricted mobility at the moment.'

It sounded a little stilted, but if I came across as awkward and meek, I reasoned this was all to the good.

Nurse Fletcher tapped her pen against her angular jaw for a few seconds. 'Can it wait until after the ward rounds, Mr . . . ?'

'Woods,' I said. 'And unfortunately, I don't think it *can* wait.'

Nurse Fletcher wrinkled her nose. 'I'm afraid, Mr Woods, your friend is not supposed to leave his bed without proper medical supervision. Doctor's orders. The last thing we want is to risk him having another fall.'

'I've been caring for him for some time. I can assure you that he won't be falling on my watch.'

Her eyes flicked back to my cheek for a few seconds. 'Forgive me for asking, Mr Woods, but have you been in a fight?'

'No. I'm a pacifist.'

'Did someone hit you?'

'Yes, a friend.'

Nurse Fletcher let this slide. She got up and produced from somewhere under the desk a vase-shaped receptacle made of thick cardboard. 'Perhaps this might be adequate for Mr Peterson's needs?'

I coughed delicately. 'No. I'm afraid it's the other sort of toilet he requires.'

Nurse Fletcher's expression remained neutral. She tapped her pen a few more times, then said: 'Oh, very well. Take a chair. But if you have any problems getting him in or out, wait for one of the nurses to assist you. We don't want any mishaps.'

I didn't hang around for her to change her mind. I grabbed the nearest chair from the alcove and hurried back to Mr Peterson's bed.

'Sorry,' I said. 'It took a little longer than I expected.'

Who's on reception? Mr Peterson wrote.

'Nurse Fletcher.'

Great. The humorless Nurse Fletcher. Let's not engage her in conversation if we don't have to.

'Agreed,' I said. 'Have the others been round yet?'

Mr Peterson shook his head. He'd already moved his bed into the upright position and was now gesturing hurriedly at the wheelchair. Despite Nurse Fletcher's warnings, transferring him wasn't too difficult. He had to lean on my shoulder with his left arm and on the bedside table with his right, but once he was on his feet, he only had to manage a couple of steps and a half-turn to lower himself safely into the seat.

When one of the nurses arrived at the bed, a few minutes later, she immediately wanted to know why Mr Peterson was out of bed and why we'd not waited for assistance. She addressed these questions to me, but we made her wait so that Mr Peterson could explain in writing and at length. We'd already agreed that part of our strategy should be to hold up our nurse until her colleague had finished with the patient in the bed adjacent and was ready to move along to the next room. We also thought that a long, tedious exchange was the best guarantor against her offering any further assistance.

'Nurse Fletcher said it was okay?' our nurse asked when Mr Peterson had handed her his elaborate missive.

Yes, she said that it was fine. Alex is going to assist me. He's quite capable. As soon as I've had my codeine we'll be on our way. Can I have it, please?

The nurse wordlessly handed him the small plastic beaker containing his medication.

Thank you, Mr Peterson wrote.

The nurse turned to me. 'Visiting hours are over in fifteen minutes. You shouldn't be here after that.' Then she and the other nurse wheeled the medication trolley back out into the corridor.

Let's go, Mr Peterson wrote. *Remember – walk past confidently, but don't rush. If she says anything, stick to the story.*

'Okay,' I said.

In the corridor, we veered right and proceeded at what I thought to be an appropriate, confident pace. I kept my back straight, my head up, and my eyes focussed on the double doors that marked the ward's terminus. I didn't cast a glance at reception as we approached, but I was dimly aware of Nurse Fletcher in my peripheral vision. She was still sitting at her post, hunched over her paperwork, but I had no idea if we had registered on her radar. The next five seconds would give me my answer. I held my breath and pressed forward. I was gripping the handles of the wheelchair so tightly that my knuckles had gone white. Two paces, three paces. My legs were no longer my own. They felt as rigid as stilts. But they only had to manage another ten metres to the doors. Reception slid past. My footfalls were barely perceptible in the enfolding silence. A dozen more steps and we'd be free.

'I'm not sure where you think you're going, Mr Woods,' Nurse Fletcher said.

I stopped and turned to face her. I had no choice.

'The last time I checked, the toilet was back that way.'

'Occupied,' I said cheerfully. 'We thought we'd just use the one on 6A.'

Nurse Fletcher tapped her pen against the desk. 'The toilet on 6A is for the patients on 6A. I'm sure that Mr Peterson can wait five minutes if he has to.'

I glanced down for help. Mr Peterson was already scribbling. He passed me his hastily torn-out note, which I handed on to Nurse Fletcher.

Mr Peterson can't wait.

I tried to make my tone conciliatory. 'As you can see, the situation's a little urgent.'

Nurse Fletcher curled her lip. 'I'm afraid it's out of the question. Mr Peterson is not meant to be out of bed without proper medical supervision. I certainly can't have the two of you gallivanting all over the hospital looking for an unoccupied lavatory, not when the facilities on the ward are more than adequate. If you go back now, you'll probably find that the toilet has already been vacated.'

Mr Peterson had started scribbling furiously.

This is ridiculous! We're going. I will not be treated like a child or an invalid!

I passed the note on. Nurse Fletcher read it, quite calmly, and then, without a moment's hesitation, raised the drawbridge to her desk and stepped out to join us in the corridor, positioning herself pointedly between ourselves and the exit. She looked quite prepared to wheel Mr Peterson back to his bed herself if needs be.

I stood like a statue. I could see the plan crashing and burning before my eyes.

Nurse Fletcher folded her arms. 'Mr Peterson,' she began, 'I can appreciate that you're distressed, but I'm afraid this is *not* open to discussion. The doctors have assessed your situation and advised us accordingly. They've been extremely clear in their instructions. You can't leave the ward unsupervised. I'm sorry, but we're acting with your best interests in mind.'

Alex, give this to Nurse Fletcher, Mr Peterson scrawled. *Since time is limited and she clearly has no interest in listening to me, I'm giving you permission to speak on my behalf. Please explain to her that we're leaving. Right now.*

I handed the note across. Nurse Fletcher looked at it and shrugged. 'I'm sorry, I can't understand this. It's not legible.'

'It says that I'm to speak on Mr Peterson's behalf,' I said. 'He's had enough of trying to talk to someone who has no interest in what he has to say.'

Nurse Fletcher raised her eyebrows in a way that told me I'd just crossed a line. But I pressed recklessly on.

'We're leaving,' I said. 'Mr Peterson doesn't care to stay here any longer. We're discharging him.'

Nurse Fletcher's voice was very calm and cold. 'No. That's simply not possible. He's in no state to be going *anywhere*.'

'I'm afraid that's not your decision to make,' I said. 'It's no one's decision but his. Please go and fetch the necessary paperwork.'

'Young man, I don't know what game you think you're playing here, but this is an extremely serious situation. Mr Peterson is going nowhere. You cannot discharge him without proper authorization.'

I held her gaze for a few icy moments. Mr Peterson passed me another note.

Tell her to call a doctor.

'What?' This was going way off script.

Mr Peterson was writing like a man possessed.

Insist! We need her behind that desk. As soon as she's on the phone, get me out of here.

I folded the note in my pocket.

'He'd like you to call a doctor, please.'

'Excuse me?'

'He wants you to call a doctor. Immediately.'

'Mr Woods, I've had quite enough of this now. This is not an emergency, and I'm not going to call—'

'It *is* an emergency. You've made Mr Peterson extremely distressed. You've said that he can't leave without a doctor's permission, so now we're asking you to call a doctor.'

Nurse Fletcher closed her eyes and exhaled through her tightly pursed lips. 'If you'd kindly take Mr Peterson back to his bed, then I assure you I'll get a doctor over to see him at the next reasonable opportunity.'

I looked at Nurse Fletcher for about five seconds, then I backed up a couple of paces and parallel-parked Mr Peterson's wheelchair against the reception desk. I made a big show of applying the footbrake.

'We're not going anywhere,' I said. 'Make the phone call and find out how long it's going to take to get a doctor across. If the answer's acceptable, *then* Mr Peterson will consider returning to his bed.'

For a few awful moments it seemed that Nurse Fletcher was

going to remain immovable. It had never been discussed at any stage of the planning, but I was fast coming to the conclusion that I might have to ram her.

And then, quite suddenly, she unfolded her arms and spun on her heels. 'Very well.' The drawbridge was up. She was back behind her desk, reaching for the telephone. 'I can tell you exactly what the doctor's going to say. But if this is what it's going to take, then so be it.' She punched in the four-digit extension code. Out of her eye-line, I slipped the footbrake off. 'Yes, hello. This is Nurse Fletcher on 6B. I need to get hold of doct—'

I ran.

The double doors held us up for less than three frantic heartbeats. I accelerated through a reckless ninety-degree turn, braced my legs and launched us towards the lifts. The momentum we'd accrued five seconds later was almost enough to pull my arms from their sockets. I overshot the near lift by a good two metres. Mr Peterson lurched dangerously in his chair. I fell forward and felt a handle burying itself in my ribcage, but there was no time to catch my breath. I backed up and jabbed the call button six or seven times. The torture of waiting for the lift to ascend five floors was instantly assuaged when the doors opened to reveal an empty interior. By the time we were in and I'd hit the G button, I could hear rapid footfalls echoing amidst the blood surging in my ears. I spun to witness Nurse Fletcher and a gangly porter hurtling into the narrowing frame of the closing doors. I couldn't begin to imagine where the minion had materialized from, but his arrival was too late to make a difference. The floors counted down to zero, then I exploded from the lift like a rocket. It was completely unnecessary by this point. The foyer was still deserted, and had it not been, my actions would most likely have proven counterproductive. But I couldn't help myself. There was so much adrenaline in my bloodstream, so much oxygen being pumped to my brain and arms and legs, that *not* running was unthinkable. No paramedic could ever have wheeled a patient into that hospital as fast as I wheeled Mr Peterson out. I took the hairpin bend of the exit ramp like a rally driver, shot past a bemused smoker and screeched to a halt twenty metres later, barely a foot from the passenger door of our waiting car.

There was no discussion, no hesitation. Mr Peterson felt virtually weightless as I helped him in. Unthinkingly, I folded the wheelchair and crammed it into the back. Three minutes later, I'd circled the hospital roundabout and pulled off the dual carriageway into the Tesco garage, where we were safely shielded from view by a row of tall trees.

I flicked on the interior light and waited for my hands to stop shaking.

Mr Peterson passed me a note: *You did great. I'm proud of you.*

I wiped my eyes and took about ten huge breaths.

'I don't know what came over me with the wheelchair,' I confessed. 'I meant to leave it in the car park. I guess I'll just have to return it when this is all over. I don't feel good about stealing from the NHS.'

Mr Peterson started making a strangled choking noise. It took me several moments to realize that he was laughing, and even longer to realize that I was laughing too. Not the kind of laughs you make at a joke, but huge, hysterical, hyena laughs that wracked my whole body and sent tears streaming down my cheeks. It was several minutes before my head had cleared enough to allow me to read his next note.

You're OK?

'I'm okay.'

Great. So let's get out of here.

I flipped the ignition and pulled back onto the road. Ten minutes later, we were on the A303, racing east into the deepening night.

ELEMENTARY PARTICLES

When we disembarked in Calais, it was about 6 a.m., local time, and the eastern horizon was just starting to brighten. We left the port a few minutes later, passing the customs gate unhindered, and then drove a hundred miles before stopping for breakfast just outside Saint-Quentin.

The Channel had been calm and the crossing unremarkable. By the time we'd boarded the ferry, Mr Peterson's lack of sleep had finally caught up with him. I left him dozing in his wheelchair in a secluded corner of the lower passenger deck while I went upstairs to the open upper deck. It was the first time I'd been on a boat. It was the first time I'd been further from home than London. I spent most of the next ninety minutes towards the bow, watching the black water swelling beneath me and the stars ascending before me. I was quite alone; the few other passengers on board were all below deck. There were no distractions, just the sound of the sea and the unhurried rotation of the sky. With only minimal on-deck lighting, it was dark enough to make out the broad, silver arch of the Milky Way, which materialized over the stern in Cassiopeia, swept high overhead, and then cascaded south into Sagittarius and the sea. Saturn was sinking starboard in Virgo as Venus was rising in Pisces over the port bow. The flat horizon afforded a novel symmetry and harmony to the sky. It made me think, fleetingly, of my mother – I was sure that she'd have some unfathomable theory about what was going on up there. But this was just a stray thought that came and passed like a mist. For the most part, I didn't think at all. I just watched, letting my mind drift from sensation to sensation, like a butterfly caught on a warm breeze.

My head was in a curious place. I wasn't thinking about what lay ahead; and everything that had gone before – at the shop and the hospital – had already taken on the character of a quickly fading dream. Only now seemed real. The adrenaline of escape had long since departed, but it seemed to have somehow flushed out my system, leaving me perfectly calm and alert. Or that was my working hypothesis. I'd also drunk eight cans of Diet Coke since Yeovil, and I wasn't discounting the possibility that this might have played some role in keeping my mind clear and focussed. Whatever the case, I didn't need to sleep, and, more than this, I didn't *expect* to need any sleep until we got to Zurich. It's hard to explain this expectation without sounding like my mother, but the simplest way I can put things is as follows: getting Mr Peterson to Switzerland was my job; it was the task I'd been appointed to; and once I'd accepted this, I knew that I'd be able to hold myself together for as long as it took. If I had to drive seven hundred miles to Zurich without sleep, then I would. If I'd had to drive to China or New Zealand, or the far side of the moon, I would have done that too. I knew our goal, and I was going to get us there. It was that simple.

I wasn't tired when we left the port, and I wasn't tired when we pulled off the *autoroute* at Saint-Quentin. But I *was* ravenous. In the service-station restaurant, I ate about five pains au chocolat, washed down with more Diet Coke, while Mr Peterson managed to eat a croissant by dunking it first in his coffee; because of his difficulties with swallowing, it wasn't easy for him to eat dry food. After that, he sat with the car door open and smoked some of his marijuana while I found a grassy hillock where I could meditate. The grass was a little wet, but I had a blanket wrapped round my shoulders to keep me warm. The constant rush of traffic became the rhythm of my breaths, rising, falling and eventually fading to nothingness.

We continued in the same vein all the way to the Swiss border, driving in ninety-minute, hundred-mile bursts, stopping at various service stations and small towns along the way so that I could stretch my legs and Mr Peterson could have another smoke. He smoked much more than usual during that ten-hour drive across Europe. He said it was because my final harvest was *an exceptionally smooth and mellow smoke - much too good to waste*, but I thought that there was probably something more going on. I didn't know for sure that Mr Peterson was experiencing more pain since leaving the hospital, but he was definitely in a certain amount of physical discomfort. The fall had shaken him, and the subsequent two and a half days he'd spent bedbound had taken an additional toll on his mobility. It seemed that even that short period of inactivity had led to some kind of deterioration in his muscles or neural pathways. He was suffering from stiffness and cramps that he struggled to alleviate. It was a visible effort for him even to manoeuvre his legs from the footwell to the ground outside the passenger seat so that he could face the open air as he smoked.

For this reason, and despite my residual guilt, the stolen wheelchair was turning out to be a godsend, and Mr Peterson had been quick to accept the practical arguments for its continued usage. I wheeled him in and out of the services, and we progressed steadily southeast across the country.

The farmland of northern France was more expansive but not otherwise very different from the farmland of southern England. Were it not for the signs and the tollbooths and driving on the right-hand side of the road, it would have been pretty much indistinguishable. But things started to change as we moved into the wine-growing regions further from the coast. By Lunéville, where we stopped for lunch, it didn't seem so much like England any more; and by the time we stopped at Saint-Louis, just west of the Swiss border, I felt sufficiently in another country to think about calling my mother.

I don't know what I can tell you about that phone call. It did not go well. Beyond that, there's not much to report.

It was around 3 p.m. local time, 2 p.m. British Summer Time, and I thought that the five hours I'd left for her to read and digest the contents of my letter might be enough to dampen down her initial reaction. But there was little evidence that this strategy had worked. She started crying the moment I started speaking, and she was still crying when I hung up. In between, she managed only a handful of stuttered sentences. She said, 'Oh, Alex,' a lot. She asked where I was and told me that I needed to come home, that nothing bad was going to happen as long as I came home right away. I didn't know what she meant by this, and I'd already decided that I couldn't tell her where I was. I could only tell her that I was safe and I'd be back by the end of the next week, but this reassurance did nothing to improve the situation. If anything, it made matters worse. Eventually, after I'd waited a couple of minutes to see if my mother was going to cry herself dry, I asked to speak to Ellie, but it wasn't even evident that she had heard me.

'I think perhaps I should speak to Ellie,' I repeated. 'Can you put her on?'

My mother continued to cry.

I hung up. There wasn't much else I could do.

We crossed the border mid-afternoon and entered Zurich an hour later. The traffic was slow-moving and the urban Swiss were calm and considerate drivers, which gave me plenty of time to find my landmarks, spot street signs and orientate myself within my mental map, which, I should tell you, was extremely comprehensive. I'd decided previously that it would be sensible for me to memorize the entire roadmap of the city. This had been an ongoing project for the past month. I'd spent several evenings and lunchtimes hunched over the Michelin map learning by heart various long and elaborate street names such as Pfingstweidstrasse and Seebahnstrasse and Alfred-Escher-Strasse and so on; and then I'd spent several more evenings and lunchtimes familiarizing myself with the different metropolitan districts and their subdivisions. The main districts were numbered one to twelve, and formed two nested arches around the northernmost tip of Lake Zurich, with District One – the Altstadt – acting as the keystone and the other districts counting clockwise in twin layers from base to base. I found this a reassuringly practical approach to town planning; from what I'd been able to ascertain online, the Swiss were a reassuringly practical people. They had a long, proud history of staying out of wars, preferring to devote themselves to more constructive endeavours like science, secure banking and building extremely accurate clocks.

Anyway, although memorizing the Michelin map allowed me to feel instantly settled on the city's roads, in hindsight, my preparations may have been a little over the top. In case you didn't know, Zurich is a very distinctive city. It sits in a natural bowl formed by the Limmat river basin and, as I've mentioned, is shaped like a tall bridge, or broad horseshoe, with the north tip of the lake forming the thin central hollow. The Limmat bisects the centre of the Altstadt along a straight north–south line, splitting the city into neat, almost symmetrical halves, and the Alps rise thirty kilometres due south from the river mouth. With all these natural signposts, Zurich is not a particularly difficult city to navigate. Or that was my experience.

It probably helped, too, that the District Eight hotel Herr Schäfer had recommended to us was very easy to access by car. Most of the hotels in Zurich are clustered around the Limmat in the middle of town, but ours was located just off Utoquai, the main thoroughfare that runs down the northeastern shore of the lake. Herr Schäfer had a bank of about a dozen hotels that he could recommend according to the varying requirements and budgets of his clients. He had a lot of experience catering for foreigners who came to Switzerland to die.

As for Mr Peterson's requirements, these were relatively simple. I'd typed them into an email for him about a month earlier, just after confirmation of his appointment date came through. He needed a hotel that was in a reasonably tranquil location, with good road links, onsite parking and facilities suited to the mobility-impaired. His room would have to be spacious and similarly handicapped-friendly, with handrails in the bathroom and at least one sturdy, high-backed chair. In addition, he was keen to get a room with a balcony, and didn't want to stay in 'the kind of place you'd go while waiting to die'.

If you can think of a more appropriate way to put that, he'd told me, *please do.*

Unfortunately, I could not, and I thought it better to state his wishes candidly than to risk a misunderstanding. The phrasing above is the phrasing we went with, and when we arrived at the hotel, I thought that this criterion had been pretty well met, although this was another area in which I had little expertise. I'd never stayed in a hotel before – I'd only seen them in films – so I didn't really know what the kind of hotel you'd stay in while waiting to die would look or feel like. All I can say is that our hotel seemed like a very good hotel to me. It had a big lobby with a high ceiling and tall stone columns and a floor that was made either from marble or a convincing marble substitute. The reception desk had a thick counter of dark, polished wood and a golden sign that had been engraved in German, English and French. It read:

Empfang / Reception / Réception

But I thought that at least one of these translations was probably superfluous.

'*Guten Tag, mein Herr,*' I said to the desk clerk in my brisk, competent German. '*Wir haben zwei Zimmer reserviert. Der Name ist "Peterson".*'

He was a small, tidy man wearing a creaseless suit and a

thin, professional smile. And he replied in precise, barely accented English: 'Ah, yes. Mr Peterson. Welcome to the Hotel Seeufer. I trust that your stay with us will be a pleasant one.'

'*Ich bin nicht Herr Peterson,*' I corrected him. '*Herr Peterson ist der Mann im Stuhl.*'

The clerk nodded. 'Yes, I see. My apologies for the confusion.'

'*Das macht nichts. Können Sie uns mit unserem Gepäck helfen?*'

The clerk twitched nervously. 'Yes, of course. I will have one of our porters attend to you immediately. In the meanwhile, there are just a few forms that perhaps you would be willing to complete?'

'*Ja. Das wird kein Problem sein.*'

It was a strange, ping-pong conversation that continued in this vein for some time. The clerk's refusal to speak German I put down to some obscure facet of hotel etiquette that I was unfamiliar with. His slightly edgy disposition I put down to my over-zealous, war-film accent. But I left the encounter satisfied that I'd at least been able to make myself understood.

Mr Peterson's room was on the first floor and was extremely large. It had a tall, arched window and a balcony looking west across the lake, and because it was late in the afternoon, the whole room was flooded with sunlight, like in one of those bad car adverts where the photography's so overexposed that it hurts your eyes. I had to wait a few moments before I could take proper stock of the interior, but my first impression was that it met all of Mr Peterson's needs. There were two broad, high-backed chairs, as well as one of those strange sofas with the narrow, stubby legs and only one armrest. The furniture was all separated by ample floor space for ease of access, and there were two up-lighting lamps on metal stands. On one wall was a painting of an unnaturally tall and slender woman with an unnaturally long and thin cigarette, and on another was a mirror constructed from five symmetrically arranged panes of glass – four trapezia and a central pentagon – which looked like the kind of mirror Superman might have in his Fortress of Solitude. All the décor followed this curiously geometrical design, and somehow managed to look very modern and very old-fashioned all at once. Even the chrome handrails in the bathroom looked like freshly sculpted antiques.

Holy shit, wrote Mr Peterson.

'It doesn't feel like the kind of place you'd come to die,' I ventured.

No, it doesn't.

'To be honest with you, I think Herr Schäfer's met the brief pretty well.'

He must have one hell of a sense of humor, Mr Peterson wrote.

My room was just across the corridor. It was classified as a 'standard' room, but really this was all quite relative. It didn't have a balcony or a lake view, and it was perhaps only two-thirds the size of Mr Peterson's disabled room, but otherwise, it was more or less the same. It had one of those blocky, bright red armchairs and an en-suite bathroom and a dark wooden desk with a lamp next to it. It had an old-fashioned telephone with a cradle and a circular dialling mechanism, and a twenty-eight-inch wall-mounted LCD television with lots of German, French and Italian channels as well as MTV and CNN and BBC News. It also had a mini-fridge hidden in the central cabinet of the desk, just below the safe. It contained four twenty-five-centilitre bottles of wine, which I relocated to the wardrobe to make space for six cans of Diet Coke.

After we'd eaten and I was alone and settled into my room, it was around ten thirty Central European Time. I phoned Ellie, who didn't deviate from the standard greeting I'd come to expect.

'Fuck, Woods!' she said. 'I told you not to call me!'

'You told me not to call until I'd spoken to my mother,' I pointed out. 'We spoke earlier.'

'Yes, I'm aware of that. I had to hold her hand through the whole fucking ordeal!'

'I told you calling her was a bad idea.'

'*That* wasn't the bad idea. You know, she only left about an hour ago. It took her that long to calm down. She didn't even open the shop today.'

I took a moment to let this sink in. In a way, it was a more damning indictment than the five minutes of continuous crying I'd experienced earlier. In the past seven years, my mother had closed her shop precisely zero times, and before that, it had taken a meteor impact to get her to take some time off work.

'She hasn't even been able to use her cards,' Ellie continued. 'She tried, but they've stopped talking to her.'

I didn't know what to say to this. So I said nothing.

'Woods? Are you still there? You're not gonna hang up on me too?'

'I thought you didn't want to talk to me,' I pointed out.

'That's not what I said. Just shut up and listen a moment. There's something else you need to know. The police have been round.'

'The police?'

'They were here a few hours ago, asking all sorts of questions. I think you might be in a whole heap of shit.'

My mind did a strange, clumsy dance. 'She called the police?'

'Who called the police?'

'My mother?'

'Don't be retarded!' I could hear Ellie's eyes rolling down the phone. 'Your mum didn't call the police. Of *course* she didn't! Do you really think she'd do that?'

'I don't know.'

'You don't know? That's your problem, right there. Sometimes you're just completely fucking clueless!'

'Yes, I understand that.'

'The hospital called the police.'

'What did the police say?' I asked.

'What do you think the police said? They asked about your "state of mind". They wanted to know where you might go or what you might be planning. They made your mum show them that ridiculous note.'

'They've seen the note?'

'Stop repeating me! Just listen. They've seen the note and they've taken it away as "evidence". They said that the wording gave serious cause for concern, or somesuch shit.'

'It was the best wording I could come up with.'

'Yes, *I* realize that. And I think at some point your mum might realize that too. But to someone who doesn't know you . . . Jesus, Woods, it reads like it was written by Hannibal Lecter!

There're some things you really don't want to appear too cool and casual about.'

'I'm not cool *or* casual,' I said. 'You know that.'

'*I* know that. The police don't. They think you're made of ice. They wanted to know if you're the kind of person who can be reasoned with. They want to put out an appeal – you know, like they do when there's a hit-and-run or some pervert abducts a child. They want your mum to go on the news asking you to come home.'

'Is she going to?'

'I don't know. I don't think *she* knows right now. But if she doesn't, I think the police are gonna go ahead with the appeal anyway. You know what the police are like. They're the same as the hospital: they have to cover their arses. They don't want it to look like they're doing nothing.'

I thought about this for a few moments. 'Would it be okay if I called you back tomorrow?'

'You'd *better* call me back tomorrow!' Ellie threatened. 'If you're not gonna speak to your mother, you have to speak to someone.'

And the line went dead. Ellie ended her phone conversations the same way she ended her regular, face-to-face conversations. Abruptly.

I realized at that moment that I was completely exhausted. Forty hours without sleep didn't creep up on me. It just hit me: all over my body, all at once. I used the last of my strength to return the phone to its cradle, then fell asleep in my clothes on top of the bed sheets. I did not dream.

* * *

The following morning, Herr Schäfer met us, as arranged, at ten o'clock in the hotel bar. It was, he later told us, his policy to try to meet with every one of his clients in the days before their appointments. Since he'd started in his line of work, around twelve years earlier, he had helped one thousand one hundred and forty-seven foreigners to die in Switzerland (Mr Peterson would be one thousand one hundred and forty-eight), and the only clients he *hadn't* met beforehand were those who'd explicitly stated this was against their wishes.

My first impression of Herr Schäfer was that he was much larger, in all dimensions, than I'd expected. He was a tall, well-built man whom I estimated to be in his early sixties. He had thick-framed glasses, silver-grey hair and very dark, serious eyes. Even when he was talking about something inconsequential, his eyes remained grave. He wore a charcoal-grey suit with a dark blue tie, and his handshake, I noted, was a precise mirror of my own: two solid up-down movements and eye contact throughout. When he spoke, his English was fast and fluent, although his wording of certain phrases was slightly odd, and he had more of an accent than the hotel desk clerk: he elongated and Germanized some of his Ws, and there was a soft buzz that attended about seventy-five per cent of his initial Ss, so that 'will' became 'veal' and 'suicide' 'zooicide'. You can imagine these sounds if you wish, but for the sake of clarity, I won't try to transcribe them.

Beyond saying *Guten Morgen*, I did not attempt to speak much German with Herr Schäfer. I was okay with subject areas that I'd had time to rehearse, but struggled when I had to improvise, and many of the subjects we'd be discussing with Herr Schäfer were not well covered by the online syllabus I'd been using.

'I hope that you are both finding the hotel to your satisfactions?' Herr Schäfer asked after the handshakes were over and we'd taken our seats.

Mr Peterson nodded.

'Mr Peterson finds it difficult to speak,' I explained. 'Also he struggles a bit with eye contact because of his condition, so he prefers to communicate in writing.'

Herr Schäfer gave a reassuring smile. 'It is of no matter. You must communicate in the way that is the most comfortable for you.'

Thank you, Mr Peterson wrote. *The hotel's very nice.*

Herr Schäfer nodded thoughtfully. 'It is not a hotel that I use very often, but it is one of my particular favourites nonetheless. I thought it would be well suited to your requirements. I find that the art deco interiors are very elegant but also very practical.'

Art deco turned out to be the name of the strange modern-antique style of furniture in the rooms. Herr Schäfer discussed this at some length, telling us that the hotel had first opened in 1919 and for many years had been a popular haunt for Zurich intellectuals. James Joyce had stayed there several times in the 1930s, by which time he no longer lived in Zurich, but visited frequently for appointments with his optometrist. From 1915 to 1917 he'd lived just round the corner, at apartments on Kreuzstrasse and Seefeldstrasse. I told Herr Schäfer that I'd heard of James Joyce, but only because of quarks, which were elementary particles named after a word that James Joyce had invented for some reason. This information seemed to please Herr Schäfer very much.

'But now, I think, we must get down to our business at hand,' he said, bringing this short diversion to an end. 'Your first doctor appointment is booked for six o'clock this evening, and the next for seven o'clock tomorrow evening. I hope that you will not find the delay too much of an inconvenience. I know that for some people it is difficult, but we are required by law to have this separation between appointments.'

We're not in a rush, Mr Peterson wrote.

Herr Schäfer smiled, but his eyes remained grave. 'You understand that this protocol is intended as a safeguard. Only a doctor can prescribe you with the medication that will end your life, and she must be satisfied that these are indeed your wishes and there is just cause to do so.'

Is there any chance she'll decide that I don't have just cause to end my life? Mr Peterson asked.

'No, I don't think so,' Herr Schäfer replied. 'Doctor Reinhardt is acquainted with your file, and she is a sympathetic woman. She will only need to make certain that you understand the choice you are making and that it is a choice you have given its due consideration. And you must understand that you are free to change your mind at any point. It is never too late to turn back from this path you are walking.'

Thank you, Mr Peterson wrote. *My mind is set.*

Herr Schäfer nodded. 'Yes, of course. But you understand, I'm sure, why we have to be very clear on this point. You will be asked the same questions many times, today, tomorrow and the next day.'

I understand. What happens once the doctor has agreed to write a prescription?

'After that, we will be free to proceed the following day.

You will sign an authorization for a member of our staff to pick up the prescription on your behalf, and then we will take care of everything. We have a comfortable, private house just outside of the city where you will be met by two of our escorts. They are very experienced and will be able to assist you at every stage of the process. The only thing they cannot help with is the final administering of the medication. They will be present, but the final action that ends your life must be your own. And you must decide when it is time to do this. Our staff will not prompt you. They will not put pressure on you in any way.'

What about Alex?

'Alex can be there the whole time if that's what you both want. Our experience has shown that usually it is a great comfort for the friends and family to be there at the end – in fact it is a comfort for everyone involved. But again this is your decision to make.'

I meant afterwards. What will happen to Alex afterwards?

'Our staff will take good care of him. They have lots of experience in this area. We always have two escorts present so that one can stay with the family while the other deals with the practicalities. The coroner and the police will have to be contacted, as is the case in all suicides, but Alex will not be required to speak with them. Our testimony and the papers you will have signed will be sufficient evidence that everything was done in proper accordance with the law. Don't worry: we make the protection of our clients and their loved ones our first priority.'

Thank you, Mr Peterson wrote. *That's what I needed to know.*

This was the point at which I asked Herr Schäfer how many people he'd helped to die. A quick calculation told me that it translated to approximately one person every four days.

'Yes, that sounds correct,' Herr Schäfer confirmed.

You're running an efficient business, Mr Peterson wrote.

'I hope I am to take this as a compliment?' Herr Schäfer asked.

Mr Peterson nodded.

'Thank you,' Herr Schäfer said. 'You should know that many people would *not* mean that as a compliment. They think, rather strangely, that there should not be this efficiency in the death business – that it shows a lack of compassion. But I hope you can see that this is not the case. Let me put it this way: at your funeral, would you rather have the pall-bearer who keeps a steady hand or the one who is so overcome by grief that he drops the coffin?'

Mr Peterson nodded. Herr Schäfer's eyes remained serious throughout.

'Good, so I think we are in agreement. We tolerate a certain amount of incompetence in our politicians and public servants, but we should not tolerate it in the death business.

'But now, unless you have any more questions, perhaps we should bring our meeting to a close? Your time is, after all, precious. Have you thought about how you are going to spend the hours between your appointments?'

'We're going to take a look around Zurich,' I said.

Herr Schäfer nodded. 'Good. It is a city of many charms. And what about tomorrow evening? Do you have plans for dinner? There are many excellent restaurants I can recommend to you if that is something you would like? Alternatively, I cook a rather good *boeuf bourguignon* and would be happy to offer you my personal hospitality.'

I looked at Mr Peterson. He shrugged. He had a kind of wry smile on his face. I shrugged too. 'We'd like to accept your offer,' I said, 'but you'll have to provide us with good directions. Unfortunately, we don't have satnav.'

We managed to get all around Zurich without really doing anything in particular. We wandered through the Altstadt, looking at a multitude of squares and churches and clock faces. We crossed and recrossed the Limmat about half a dozen times. I wheeled Mr Peterson on and off the tram and we hunted down the Opernhaus and the Rathaus and the Kunsthaus and the house on Unionstrasse where Einstein had lived as a student. There was a small plaque next to the door, which read: *'Hier wohnte von 1896–1900 der grosse Physiker und Friedensfreund Albert Einstein.'*

I translated this for Mr Peterson as follows: 'Here lived from 1896 to 1900 the great physicist and friend of peace Albert Einstein.'

Friend of peace? Mr Peterson queried.

'Friedensfreund,' I said. 'I think that's an accurate translation. *Freund* is definitely "friend" and I seem to remember that *Frieden* is "peace".'

Pacifist? Mr Peterson suggested.

'Yes, I suppose that's a better translation,' I conceded.

We didn't go into Einstein's house. We didn't go into any of the museums or churches or galleries that we passed. Mr Peterson said that he didn't want to be indoors more than necessary, and he especially didn't want to go anywhere quiet. He was happier in the fresh air and bustle, just moving from place to place. He didn't want to stay still for too long.

We were back at the hotel in plenty of time for our first appointment with Dr Reinhardt, which took place in Mr Peterson's room. We both sat in the blocky art deco chairs while Dr Reinhardt perched a few feet away on the one-armed, stubby-footed sofa. She was, as Herr Schäfer had told us, a sympathetic woman, but she was also very thorough in her questioning. And because Mr Peterson often had to provide quite detailed responses, the interview lasted a long time.

Dr Reinhardt asked about the injury to Mr Peterson's left hand, and he told her that he'd fallen a few days earlier and had received treatment in hospital. (He omitted the second half of this story – quite wisely, I thought.) Then she asked him lots more questions about his PSP and the impact it was having on his life. This was probably the easiest part of the interview. The facts were simple and indisputable. Much trickier was negotiating the dark waters surrounding Mr Peterson's previous suicide attempt and subsequent hospitalization – his six-week stay on the psychiatric ward. These facts were, of course, well documented in his medical record, and they drew us deep into *Catch-22* territory.

Under Swiss law, Dr Reinhardt explained, the prescription of narcotics and anaesthetics was very tightly regulated. The specific law that controlled such prescriptions was a formidable piece of legislation, and it had a similarly formidable name. It was called *die Betäubungsmittelverschreibungsverordnung*. This name was considered formidable even by native German-speakers, who were used to long words. Nevertheless, Dr Reinhardt assured us that, once you got to grips with it, *die Betäubungsmittelverschreibungsverordnung* was not all that complicated – or not in the section dealing with physician-assisted suicides. In essence, there were three sensible rules: the patient must have expressed explicitly his desire to die, this desire had to be persistent, and the patient had to be of indisputably sound mind. It was this final point that caused the problem, of course, because it was standard medical practice – sanctioned by *The ICD-10 Classification of Mental and Behavioural Disorders* – to regard the desire for self-destruction as evidence of poor mental health.

Mr Peterson wrote an elaborate page and a bit explaining how he'd been hospitalized and forced to take Prozac for six weeks, but he'd never actually felt himself to be 'depressed' – or not until he'd been handed to the psychiatrists.

It was being sectioned that made me depressed, Mr Peterson concluded, *not vice versa.*

Fortunately, Mr Peterson's past diagnosis of 'depression' was not deemed to be a critical factor, and Dr Reinhardt was more than satisfied with his explanation. She only had to be sure that he was thinking clearly in the present, and that his desire for death was not the product of a short-term depressive episode. The fact that he'd been a member of an assisted suicide clinic for the past fifteen months suggested it was not. Dr Reinhardt felt confident that she could write him a prescription without violating the terms of *die Betäubungsmittelverschreibungsverordnung*.

She had greater concerns regarding whether or not Mr Peterson would be physically capable of ending his own life. The medicament – she did not refer to it as a 'medicine' – that was prescribed for assisted suicides was sodium pentobarbital, and since most patients would not be able to administer it safely to themselves as an intravenous injection, it had to be taken orally. The medicament would be dissolved in about sixty millilitres of water, which then had to be drunk down quickly, preferably in one attempt. This would cause a peaceful loss of consciousness in a matter of minutes, followed by respiratory failure a few minutes later. It was completely painless and risk-free, Dr Reinhardt assured us, but the sodium pentobarbital had to be swallowed quickly and in its entirety. Sipping the solution or taking an incomplete dose would be likely to result in a loss of consciousness, or even an anaesthetic coma, but it would not guarantee death.

The problem, of course, was that swallowing thin liquids was not easy for Mr Peterson. The same neurodegeneration that caused the difficulty with his speech also affected his ability to control his throat muscles. Sixty millilitres of water was not a lot, but the dissolved sodium pentobarbital had a very bitter taste, and this increased the chance of a choke reflex.

Dr Reinhardt had to be confident that Mr Peterson could knock back a small glass of water without complications, so she made him do two trial runs. The first was a bit of a struggle, but he managed it in less than seven seconds, which was deemed a satisfactory time-frame. In the second run, Dr Reinhardt suggested that he use a straw while I held the glass. (This kind of assistance was acceptable, as long as I didn't *pour* the drink; the action that ended Mr Peterson's life had to be his own.) Because he was no longer worrying about his hand–eye co-ordination, Mr Peterson could focus all his attention on his throat, and consequently, found the straw method much easier. Dr Reinhardt was satisfied and left with the promise that the next evening's appointment would be much shorter. We would run through the practicalities once more, Mr

Peterson would reconfirm his decision to die, and after that, the prescription would be written. There would be no further obstacles.

It wasn't so late when I phoned Ellie that evening. I don't think it was even nine o'clock, less than twenty-four hours since our previous conversation, but already, in this short time, things had started to move.

The police had gone ahead with their 'appeal' that morning: they wanted me, or anyone else who knew of my whereabouts, to contact the Somerset and Avon Constabulary immediately. My mother had declined the police's invitation to deliver the appeal personally; her only involvement had been in supplying them with a recent photograph of me. According to Ellie, it was not a good one.

'I guess it was the most recent photo she could find,' Ellie told me. 'Or maybe the only photo she could find. I don't see why else she would have given them *that*.'

The photo showed me sitting at home with Lucy on my lap. 'That's probably the only time she could get me to stay put for a photograph,' I reasoned. 'She knows I don't like having my photo taken.'

'Yeah. It shows.'

'Do I look pissed off?'

'No, you don't look pissed off. I mean, you've got this kind of *snarl* going on – your face is really screwed up – but I wouldn't say you look pissed off. That would be an improvement. To be honest with you, you look fucking sinister.'

'At least the cat's there,' I reasoned. 'I suppose that must humanize me a bit.'

'The cat makes you look like a Bond villain.'

'Oh.'

'They've been showing it on the news – and not just the local news. By this evening it was on the *national* news. Seriously, this is a big story, and it's gonna get bigger. You can tell. It's got "public interest" written all over it. The details are just fucked up enough to grab people's attention. We've already had a couple of journalists phoning the shop. Trust me: this story isn't going away.'

Once more, I didn't relay any of this information to Mr Peterson. I didn't think it would do him any good. And despite Ellie's dramatics, I still felt reasonably insulated from whatever was going on at home. I doubted that anyone in Europe paid too much attention to what was happening in the UK, much less Somerset. Nevertheless, when Mr Peterson told me the following morning that he wanted to get out of the city for the day, I decided that this was not a bad idea.

I don't really care where we go, he told me, *but I think I'd like to see those mountains a little closer up.*

'You want me to drive you into the mountains?' I asked.

No, I thought we'd walk.

'Oh.'

I'm kidding.

'Right.'

I'll leave the itinerary up to you. We can go wherever the hell you want. Just so long as it's away from the city.

I thought about this for a few seconds. 'How do you feel about CERN?' I asked.

* * *

So we drove to CERN. It was a four-hundred-mile round trip, but luckily when it came to car travel, Mr Peterson still had what he termed an 'American mindset'. With eleven hours to spare, he did not regard a journey halfway across Switzerland and back as a daunting prospect, and neither did I.

Sticking to the *Geschwindigkeitsbegrenzung* and taking the A1, the *Autobahn* that cuts straight across Switzerland's central plateau, linking Geneva, Bern and Zurich, the return leg of our journey took a little under three hours. But on the outward leg we took the four-hour scenic route, skirting the foot of the Alps with a halfway stop at Interlaken, which looked like a postcard – as did most of Switzerland, in fact. It was the kind of country where you couldn't imagine anyone ever dropping litter, a country of crisp air and castles and jagged mountains and lakes like mirror-glass, reflecting only pristine hues of blue and green and white.

Of course, by the time we'd reached CERN, at the French border just northwest of Geneva, the landscape had diminished somewhat, but the surroundings were still pleasant enough. There were rolling hills covered by vineyards and scattered trees and villages, and you could still see the Juras to the north and Mont Blanc rising fifty miles to the southeast. As for CERN itself, my first impression was that it looked like a large but otherwise normal workplace – the kind of business park you'd find outside any city or large town. It had a bus stop and a supermarket-sized car park filled with fuel-efficient hatchbacks. It had a reception and lots of blocky, flat-roofed buildings that looked like regular offices, and a handful of workers drifting around outside who didn't look exactly *ir*regular either, aside from the fact that none of them was wearing a tie. (As you probably know, scientists don't wear ties unless they're giving evidence to a parliamentary inquiry or receiving a Nobel Prize.) The only noteworthy things about the complex were the twenty European flags flapping over the central boulevard and the thirty-by-forty-metre wooden globe that sat across the road from reception. But, of course, this was just the surface; I knew that most of what was interesting about CERN was buried a hundred metres below us.

We weren't allowed to go down to see the Large Hadron Collider because it was the most expensive science experiment in human history and not open to the general public. The receptionist directed us instead to the Globe of Science and Innovation, the vast wooden structure over the road, which housed a permanent exhibition on CERN and particle physics.

What is a large hadron, anyway? Mr Peterson asked as I was wheeling him across.

'It's not the hadron that's large,' I explained, 'it's the accelerator. A hadron's just a proton or neutron or similar particle, and they come in regulation sizes, like ping-pong balls. They're exactly like ping-pong balls except they're about twenty-five trillion times smaller.'

That number means nothing to me.

'Two point five times ten to the thirteen: twenty-five followed by twelve zeroes.'

That's even more meaningless.

'If you scaled up a proton so it had the diameter of a ping-pong ball,' I clarified, 'then a ping-pong ball, in comparison, would have a diameter seven hundred times the diameter of the Sun. It would be approximately the same size as Betelgeuse.'

That's just plain ridiculous, Mr Peterson wrote.

Although it was very austere on the outside, once we'd made our way through to the exhibition area, the Globe of Science and Innovation looked like the command centre of an alien spacecraft. Mr Peterson found it to be *vaguely hallucinogenic*, and while it had little in common with any of the hallucinations I'd experienced, I knew what he meant nonetheless. The interior was a vast circular arena dotted with variously sized orbs and screens and interactive display pods, with everything illuminated by coloured spotlights that shifted and faded and brightened as you moved around the room. The lights were all in very dramatic, futuristic tones like turquoise and violet and electric blue, and, inevitably, there were lots of strange, ambient noises humming and fizzing in the background – all the standard devices that marketing teams and PR men use to 'sex up' particle physics, as if this were a subject that needs such interference. Nevertheless, I had to admit that the audiovisuals *were* impressive, and the exhibition itself was very well put together. The interactive display pods had an English audio option, which meant Mr Peterson didn't have to struggle to read anything. One touch of the screen elicited a two- to five-minute lecture on topics such as antimatter and dark energy and Heisenberg's Uncertainty Principle and so on. There was plenty of information, but since Mr Peterson didn't have the benefit of the onscreen graphics, which moved too quickly for his eyes to follow, I still found myself adding bits and pieces wherever I could. It started off with simple explanations of what was going on onscreen, but grew increasingly complicated from pod to pod. I don't know why, but the more I talked, the less I felt like stopping. And, unusually, Mr Peterson seemed in no hurry to stop me either. He even asked questions.

I suppose the ping-pong ball analogy must have whetted his appetite for more of the same. For some reason, he seemed to get a kick out of these ludicrous comparisons – not to mention all those mind-boggling numbers and scales in which fundamental physics excels. Of course, the display pods already gave us a fair number of statistics and analogies. There was the standard example used to illustrate the structure of the atom, namely: if you scaled an atom up to the size of a football stadium, its nucleus would be a single pea placed on the centre spot and its electrons would be dust motes orbiting close to the furthest seats. Everything else would be empty space. Then there was the terminal velocity to which the hadrons were accelerated in the LHC: 99.999999 per cent of the speed of light. At this speed, the hadrons would be looping the twenty-seven-kilometre accelerator tunnel approximately eleven thousand times every second. But Mr Peterson was not satisfied with this information alone. Before long, he had me working out all kinds of ridiculous maths problems.

How long would it take one of those hadrons to get back to Zurich? he asked.

I scribbled my calculation on the back of his notepad, which I'd had to hold up to the display screen to read. 'If it took the A1, just under a thousandth of a second,' I answered. 'In comparison it's going to take us about three hours in the car.'

How about from Zurich to the Sun? Mr Peterson asked.

'Eight minutes twenty seconds.' (I didn't have to figure that one out.)

How about us?

'Driving?'

Yes, driving.

This calculation took a little longer. The answer I came up with was a little over one hundred and forty years, if we drove twenty-four hours a day and stuck to the motorway speed limit.

But I think the number that made the biggest impression on me concerned the lifespan of the 'exotic' particles created in the LHC. The longest-lived of these particles could exist for only a few hundred-millionths of a second before decaying; the shortest-lived were so unstable that their existences couldn't even be 'observed' in a conventional sense. They popped into being and were gone in the same tiny fraction of an instant, so quickly that no instrument had yet been invented that was sensitive enough to register their presence, which could only be inferred post mortem. But the more I thought about this, and the more I thought about how old the universe was, and how old it would become before it suffered its final heat death – when all the stars had gone out and the black holes had evaporated and all the nucleons decayed, and nothing could exist but the elementary particles, drifting through the infinite darkness of space – the more I thought about these things, the more I realized that *all* matter was akin to those exotic particles. The size and scale of the universe made everything else unimaginably small and fleeting. On a universal timescale, even the stars would be gone in much less than the blink of an eye.

But this was not an analogy I felt like sharing.

When I called Ellie that evening – after the second appointment with Dr Reinhardt but before Herr Schäfer's *boeuf bourguignon* – she told me that my story had 'gone viral'. A couple of journalists phoning the shop had, overnight, become a dozen transient reporters who took turns doing their pieces to camera in front of the shop and haranguing my mother for an interview. So far, she'd answered only one question, which had caught her off-guard as she was opening up in the morning. She'd been asked how she was feeling.

'I'm upset, obviously,' she'd replied.

A thesaurus was consulted, and by mid-afternoon my mother was quoted as being 'distraught'. After that, she said nothing at all, which was taken as further confirmation of just how dismayed she was feeling. People wanted to empathize with her suffering, and a wall of silence was not going to deter them.

'I told you,' Ellie said. 'This story's got "public interest" written all over it. It's going nowhere. The appeal's still running every hour. They're still showing that fucked-up photo and making references to your "disturbing" note.'

'Things like this have a lifespan,' I philosophized, 'and it's not—'

'You're all over the internet too,' Ellie ploughed on. 'People are *discussing* you on forums! I'm surprised you haven't seen. They do have the internet in Switzerland, right?'

'They invented the internet in Switzerland,' I said. Then my heart fluttered against my ribcage. 'Who said anything about Switzerland?'

'Everyone! That's where everyone's saying you've gone. Apparently, it's the only country in the world that will provide medical assistance to foreigners who want to kill themselves. I assume that's what's going on here? If you were planning to drive the old man off a cliff, you could have done that in Dorset. No need to go abroad. Even the police have that part figured out.'

'Oh.'

I didn't know what else to say. I thought I could hear Ellie lighting up at the other end of the line.

'Listen,' she said. 'It said on the news that they've been in touch with the Swiss authorities.'

'Who have? The police?'

'The police, the Home Office – whoever it is who deals with this kind of shit.'

I thought about this for a few moments. 'I don't think they can do anything while I'm here. Under Swiss law, what we're doing is perfectly legal. That's the point.'

'You're seventeen. *That's* the point the police are making. They're saying it's a special case and the Swiss authorities should intervene.'

'The Swiss aren't big on intervention,' I pointed out.

'Oh, stop being so fucking cool about this! There might be people looking for you – you need to understand that.'

'I do understand that. But I only have to make it through the next twenty-four hours. After that—'

'Stop!' Ellie interjected. 'I don't want to know. I *really* don't want to know. Just be careful: that's all I'm asking.'

I didn't say anything.

Ellie let fly a final expletive and hung up.

I turned the television on to BBC News. I only had to wait about ten minutes before my photo flashed up. It was not a good photo. I turned off the TV and sat on the bed for five minutes, focussing on my breathing.

I reasoned that there was little I could do about this new turn of events. To my knowledge, Mr Peterson hadn't once switched on his television since we'd arrived in Switzerland.

He'd be quite oblivious to what was going on back home, and I knew I had to keep it that way. The unknown quantity was Herr Schäfer. I had no idea if he had any 'protocols' covering this kind of situation. My guess was that he did not.

It took us about fifteen minutes to reach the address, which was in the quiet eastern suburbs at the far end of District Twelve. Herr Schäfer's residence was modest and functional – another of those blocky, low-roofed, no-nonsense houses that the Swiss seemed to like. A security light illuminated a small patch of plain lawn, so well trimmed it might have been Astroturf, and inside everything was similarly tidy and low maintenance.

Although I was observing him with a hidden hyper-vigilance, upon our arrival, Herr Schäfer gave no indication that anything was amiss. He had the same demeanour as before – a strange mixture of seriousness and nonchalance that at times made his utterances sound like those of a deadpan comedian. It wasn't that he lacked the appropriate gravitas for a man in his line of work; it was more that this gravitas seeped inappropriately into other areas. He discussed death with the same solemnity that he brought to bear on the meat-to-mushroom-to-wine ratio in his *boeuf bourguignon*. And these were both subjects he talked about at length.

It turned out that Herr Schäfer had not always been in the 'death business'. He'd worked for over twenty years as a human rights lawyer, and it was his passionate belief in what he termed the 'final human right' – the right to die – that had eventually led to him giving up the law to open his private clinic, which was almost unique in its willingness to offer its services to non-residents as well as to Swiss nationals. But human rights, Herr

Schäfer believed, should not be contingent on national borders.

It wasn't a particularly 'normal' dinner, needless to say, but after a few minutes, I felt strangely relaxed. Herr Schäfer seemed very comfortable in his role as host, and having a three-way discussion with Mr Peterson was, in some ways, easier than having a one-to-one. It was slightly more involved in that he had to pass me his notes to read before I handed them on to Herr Schäfer, but it also granted him more time to write and more time to rest. And having accepted this practice the day before, Herr Schäfer no longer seemed to give it a second thought. He acted as if this were a perfectly unremarkable way to conduct a conversation. He also had a lot of patience when it came to me practising my German, which I tried to do whenever I could. With a little prompting, I'd soon moved on from simple pleasantries – *es schmeckt sehr gut* – to more complex, stop-start sentences: *Keinen Wein für mich, Herr Schäfer. Ich trinke keinen Alkohol. Aber ich habe eine grosse Lust auf Coca-Cola. Keine Angst – ich habe einige Dosen im Auto.*

But while he had a high tolerance for these halting exchanges, Herr Schäfer was less keen on the way in which I addressed him, which apparently was much too formal.

'Now that we know each other better, you should call me Rudolf,' he insisted.

I told Herr Schäfer that this didn't sit too comfortably with me. 'It's a little bit too . . .' I tried to think of a word that wasn't 'reindeerish', failed and said: 'Perhaps I could call you Rudi – if that's okay?'

'Yes, this is acceptable for me,' Herr Schäfer agreed. 'Actually, this is what both my grown-up daughters call me.'

I found this fact a little odd, but said nothing.

Herr Schäfer went on to tell us about his daughters, both of whom still lived in Zurich, as did his ex-wife, whom he'd amicably divorced ten years earlier, and it was during this seemingly innocuous line of conversation that matters took their sudden, dangerous turn.

'My wife was never very happy with my change of career,' Herr Schäfer was telling us. 'Or perhaps I should say that she was not happy with the media attention that my work unfortunately has brought. I'd like to say that this has become easier with the passing of the years, but as you must realize, there are still these cases that remain controversial.'

One look was enough to tell me that Herr Schäfer was no longer talking in generalities. I shot him a panicked warning glance, which I hoped Mr Peterson wouldn't notice, and as far as I could tell, he didn't. The problems with his eyes made it difficult for him to pick up on these quick, non-verbal exchanges.

Herr Schäfer sipped his wine without breaking eye contact or changing his expression. *'Er weiss es nicht?'* he asked, keeping his tone neutral.

'Nein,' I confirmed. *'Ich denke, dass es so besser ist.'*

Herr Schäfer nodded thoughtfully.

If you two are going to speak German again, Mr Peterson wrote, *I think I'd like to go for a smoke.*

I passed the note on to Herr Schäfer and, while he was distracted, tried to shoot a second warning glance, this time aimed at Mr Peterson. Given the circumstances, I didn't think this was a good moment for a 'smoke', but my glance either missed its target or was ignored.

'I would suggest that the small patio at the back would suit your purpose,' Herr Schäfer said. 'And perhaps at the same time Alex would be willing to help with the dishes?'

'I'm not sure this is a good idea,' I told Mr Peterson after I'd parked him outside the French windows. 'Or you should at least try to be circumspect. We don't know how Herr Schäfer might feel about this.'

He's in the death business, Mr Peterson pointed out. *I don't think he's going to be offended by a bit of pot.*

'He might if he thinks your judgement's impaired.'

I got the impression that had Mr Peterson been capable of rolling his eyes, he would have. *Relax,* he scribbled. *It's pot, not acid.*

I took thirty seconds, then went back into the kitchen, where Herr Schäfer had already filled the sink with soapy water and was gesturing to a tea towel that hung above the radiator.

'So, Alex,' he began, 'it appears that we have a small situation here.'

'Yes,' I agreed.

'Of course, I knew already that these circumstances were unusual. On some rare occasions we will have people younger than you – children or grandchildren – who wish to be there at the end, to say their goodbyes. But this is in a context where the whole family is present. Your situation is unique in my experience.'

'Mr Peterson doesn't have a family,' I said. 'I'm all he has.'

'Yes, I understand that, I think. But let me get to the point. How old are you, Alex?'

'Does that make a difference?'

'Not necessarily.'

'I'm seventeen,' I admitted. 'I'm old enough to drive and procreate, but I'm not old enough to vote or drink alcohol.'

Herr Schäfer nodded gravely. 'Some would say that the driving and procreation require more responsibility than the voting or drinking. But we will leave this to one side for now.' He paused and looked at me for a few moments. 'Your age has been difficult for me to guess,' he said. 'In many ways you seem to me older than your seventeen years, but in others much younger. I hope you won't mind me saying this?'

'I don't mind. I've been told the same thing before. I don't know how to be any different.'

'You shouldn't be any different,' Herr Schäfer said. 'You should be just as you are. In German, we would describe you as *ein Arglose*, but this does not translate very well into English. "An innocent" is a close approximation, but really this is not quite right. *Ein Arglose* has more the meaning of "one who is without cunning". It means that you are just as you appear to be – you have no thoughts of deception.'

I shrugged. 'I *do* have thoughts of deception. It's just that I'm incredibly bad at it, so there's not much point bothering.'

Herr Schäfer nodded. 'I think this is merely another way of saying that it is not in your nature.'

I thought about this for a while. 'Perhaps,' I concluded, 'but not always. I mean, I'm not being completely honest with Mr Peterson right now. Is that what you're getting at?'

'No. I think we both know that this is a different thing entirely. Have you lied to him?'

'No. I just haven't told him certain things.'

'And this is because you want to protect him? Am I right in thinking that?'

'Yes,' I admitted. 'I think if he knew what's happening back home, it might force him into a bad decision. And he'd be doing it to try to protect *me*, except he wouldn't be. It wouldn't be good for anyone.'

Herr Schäfer nodded again. 'You understand, I'm sure, the possible consequences of your actions? Now that the British police are involved, you may face prosecution when you go home. You will no longer be protected under Swiss law.'

'Yes, I know. I don't mind facing those consequences. I just don't want to put that burden on Mr Peterson. He shouldn't have to think about those things. Not now.'

'Okay,' Herr Schäfer said, 'so let me ask you another question. You know that there may be consequences, but you still wish to be here? Is that correct? You are not having thoughts about leaving now?'

'No. I want to be here.'

'Is that because you feel obligated to be here?'

'No. It's because I think what I'm doing is right.'

I dried the last plate and Herr Schäfer gestured to the kitchen table. We both sat.

'You know, Alex,' he said, 'my opinion is that if you're old enough to want to be here, then you're old enough to be here. I'm what most people would call a libertarian. Do you understand what that means?'

I considered the term. 'I think it has something to do with believing in the virtue of the free market,' I said. 'Is that right?'

Herr Schäfer smiled. 'Not so much in my case, no. It means

383

that I think every individual should be free to make their own decisions – without other people telling them what they must or must not do. The only restriction is that people are not free to hurt or exploit other people – and this is where it is quite different from the free market.'

Herr Schäfer poured himself a glass of wine before continuing. 'In this instance, what I'm trying to say is that you must be free to make your own choices, just as your friend Isaac must be free to make his. No one should interfere with that.'

I let this sink in. 'Does that mean you're *not* going to send us home?'

'That would be against everything I have stood for over the last twelve years. The only reason I ever send people away at this late stage is if I or Dr Reinhardt think they are not here by their own free will or they don't understand the choice they are making. But in this case we have no doubts.'

'What about all the stuff that's been on the news? You're not going to tell Mr Peterson?'

'No. I think my duty lies in the other direction. It is not my place to influence him one way or the other. His decision should be free from outside pressure. My mind is very clear on this. I will not tell him anything.' Herr Schäfer paused and sipped from his wineglass. 'However, you must understand that your circumstances are not the same as mine. You are carrying a different burden.'

'Do you mean that *I* should tell him?'

'No. This is your decision, not mine. All I'm saying is that you should give these matters some extra thought. Tomorrow will be difficult for you. You need to be prepared. You need to be sure in your own mind that you are doing the right thing.'

I looked out across the open-plan living room through the patio doors. 'I'm doing the right thing,' I said.

And I knew that this thought and this thought alone had the power to carry me through the next twenty-four hours. Without it, I would have broken down.

THE HOUSE WITH NO NAME

The house had no name and no number. Since no one lived there, and no one ever stayed there for more than a few hours, a name would have been superfluous. For the purpose of deliveries, if deliveries were ever made, I suppose they probably got by just referring to it as 'the house'. There were no other houses in the area with which to confuse it.

It was located on a small industrial estate about twenty minutes' drive east of Zurich, and the industrial location was required by law. While the majority of the Swiss believed that such a place should, in principle, be allowed to exist, there were few who thought it should be allowed to exist in their backyard.

So the house had been purpose-built out of town and rose incongruously among the warehouses and small factories that buttressed the intersection of two noisy highways. But despite the setting, efforts had been made to ensure that the house appeared as normal as possible. Outside there was a little driveway and hedges and a front porch. Inside there was a kitchenette and a bathroom and most of the domestic comforts you'd expect to find in any house, anywhere: a couple of long sofas, a couple of beds, a round table with four chairs, cushions, lamps. There was landscape art on the walls and large windows and patio doors admitting lots of natural light. There was a stereo for those who wished to listen to music and even a small back garden with shrubs and a trickling fountain. It was fenced off from the surroundings, but you could still hear the traffic along the main road, which hissed rhythmically, like the sea.

After we'd pulled up in the front driveway, Mr Peterson told me that he wanted to leave the wheelchair in the boot. *It's important for me to walk*, he wrote.

I nodded.

He used a single crutch in his right hand and wrapped his left arm around my shoulder, and in this fashion, we made a slow, shuffling progress up the drive. Mr Peterson had done very little walking over the past week. It took a long time.

My mind was extremely alert – as alert as it had been on the night we'd escaped Yeovil Hospital, although once again I'd had no sleep. Once we'd got back to the hotel, I'd sat up thinking about what Herr Schäfer had said until about two in the morning, and after that, I simply hadn't felt tired. I drank about five cans of Diet Coke and stayed up reading a fifty-year history of CERN, which I'd bought from the centre's gift shop. By 6 a.m., I'd reached the creation of antihydrogen in the mid-1990s and still wasn't tired. I went for my morning meditation down by the lake, just as the sun was coming up. There was hardly anybody else about – just a couple of joggers and a family of swans and cygnets bobbing on the water. The promenade on the lakeside had been planted with lilacs, which were just coming into bloom and fragrancing the air with a cool vanilla scent.

Several doses of marijuana had helped Mr Peterson sleep peacefully until around seven. By that time, I was back at the hotel, where I helped him wash and dress. He wrote that he wanted to look presentable. It was another of those things that felt important to him.

'How are you feeling?' I asked.

Calm, he wrote. Calm and resolved. How about you?

'The same,' I said.

Are you sure?

'Yes.' I managed a thin smile. 'I'm resolved too.'

And as I walked him those final few steps towards the front door of the house with no name, my resolve had only strengthened. I had a task to do, and I'd hold out for as long as it took. If there'd been any doubts about whether I should tell Mr Peterson about what was going on back home, these had now evaporated. The crux of the matter was clear as oxygen: if I told him, then, one way or another, whatever decision he made, he was going to suffer. We were both going to suffer, much more than was necessary. Avoiding such needless cruelty didn't strike me as the kind of thing that required a complex moral justification. It was just common sense.

After she'd made cups of coffee for herself and Mr Peterson, Petra – one of the two escorts who had met us at the house – sat with us at the small round table. Linus, the other escort, did not. The only time I really saw him was when he greeted us at the door. He spent the rest of the time 'backstage', preparing paperwork and taking care of other practicalities. Later on, it would be Linus who dealt with the Swiss authorities, registering the death and arranging for the transportation of Mr Peterson's body to the crematorium. Petra's role was to be available to us at all times – to talk us through every stage, answer any questions and generally look after us throughout the appointment. When the time came, she would also be the one who prepared and handed over the sodium pentobarbital, but this could only be done at Mr Peterson's explicit request. No one else was allowed to initiate this action.

My first impression of Petra was that there was nothing to her. She couldn't have been much more than five feet tall, and she was as skinny as Mr Peterson, but with no trace of the wiry strength he'd once possessed. Her hair was ash blonde and tied back in an efficient ponytail, and her skin would have looked pale in an English winter. Her voice was light and soft, and she was wearing very little make-up, just a tiny hint of eyeliner, and this had the effect of making her appear even paler, smaller and younger than she probably was. But despite her diminutive stature, she carried herself with a brisk self-confidence that put me at ease. It was strange, but except for the calm, reassuring quality she had about her, she reminded me of my mother.

I spent a very long time wondering about Petra and how she'd come to this job – whether there were newspaper adverts and interviews, just like any other normal job. Eventually, I got tired of wondering and just asked her.

Alex likes to know how things work, Mr Peterson apologized.

'She did say we should ask questions,' I pointed out.

'I did,' Petra agreed. She spent some time looking at Mr Peterson's blind-written note – she still found this trick an interesting novelty – and then told us that she'd trained as a nurse before joining Herr Schäfer's clinic seven years ago; she'd made a 'speculative application' having read about his work in a national newspaper. 'I thought it was important work and something I could do well,' Petra concluded.

All of Petra's utterances were like this. She was direct and plainspoken, yet, with her featherlight voice, she managed to project compassion in the simplest, shortest sentences. I suppose this was one of the reasons she was suited to her job.

She had to go through most of the questions that Mr Peterson had already been asked two or three times before, but these questions were now raw and immediate. 'Do you want to die today?' Petra asked. 'Is your mind clear? Is this your own decision?' After that, there came the repeated insistence that there was no pressure to continue – the decision could be reversed at any point, right up until the poison had been taken. Petra didn't refer to the sodium pentobarbital as a medicine or medicament. At this late stage, there was no room for ambiguity.

Mr Peterson had to write his answers to all these questions and then sign about half a dozen different documents, reconfirming his intentions and giving the escorts the legal right to deal with the Swiss authorities after his death. After that, I helped him to the bathroom (*I don't want my last thought to be that I need to pee*, Mr Peterson wrote), and when we got back, he told Petra that he was ready to take his anti-emetic. This was a standard precaution to ensure that the sodium pentobarbital – which had an extremely unpleasant taste – stayed down. On this point, Petra was typically forthcoming. 'The pentobarbital tastes poisonous,' she told us. 'The stomach's natural response is to throw it up.' Anti-sickness medication was always taken first, and it had to be taken at least half an hour before the poison – to allow its full effects to manifest.

And then we had to wait.

And there were a million things I thought I should say, but I couldn't get any of them straight in my head. I didn't know where to begin. I suppose I must have looked agitated, because after a while, Mr Peterson passed me a note.

I understand. You don't have to say anything at all. Just being here is enough.

I nodded. I thought he was right. Sometimes words aren't needed.

You should put on some music, Mr Peterson wrote.

'What would you like to hear?'

Mr Peterson gave a kind of crooked half-smile. *Lots of things. I think the decision's too big for me right now. You choose.*

I thought about this for a minute. 'I suppose you could do worse than Mozart,' I said.

Mr Peterson nodded. *Agreed.*

So I put on Mozart's Piano Concerto No. 21 in C major. Mr Peterson closed his eyes and listened. I sat and watched a couple of sparrows through the patio doors as they darted back and forth between the slender saplings of the back garden, their shadows flittering below them like dark puppets. The double-glazing cut out all the noise from the roads and factories. There was no whisper of the outside world, no sound in the room but the shimmering layers of Mozart and the slow rise and fall of my breath.

When the music had finished, Mr Peterson gestured for

me to call back Petra from the corner chair to which she'd retired.

I'm ready to die now, he wrote. *I want you to prepare the poison for me.*

I helped him across to the small leather sofa that looked out onto the garden.

'Do you want me to put some more music on?' I asked.

Play the Mozart again, Mr Peterson wrote. *It's perfect.*

Within a few minutes Petra had returned with the small glass of dissolved sodium pentobarbital. It was clear and colourless, like normal tap water. She placed it carefully on the table next to Mr Peterson, along with the drinking straw that his medical notes had said to provide.

'Between two and five minutes after drinking this, you will lose consciousness,' Petra said. 'And after that, you will die. Do you understand?'

Mr Peterson nodded.

'I need you to write it,' Petra said.

I understand, Mr Peterson wrote. Then, after he'd torn out the page, he wrote a second note, to me. *You going to read for me?* it said.

'Yes,' I confirmed. I already had *Slaughterhouse-Five* prepared. I was going to start reading it after he'd taken the poison, and he'd told me to keep reading until he was fast asleep. I think he'd thought of this for me as much as for him. He knew I needed something to do, to keep my mind focussed.

Thank you, Alex, Mr Peterson wrote.

'I love you,' I said. 'I love you and I'm going to miss you.'

I know. Me too. You're going to be OK.

'Yes.'

You take good care of yourself. Make sure you drive home safely.

'I always drive safely,' I said.

Mr Peterson nodded, barely more than a tiny dip of his head.

I guess I'll see you on the other side,

he wrote. And that was the last thing he wrote. It was a lousy joke, but I was glad he'd made it all the same.

'See you on the other side,' I said.

I held the glass steady while Mr Peterson drank the sodium pentobarbital through the straw. I made sure that all the liquid had disappeared before I returned the glass to the table, and then I started reading.

Listen, I read.

Billy Pilgrim has come unstuck in time.

Billy has gone to sleep a senile widower and awakened on his wedding day . . .

Mr Peterson listened. Mozart continued to play. I kept reading for three more pages.

The most important thing I learned on Tralfamadore was that when a person dies he only appears *to die. He is still very much alive in the past, so it is very silly for people to cry at his funeral. All moments, past, present and future, always have existed, always will exist. The Tralfamadorians can look at all the different moments just the way we can look at a stretch of the Rocky Mountains, for instance. They can see how permanent all the moments are, and they can look at any moment that interests them. It's just an illusion we have here on Earth that one moment follows another one, like beads on a string, and that once a moment is gone it's gone forever . . .*

By the time I paused in my reading, the Piano Concerto

No. 21 had reached its second movement. Mr Peterson's eyes had closed and his breathing had slowed to the rhythm of deep sleep. After that, it didn't take long for him to die.

I picked up the ashes the following morning. It doesn't take much time to cremate a body – about two hours from start to finish – and in prearranged assisted suicides, those which have been properly documented, there's no delay in getting the death certified and a cremation permit issued. The medical examiner just has to confirm the death and check that all the paperwork is in order – and, in Mr Peterson's case, it was. All the evidence was there in black and white: the declaration of intent, the passport to confirm his identity, the signed testimonies of Linus and Petra and Dr Reinhardt. The death and cause of death were certified in a matter of minutes. If I hadn't felt so drained, I might have been able to collect the ashes that same afternoon.

Instead, I returned to the hotel and slept for twelve hours straight. When I awoke, it was dark outside. I guess it was around three in the morning. My sleep routine was shot to pieces; though, at that time, I hadn't noticed any signs that a seizure was imminent. I was still in a bubble. Either nothing felt strange or everything did. I couldn't decide which.

I still hadn't cried, even though Petra had insisted that I should. She said that I should 'let it all out', that there wasn't any need to be strong any more. I told her the truth: I wasn't trying to be strong. I just didn't feel like crying right then.

I went for my morning meditation in the same spot as the day before, where nothing had changed. There were the same swans on the lake, the same lilacs perfuming the promenade. The only difference was that the meditation didn't really work.

The idea is to clear your mind of clutter, but my mind was already blank to begin with. There was nothing to clear.

So, after about half an hour, I went back to the hotel and packed my bags. There weren't so many this time. Mr Peterson's clothes and suitcase had been left to the Red Cross.

I went to check out just before eight and found the same desk clerk working – the one who'd checked us in three days earlier and refused to speak German with me.

'Where is Mr Peterson?' he asked me. I thought it was an odd question to ask; I assumed he'd already seen that my room was booked for an extra night.

'*Herr Peterson hat gestern ausgecheckt,*' I told him. Mr Peterson checked out yesterday.

I turned up at the crematorium at nine, when it opened. Everything had been paid for in advance, so it didn't take long to get the remains handed over. There was just one release form to sign. I was back on the road ten minutes later.

I didn't really have a plan about when or where I'd stop. I thought I'd just keep driving until I was tired or needed to stretch my legs – assuming I made it across the border. I knew that wasn't a given, although I thought the bigger problem would be trying to buy a ferry ticket in Calais.

As it happened, I'd been driving for less than an hour when I was forced to pull off the *Autobahn*. It hit me without warning as I was driving through the Bözberg Tunnel. Suddenly, I was smelling lilacs again. I got off at the next junction and parked up a mile or so from the motorway, just on the edge of a quiet, seemingly deserted village. I stood in the fresh air with my hands on the bonnet and tried to count my breaths, but somewhere around five or six, I found that I was shaking and I couldn't stop.

And then I cried. I don't know how long for. Maybe a minute, maybe ten. I sat in the gravelly road with my back against the bumper and I cried for as long as I needed to, until the shaking had stopped and my head was clear again. Then I got back in the car, placed Mr Peterson on the passenger seat beside me and drove north to meet my fate.

WILL

My mother arrived at Dover Police Station around four in the morning, looking very much like she'd been shot from a cannon. By that time, I'd been talking in circles with Chief Inspector Hearse and Deputy Inspector Cunningham for at least two and a half hours. They let her into Interview Room C, where she wasted no time on pleasantries. She rushed straight over to where I was sitting and crushed my head into her stomach. And she kept on holding me for at least three minutes. I don't know which of us felt most awkward about this – me or Chief Inspector Hearse or Deputy Inspector Cunningham – but after a while, I stopped trying to twist my neck back into a sensible position and just kind of accepted the arrangement. Despite the contortion, I decided that being mauled by my mother was preferable to being mauled by the police.

'Mrs Woods,' Chief Inspector Hearse began, 'if you'd like to take a seat, then we can bring you up to speed with th—'

But my mother didn't want to be brought up to speed. And

she didn't want a seat either. 'I'd like to take Alex home now,' she said.

The policemen exchanged a glance before Chief Inspector Hearse continued: 'I appreciate that this must be a difficult situation for you, Mrs Woods, but there are still questions that we need to ask. You can sit in, of course, but I'm afraid that the interview is not finished yet.'

'I see.' My mother released my head and planted her fists on her hips. 'And what exactly has he been charged with?'

'He hasn't been charged with *anything* yet,' Chief Inspector Hearse stated. 'At this point, we're just asking some questions, and with your co-operation we'd—'

'You don't have my co-operation,' my mother interjected. 'If you haven't charged him, I'm taking him home.'

Deputy Inspector Cunningham stepped in: 'Mrs Woods, you should be aware that we *can* hold your son for up to forty-eight hours without bringing charges against him. But this process will be—'

'This is appalling!' my mother snapped. 'Can you even begin to imagine how hard this past week must have been for him? It's the middle of the night. He's seventeen. Have some compassion! At this rate, you're going to end up giving him a seizure!'

'Actually, I've already had a seizure,' I said.

'He's already had a seizure!'

'It was only a partial seizure,' I clarified. 'It passed after a couple of minutes. I don't think I should drive home, though – just to be safe.'

'Of course you're not going to drive home! *I'm* going to drive you home.'

'Mrs Woods—' Chief Inspector Hearse began.

'This is appalling!' my mother reiterated. 'What kind of operation are you running here? It's tantamount to torture! Look at him: he's ill; he's sleep-deprived. I don't suppose you've offered him the chance to see a doctor, let alone a lawyer?'

Chief Inspector Hearse tried to wrestle the situation back under control. 'Mrs Woods, I assure you: your son has not shown any signs of illness while we've been dealing with him. If he does, then of course we'll make a doctor available to him. And the reason he hasn't been offered a lawyer is that he hasn't yet been charged, as I've said.'

'He had a seizure!'

'Neither of us was present when the seizure is alleged to have taken place. And—' This time, Chief Inspector Hearse raised a stern finger to forestall my mother. 'And there are also certain circumstances that you are not yet aware of.' He gestured to Deputy Inspector Cunningham, who, for a second time, retrieved the bag of cannabis and dropped it in the centre of the table.

'It's marijuana,' Chief Inspector Hearse pointed out, very solemnly.

'I know what it is, Inspector,' my mother said. 'I'm not an imbecile.'

'We found it in your son's car. We think it may go some way to explaining his "seizure".' (We could all hear the quote marks.)

'That's absurd,' my mother spat. 'Alex does *not* use drugs.'

'It was Mr Peterson's,' I explained.

'Yes, that makes a whole lot more sense,' my mother agreed.

'With respect, Mrs Woods . . .' Chief Inspector Hearse began, rather ominously. 'With respect, parents are often ignorant of what their children get up to. They don't want to think—'

'Let me stop you there, Inspector,' my mother said (and it was the kind of tone that forced you to stop, a tone with which I was very familiar). 'Firstly, it's cannabis. It's rather trivial given the circumstances, and its presence here does not make my son a miscreant, as you seem very keen to imply. If you're telling me that it's only miscreants who have ever used narcotics, and not thousands of politicians and judges – and policemen too – then I'm calling you a liar and a hypocrite.' There was a chilly silence. My mother didn't like liars, and she especially didn't like hypocrites. 'Secondly,' she continued, 'if you're telling me that after the few hours you've known him, you have a better understanding of my son than I do – enough to tell me that *I'm* ignorant of his character – well then, frankly, you need your head examined.'

Chief Inspector Hearse had gone very red. His mole was throbbing. 'Mrs Woods! What I'm telling you is that your son is not the angel you seem—'

'I'm not saying he's an angel. I'm saying he's a puritan. The idea that he'd take drugs – that he'd take any substance that hadn't been certified by someone with three PhDs – is laughable. He sees drinking alcohol as a major character defect!'

There was a small, uncertain silence. I think that Chief Inspector Hearse and Deputy Inspector Cunningham were surprised at my mother's outburst, but I was gobsmacked. Contrary to everything I'd always assumed, it seemed that my mother really *did* know me quite well.

It was Chief Inspector Hearse who regrouped first. 'Mrs Woods, I think we're getting off the point here. This isn't just about possession for personal use. Your son has already admitted that he grew and supplied the marijuana in question. And this has been going on for quite some time.'

'I only supplied it to Mr Peterson,' I clarified. 'And he'd been smoking marijuana since 1965. It's not like I pushed it on him. Also, I wasn't selling it. I was just helping him grow it when he couldn't get up to the loft any more.'

'There you go!' my mother said. 'It wasn't for profit or personal gain. I don't know what you're trying to tell me here, Inspector, but this whole situation is ridiculous. I'm taking my son home. If you need him for further questioning, I will bring him in personally. But right now we're leaving. If you want to stop us, you'll have to arrest us both – and rest assured that when I get out, I'll be writing a letter of complaint the likes of which you've never seen. You'll be lucky to have jobs at the end of it. The way you've conducted yourselves tonight is appalling! You should be ashamed. Come on, Lex, we're leaving!'

And I got up and I followed my mother out the door. Neither of the police officers tried to stop us. Chief Inspector Hearse started to say something but we were gone before anything much had registered. It was that simple.

In the car, as we drove west, with the sky gradually brightening behind us, I told my mother everything. I tried to explain to her why I'd done what I'd done, but she seemed to know that already. She just wanted to understand exactly how things had happened. And when I'd finished, she only criticized me once. She said that I should have told her all this much earlier.

'I thought you'd try to stop me,' I said.

'I wouldn't have tried to stop you,' she replied. 'You're essentially grown up. I can't make decisions like that for you any more.'

'You didn't say that in the police station,' I pointed out. 'You said that I was *only* seventeen.'

'I'm your mother,' my mother said. 'I just wanted you out of there. How are you feeling now?'

'Better,' I said. 'I mean, I still feel sad, obviously. But now it's a good kind of sad, if that makes sense.' I thought for a bit. 'What I mean is, I wouldn't change anything. I don't mind what happens with the police. They could lock me away for a thousand years and it wouldn't make any difference. I don't think I've done anything wrong.'

'Neither do I,' my mother said.

There's not much left to tell. I could go into more detail about the months that followed – the various shifts in my case, the many letters of support I received from both strangers and people I knew (Dr Enderby, Dr Weir, Herr Schäfer), and the equally numerous letters of condemnation that prayed with fervour for the salvation or damnation of my immortal soul. I could talk more about these details, but, by now, you probably know most of the things that are worth knowing. My case started with a bang but it ended with a whimper. After close to four months of meetings and 'further enquiries', long after the media glare had diminished, my case was effectively dropped. It was not deemed in the public interest to prosecute me for abetting a suicide. For the production and possession of illegal narcotics with the possible intent to supply, I got a caution. Dr Weir told me that this would not prevent me from getting into a good university and pursuing a career as a theoretical physicist.

But, really, none of this should have dragged on for as long as it did. It might have all been settled in a matter of weeks – had it not been for the existence of the will. This was the complicating factor that I hadn't foreseen. And it's the last thing I have to tell you about.

It had never occurred to me that Mr Peterson would have a will. I didn't even know that he had a lawyer, not until I met her in her small, tidy office in Wells, on the day of my eighteenth birthday. Prior to that, I hadn't been allowed to see the contents of the will. I only knew about it because the police had brought it to my attention. They'd got some sort of special legal permit to obtain a copy because it was deemed 'potentially' (and later 'extremely') relevant to their investigation.

In short, it turned out that I was a major beneficiary of the will – one of only two beneficiaries – and this gave me a 'plausible motive' for wanting Mr Peterson dead (beyond all the very clear motives I'd already laid out in my various statements). I tried to point out to the police that this motive was only plausible if I'd known about the will beforehand – otherwise it was not only *im*plausible, but also violated causality in quite a major way – but I got the impression that they saw this as a weak defence. Luckily, my lawyer told me I didn't have to prove that I didn't know about the will; the police had to prove that I did.

'How could they possibly prove that?' I asked.

My lawyer shrugged. 'If you confess.'

'I could confess to anything,' I pointed out. 'I could confess that my father's the Pope. It wouldn't make it true.'

My lawyer conceded this point but counselled that until this matter was laid to rest, I should remain patient and humourless, which was usually the best approach when dealing with the law.

So the day I finally got to see the will was, as I've said, the day of my eighteenth birthday. It was only then I got to discover what it was that the police had wanted me to confess to. My mother and Ellie came with me for moral support. It was a sunny Friday morning, the autumnal equinox, and the third time in living memory that my mother had decided to close her shop on a work day.

The will was set out in complicated legal jargon, of course, but the thrust of it was very simple. All the information I needed to know was laid out in a letter that Mr Peterson had left with his lawyer. I enclose a copy:

Dear Alex,

Well, if you're reading this then I guess everything went to plan and I can no longer number myself among the living. It's pretty funny to think about. Writing this now, I still feel very much alive. It's a beautiful spring day and, apart from the fact it's a little tough to follow what I'm writing, I've not really noticed any symptoms since I woke up. I think maybe my brain's decided to cut me a break for just long enough so I can get this down on paper. What do you think? Does that idea fly in the face of medical science or what?

But back to the point:

I know now I'm dead. What I don't know, obviously, is how much longer I had. I hope it was many more months. On a day like today, it feels very possible. And the fact that I'm in a position to hope for more time, the fact that I can think like that, is mostly down to you. I want you to know that. I don't know how much time I have left, but I do know that things are going to end well. I don't doubt that for a second. As you know, I've never been one for faith, but I do have faith in you.

In the grand scheme of the universe, I doubt there are very many animals who've had the privilege of a peaceful, painless death. Unfortunately, the universe doesn't work like that, as we both know. There's nothing natural about a painless death, and the fact that I'm going to get one – the fact that I did get one – that's something that makes me feel very blessed.

Don't worry; I don't plan to go on in this morbid vein much longer. I just want you to know that I die contented, and a few years ago (a few months ago, even), that idea would have seemed unthinkable. As lives go, I think mine was mostly a good one. I enjoyed the uneventful parts especially.

But as I've said, time is pressing. Let me cut to the chase:

I've left instructions with my attorney concerning what she should do with my 'estate' in the event of my death. (That's what they call it in legalese, an 'estate'. I'm not getting delusions of grandeur.) The short of it is as follows:

I've got a real estate guy in town who should've

been contacted now that I'm dead. He's to oversee the sale of my house, and from the resultant capital, along with whatever savings I have left, you're to receive £50,000. The rest (the lion's share, I'm afraid) is going to Amnesty. But I'm sure you won't begrudge them that.

I figure that £50,000 will just about cover an education these days, even a London education, I hope. And this is the only condition I place on your receipt of the money. You're to spend it on your continued education. I'm sorry, but I'm adamant about this. If you're going to work on that Theory of Everything, you'll need time and space and no distractions. That's what I'm buying for you.

From a personal standpoint, I'm not too disappointed to be leaving the universe before you've had a chance to figure it out. I suspect that the Final Answer is just going to be a lot of disappointing math. But this is probably one of those areas where we'll have to agree to disagree.

All that's left for me to say is: thank you again, Alex. I hope that your mother understands the decision we made, and that she'll forgive me for allowing, and needing, you to be a part of it. I hope also that none of this caused you any difficulty with the law. I know we've discussed this enough already, and I'm sure you're right: there's no reason there should be any trouble. If there's no victim, there's no crime. It's common sense. But you'll forgive me, I hope, if I still worry a little.

In the long history of human affairs, common sense
doesn't have the greatest track record.
   And on that thought, I'll leave you.
   Your friend,
   Isaac

I imagined that Mr Peterson had had quite a lot of fun writing that letter. I passed it to my mother, who read it and started crying. She passed it on to Ellie. Ellie did not cry. She cast a quick, critical eye over it before handing it back to me with a brisk shake of her head.

'That's some kick in the balls,' she said. I think she was referring to the clause regarding how I was to spend the money.

After that, we left the office and walked back to the car, which was parked not far from the cathedral. My mum had hold of one hand and Ellie had the other, and I can't remember any of us saying anything more. I only remember looking up at the cathedral and the sky above and thinking about a whole lot of different things. I thought about architecture and all the beautiful things human beings had managed to build. I thought about London and the Natural History Museum, Charles Darwin and Theories of Everything. I thought about the future.

All these thoughts drifted like clouds through the virtual space of my mind's eye – tiny electrical and chemical signals that combined to create an entire world – but then, after a while, everything just kind of melted away. All that was left was a calm blue void. I felt very happy.

ACKNOWLEDGEMENTS

Firstly, huge thanks to Donald Farber, Trustee of the Kurt Vonnegut Copyright Trust, and to all the good people at Jonathan Cape for their generosity in allowing me to use the various quotations from Mr Vonnegut's work that appear throughout this novel. Needless to say, Kurt Vonnegut has been a massive inspiration to me, and my debt to him is considerable. Thanks also to the Joseph Heller Estate for granting permission for the *Catch-22* quotes; your generosity is likewise very much appreciated.

In chapter five, Alex reads and quotes from 'Martin Beech's meteorite book'. This is a genuine book by a genuine man. The full title is *Meteors and Meteorites: Origins and Observations*, and it was my primary source for a wealth of information concerning meteoroids, meteors and meteorites. My sincere thanks to Dr Beech, and apologies, again, for demoting your fictional counterpart (whom Alex refers to as 'Mr Beech'). I was also guilty, in one or two places, of altering the science to suit my own purposes – any inaccuracies are entirely my own work. Additional thanks to Ken Hathaway at The Crowood Press, who gave me permission to use the direct quotation.

Now some more general thanks.

To Stan, my agent at JBA, who took me to the pub and made all sorts of crazy promises about my book – all of which he has so far managed to keep.

To all the people at Hodder who have devoted so much time, energy and enthusiasm to *Alex*. I'm a bit fearful of singling people out, in case I miss anyone, but I feel there are a few names I have to mention in particular: Alice and Jason, who have done wonders with the foreign rights; Naomi and Rosie, who, at the time of writing, are shepherding me through marketing and publicity; Clive, who sent me a nice, reassuring e-mail after the birth of my daughter, just when I needed it; Amber, a very thorough and perceptive copyeditor; and Harriet, who has chased up permissions, made travel arrangements, and taken care of at least a dozen other practicalities. As someone whose organizational skills are occasionally lacking, I'm very appreciative of this.

Special and separate thanks to Kate Howard, my very wonderful editor, who loved *Alex* from day one, and whose unwavering enthusiasm has been driving things forward ever since.

My mum proof-read the third draft, found lots of errors, and then said many encouraging things, for which I'm very grateful. Thanks also to the rest of my family – to my dad, for never telling me to get a 'real' job, and to my siblings, Siân, Kara and Ciaran, who have been generally supportive in innumerable ways.

Finally, the biggest thanks have to go to Alix, my only reader for three years, whose unconditional love and support made this book possible. Without her, there would be no acknowledgements to write.

Gavin Extence was born in 1982 and grew up in the interestingly named village of Swineshead, Lincolnshire. From the ages of 5–11, he enjoyed a brief but illustrious career as a chess player, winning numerous national championships and travelling to Moscow and St Petersburg to pit his wits against the finest young minds in Russia. He won only one game.

Gavin now lives in Sheffield with his wife, baby daughter and cat. He is currently working on his second novel. When he is not writing, he enjoys cooking, amateur astronomy and going to Alton Towers.

twitter@thingsalexknows
www.alexwoodsbook.co.uk

© Alix Extence

We asked the book groups who read early copies of the novel to tell us the questions they would urge others to consider after reading *The Universe versus Alex Woods*.

This is a very character-based novel. Whose relationship changes the most significantly throughout the book – the one between Alex and his mother, or Alex and Mr Peterson?

Why is the meteorite incident important in Alex's story?

Did Mr Peterson assume the role of father in his and Alex's relationship? Why do you think the friendship between them developed, even after Alex lost the precious book Mr Peterson's wife gave him many years ago?

Was it okay that Mr Peterson relied on someone so young for such an enormous responsibility and the consequences that followed?

Bramble Book Club

Did reading about euthanasia within the context of the book and getting to know these characters affect your previously held views on the subject in any way?

Alex's quirky, unusual personality and stance as a social outsider was used to encourage the reader to explore the concept of euthanasia. What other literary devices were used and what effect did they have?

Gourmet Readers

If you were seventeen, do you think you would have been able to do what Alex did?

Bookerpie

Jasper Sutcliffe of Foyles Bookshops (www.foyles.co.uk) talks to Gavin Extence.

Alex is a very bright boy but very unworldly. Is this why you chose him as the narrator?

I loved the contradictions in Alex's character, and in particular, the mixture of naivety and academic intelligence. Alex has the capability and desire to understand the world on quite a deep level, but he's also an innocent in lots of ways. Consequently, I think his voice brings a real freshness to the narrative. In general, I'm a big fan of teen narrators because they tend to have this dual perspective that comes from having one foot in adulthood and the other in childhood. Adolescence is really the point at which you start to form your own opinions about morality, religion, politics and so on – and having Alex as narrator allowed me to tackle a lot of big, important issues in (I hope) an accessible and unassuming way.

Meteorites, marijuana factories, abduction and euthanasia: that's a lot to tackle in a first novel. Did you ever feel that you'd bitten of more than you could chew?

Yes, at times. But I've never been a fan of the 'write what you know'

dictum, which strikes me as offering a very limited scope for a first novel. For me, one of the great pleasures of writing fiction is that you're free to go wherever your imagination takes you. It probably helps, too, that I have a background in research, so I wasn't intimidated by having to find out about subjects in which I have no specific expertise.

Euthanasia is an immensely controversial subject and highly divisive. Why did you feel you wanted to tackle this topic?

Oddly, I didn't set out to write about assisted suicide. My starting point was Alex. I had the vague notion, early on, that I wanted him to do something unconventionally heroic; and although assisted suicide is a highly divisive topic, I'd like to think that Alex's heroism still stands regardless of the reader's personal views. After all, his actions are almost entirely selfless: he sacrifices his own wishes to help fulfill someone else's, and is willing to face whatever consequences follow.

You use humour to great effect in the book allowing the reader to bare some very intense scenes. Do you prefer writing humour or the more emotional passages?

As a rule, I prefer writing humour because it provides a rhythm and structure that I'd otherwise miss. That said, I don't actually think of humour and emotion as distinct categories. Tragedy and comedy are more like two sides of the same coin. You can take almost any situation – no matter how horrific – and push it to a point where it becomes outrageously funny: the crucifixion scene at the end of *The Life of Brian* springs to mind. Then, by the same token, lots of comedy sails perilously close to tragic territory. There are scenes in *The Office* that have an almost unbearable level of pathos.

The point, I think, is that when faced with extreme and unpleasant situations, laughter is as instinctual a response as tears. Kurt Vonnegut called laughter 'the soul seeking release', and I think that's spot on. There are some things in life that are so bleak that I can't imagine how any of us would deal with them without humour. I think it's a human quality that should be valued very highly.

Will Alex's adventures with the universe and the law continue?

In a word: no. The book was written as a stand-alone novel and I think the story wraps up exactly where it should. Alex can live the rest of his life off-stage.

When do you write?

Usually 9–5, but I tend to be most productive in the morning.

Pen and paper or on a computer?

Pen and paper – for a first draft, I much prefer working longhand.

Favourite location (kitchen, office, shed)?

On the sofa in my lounge, next to the fish tank.

Why did you start writing?

I've loved writing ever since I was a child. Writing a novel was a long-held ambition.

Do you have any peculiar writing habits?

I wrote my debut mostly in my dressing gown. I couldn't afford to have the heating on and needed the extra layer.

If you weren't a writer, what would you be?

I'd like to say astronaut, but more realistically, a teacher or a librarian.

Which book do you wish you had written?

The Gruffalo.

Who was the first person to read this novel?

My wife – she read it as a fortnightly serial as I was writing.

THINGS ALEX KNOWS

A collection of the incredible, sometimes unbelievable, often strange things that Alex Woods knows, taken from the book's very own Twitter feed – @ThingsAlexKnows

Lewis Carroll had Temporal Lobe Epilepsy, which was probably one of the reasons he had such a strange imagination

If extraterrestrial life were discovered, it would likely be microbes in the sunless seas of Europa or the frigid methane lakes of Titan

Newton came up with gravity and his Laws of Motion while he was locked away at home, hiding from the plague

The brain is the most complicated collection of atoms in the known universe

It would take over 140 years to drive to the sun, if you drove 24 hours a day and stuck to the motorway speed limit

The more stuff you try to force into it, the less accommodating time becomes.

A standard two litre bottle of cola has about seventy-five teaspoons of sugar in. That's the same as a chocolate cake 8 inches in diameter

Did you know that the average human body contains enough sulphur to kill all the fleas on a dog?

The probability of getting struck by a meteor heavier than a gram, if you live for 100 years, is about 1 in 2 billion?

Longest place name in the world - Taumatawhakatangihangakoauauotamateaturi pukakapikimaungahoronukupokaiwenuakitanatahu.

The first thing I learned today was this: what you think you know about a person is only a fraction of the story

There are approx 1.5 million ants for every person

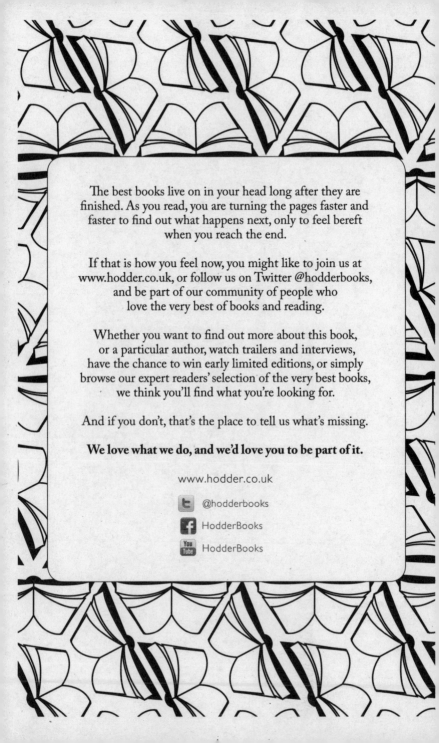

The best books live on in your head long after they are finished. As you read, you are turning the pages faster and faster to find out what happens next, only to feel bereft when you reach the end.

If that is how you feel now, you might like to join us at www.hodder.co.uk, or follow us on Twitter @hodderbooks, and be part of our community of people who love the very best of books and reading.

Whether you want to find out more about this book, or a particular author, watch trailers and interviews, have the chance to win early limited editions, or simply browse our expert readers' selection of the very best books, we think you'll find what you're looking for.

And if you don't, that's the place to tell us what's missing.

We love what we do, and we'd love you to be part of it.

www.hodder.co.uk

@hodderbooks

HodderBooks

HodderBooks

Michael ROSEN'S
BIG BOOK
of
BAD THINGS

Illustrated by **Joe Berger**

PUFFIN

For Connie, my mum (1919–1976), Harold, my dad (1919–2008), and Brian, my brother; and for Emma, Elsie and Emile

PUFFIN BOOKS

Published by the Penguin Group
Penguin Books Ltd, 80 Strand, London WC2R 0RL, England
Penguin Group (USA) Inc., 375 Hudson Street, New York, New York 10014, USA
Penguin Group (Canada), 90 Eglinton Avenue East, Suite 700, Toronto, Ontario, Canada M4P 2Y3
(a division of Pearson Penguin Canada Inc.)
Penguin Ireland, 25 St Stephen's Green, Dublin 2, Ireland (a division of Penguin Books Ltd)
Penguin Group (Australia), 250 Camberwell Road, Camberwell, Victoria 3124, Australia
(a division of Pearson Australia Group Pty Ltd)
Penguin Books India Pvt Ltd, 11 Community Centre, Panchsheel Park, New Delhi – 110 017, India
Penguin Group (NZ), 67 Apollo Drive, Rosedale, North Shore 0632, New Zealand
(a division of Pearson New Zealand Ltd)
Penguin Books (South Africa) (Pty) Ltd, 24 Sturdee Avenue, Rosebank, Johannesburg 2196, South Africa

Penguin Books Ltd, Registered Offices: 80 Strand, London WC2R 0RL, England

puffinbooks.com

First published 2010
005

Text copyright © Michael Rosen, 2010
Illustrations copyright © Joe Berger, 2010
'The Difference' and 'The Noise' previously published in *Michael Rosen's A to Z* by Puffin Books 2009,
copyright © Michael Rosen, 2009
All rights reserved

The moral right of the author and illustrator has been asserted

Set in 13/16 pt Bembo MT Pro
Typeset by Palimpsest Book Production Limited, Grangemouth, Stirlingshire
Made and printed in England by Clays Ltd, St Ives plc

British Library Cataloguing in Publication Data
A CIP catalogue record for this book is available from the British Library

ISBN: 978-0-141-32451-7

www.greenpenguin.co.uk

Contents

See Michael
performing some of the poems

from

live
on this website!

www.bbc.co.uk/scotland/learning/authorslive/michael_rosen/video/

Just look for the bendy, bendy toothbrushes . . .

Foreword

When I do my shows, I tell a story called 'Michael's Big Book of Bad Things'. I thought it would be good to write it down. You'll find it here: chopped up into several long bits, and spread out through the book. It's full of noises. Noises are very hard to spell. When you read it, perhaps you can make up the noises you think will best match my spelling.

In a way, for people reading poetry, poems are like that: thinking up the sounds to match what's been written. That's the way poems come alive.

Michael Rosen

Michael's Big Book of Bad Things Part 1

I noticed that my mum and dad were different.
This is how it was:
I go to the bathroom. I'm cleaning my teeth.
Chooka chooka chooka.
Shee shee shee.
And I notice that the toothbrush
is a bit wobbly.
Mmm, it's a bit wobbleee.
Take it out of my mouth.
Bend it.
Bendy bendy bendy
Bendee bendee –
CRACK!
Try to stick it back together.
No good. I'll have to tell Mum.
Better make up a story . . .
'Er . . . I was cleaning my teeth
REALLY HARD . . . and . . . er . . .
The toothbrush broke.'
Yes, that's what I'll say.

Go downstairs with the two bits of
toothbrush.
Into the kitchen.
'Hi, Mum . . . well, er . . . I was cleaning my
teeth
REALLY HARD . . . and . . .'
I open my hands to show her the two bits
of toothbrush.
She looks at them.
'Not to worry,' she says,
'it's only a toothbrush.
It's no big deal. We'll just get another one.'
And that's that.

But . . .
a few minutes later my dad comes in.
'Hi, everybody. Anything happen today?'
'No, no, no,' we say, 'nothing much.
Sky's still blue.'
'Nothing at all?'
'Nope. Nothing at all.'
But then my mum says,
'Oh, hang on. Yes, there was something.
Something funny. Michael was in the
bathroom
cleaning his teeth so hard the toothbrush
broke.

And my dad says,
'Cleaning his teeth so hard the toothbrush
    broke?
I've never heard of anyone cleaning their teeth
so hard that the toothbrush broke.
Michael, what's all this about
cleaning your teeth so hard the toothbrush
    broke?'
And I say,
'Oh yeah, right. Yeah. Look. You see,
I noticed that the toothbrush was a bit
wobbly and . . .'
And he says,
'Wobbly? Wobbly? How do you mean
    wobbly?'
And I say, 'Yeah, and I was interested to see
if it was a bit bendy and . . .'
And he says,
'What's that you're doing with your hands?
That bendy thing?'
And I say,
'Oh yeah, right, I was just trying to see if . . .'
And he says,
'Oh, I'm beginning to get the picture:
bendy bendy bendy –
CRACK!'

You see, he's got it out of me.
He's taken me in for questioning
and he's found out exactly what happened
without me telling him.

And then he REMEMBERED IT.
He remembered and remembered and
    remembered it,
so the next time I did a
BAD THING
he could remind me of it.
So, maybe I was sitting on my brother's head
for half an hour or something
and he comes in and says,
'What do you think you're doing?'
And I say,
'Oh yeah, I'm sitting on my brother's head
for half an hour.'
And he says,
'Oh yes, like the time you went to the
    bathroom
and
bendy bendy bendy –
CRACK!'

It's like he had written it down
in a book.
Michael's BIG BOOK of BAD THINGS.

One Second Late

Oh no.
I'm one second late for school.
One whole second.
And now I'm in trouble.
Serious trouble.
Big, big, big serious trouble.
They've fetched the school guards.
There are six of them.
They've arrested me.
They're holding me by the arms
and marching me off somewhere.
Where am I going, guys?
Oh no.
We're going to the . . .
to the . . .
. . . school prison.
No, please, not the school prison.
It's under the school hall.
And it smells of feet.
Please don't put me in the school prison.
I was only one second late.
Do you hear me?
One second late.
That's not so bad, is it?
What are you doing now?
Not the wall bars.

Don't string me up from the wall bars.

Oh!

Now you've strung me up from the wall bars.

And I said, don't.

You guys never listen.

Where are you going?

You're not going to leave me here, are you?

But it smells of feet down here.

Look, I was only one second late.

Everyone is one second late sometime in their
life.

I've heard of babies being born one second
late

and no one puts them in a prison.

There isn't a babies' prison for late babies, is
there?

Is there?

Hello? Anyone there? Can anyone hear me?

Look, I've been in here for three weeks now.

And I'm getting hungry.

No food or drink for three weeks.

Just because I was late?

One second late, and that's what you get?

Three weeks strung up from the wall bars.

In the school prison.

With nothing to eat?

Hey, and what's that?

WHAT IS THAT?!

It's rats. There are rats in here.

Can anyone hear me?
There are rats in here.
And, look!
They're nibbling my toenails.
That's not fair.
Look, I don't mind there being rats in here.
I can live with that.
But not if they nibble my toenails.
That's going too far.
What do you think?
Can anyone hear me?
Is anyone listening?
Hellooooo?
Hellooooo?

Put Your Hand Up

My three-year-old says to us,
'Put your hand up if you want to be a
  sandwich.'
I put my hand up.
'Good,' he says, 'now I'll eat you.'

Sea-slugs

I know a man
who lived off sea-slugs.

Each soft brown blob
he swallowed, then sighed.

His furry tongue
met their furry skins.

The soft sea-slugs' horns
tickled his throat.

He tried anemones
but didn't like their frills.

The way they seemed
to invite him in.

The sea-slugs just waited,
giving no sign.

He thought of them
as his pet plums.

He loved them
as if they were his children.

He had children.
He loved them too.

Stories and Illnesses

You tell me a joke; I tell you what happened.
You catch on; I catch your cold.
You tell me a secret; I give you a headache.

I laugh; you sneeze.
You cry; I cough.
I talk; you ache.
You whisper; I sweat.

Our stories fly between us like germs.
Our germs fly between us like stories.
We are houses looking after stories.
We are houses looking after germs.
Tell me a secret and I will keep it in my house.
My germs are secret and you will keep them
    in your house.
Do you want to know a secret?
There's a germ of a story here.

Air

The yawn in the morning filling your mouth
with no one to start you yawning

air in my hair
air in the air
fffffffffffff

The swing in the playground swinging
with no one on the swing to swing it

air in my hair
air in the air
fffffffffffff

The balloon with its skin blown up tight
with no one blowing to tighten the skin

air in my hair
air in the air
fffffffffffff

The open window where the cool blows in
with no one to blow the cool

air in my hair
air in the air
fffffffffffff

The flame on the candles flaming
with no one to fan the flames

air in my hair
air in the air
fffffffffffff

The sleepers breathing all night long
with only sleep to make them breathe
ffffffffffffffffffffffffffffffffffffffffffff

The Stranger on the Road from Jack and the Beanstalk

In this pocket, beans that grow into palaces
where a giant woman will do all she can for you.
In this pocket, a needle that will sew your finger
back to your hand, when an axe chops it off in the forest.
In this pocket, the hairs from a bald man's head
that will make you a scarf when the frosts come.
In this pocket, a chain that will lock up the jaws
of the man who tells lies about you.
In this pocket, crumbs of black bread
that will find you friends who will never leave you.
In this pocket, seashells that will sing you songs
sadder than your grandmother's grave.

The Stranger Who Met Jack Meets Someone Else

Sorry, I have no food to sell, sir. I gave all that I
   had left
to a boy I met on the road. He was hungry.
I gave him some beans. I couldn't refuse him,
   poor thing.

I'm like that, sir. I'm happy that I was able to
   help another.
You're looking at my cow, sir. No, she's not for sale.
She's too precious to me. She comes with me
   wherever I go.

My dear grandmother (may she rest in peace!)
gave the cow to me on the day she died,
telling me that she will always bring me good luck.

I can see, sir, that you're still looking at her.
Yes, look into her eyes, deep, deep into her eyes
and you will see things you've never seen before.

Oh, sir, no, how could I? Five gold pieces?
She means more, much more, than gold.
Twenty gold pieces. You're too kind, sir.
Take her, and may you live to love and love to live.

The Messenger

Beware the messenger.
He tells you bad news
to make himself
feel less bad.
Beware the messenger.
He tells you sad news
to make himself
feel less sad.

When he talks of things
being confused,
for him, it makes things clear.

So that he'll be less afraid,
he says he's full of fear.

If you tell him
his words made you
feel bad
or sad
afraid
or confused,
he'll say
what he's doing
is just bringing
the news.

The Space on the Page

The space is a friend.
I tell it what hurts.

I tell it why I'm not good.
The space is a friend.
I tell it the bother I'm in.
It won't let me tell lies.

The space looks at me.
It never says I'm bad.
It never says I'm good.
It never asks me the kinds of question
I don't know the answer to.

The space never shames me.
The space never laughs at me.

When there is something in my head
making me sad or wild,
the space takes it.

The space takes it
till it's a space no more,
till it's full of what I wanted to say,
till it's full of what I didn't know
I wanted to say.

Then it's there in front of me
talking of how I am
so the bother or the sadness or the wildness
can be quiet for a while.

Tell me that's not a friend?
I don't think so.

That's a friend.

Fox

Fox thought Dog was lucky
to be given food every day
but when Dog explained
why he wore a collar,
Fox ran away.

Alligator Problem

If an excavator
excavates
and a motivator
motivates
and a rotivator
rotivates
and an operator
operates
and an indicator
indicates
and an investigator
investigates,
what does an alligator do?

Fish

All on his own
he stared at the fish.
All on its own
the fish stared at him.
Hour after hour
they stared at each other.
They forgot to eat.
All they did was stare.
No one knows
how long it went on.
It must have been days.
It could have been weeks.
When he was found,
all he could say was:
'Water, water,
underwater water.'
The fish
couldn't say anything.

Eddie Dream

It was the one again:
and he's younger than he was
when he died,
but he's got something we both know is
   deadly
and I think he's had it before
and we're talking about
getting him better
and he's being strange,
old for his age,
but mucking about
and I'm letting him
because
I know that this may be
the last day he's alive
and he knows that I know
that this may be the last day
he's alive
but neither of us says
that this may be the last day
he's alive
and I notice he's wearing
the green woollen top
he wore when he was very young . . .

And now in daylight
and the dream is over
I realize I haven't thought of this top
for years.
My picture of it must have been stored away
in my head
without my knowing it was there.
But that's the least of it.
It's sitting on the edge of my bed
knowing that
he's not here
he'll never be here
and that moment in the dream
where I let him fool around
was about loving him being here.

The Book

I opened a book
and a hand fell out.
I turned a page
and heard a shout:
'I'm lost in a wood;
my mother's no good.'
I couldn't bear to look
so I closed the book.

But the girl called out:
'Don't leave me here;
I need you to help me.'
I was cold with fear
so the book stayed shut.
I put it back on the shelf;
put it out of my mind
but then –
it opened itself.
Right there in front of me
it opened up wide
and I heard a voice say,
'Come inside.'

The hand that fell out
jumped back in the book,
the girl inside

gave me a long, cool look
and before I knew it
I was in that wood,
running and running
as fast as I could,
running and running
as fast as I could,
running and running
as fast as I could . . .

Car School

One day a car pulled up at our school
and said,
'I'm your new head teacher.'
The old head teacher was taken out the back
and put in a skip
and the car drove into her office.

The car changed the name of our school.
It was called Car School
and we got a new uniform that had
a picture of a car on the front pocket.

The mayor came to our school
and said how lucky we were
that the car had come
and was sharing with us all that it knew
about cars.

Car School was in the local newspaper.
Everyone wanted to go to Car School.
To get in you had to do a Car Test.
There were questions about cars.

The mayor said that cars had a lot
to offer to the community
so that we could all move forward.

Some of the old teachers left
and the new teachers were cars.
Blue, red, silver, dark green.

A boy in my class wrote a story
about a car that ran someone over.
He was asked to see the head teacher
and we never saw him again.

A woman came to the school
to talk about road safety
and she said how going by bus
was a good idea.
One of the cars stood up
and said that what she was saying
was unbalanced and unfair.

I go to Car School.
Brrrrrrrmmmm.
Brrrrrrrrmmmm.
That's our school song.

Win This Car

I saw a car
and it said on it:
WIN THIS CAR!!!
You had to do a quiz
to win it.

But I don't want to
win a car
with
WIN THIS CAR
written all over it.

Who wants
to drive around the streets
in a car with
WIN THIS CAR
written on it?

Not me.

If a Computer . . .

If your computer laughs
when the clown gets hit
by custard pies,
if it can't stop itself
from telling lies,
if it says it wants
to be your friend,
if it likes stories
but cries at the end,
if it makes mistakes
but carries on
and then suddenly says,
why did I go wrong?,
if it says,
don't leave me behind,
if it makes plans
but changes its mind . . .

it's not a computer.

What Is a Window?

What is a window?
A word beginning with 'w'
like the word 'what' and the word 'word'.
A word ending with 'w' like 'ow!'
(but 'ow!' rhymes with 'cow' not 'window').
Window
is a word with two syllables – 'win' and 'dow'.
Windows don't usually win anything
though you could have a prize window
that won a window competition,
but there's no such thing as a 'dow'.
There is something called a 'dhow',
which is a boat
and 'doh!'
which is what
Homer Simpson says.
The two syllables could be 'wind' and 'ow!'.
There is the wind
which does sometimes make you say 'oh'
when it blows very hard
but 'oh' isn't spelled like 'ow'.
A famous poet once asked
'Who has seen the wind?'
In the end she didn't find out.

Most people have seen windows though.

They're all over the place on the sides of
   houses and buildings.

Just guessing,

I would say that there are a million types of
   window.

Here are some: casement, sash, mullion,
   windscreen, porthole, skylight.

The first people to call a window a 'window'
lived in Scandinavia.

Some of them sailed across the sea to Britain.

When they landed,

if they built a house that had a window,

or if they threw something at a window,

they said 'window'.

The people living in Britain at the time
didn't call windows 'windows'.

After a while,

the people living in Britain did start calling
windows 'windows'.

No one knows why.

Are windows windowy?

Is an elbow elbowy?

Is a chair chairy?

I don't know about elbows and chairs

but a window is windowy.

In Scandinavia, people knew that it meant
   wind–eye.

A window is an eye through which the wind
   blows.
Or is it an eye that sees the wind?
Or is it the eye of the wind?
The thing the wind sees with?
What does the wind see?
The famous poet could have asked,
'Who has seen the wind see?'
But she didn't.

Words Are Ours

In the beginning was the word
and the word is ours:

the names of places,
the names of flowers,
the names of names,
words are ours.

Page-turners
for early learners

How to boil an egg
or mend a leg

Words are ours

Wall charts
Love hearts

Sports reports
Short retorts

Jam-jar labels
Timetables

Words are ours

Following the instructions
for furniture constructions

Ancient mythologies
Online anthologies

Who she wrote for
Who to vote for

Joke collections
Results of elections

Words are ours

The tale's got you gripped
Have you learned your script?

The method of an experiment
Ingredients for merriment

W8n 4ur txt
Re: whts nxt

Print media
Wikipedia

Words are ours

Subtitles on TV
Details on your CV

Book of great speeches
Guide to the best beaches

Looking for chapters
on velociraptors

Words are ours

The mystery of history
The history of mystery

The views of news
The news of views

Words to explain
the words for pain

Doing geography
Autobiography

Arabian Nights
Fighting for your rights

What to do in payphones
Goodbyes on gravestones

Words are ours.

The Tents

The tents were worried it was going to rain.
The tents were tense.
We said,
'Relax, tents, relax.'
But these tents were tense.
They were so intense.

Perhaps
the tents were worried about us.
Would we get wet?
After all,
we were in tents.

Tabby and Grey and Tortoiseshell

The Tabby Cat
chased the Grey Cat out of his house
so the Grey Cat went off to another house.

But the Tortoiseshell was living in that house.

You would have thought
that the Grey Cat would know
what being chased out felt like
but the Grey Cat kicked
the Tortoiseshell Cat out anyway.

1954

The wonder of Baker Street station:

arriving in a train
that's fitted with brass handles and plates
each with curly writing engraved on saying:
'Live in Metroland'
'Live in Metroland'
'Live in Metroland'.

The giant electric noticeboards
with the names of every station
in Metroland,
flashing on and off
electrically
electrically
electrically.

A black bomb
from the Second World War
with a hole in the side
for you to put your money in
for wounded soldiers.
A black bomb.

And a cinema
that shows cartoon films

all day.
In the station.
All day.
In the station.
All day.

The wonder of Baker Street station.

Red Sheep

Edinburgh to Glasgow
is a long, long road
and they're worried
about drivers falling asleep
as they stare
at the road
ahead.
(True!)

A farmer with fields
alongside the road
was worried too,
so he painted
his sheep
red.
(True!)

There they stand
and watch the cars:
red sheep
on green grass.
Green grass,
red sheep.
Red sheep,

green grass –
keeping you awake,
singing:

'Oh you won't fall asleep
you won't fall asleep
you won't fall asleep
when you see red sheep.

Oh you won't fall asleep
You won't fall asleep
You won't fall asleep
When you see red sheep.'

But what if . . .
you turn your head
to see the red sheep?
And you turn off the road?
(Yaaaaaaaaaaaaaagh!)

Then at night
as you close your eyes
and wait for sleep

you hear
Red Sheep?
Singing:

'We are red
we are red
red eyes
red legs
red teeth
red heads

red eyes
red legs
red teeth
red heads.

Oh you won't fall asleep
You won't fall asleep
You won't fall asleep
When you see red sheep.'

We're Walking

We're walking, we're walking,
we're walking away,
we're walking away from the bullets.

Bullets don't grow in the ground.
There is no fruit where the bullet is found.

We're walking, we're walking,
we're walking away,
to where we know
that something will grow.
This is why
we said goodbye
to the ones we loved who were found
lying still on the ground.

We're walking, we're walking,
we're walking away . . .

The Balloon

They've invented a balloon that stays on the
    ceiling.
They've invented a balloon that stays on the
    ceiling.

Nevermore will I have that morning bring-
    down feeling:
waking up and seeing
balloons I bought the day before
lying on the floor.
No feeling bad.
No feeling sad.
Now it stays
for days and days
and nights and nights
hanging out by my bedroom light.

Nevermore will we laugh
at the balloon that couldn't last
and floated in mid-air
halfway between the ceiling and floor,
the balloon that couldn't make its mind up
whether to sink or soar.

Now we have:
Mr Perfecto,

Numero Uno,
The Clever-Dick
with its one stay-in-the-air trick,
never dropping,
never stopping topping,
never fated
to be deflated,
forever over our heads
and over our beds,
scarcely budging,
gently nudging,
unbearably slow,
the guest who won't go.

It's not a balloon.
That's a lie.
It's a spy.
Watching us as we sleep,
as we snore,
wanting to know about us
more and more,
a balloon that can see
like CCTV.

So I say:
bring back the bring-down,
the balloon going to ground,
the balloon that wrinkles
and crinkles,

the balloon that would often
soften.

I don't want to live with:
the horror
of the balloon that'll be up there 'tomorrer',
the plastic freak
up there next week,
me with the fear
it'll be up there next year.

I want to keep my appointment
with disappointment.

The Draught

I left my shoes by the front door overnight.
In the morning they were full of draught.

It slid in under the door but the shoes were
    waiting.
They drank it down and it sat in their bellies.

When I poked my toes and soles inside
my shoes swallowed my feet with a silent gulp.

Today; One Day

Today
The rain has died
My shoes have died
The sun has died
My coat has died
The earth has died
Today.

One day
The rain will flower
My shoes will laugh
The sun will sing
My coat will fly
The earth will dance
One day.

Two Plus Two Is Five

Two plus two is four. Two plus two is four.
Two plus two is four. Two plus two is four.

But is there any way
we can make it say:
two plus two is five?

Imagination leads to transformation.
Transformation follows imagination.

Transformation is a volcano roaring out of the sea;
a mountain stands where there was only sea before;
a young eagle flying is learning for the first time
what it feels like to soar.

Transformation is a smile turning into tears.
Transformation finds freedom where we only
   had fears.

If I imagine,
I transform what I know into something I didn't
   know before.
If I transform what I know, I transform myself.
If I transform myself I'm alive.
With imagination, I'll turn two plus two into five.

Watch me!

Two point four is nearer to two than three.
So if you had to choose between calling it two
    or three
what would you call it? Yes, you!
You'd call it two, wouldn't you?
But remember it was two point four – before!

Imagination leads to transformation.
Transformation follows imagination.

If I imagine, I transform what I know
into something I didn't know before.
If I transform what I know, I transform my mind.
If I transform my mind, I transform myself.
My mind will change. I change my mind.

Right!
Let's change minds. Let's change ourselves:

Two point four (which we called 'two')
plus two point four (which we also called 'two')
is four point eight.
Four point eight?
Well, four point eight is nearer to five than four,
wouldn't you say?

So, if you had to choose between calling it four
    or five,
what would you call it? Wouldn't you call it five?

So two plus two is five.
We're alive!
Two plus two is five
We're alive!
Two plus two is five.
We're alive!

Talking Cat Language

What do our cats think
when I go up to them and say 'miaow'?
Do they think I'm talking to them?
They do look at me
when I say 'miaow',
but when I say 'miaow' again
they look away.

I think that they can hear
I'm talking some kind of cat language
but I think they think,
He hasn't got anything very interesting
to say.

Perhaps they think I'm doing that thing
dads do when they meet someone:
'We took the A23 as far as we could
but we had to turn off on another road
and, you know, it was clear all the way . . .'

No point in listening to that.

Or maybe
I don't make sense
when I say 'miaow'

and they think I'm saying
'rubble dubble'.
So they look up, thinking,
This may be interesting. Let's see.
He might say, 'Breakfast's ready.'
Then I say 'miaow' again
and for them it's 'rubble dubble' again.
So they think,
Yeah, well, we won't bother with that.

Bob Dylan Once Said That He'd Let You Be in His Dreams if He Could Be in Yours

You told me there was a fog
where an owl made echoes in a box.
A leaf tried to bite you.
A dog said hello.
And a horse floated across the sky.

I told you there was a tunnel
where a shopping trolley took me to school
and taught me my ten times table.
A dead man gave me his jacket
and the old school clock chimed, 'Wrong,
    wrong, wrong.'

You told me there was a river
where you were going to drown.
I told you there was a school hall
where I was going to burst.
I didn't believe me.
You didn't believe you.

The Lesson

Whatever my brother learns at school
he teaches me.
He's four years older than me
and doing so well at school
that they've put him in a year ahead.
So he's doing stuff that
I won't be doing
until five years' time.

It's called
calculus.
I'm ten.
He says: 'Dy by dx –
it's like a car going faster more slowly.'

'What?!

Either a car's going faster
Or it's going more slowly.
It can't go faster more slowly.'

'Oh yes it can,' he says,
'd2 by dx squared.'

I don't get it.

'It's calculus,' he says.

I go to bed.
I lie in bed thinking . . .
. . . calculus, calculus
the octopus that calculates
the calculating octopus
here comes the calculus
the calculating calculus . . .

YAAAAAAAAAGHHHHHHH!

The Clock

The clock is broken.
It never tells the right time.
Whenever we look at it,
it's wrong.
We go off thinking it's 8.30
when really it's 8.15.
We get there too early
and we hang about
with nothing to do.

That clock
is a waste of time.

The Lift

At the second floor
we heard a voice inside the lift say:
'Second floor, going up.'
But the second floor
was the top floor.
Where were we going?

What's in Your Bag?

Hey, mister,
What's that you've got in your bag?
An elephant?

OK, OK, it is a big bag.
But now that you've asked
In my bag there could be . . .

An elephant, shrunk
Or just its trunk
Or a thing that goes clunk

A superhero figure
A small yellow digger
An ant that got bigger

There could be a you-know-what
A thing that's not
And a dream I forgot.

Some armadillos
A pair of pillows
A wind in the willows

A nest of rooks
Some worried looks
Too many cooks

A cha-cha dance
The South of France
My last chance

The sound of a car
The morning star
A step too far

My middle name
The rules of the game
More of the same

The grate of a grater
The skate of a skater
The wait of a waiter

Something cracked
Some brains I wracked
A matter of fact

A snip I snapped
A zip I zapped
A rip I wrapped

A bit of a mess
A more or less
A definite yes

The cream of the crop
A tip for the top
A full stop.

Like I said,
I know it's a big bag.'

Not Santa

You're no Santa.
You're just as I feared,
sitting there
with your cotton wool beard,
with your little pointy red hat
and, hey, no one talks like that.

You haven't got a proper sack
It's a polythene bag . . .
And that's a cushion stuffed up your shirt.
Look, it's started to sag.

No mistake.
You're a fake.

And, anyway,
it's not Christmas Day.

Take the Thing into Your Hands

Take the thing into your hands
and open it.
You can open it any way you like.
Many people say that there is a front
and a back,
a right way up
and an upside down
but don't be put off by that.
You can open it any way you like.
You see that door in the side of your head?
Open it.
Now, move the thing in your hands
in any way you like:
side to side, round and round,
over and over.
Perhaps you'll see that there are
sheets that can be turned over.
You can turn them over and back.
You can also hold it still
and move your head.
You can hold your head still
and move your eyes.
Has anything started to come through

the door?
I hope so.
If things do start coming through
the door,
I'm fairly sure that they will
start dancing in the room inside,
or sitting on the chairs
or standing on the table
or shouting
or being rude to people you don't like
or even being rude to people you do like
or kissing
or dying
or going on a boat
or taking things out of their pockets
and showing them to you.
Some of these things
you may have never seen before
but now you know them.
Some are as familiar to you as potatoes,
but these potatoes are different.
When you get tired of all this,
why not put down the thing in your
   hands?
And close the door.
Some of the things that came inside
will stay.
You may well start dressing them up
in things that you like.

You might change the tune they were
dancing to.
You might ask them to keep
taking things out of their pockets.
One day
you might find yourself saying the same
rude things.
Or you might change the words round
to make them ruder.
You might go on the boat.
You might start kissing.
I won't say any more about what else you
    might do.
If you've liked doing all this,
I think you'll probably try to take
another one of these things into your hands
and start all over again.
And then the things that come through
the door the next time
will meet the people who came through
the door last time.
You may even start turning them into each
other.
Look, there's a man hiding under a sheep
so that a giant won't eat him.
And there's a boy running away from
a giant down a beanstalk.

And now you've gone and made the man under
the sheep
run down a beanstalk.
Well, well, well.

This Is the Place

This is the place
I don't want to be
but it's the place where I am.

This is the thought
I don't want to think
but it's the thought that I'm thinking.

This is the memory
I don't want to remember
but it's the memory I'm remembering.

This is the person
I don't want to be
but I am what I am what I am.

Once you said I couldn't.
You said I couldn't but I can.

Jellyfish

The jellyfish
dances through the water
waving its frilly underwear.

We found one on the beach.

It had become a polythene bag
full of water.

Its frills lay on top
like party ribbons
after the dance is over.

You Can't; You Can

You can't do something yesterday.
You can't do something tomorrow.
You can only do something now.

You can remember something from yesterday.
You can plan something for tomorrow.
You can only do something now.

What you did yesterday
can help you choose
what to do now.

What you did yesterday
and what you do now
can help you plan
what to do tomorrow.

But you can only do something
now.

Please Leave

Please leave my mind
Step through the door
Don't hang about
Please leave my mind
Go
I don't want you here
Leave now
The door is waiting
Leave
Close it behind you.

But you stay.

It's
because I won't open the door
for you to go through.
I don't know how to open the door
I don't know where the door is.
I don't know if there is a door.
I don't know
whether
if there is a door
I could open it.
I don't even know whether
if I could open it
I would open it.

So because I know how to say
'leave',
I say:
Please leave my mind
Step through the door
Don't hang about
Please leave my mind
Go
I don't want you here
Leave now
The door is waiting
Leave
Close it behind you.

Michael's Big Book of Bad Things Part 2

My dad had a favourite page
in
Michael's BIG BOOK of BAD THINGS.
Page one.
On page one, it said:
'Oh yes,
like the time you threw your mother's best
    ring
out of the window.
It was her grandmother's!'
I know that sounds bad,
but I was only two.
It was page one
in
Michael's BIG BOOK of BAD THINGS.
I must have been sitting on the floor,
seen the ring
and
fweeeeeeeeeeeeeeeeeeeeeeeeee
out of the window.
And it was worse than that.

We lived in a flat over a shop,
so, when it went flying out of the window,
it landed in the . . .
street.
WHERE IT WAS NEVER FOUND AGAIN.

And it was worse than that.
My mother and father could speak another
    language
that some Jewish people can speak:
Yiddish.
Perhaps your mother or father or grandparents
speak another language
And when they speak English,
every now and then a word from the other
    language
pops into what they're saying.
That's how it was with my dad.
He didn't say the word 'grandmother',
He used the Yiddish word
And it made it sound all ancient.
This is how it went:
'Oh yes,
like the time you threw your mother's best
    ring
out of the window.
It was her . . . BUBBE'S!'
YAAAAAAAAAAAAGH!
It felt like the room filled up with

old BUBBES!
And they were all standing round me saying,
'You threw your mother's best ring out of the
   window?
And it was her . . . BUBBE'S?
Oy yoy yoy yoy yoy.'

So what happens next time
I do a
BAD THING?

Staying Over

At Malc's flat
there's raisins and tangerine pieces
to have in bed.

At Mart's house
there's a train set in his bedroom.

At Chris's flat
there's a lift to play in till bedtime.

At Malc's
we go over to his Armenian Granny's
and she cooks us pilaff.

At Mart's
we make tunnels
for his train to go through.

At Chris's
we go down to the playground
and play football-tennis for hours.

At Malc's
we talk about places far away

like Czechoslovakia and Bulgaria
where his dad goes.

At Mart's
we talk about the two lakes in France
where me and him got lost
in the mud and bullrushes
but got back to the campsite OK in the end.

At Chris's
we talk about Arsenal and Spurs;
he's Spurs
I'm Arsenal.
We imagine what it would be like
if Arsenal played Spurs in the Cup Final.

At Malc's
his mum and dad are Peggy and Francis
and I love it
when Francis comes into our bedroom
at bedtime and sings us,
'Barnacle Bill the Sailor'.

At Mart's
his mum and dad are Lorna and Fred
and I love it
when Fred stops wasps stinging me
by grabbing them with his fingers.

'You've got to be quick,' he says,
and Lorna says, 'Oh, Fred, please!'

At Chris's
his mum and dad are Rene and Moishe
and I love it
when Rene plays the trick with the plastic egg
that she serves up in a plate of baked beans
and I believe it's real and try to stick my fork
in the plastic yolk.

Not so good at Malc's
when we drew pictures on Armenian Granny's
   doorstep
and she said she couldn't wash it off
and Uncle Felix with the beard
went off in a big huff
and didn't talk to us.

Not so good at Mart's
when I threw Mart's baby brother's
Special Extra-fast Yo-yo over the fence
and when I pretended to put it back
on the shelf,
Lorna saw that my hand was empty
and did a whole tut-tut-tut thing.

Not so good at Chris's

when we came back from
Spurs v Arsenal
and this group of kids surrounded us
and poked and prodded us and
called us names
and we came back and sat on the sofa
and felt bad all evening.

I love it that my parents
let me go and stay
at Malc's, Mart's and Chris's.

The Seagulls

The seagulls think we live at the seaside:
the tower blocks are their cliffs;
they swoop for fish in the gutter
but are happy that it's last night's fried rice.
They stand about screaming on the pavement
   beach
and ride the sea-breezes pumped out
by the cinema air-conditioning.
They hover over the waves of cars
and if you stare at them,
wondering what they're doing
so far from home,
they stare back:
'This is our home now.
That kebab
is a crab.'

They Don't Love You

You're thinking that your mother loves your
    brother more than you
You're thinking that your father loves your
    sister more than you
You're thinking that your mother loves you
    less than him
You're thinking that your father loves you less
    than her

You can prove it
You can prove it
You can prove it
He was asked if he wanted more
He got the present that cost more
No one shouts at *her*
No one hits *her*
She gets the smiles
You get the snarls
He gets told he did really well
You get told you should've done better
He's allowed to do what he wants
You're not allowed to do anything

You're thinking that your mother loves your
    brother more than you

You're thinking that your father loves your
	sister more than you
You're thinking that your mother loves you less
	than him
You're thinking that your father loves you less
	than her

But there's no one there to see it
There's no one to believe it
It's something you know and it's something
	you say
Bu they think you're mad and they say
	you're lying
There's no point in trying to get them to
	love you
'Cause they don't and they won't and they
	won't and they don't
So you might as well be a pig.

On the Move Again

You know
You gotta go.
No time to grieve
You just gotta leave.
Get away from the pain
On the move again.

You gotta move it
To prove it.
Prove it
To move it.

Take the train.
Catch a plane.

Make the trip
In a ship.

Take a hike.
Ride a bike.

Go by car.
Going far.

Use your feet
On the street.

Get stuck
In a truck.

You gotta move it
To prove it.
Prove it
To move it.

Then you arrive
And you're alive.
You arrive.
You're alive.

What you leave behind
Won't leave your mind
But home is where you find it.
Home is where you find it.
Home is where you find it.
Home is where you find it.

Corned Beef

Why does Mum keep cans of corned beef
in the cupboard?
Not just one or two cans –
stacks of them.
Does she think that one day we'll
have a corned beef party?
Does she think that
people will come over
and she will say, 'Surprise!',
pull back a cloth
and there, in front of everyone,
the table will be full of
cans of corned beef?
And then everyone will sit round
opening cans of corned beef?
And we'll sit and eat it saying,
'Corned beef. This is nice.
Mmmmm. Nice party.'

Or does she think that one day
all the shops will be closed
and we won't be able to buy
any food, but we'll be all right
because we'll be able to eat
corned beef?
Every day.

For months and months.
And people will be jealous of us
and they'll be queuing up outside
our house, shouting,
'Let us in.
We want corned beef.
We want corned beef.'

I don't like corned beef.
I don't like the way
there are these chunks of fat
sitting on it.
And when you eat it
it sticks to the roof of your mouth.

And now I think of it
I've never seen Mum eating it either.

Why does Mum keep cans of corned beef
in the cupboard?

Once, there was a terrible disease in the
country where corned beef comes from.
It was an 'outbreak of Typhoid', they said.
In the newspapers and on the TV
they kept saying to us,
'DON'T EAT THE CORNED BEEF,
DON'T EAT THE CORNED BEEF.'

Mum went to the cupboard,
took down one of the cans and said,
'Hmmm, better not open that
till the typhoid outbreak is over.'

Why does Mum keep cans of corned beef
in the cupboard?

Daddy-long-legs in a Hotel Room

Everyone's ducking out of the way
of you and your furry legs.
You are like eyelashes
with wings,
fluttering and flittering about,
bumping into lampshades:
tutta tutta, ta-ta tutta,
a jerky drum solo.

You feel like a spider's web
when you brush across our faces:
tutta tutta, ta-ta tutta.

– Kill it, Dad.
– Kill it, Dad.

They think your hairs
could bite and sting.
We stare at your
up-the-wall, down-the-wall dancing.
If we're not careful
you could jitterbug down our necks:
tutta tutta, ta-ta tutta.

I switch out the light.
It's quiet.
We lie and wonder if
there'll be a moment
when we'll feel your
whiskers
whisper across our skin:
tutta tutta, ta-ta tutta.

In the morning
the bathroom is white and glarey.
You're flat out on the tiles,
your legs splayed.
The jazz is over.

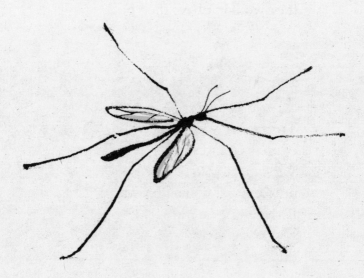

Dinosaur Problem Solved

My three-year-old
holds a wooden block up to his ear
and says,
'It's a dinosaur telephone transformer.'

Wow!
One moment it's a telephone
then –
click click click –
it's a dinosaur.

If the dinosaurs had known
how to turn into telephones,
they wouldn't have died out.

Satnav

In the future
we'll have satnav clothes.

You could have satnav shoes
or satnav trousers
and they'd talk to you:

'The bathroom is the second door
on the left.
Second door on the left.'

'When you get to the table,
sit down.
Sit down.
Eat the broccoli.
Eat the broccoli.

You smell.
Change your shirt.
Change your shirt.'

If you lost your socks,
you'd type in 'socks'
and your satnav trousers would say:

'Your socks are where you left them,
screwed up
on your bedroom floor.
On your bedroom floor.'

Then you'd get up to go and see your friend
and the satnav trousers would say,

'Do not go out.
Do not go out.
Your friend doesn't like you.
Turn round, go back.
You haven't done your homework.
You haven't done your homework.

Your socks are where you left them.
Go to bed.
Go to bed.

Have a bath.
At the end of the passage,
turn left.
The bathroom is the second door on the left.
Open the bathroom door.
Run the bath.
I know what you're thinking:
you're thinking that
you could get away with running the bath,

splashing it about a bit with your hand
and then letting the water out.

I'm not that easily fooled.
I'm watching you.
I'm your satnav trousers.
I know everything.'

The Corner of the Sheet

Sorry, Mum,
I can't stop myself
but it all starts
when I nibble the corner of the sheet.
It seems to go on when I'm reading in bed
and I don't even know I'm doing it.
I chew the corner more and more,
and more and more sheet goes into my
　　mouth.
I'm sorry, Mum,
but it gets juicy
and soon there's a whole mouthful of sheet
that I'm chewing on, making sklewshy noises.
I'm sorry, Mum,
I can't stop myself.
I clench my teeth round the sheet,
I close my lips and suck,
open my lips, open my mouth,
and the mouthful of sheet cools,
so when I next clamp my mouth
round the corner it tastes cool.
And this goes on and on and on
till I fall asleep.

In the morning
it's cold and I try not to touch it.

By the evening it's gone crisp
and dry.

Some of the sheets
now have tiny holes near the corner.
I think this is something to do
with the chewing
but I'd rather not think about that.

Sorry, Mum.

School Haiku

At school we learn ways
how to say horrible things
to one another.

Shane

Look out.
There's Shane.
Shane fights in the playground.
He roars.
We're scared.

If you're walking along
the pavement and Shane's
coming towards you,
cross the road.

When you're on your own
and it's dark
and you're feeling lonely,
don't think of Shane.

He's got a black jacket
with little white marks on it.
Little dots.
Little flakes.
Like snow, or flour
or that sweet stuff
we buy in a yellow tube
with a straw made of liquorice.
Sherbet.
You suck it up through

the liquorice straw
and when it gets to your mouth
it fizzes.
Sherbet.

Harrybo calls Shane
'Sherbet-Jacket'.
Shane is scary.
Sherbet-Jacket
is not so scary.

The Difference

In Glasgow
the hotel gave us something called
'Soap'.
In Edinburgh
the hotel gave us the same stuff
and it was called
'Skincare Bar'.

Our Flat

In our flat
faces speak
of places across the sea.

In our flat
voices walk in
talking, but not like me.

In our flat
books fly around us
saying, 'Never stop saying "Why?".'

In our flat
stories stroke us
until we cry.

In our flat,
there was a mother and father
who were born so poor
they told us:
even if we now have more
no one is worse than you;
things could be fair
if we learned how to share,
and they sang a sweet song
that said war is wrong.

Find out what's possible, they said.
Find out what's possible.
Find out what's possible, they said.
Find out what's possible.

The Alley

We come from the flats
from above the shops.
Here is the alley for the vans
bringing stuff for the shops.
We live in the alley.

We spy on the man in the van
loading tables and chairs.
He accelerates past the dustbins
so fast that my brother calls him
'Accelerating-Past-The-Dustbins'.
'Look out,' he says, 'here comes
Accelerating-Past-The-Dustbins!'

We say that
Accelerating-Past-The-Dustbins
fills the legs of the chairs and tables
with diamonds and gold
and we're the only ones who know.

That's the fence
we kicked the ball over and
we climbed over and into the church
that burned down on the night
I was born and we're not allowed
to go in there,

but we do go in there to find treasure:
melted glass, yellow tiles, twisted iron.

The treasure that we find –
the melted glass, yellow tiles, twisted iron –
we hide.
We hide it from
Accelerating-Past-The-Dustbins
in case he steals it from us
to put in the legs of the tables and chairs
that he's smuggling to America.

There are bushes by the fence
and once a year they're covered
in fat white berries, which we pick
and pile up so that we can throw them
at each other and into the van of
Accelerating-Past-The-Dustbins.

My Dad

My dad is a map:
follow this road
cross this bridge
go round this lake
don't fall down this cliff
climb this hill
stop and look at this view.

Today
I've got to
follow this road
cross this bridge
go round this lake
not fall down this cliff
climb this hill
stop and look at this view
without a map.

Perhaps

Perhaps he thinks that saying he loves us
  will make us weak.
Perhaps no one ever said they loved him
  when he was a boy.

The Rhythm of Life

Hand on the bridge
feel the rhythm of the train.

Hand on the window
feel the rhythm of the rain.

Hand on your throat
feel the rhythm of your talk.

Hand on your leg
feel the rhythm of your walk.

Hand in the sea
feel the rhythm of the tide.

Hand on your heart
feel the rhythm inside.

Hand on the rhythm
feel the rhythm of the rhyme.

Hand on your life
feel the rhythm of time
hand on your life

feel the rhythm of time
hand on your life
feel the rhythm of time.

Don't Drown

Don't drown.
Practise swimming for a long, long time.
Don't drown.
Practise shouting, 'Help!'
Don't drown.
Keep the water out.
Don't drown.
Call for help.
Don't drown.
If you see the water rising,
leave.
Don't drown.
If you think you're sinking,
grab something.
Don't drown.
If you think there's no way out,
you're probably wrong
and there is a way out.
Find it.
Don't drown.
If you think you're stuck,
probably you're not.
Don't drown.
If you think you can't go on,
probably you can.
Don't drown.

The Newborn Child

This is the newborn child.
This is the child just come into the world.
Was it born in a hotel suite?
Was it born on to the ground and left there
as its parents ran from guns and bombs?

What shall we do with the newborn child?
What shall we make it? A boy or a girl?

Shall the child live in the city with the sound
    of trains, trams, buses and cars?
Shall the child live in the country with the
    sound of tractors, dogs and chainsaws?
Shall the child live up a mountain?
Or on a beach?
Shall the child live in a house, an apartment, a
    tent or a hut?

Shall the child live with a mother who hasn't
    eaten for three months?
Shall the child live where there is a bath on
    every floor?
Shall the child drink dirty water every day?
Shall the child live?

You choose.
This is the newborn child.
What kind of child is this child?

They Said; I Say

Whenever my mother left the house,
she'd say, 'Where's my hat? I'm going.'
I didn't understand.
'But you haven't got a hat,' I'd say.

Whenever I had wrinkles in my socks,
my mother would say,
'Take the bagels out of your socks.'
I didn't understand.
I'd say, 'I haven't got any bagels in my socks.'

Whenever we sang in school,
'There is a green hill far away
without a city wall.'
I didn't understand.
I'd say, 'Green hills don't have city walls.'

Whenever our history teacher lost her temper,
she'd say, 'Great Scott! You're for the high
    jump!'
I didn't understand.
Who was Scott? Why was he great?
And why did we have to do the high jump?

As we leave for nursery school in the morning,
I say to my four-year-old daughter,

'Where's my hat? I'm going.'
And she says, 'But you haven't got a hat.'

I look at her socks and say,
'Take the bagels out of your socks.'
And she says, 'I haven't got any bagels
in my socks.'

Along the way, I sing:
'There is a green hill far away
without a city wall.'
And she says, 'Why has the green hill
got a city wall?'

And when I say goodbye to her,
I say, 'Great Scott! You're for the high jump!'
And she says,
'No I'm not.'

The Mirror

When Dad looks in the mirror,
he says, 'Hiya, handsome, and
how are YOU today?'

When birds look in the mirror,
they start attacking the picture
that they see of themselves in the mirror,
and they peck, peck, peck at the glass.

What if Dad started doing the same thing
when he looks in the mirror?
'Hey, you! You're stressing me!'
WHAM!

Wet Concrete

The fact is
where there is wet concrete
people walk in it.
Sometimes it looks as if it's a mistake
and it's just the edge of a heel
or the tip of a toe.
Sometimes it's a dog's paw print.
I don't suppose the dog thought,
'Hey, this could be fun.
Why don't I go and step in that wet concrete?
You know, leave my mark for the next fifty years?
OK, not many people know me around here
and when I die not many people are going to
    remember me
but at least my paw print is going to be there.'

No, I don't think dogs work things out like that.

But with people it's different:
Sometimes you see a whole line of footprints.
That person must have known.
They must have felt their foot go plop plop plop
in the wet concrete
and they chose not to get off:

'Hey, look at where my feet went.
And the soles of my shoes must be brilliant
to make tracks in the wet concrete like that,
full of little lines and holes.'

Not far from where I live
there's one small patch of concrete.
Just a tiny patch between a drain cover and a
      wall.
Only just big enough for a foot to fit on it.
And you know what?
Someone has done just that.
Fitted their foot right in it.
He must have seen the wet patch
tucked in there next to the wall,
carefully got himself lined up
and lowered his foot down
on to that smooth, wet concrete:
pressed it down
lifted it up
then buzzed off.

A real precision job.

'Hey, Harry,' said his friend at work,
'you've got some stuff on your shoe.
You must have stepped in something.'

'Oh jeez,' says Harry,
'I must have stepped in some wet concrete.
Now, how did that happen?'

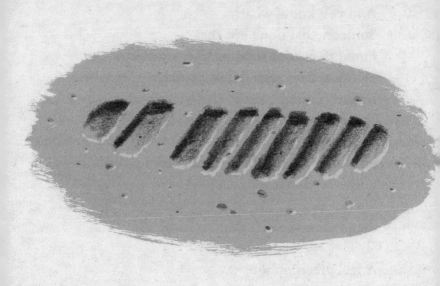

The Child

The child is happy.
She is jumping up and down.

Is she jumping up and down
because she is happy?
Or is she happy
because she is jumping up and down?

Something Changes

When you're born
your folks think you're amazing.
They scream:
'It's a BABY!!!
Quick, quick, quick,
come and have a look.
IT'S A BABY!!!'

Then a few weeks later,
maybe you lift your head up
a tiny, tiny, little bit
and they scream:
'LOOK!!! THE HEAD!!!
Quick, quick, quick,
come and have a look.
IT'S AMAZING!!!'

Now I don't want to say
anything to disappoint you.

But something changes.

Wind forward a few years.

You get back from school.
You open the door.

You chuck your bag on the floor.
Urgh!!!
You walk into the living room.
Slump down on the sofa.
Urgh!!!
You switch on the TV.
Urgh!!!

Your folks don't say,
'LOOK!!!
HE'S SWITCHED ON THE TV!!!
FIRST HE DUMPED HIS BAG
AND NOW HE'S SWITCHED ON THE
   TV!!!
QUICK, QUICK, QUICK,
COME AND HAVE A LOOK!!!'

For some reason
they're just not as excited
about every little thing you do.

Michael's Big Book of Bad Things Part 3

Ah bedtime.
I had a problem with bedtime.
When my mum said the word 'bed'
or 'bedtime',
I couldn't hear it.
My ears wouldn't work.

So there's me and my mum
sitting on the sofa, watching television.
(Why do people watching TV
get that funny smiley staring look,
when they're watching TV?)
And my mum says,
'Michael, it's time for bed.'
And all I hear is:
'Michael, it's time for –'
So she says it louder,
'Michael, it's time for bed!'
And I go on watching TV with the smiley
    staring look.
'Michael, IT'S TIME FOR BED!!!'

And I say,
'OK, Mum, no need to shout about it.'
And I get up
and start to walk off
but when I get behind the sofa
I think, 'If I'm really quiet,
she won't know I'm here
and I can go on watching TV.'

So I stop breathing.

And she says,
'Michael, I know you're there.'
And I say,
'I'm not.'
And she says,
'What are you talking about?
Standing there saying you're not there!
You must be there if you're standing there
saying you're not there.
What? You take me for stupid?
Now go to bed.'

So I go out the room.

But when I'm out the room,
I think, 'If I make that noise on the floor
that sounds like I'm going upstairs,
she'll think I've gone upstairs

and I can creep back in, peep round the edge
    of the door
and go on watching television.'

So I stand outside the door
and go stamp, stamp, stamp
on the floor with my feet.
And I'm standing there stamping away
and I don't realize that she's come up behind
    me
and she's standing over me and she says,
'What do you think you're doing?'
And I say,
'I'm just going upstair– Well, actually, I'm not.'
And she says,
'That doesn't sound anything like going
    upstairs.
So go up there,
go to the bathroom,
wash your face,
clean your teeth
and go to bed.
I can't stand looking at you
ANOTHER MINUTE!!!'

And she means it.

So it's
up, into the bathroom,

shut the door and
yeahhhhhhhhhhhhhh.
It was time to muck about.

Put the plug in:
fippp.
Turn the taps on:
bsssshhhhhhhhhhhhhhht.
Flick water at the mirror:
blip blip blip blip.
There's drops of water on the mirror
and the drops start turning into drips
and one drip is going faster than another drip
and it's a race!
And I start doing a running commentary
like the horse racing on the TV:
'And here comes Fancy Pants. Here comes
    Fancy Pants.
And closing on Fancy Pants it's Nosehead. Yes
    it's Nosehead.
Nosehead is closing –'
And I hear my mum from downstairs
shouting up at me:
'Michael! What's that silly noise going on up
    there?'
And I say,
'Oh yeah. Right.
I was just looking for the flannel.'

And I carry on . . .
'Yes, it's Nosehead overtaking Fancy Pants on
  the inside . . .'

Now, when a man shaved when I was a boy,
this is how they did it:
plug in:
fipppp.
Taps on:
bsssshhhhhhhhhhhhht.
Little brush
into the water:
cafloffapupp, cafloffapupp, cafloffapupp.
Into a special jar of shaving soap:
chooff chooff chooff.

Now I loved this shaving soap.
If you held it up to the light,
it was all
Twinkly.
Smell it
and it was all
perfumey.
Prod it:
thppppbbbb.
It was all
squidgy.
So I'm prodding it –
thppppbbb, thppppbbb, thppppbbbb –

and I start to make a hole in it,
so I shout,
'I'm drilling for oil!'
And I hold it up to my eye to get a view into
    the jar.
'Hey, you can't see the hole from the outside.
That's a-mazing.
Hey, I could bury something in there.
What could I bury?
I know.
The top of the toothpaste.
Good thinking.'
So I unscrew it:
chooka chooka chooka
and then into the shaving soap:
thppppbbbb
and smooth over the top:
Shhhhhhhhhhhhhhhh.
Hold it up to my eye to look into the jar.
'Wow, that's like, that's like,
buried treasure.
Pirates would come along looking for it.
singing their song:
'Yo ho ho and a bottle of rum
Yo ho ho and a –'
And I hear my mum from downstairs
shouting up at me,
'Michael! What's that silly singing going on
    now?'

And I say,
'Oh yeah. Right. I was just glad I found the
   flannel.'

Quick! Wash my face. Clean my teeth . . .
. . . Hey, the toothbrush is a bit wobbleee
and a voice inside me says,
'No, Michael, don't do it.'
And I say,
'No, I've got to. I've got to do it.'
And the voice says,
'Michael, don't do it.'
And I start to bend the toothbrush:
bendy bendy bendy.
'Michael, stop, stop.'
'I've got to do it . . .'
Bendy bendy–

But then I stop.
Quick, finish off my teeth
and then off to bed.

Chazze Bupke

My mum and dad can speak a language
I don't really understand.
I know some of the words
but not all of them.
So my dad plays games with the words,
like this.

He's cooking some beans in some kind of mix
in a frying pan.
'What's that?' I say.
'Chazze bupke,' he says.
'What's chazze bupke?' I say.
'Tigers' eggs,' he says.
'What are tigers' eggs?' I say.
'Chazze bupke,' he says.

I'm Tired

Dad says,
'Phew! I'm tired.'

Mum says,
'You're tired? I'm tired!'

Dad says,
'I've never, ever been as tired as this.'

Mum says,
'You don't know what "tired" is.
I'll tell you what "tired" is.
It's me.
That's what tired is.'

Dad says,
'I'm tired all over.
It's my legs. It's my head.'

Mum says,
'My tired isn't just inside.
Everywhere's tired.'

Dad says,
'I haven't even begun to tell you
how tired I am.'

Mum says,
'I know how tired
you are.
You've told me.
You know something?
You telling me you're tired
makes *me* tired.'

Dad says,
'And that's it.
No one understands how tired I am.
No one listens.
In the end I get tired,
saying, "I'm tired."'

Mum says,
'What you don't know
is that before I was this tired
I didn't know a person could be this tired.
If I had known then
how tired I was going to be
I wouldn't have let myself get this tired.'

And I say,
'Anyone round here tired?'

The Raft

Mart and me
made a raft for the river:
thick branches criss-crossed
and tied with rope.
Empty cans on top
to help it float.
Mart and me
would row about on the water.
We'd cross to the other side.
We'd row
downstream,
upstream,
under the trees,
between the fields.
We'd be river rovers.
The river would be ours.

We made the raft at the water's edge.
We pushed it out into the shallows.
Mart got on.
'Are you getting on?' he said.
'Not yet,' I said.

And then it flipped.

It flipped right over.
He was under the raft.
The raft was on top of him.
He was underwater.
I couldn't lift it off him.
The criss-cross branches
were like a cage holding him down
in the river water.
His face came up into a space
between the branches.
He called out.
He went under again into the river.
I tried to lift the raft
but he was clinging on to it
underneath.
I couldn't lift the raft.
His face came up into the space again.
I could see his hands
gripping the branches.
He was trying to get air
but he couldn't get his mouth
up high enough into the space,

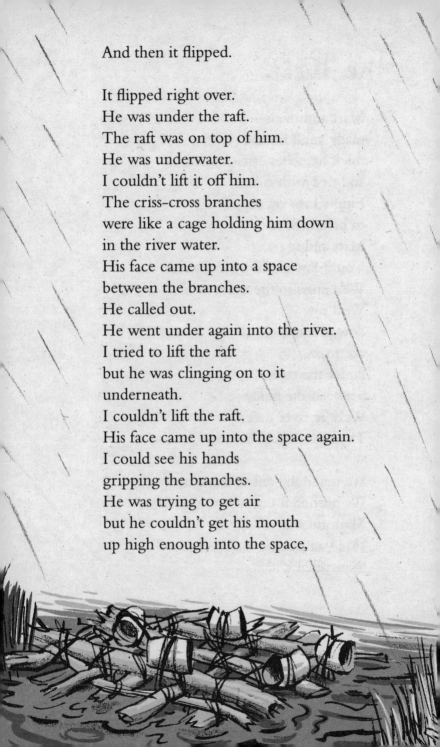

so his mouth
was filling up with river water.
Then he went under again
and the space where his face had been
was river brown.

Mart's brother Tony
stepped into the shallows,
grabbed the raft
and hoisted it up
with Mart
still clinging to it.

Mart choked and coughed and spat.
He sat on the riverbank
shuddering.
His clothes stuck to him like
another skin.

Mart's mum and dad
and my mum and dad
had a conference.
They decided that
there would be
no rafting.

We broke the raft up.
The river wasn't ours.
I should have been better
at helping Mart.

The Rains

In the Jura Mountains,
it rained
and rained
and rained.
Every day,
every night.
We lay in our tents
and listened to the rain:
rain raining
rain raining
rain raining.
The earth was a sponge.
The paths were rivers.
Our sleeping bags were damp.
Underneath the tent
it started to smell of old cabbage.
Our feet wrinkled.

My father got up in the night
and shone a torch
into the rain
and dug a ditch
round the tent
so that the water
would flow away

but the ditch filled up
and one night
it flowed into the tent.

We lay in the dark
while the rain rained
on and on.
Rivulets of rain
trickled through the tent,
the lightning lit up our faces,
the thunder rolled round the mountains.
I thought there could be waves of rain
and we would float away.

When I woke up,
the rain had stopped.
There was no pattering
on the tent roof.
There were birds.
It was light.
Warm in the sleeping bag.
Cold on our faces.
I pulled my hand out of the bag.
I touched the tent.
The wall was wet and tight.
I wondered what was outside
on the other side of the wall.
I didn't mean to press too hard.

Or perhaps I did.
The wall of the tent was so wet and so tight
that I poked a hole straight through it.

I didn't know
but Dad was standing right there
and he saw my finger burst through.
He heard it rip the tent wall.

'For God's sake,
WHAT HAVE YOU DONE NOW?!'

I looked through.
He was on the other side,
staring in,
his eye, big in the hole.
'Oh, sorry,' I said,
'I didn't mean to, honest.
Oh, there's dry land out there . . .'

Cosmo Caff

We live next door to the Cosmo Caff.
Sausage and mash
Peas and carrots

Men in overalls
and dungarees
file in at lunchtime:
clomp clomp clomp.
Beef and potatoes
Sausage and mash
Peas and carrots

First thing in the morning
we see Mrs Conroy
tipping spuds into the
peeling machine
in the Cosmo backyard:
budda budda budda.
Bacon
Bacon and egg
Bacon, egg and beans
Bacon, egg, beans and chips
Beef and potatoes
Sausage and mash
Peas and carrots

The peeling machine
in the Cosmo backyard goes
round and round and round:
drubba drubba drubba.
Apple pie and custard
Bacon
Bacon and egg
Bacon, egg and beans
Bacon, egg, beans and chips
Beef and potatoes
Sausage and mash
Peas and carrots

And out come the spuds
gleaming and oval
like big birds' eggs
in the rain:
spadder spadder spadder.
Ice cream, jelly
Apple pie and custard
Bacon
Bacon and egg
Bacon, egg and beans
Bacon, egg, beans and chips
Beef and potatoes
Sausage and mash
Peas and carrots

Then into the chipper
with the big lever
squeezing the spuds
through the grille:
karrunch karrunch karrunch.
Cup of tea, mug of tea
Ice cream, jelly
Apple pie and custard
Bacon
Bacon and egg
Bacon, egg and beans
Bacon, egg, beans and chips
Beef and potatoes
Sausage and mash
Peas and carrots

And we hear the white chips
tumble into the hot oil
in the fryer:
tsssssssssssssssssssss.
Lemonade, orangeade
Cup of tea, mug of tea
Ice cream, jelly
Apple pie and custard
Bacon
Bacon and egg
Bacon, egg and beans
Bacon, egg, beans and chips
Beef and potatoes

Sausage and mash
Peas and carrots

And out come the chips
all crisp and brown
like autumn twigs
on to the plates:
chooff chooff chooff.
Slice of bread, slice of toast
Lemonade, orangeade
Cup of tea, mug of tea
Ice cream, jelly
Apple pie and custard
Bacon
Bacon and egg
Bacon, egg and beans
Bacon, egg, beans and chips
Beef and potatoes
Sausage and mash
Peas and carrots

We sit shoulder to shoulder
in Cosmo Caff.

We live next door
to Cosmo Caff:
clomp clomp clomp
budda budda budda
drubba drubba drubba

spadder spadder spadder
karrunch karrunch karrunch
tsssssssssssssssssssss
chooff chooff chooff

Time to Write

They say don't forget to write your name on the
  paper.
Why? Are they worried I might forget it?
Hey, what if I wrote, 'I dunno.'?
What would happen?
Or what would happen if I wrote, 'Me'?
I'm me, so fair enough.
Or what if I didn't write my name . . .
I could write someone else's name.
My name's Michael. I could write 'Rosemary'.

And then it's time to write the date.
Why? It's always today.
It's never yesterday.
It's never tomorrow.
So I could write 'Today'.
But then . . .
what if I wrote 'Tomorrow'?

And then comes the title.
I always find that the hardest.
One thing I've figured out:
if I'm writing about my mum
I shouldn't write 'My Dad'.

Where Do We Come From?

I come from when houses were ruined,
the skies had stopped exploding,
my father in Germany meeting
the skeleton of a dinosaur in the snow
in the wrecked Berlin Natural History Museum,
my mother holding on to my brother,
having lost a living, walking, just-talking toddler
to a never-ending cough,
my parents who grew up when you could buy
a live chicken in Hessel Street,
my father sharing his bedroom with his Uncle Sam
but never talking to him because one day
Sam had grabbed the cap my father had bought
down Petticoat Lane, and turned it inside out.
'Who switched the light off, Father?'
'Neither of us. We didn't have lights.
We had a candle.'
My mother having to bring flowers to school
for Harvest Festival but she had no garden,
so she walked down Globe Road
looking for a flower to pick
but there were none,
and there were Mosley's Men out too,
looking for Jews like them to give a beating to
for being Jews,
and the uncles who never came back

from camps in Poland, just vanished, gone,
but I was here, made from this, all this,
it goes on, it hadn't stopped,
there was my father swearing in Yiddish:
'*Chaliera zolste nehmen.*'
'Don't say that, Harold!' my mum says to him.
And now I can say it too.
And now I can say it too.

Fly Racing

We lie on our backs in the tent,
looking up at the roof
where the flies walk and hop and fly.
There are bluebottles and horseflies
and houseflies and midges.
My brother says it's a race
and he gives them names:
the housefly he calls Joe Soap;
the horsefly he calls Thugger;
the midge he calls Tiddlybottom.
Then he starts the racing commentary:
'. . . and Joe Soap is heading for the line,
oh no, he's turning back, Tiddlybottom
is stuck, Tiddlybottom hasn't moved,
Thugger is powering into the lead . . .
and little Tiddlybottom seems to be stuck . . .'

And I'm giggling
and he's shouting
and I'm giggling
and my dad suddenly puts his head
through the tent door:
'You've woken us up.
It's half past five in the morning.
We come on holiday to rest and relax
and all we can hear is you two roaring

your heads off in the middle of the night.'
And my brother says,
'But you said it was half past five
in the morning;
that's not the middle of the night.'

'Enough!' says my dad,
and his head disappears from the tent door.
'We'll talk about this later.'

Oh no. Not the 'Later' Thing!

And I lay there pointing up
at Tiddlybottom.
He hadn't moved.
He was still there.
And we lay there laughing so hard
but oh so quietly
that there were tears streaming
out of our eyes
and we buried our faces
in our sleeping bags.

Later, we got the 'Later' Thing.

Great Expectations

'Listen to this,'
my father said.
He pumped up the Tilly lamp
in the tent
and opened the book.

Ten of us round him
in the tent
at night.

'Listen to this,'
my father said.

A boy called Pip.
An uncle called Pumblechook.
A convict in chains.
A rich old woman
all on her own
still wearing the wedding dress
from the wedding that
never happened.
On the table,
the mouldy wedding cake
not eaten.
Love, death, money.
Money, love, death.

'Listen to this,'
my father said.
And he does all the voices:
'What larks!'
'Don't know ya!'
'Beggar him, boy!'
'How much do you want?
Fifty pounds?'
'Oh, not nearly so much.'
'Five pounds?'

The Tilly lamp.
The book.
The eyes.
The tent.
'Listen to this,'
my father said.
And I can hear it all
wherever I go.

> **Tilly lamp:** *a lamp that you ran on paraffin*
> *(a bit like petrol), that you made work by pushing a*
> *little pump on the side of the paraffin tank and*
> *lighting a lacy white cylinder.*

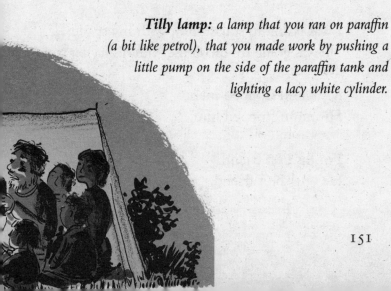

Campsite, Ladram Bay, 1952

I was six.
He was six.

I had a spade.
He had a frying pan.

I hated him.
He hated me.

I really, really, really hated him.
He really, really, really hated me.

I marched towards him.
He marched towards me.

I was going to squash him with my spade.
He was going to squash me with his frying pan.

My mum stopped me.
His mum stopped him.

I'm his best friend.
He's my best friend.

The Bell

There are forty-eight children in my class.
We sit in four rows of twelve.
We sit in twos, one next to the other,
at desks, with two lids, side by side,
one each.

Miss Williams works out where we sit.
We do tests: Arithmetic and English.
She adds up the marks
and whoever's got the best mark
sits at the top of the class
in the desk at the end of the first row,
next to the window.
Whoever gets the worst mark
sits at the bottom of the fourth row,
furthest from the window.
And she works out everyone else's place
from the mark that they get.

She does this every week.
Every week, we do tests.
Every week, we change places.
We take everything out of our desks
and move (very quietly) to where
she tells us to go.
This way, we always know

who's better than you
and we always know
who's worse than you.
Unless you come top,
when there's no one better than you.
Unless you come bottom,
when there's no one worse than you.
The same people are always in the top row.
The same people are always in the bottom row.
The same people are always in the two rows
in between.

Miss Williams says that only the top two rows
will pass their Eleven Plus.
She stands next to the last person on the
end of the second row.
She holds up her hand as if
she is helping people cross the road.
This side will pass, she says.
This side will fail, she says.

This way we know who are the
Eleven Plus Failures
and who are the Eleven Plus Passes.
We know all that
before we've even taken
the Eleven Plus exam.
Next door, there's another class.

They are all
Eleven Plus Failures.

I want to be twelfth.
This is because the person who is twelfth
sits nearest to the bell that sits
on top of Miss Williams's cupboard.
When you're twelfth,
you take the bell,
you go out of the room,
you go downstairs
and you stand in the hallway
outside the head teacher's office
and shake the bell so loudly
that the gonging fills the classrooms
and all the spaces in between.

All the children and teachers hear the sound
and come out of their classes
and walk (very quietly) down the stairs
and out into the playground.

All because you rang the bell.

I never have come twelfth.

The Fly

I heard a fly buzz
in the head teacher's office
just as he was explaining
what was wrong with me.

I heard a fly buzz
but I couldn't see it.
The head talked of things
that I wasn't doing
and they were things
that I should have
been doing.
And the fly buzzed
in the corner.

I could tell it was dying
because it wasn't the buzz
a fly makes when it's on the move.
It was the stop-start buzz:
dzzt dzzt.

The head talked of things
that I was doing
and they
were things

that I shouldn't have been doing.
It was hot.

I looked into his eyes
and I could see
that he thought I was listening.
Dzzt dzzt
dzzt dzzt
dzzzzzzzzzzzzzzzzzt.

*'I heard a fly buzz' is the first line of a poem by Emily
Dickinson. I thought I'd borrow it!*

157

The Head's Toilet

Once I was in a school
and the head teacher
said that I could use the toilet
he had next to his room.
When I went in there,
I noticed that
on the window sill of his toilet
there were three silver cups.
They were the kind of cups you get
for doing something well.
I wondered whether
the head had won them
for doing something well
in there.

Science

We were doing Science.
Properties of matter.
Solid, liquid, gas.
Ice, water, water vapour.

Everything in the universe
is
solid, liquid or gas.

Take something solid,
Warm it up enough and it'll become liquid.
Warm it up more and it'll become gas.
Cool the gas down enough and it'll become a
    liquid.
Cool it even more and it'll become a solid.

Harrybo whispered to me,
'Hey, you could freeze a fart.'
'Yeah,' I said, 'and you'd have
a little farty ice cube.'
'Yeah,' he said,
'solid fart.'

We were doing Science.
Properties of matter.

A Terrible Start

Once
I was horrible to a boy.
I got others
to be horrible to him too.
Made them laugh at him.
No reason.
It was just because I could.
Making him feel bad
made me feel good.

Then I left that school.

I went to a new school.

There was a boy there
who was horrible to me.
He got others
to be horrible to me too.
Made them laugh at me.
There didn't seem
to be any reason for it.
Unless it made him feel good
to make me feel bad.

I was angry.
It wasn't fair.

After school,
I drew pictures of him
on a wooden table
in the class.
Huge.
All over the table.
I went home.

At home
I realized
that everyone would know
it was me who had drawn
the pictures of him
on the wooden table.

I stayed away from school.

When I went back,
they said,
'Why did you draw the pictures
of him on the table?'

The head teacher said,
'By God, boy, you've made a
terrible start.
An absolutely terrible start.'

The Glare

Why do mums and dads
do the Glare Thing?
You're round at someone's house
and you say something
that you're not supposed to say,
like,
'Dad always says Auntie Mary
never gave the money back.'
And everyone stops talking.
It all goes quiet
and there across the table is
the Glare.
What are you supposed to do
with a Glare?
Do you say,
'Ah, I can see you're glaring at me.'?

I suppose they do it because
no one wants to say anything
in case they make matters worse.
So the Glare means,
'You've said something awful.
I can't say why for now,
but you wait till we get home.'

But, hang on,
if that's why they don't
say anything,
then how come you can get
the Glare at home?
That's weird.
When you're at home,
it's not as if there's a 'later'
when it'll be more OK to tell you off.
You could get told off
straight away.
But instead
it's the Glare.

What's the problem?
Are they too tired to tell you off?
Is it too much effort?
So all they can manage
is the big, mean eyeballs thing?

The Great Central-heating Mystery

The central heating
seems to break down
whenever Granny comes to stay.
So does it need mending?
Or will it work
if we send Granny away?

The Hole in the Wall

I loved sharing my bedroom with my brother
but one day my parents said that my brother
was going to move out of our room.
He was going to have:
A Room Of His Own.
We wouldn't share any more.

So he moved out the model cars he had made
and the model trains and the model planes.
They all went off to the room next door.
His room.
In there, he set up the model cars he had made
and the model trains and the model planes.

And soon he got to work making something new.
Something Really Big.

I wanted to be in there
while he was making it.
But I had to go to bed in my room.
The room that used to be our room.

So I had an idea.

I had a metal ruler, a hard steel ruler
with sharp edges and corners.

I got into bed with this metal ruler
and just where the bed meets the wall,
just out of sight of anyone looking,
I started to scratch the wall
with the hard corner of the metal ruler.
Scratch scratch scratch.
Scrape scrape scrape.
I was making a hole
through to my brother's bedroom.
I twisted the corner of the metal ruler
round and round and round.
Scratch scratch scratch.
Scrape scrape scrape.

After ages of scratching and scraping
all I had made was a tiny dent in the wall.
So I went to sleep.

The next night, I got working at it again.
Scratch scratch scratch.
Scrape scrape scrape.
The dent got a tiny bit deeper.

And the next night.
And the next.
Scratch scratch scratch.
Scrape scrape scrape.
After a few nights
I reached a bit of wood.

Should I try to scrape *through* the wood
or round it?
I decided to go over the top.
But this would make the hole wider
and maybe someone would see it . . .
. . . but I didn't care. I had to go on.
I had to make the hole.
I had to get through to my brother's room.
Scratch scratch scratch.
Scrape scrape scrape.
It was now a little cave in the wall.
A secret tunnel.

I wet my fingers in my drink
and then dabbed the dry plaster with my fingers.
The plaster went dark.
The secret tunnel was wet.
What if I could shrink myself down
and crawl through it?
Be an explorer bravely climbing through
the dangerous cave.
Will I get through
or will I be trapped in here forever?
Just then my dad popped his head
round the door.
'Goodnight, Mick!' he said all cheerily.

I hadn't heard him coming.
Oh no, he mustn't see it.

So I sat up in the bed
and quickly twisted round
to cover up my hole in the wall.
He mustn't see the hole.

But he saw me do this sitting–up, twisty–round thing.

Oh no, he's seen me!
Instead of going back downstairs
he opened the door
and walked into the room.
Still cheery, he says,
'Hey, what's that you're doing?
What are you covering up there?'
'Nothing.'
'No, come on, Mick, look at you,
I can see from the way you're sitting
you're covering up something.'
'No.'
Still cheery, he says,
'Come on, come away from the wall.
Let me have a look.'

What could I do?
I had to let him see.

So I leaned forward.
He saw it straight away:
The Hole in the Wall.

Oh no.
It's the moment when the cheery stuff
stops.
It's the moment when the cheery stuff
stops.

He stood there staring at
The Hole in the Wall.
He pointed at it.
'What's that?' he says.
'It's a hole in the wall,' I said.
'I can see it's a hole in the wall,' he says,
'but how in heaven's name
did you make a hole in the bedroom wall?'
'With this,' I said, and I pulled the metal ruler out
from under the covers.
He slapped his hand on his forehead.
'You've wrecked the wall,' he says.

He shouted for my mum:
'Connie, Connie, come and look at this.'
And of course my brother comes running along
behind her.

All three of them stood by my bed,
staring at
The Hole in the Wall.
'Look what he's done,' says my dad.
'Look at it. Look at it.

He's wrecked the wall. It's wrecked.'
'Oh, Michael,' says my mum,
and my brother is giggling and giggling,
'Wa-ha-ha-ha, ho-hee-hee, ya-ha-ha-hee!'
'It must have taken him ages,' he says.
And Mum is saying,
'But, Michael . . . what did you think you
    were doing?
Why did you do it?'
And I said,
'I was trying to get through to Brian's room.'
And my brother says,
'But, Mick,
you could have just got up,
walked out the door,
walked across the landing
and in through my door.'

The Homework Book

Miss Williams said that from now on
we would have homework
and that we were to bring
a homework exercise book to school.

This was serious stuff:
all about passing The Exam,
The Exam called 'The Eleven Plus'.
Everyone was worried about
The Eleven Plus.
Would I pass?
Would I fail?
Everyone was worried.
Teachers, parents, us.
I couldn't get to sleep.
Mum brought me hot milk.

On Mondays
Miss Williams went through
the homework in our homework books.
While she was talking, I got bored.
I drew a picture in my homework book
of a man with a big beard
right in the middle of my maths homework.
He was carrying a bag.
He put things he picked up off the pavement

into his bag.
I called him Trev the Tramp.

Miss Williams went on going through
the homework with the whole class.
This was really important.
We had to listen or we wouldn't pass
The Eleven Plus.
Everyone was listening.
Everyone was concentrating
so that they could pass
The Eleven Plus.

I bent down behind the boy
sitting in front of me.
I looked across to my friend Harrybo
and held up my picture of Trev the Tramp.
I pointed at Trev the Tramp.
I whispered, 'Trev the Tramp.'
Miss Williams saw me
holding up the homework book.

She was on to it in a flash.
'What's that, boy? What is it?!'
I quickly shut the homework book.
'Nothing, Miss Williams.'
She rushed over.
(She was brilliant at rushing over.)
She grabbed the homework book.

She flicked through the pages.
She found the picture of Trev the Tramp.
Right there in the middle of 23 x 12.

'This is it, isn't it?' she said.
'In your homework book!
I'll tell you what's going to happen
now, boy,' she said.
'You're going to take your homework book
home to your parents along with a
letter from me.'
She pointed at herself when she said 'me'.
'My goodness, you're in trouble, boy.
Serious trouble.'

For the rest of the day,
I was very quiet. I put my feet down
on the ground carefully and I made
sure I didn't bump into anything.
At going-home time, she handed me
a big white envelope.
'The letter to your parents is in there,
along with the homework book.'

But when I got home
I couldn't face giving it to my mum.
I couldn't face giving it to my dad.
I nipped upstairs and slipped it
under my bed.

All evening I was thinking
about the big white envelope
with the letter from Miss Williams,
the homework book and the
picture of Trev the Tramp.
I didn't want to give it to them.
I didn't want to see their faces
as they read the letter and looked at
Trev the Tramp.

What I did was put the big white envelope
on their bed when I went to bed.

In the morning, my dad said,
'Oh dear, you poor old thing,
you must have been so worried
about that letter, eh? I'll write one back.
I'll say some things in the letter
that will make sure you won't have
to worry about this stuff any more.
And I'll get you a new homework book.'

At school my friends said,
'Did you get in trouble?
Did you get the whacks?
What happened?'
And I said,
'My dad said I wasn't to worry.'
They didn't believe me.

And I don't know what my dad wrote,
but Miss Williams never said
anything about it ever again;
the head never said anything about it again.

My dad was a teacher
and maybe he wrote in some kind of
special teacher language
that meant Miss Williams wouldn't
ever say anything again.
Some kind of teacher code . . .
that's what must have done it.

The Noise

If my father wanted you to be quiet,
he didn't say, shhh,
he didn't say, be quiet,
he didn't say, shuttup.

All he did was put his hand up
to the side of his face
and say in a quiet voice
that sounded as if
there was some kind of terrible pain
in the middle of his brain:
'The noi–i–i–i–se!'
It was as if the palm of his hand
was trying to reach inside
his head to get at some awful thing in there.

So, we would be going on a car trip.
Dad driving, Mum next to him.
Me and my brother in the back.
My brother says,
'There's an imaginary line
down the middle of the back seat.
I'm this side.
You're that side.
You can't cross the line.
I'm this side of the line.

You're that side of the line.
So –'
'Yeah, I get the point,' I say,
'there's a line.'
'. . . and you can't cross the line,' he says.
So I say,
'Yeah yeah, I get the point.
I won't cross the line.'
And I stick my hand over the line.
'Hey,' he says, 'you crossed the line.'
'I didn't,' I say, and I stick my hand
across the line again.
'YOU CROSSED THE LINE!' he says.
'I DIDN'T,' I say, and I stick my hand
across the line again.
'MUM! HE CROSSED THE LINE!'
'I DIDN'T,' I say.

And my dad's hand goes up
to the side of his face and:
'The noi-i-i-i-se!'

My brother used to imitate it.

If I was making a racket,
my brother would walk around the house
saying,
'The NOISE! The NOISE!'

So it's breakfast.
My dad couldn't stand any noise
at breakfast.
One sniff
and it was the GLARE.

He comes downstairs,
sits down in the chair
and opens up the newspaper.
You can't see him.
He's disappeared.
One moment you've got a dad
and the next you've got a newspaper.

All you see is his hand.
It comes out from behind the newspaper,
moves across the table all on its own,
finds the cup of coffee
and disappears behind the newspaper.
He didn't even drop the newspaper
to see where the cup was.
He just knew where it was.
We used to stare at the hand
coming out, grabbing the cup,
disappearing behind the paper.

Once, my brother
moved the coffee cup.

The hand came out,
couldn't find the cup.
The newspaper came down.
'What's going on?' says my dad.
He grabs the cup
and disappears again behind the paper.

Once, I sat there and a little voice inside me said,
'Hey, why don't you practise playing drums
on the side of the table?'
And I said, 'No, that would be crazy.
Dad can't stand any noise at breakfast.'
And the voice said,
'Yeah, but you know you want to.
Go on. Pick up the knife and fork
and blam blam blam, away you go.'
'No, no, no, I couldn't.'

But I did.
Knife, fork, side of table and
blam blam blam!

The newspaper came down
and my dad's hand went up to the side of his face.
He started to say, 'The no-i–'
But my brother was in there quick
with
'THE NOISE!!!'

And my dad was left there with his
hand in mid-air still trying to say,
'The no-i-i-i-i-ise!'

Zeyde

Zeyde went to work
when he was fourteen.
He worked five and six days a week
in a place called a 'sweatshop'.
He was in a factory making
boys' school caps.
The ones with a peak on the front.
He did this all his life.
He retired
and almost straight away
he died.
When we used to go over to see
Bubbe and Zeyde,
he was nearly always tired.
He slept in the chair.

This is a life?

Zeyde: *grandfather*
Bubbe: *grandmother*

The Dump

'Come on, Mick,' says my dad,
'let's go up The Dump.'

Out the door, across the yard,
up the alley, to The Dump.
Here there are:

old sinks, copper pipes,
red bricks, yellow bricks,
concrete slabs, window frames,
floorboards, mantelpieces,
iron gutters, drain covers,
rotten beams, door handles,
bath taps and window sills.

'Nip up there and grab that,' he says.

I climb The Dump.
I grab the window sill.
I wonder what he's going to do
with a window sill.
We go back down the alley,
across the yard and indoors.

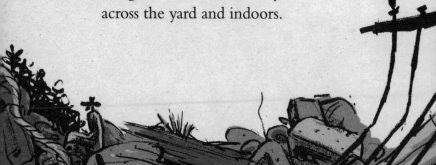

'We found a really good window sill,'
my dad says to my mum.
'Oh yes,' she says,
'and what are you going to do with that?'
'Not sure yet,' he says.
'Where have you put it?' she says.
'In the yard,' he says.

In our yard, we've got:

old sinks, copper pipes,
red bricks, yellow bricks,
concrete slabs, window frames,
floorboards, mantelpieces,
iron gutters, drain covers,
rotten beams, door handles
bath taps and window sills.

Toad in France

It hasn't rained for days.
The grass is brown.
It's hot.
We're walking slowly.

We find a toad in the house.
It's dry.
We're sure that the toad
doesn't like being as dry as that.

We take it out
and put it
in the hedge.
Later it rains.

There's a storm.
With lightning.
All the lights in the house
go out.

We run about
looking for candles.
We think the toad
likes the rain.

Make Your Bed

I was brought up before there were duvets.
When your mum says, 'Make your bed!'
you can do it in about three and a half
    seconds:
one whoosh across the sheet.
One flollop of the duvet.
One bash of the pillow.
Done.

Oh, it wasn't like that in my day.
On my bed
there was:
a bottom sheet,
a top sheet,
two blankets,
an eiderdown (a bit like a duvet)
and a coverlet
(a fluffy bedspread thing made of
something called 'candlewick').

When my mum or dad said,
'Make your bed,'
you knew it would take you about
three weeks to make it.
'Make your bed!'
and I slump up the stairs as slowly

as I can,
sit down next to
the pile of sheets
and blankets
and the eiderdown
and the candlewick coverlet.

After about a week
my mum or dad would wonder
where I had gone.
'Where's Michael? We haven't seen him
since last Monday.'
'Michael! Michael!
Where are you?'
'I'm upstairs. In my room.'
'What are you doing?'
'I'm making my bed.'
'But that was days ago.'
'I know.'
'How far have you got?'
'I'm just doing the eiderdown.'
'Don't forget the coverlet.'
'The coverlet's tomorrow.'

Bagel

On Sundays,
we go over to see Bubbe and Zeyde.
Bubbe takes me to the bagel shop to buy
    bagels.
There are hundreds and hundreds of them.
Then we take them home.
We sit down to eat the bagel,
and Zeyde says:
'Save the hole for me.'

So I eat a bit of the bagel.
Then I say,
'Do you want the hole now, Zeyde?'
And he says, 'No, there's too much bagel
    round the hole.
I just want the hole.'

So I eat some more bagel.
And I say,
'Do you want the hole now, Zeyde?'
And he says, 'No, there's too much bagel.
I just want the hole.'

So I eat some more
until all that's left is a tiny, tiny little ring of
    bagel

round the hole.
And I say, 'Do you want the hole now, Zeyde?'
And he says, 'No, I can still see some bagel
    round the hole.'

So then I eat the tiny, tiny ring of bagel round
    the hole
and there is no bagel left.

And Zeyde looks at me and says,
'So? You couldn't save me the hole?'

> **Bubbe:** *grandmother*
> **Zeyde:** *grandfather*

A Three-year-old Playing Beasties

'Daddy, you're the beastie.
No! I'm the beastie – rahhhh.
Now, I'm fighting the beastie.
Daddy, what is a beastie?'

A Three-year-old Asks a Question

'Dad, when you grow up, do you want to be a baby?'

Michael's Big Book of Bad Things Part 4

Next morning my dad comes into the
  bathroom.
He's going to have a shave.
It's . . .
plug in:
fippp.
Taps on:
bssssshhhht.
Little brush in the water:
cafloffapupp, cafloffapupp, cafloffapupp.
Into the shaving soap.
chooff chooff choo—
and he stops.
And he's looking into the jar.
And he's thinking, What's that?
How did that get there?
How did the top of the toothpaste get into my
  shaving soap?

So he comes downstairs
into the kitchen
and he goes up to my brother Brian.
And he holds out the jar of shaving soap
with the top off the toothpaste sticking out,
and he says, 'Brian. How did that get there?
How did the top of the toothpaste get in my
   shaving soap?'
And my brother says,
'I dunno. How should I know?
Why pick on me? What about him?'

So my dad comes up to me and he holds out the
   jar
of shaving soap
with the top off the toothpaste sticking out,
and he says,
'Michael, how did that get there?
How did the top off the toothpaste get in my
   shaving soap?'
And I say, 'I dunno.'
But there's a difference between my brother and
   me.
When my brother said, 'I dunno,' his eyebrows
   stayed down.
When I said, 'I dunno,' my eyebrows shot up in
   the air.
The moment my dad saw my eyebrows go up,

he knew that I was lying.
'Look at your eyebrows!' he says.

(What?! How can you look at your eyebrows?
The things dads say! 'Look at your eyebrows!'
Imagine walking along the road with your dad
and you think, 'I wonder what my eyebrows
  look like.'
And you start staggering about trying to get a look
at your eyebrows, and your dad says,
'What are you doing, son?'
And you say,
'I'm just looking at my eyebrows, Dad.'
And he'd say,
'Don't be so daft.'
But here he is, asking me to look at my
  eyebrows!)

Anyways,
I say,
'What's the matter with my eyebrows?'
And he says,
'They've gone up in the air.
That means you're lying.'
And I say, 'I'm not.'
And he says:
'And there's another giveaway.
Your voice has gone squeaky.'
And I say in a squeaky voice,

'No it hasn't.'
And he says,
'What did you think you were doing,
sticking the top of the toothpaste
in my shaving soap?'
And I said, 'Buried treasure. Pirates were going
to find it, and they were singing
"Yo ho ho ho and a bottle of —"'
And he smacks his forehead
and says, 'Crazy. The boy's crazy!'
except,
he says it in Yiddish:
'The boy's meshuggener!'

And it reminds him of something:
PAGE ONE
In
MICHAEL'S BIG BOOK
Of
BAD THINGS.
And he's saying,
'Oh yes,
like the time you threw your mother's best ring
out of the window.
It was her . . . BUBBE'S.'
YAAAAAAAAAAAAAAAAAAAAHHHHH.

The room filled up with Bubbes.
There were Bubbes flying all round the room

and they were saying,
'First, you throw your mother's best ring out
    of the window?
And then you stick the top off the toothpaste
in your father's shaving soap?
Oy yoy yoy yoy yoy yoy yoy.'

Index of First Lines

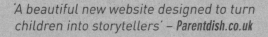

Bright and shiny and sizzling with fun stuff . . .

puffin.co.uk

WEB FUN

UNIQUE and exclusive digital content!
Podcasts, photos, Q&A, Day in the Life of, interviews
and much more, from Eoin Colfer, Cathy Cassidy,
Allan Ahlberg and Meg Rosoff to Lynley Dodd!

WEB NEWS

The **Puffin Blog** is packed with posts and photos from
Puffin HQ and special guest bloggers. You can also sign up
to our monthly newsletter **Puffin Beak Speak**

WEB CHAT

Discover something new EVERY month –
books, competitions and treats galore

WEBBED FEET

(Puffins have funny little feet and
brightly coloured beaks)

Point your mouse our way today!

It all started with a Scarecrow.

Puffin is seventy years old.
Sounds ancient, doesn't it? But Puffin has never been
so lively. We're always on the lookout for the next big
idea, which is how it began all those years ago.

Penguin Books was a big idea from the mind of
a man called Allen Lane, who in 1935 invented
the quality paperback and changed the world.
**And from great Penguins, great Puffins grew,
changing the face of children's books forever.**

The first four Puffin Picture Books were hatched in 1940 and the
first Puffin story book featured a man with broomstick arms called
Worzel Gummidge. In 1967 Kaye Webb, Puffin Editor, started the
Puffin Club, promising to **'make children into readers'.**
She kept that promise and over 200,000 children became
devoted Puffineers through their quarterly instalments of
Puffin Post, which is now back for a new generation.

Many years from now, we hope you'll look back and
remember Puffin with a smile. **No matter what your age
or what you're into, there's a Puffin for everyone.**
The possibilities are endless, but one thing is for sure:
whether it's a picture book or a paperback, a sticker book
or a hardback, **if it's got that little Puffin
on it – it's bound to be good.**

'It's

...ring really

 big ♥ knickers!'

Fabulously funny!

Further Confessions of Georgia Nicolson:

Angus, thongs and full-frontal snogging
'It's OK, I'm wearing really big knickers!'
'Knocked out by my nunga-nungas.'
'Dancing in my nuddy-pants!'
'...and that's when it fell off in my hand.'
'...then he ate my boy entrancers.'
'...startled by his furry shorts!'
'Luuurve is a many trousered thing...'
'Stop in the name of pants!'

Also available on tape and CD:
'...and that's when it fell off in my hand.'
'...then he ate my boy entrancers.'
'...startled by his furry shorts!'
'Luuurve is a many trousered thing...'
'Stop in the name of pants!'

'It's OK, I'm wearing really big knickers!'

Fabulously funny!

Louise Rennison

HarperCollins *Children's Books*

Find out more about Georgia at
www.georgianicolson.com

First published in Great Britain by Piccadilly Press Ltd, 2000
Published by Scholastic Ltd, 2001
This edition published by HarperCollins *Children's Books*, 2005
HarperCollins *Children's Books* is a division of HarperCollins*Publishers* Ltd,
77-85 Fulham Palace Road, Hammersmith, London W6 8JB

The HarperCollins *Children's Books* website address is
www.harpercollins.co.uk

17

Copyright © Louise Rennison 2000

The author asserts the moral right to be identified as the author of this work.

ISBN-13   978-0-00-721868-4

Printed and bound in England by
Clays Ltd, St Ives plc

To my dear family: Mutti, Vati, Sophie, Libbs, Hons, Eduardo Delfonso Delgardo, John S, Apee, Francesbirginia and especially Kimbo. Thanks you all for not killing me yet.

Also dedicated to my mates: Salty Dog, Jools, Jedbox, Badger, Elton, Jimjams, Jenks, Phil, Bobbins, Lozzer, the Mogul, Fanny, Dear GeH. MSH, Porky, Morgan, Alan D, Liz G, Tony G, Psychic Sue, Roge the Doge and Barbara D and the Ace Crew from school, Kim and Cock of the North xxxxxx.

An especial thank you to John, the Pope. Where would I have been without your wise advice – "Stop making such a fuss and just get on with it, you silly girl!"?

Heartfelt thanks and sympathy to Brenda, Jude, Emma and all the very fab people at Piccadilly.

And of course to Gillon and Clare – HURRAH!!

The Sex God has landed...
and, er, taken off again

Sunday July 18th
My room
6:00 p.m.

Staring out of my bedroom window at other people having a nice life.

Who would have thought things could be so unbelievably pooey? I'm only fourteen and my life is over because of the selfishosity of so-called grown-ups. I said to Mum, "You are ruining my life. Just because yours is practically over there is no reason to take it out on me."

But as usual when I say something sensible and meaningful she just tutted and adjusted her bra like a Russian roulette player. (Or do I mean disco thrower? I don't know and, what's more, I don't care.) If I counted up the number of times I've been tutted at... I could open a tutting shop. It's just SO not fair... How can my parents take me away from my mates and make me go to New Zealand? Who goes to New Zealand?

In the end, when I pointed out how utterly useless as a mum she was, she lost her rag and SHOUTED at me.

"Go to your room right now!"

I said, "All right, I'll go to my ROOM!! I WILL go to my room!! And do you know what I'll be doing in my room? No you don't, so I'll tell you! I'll be just BEING in my room. That's all. Because there is nothing else to do!!!!!!"

Then I just slammed off. Left her there. To think about what she has done.

Unfortunately it means that I am in my bed and it is only six o'clock.

7:00 p.m.

Oh Robbie, where are you now? Well, I know where you are now actually, but is this any time to go away on a footie trip?

On the bright side I am now the girlfriend of a Sex God.

7:15 p.m.

On the dark side, the Sex God doesn't know his new

8

girlfriend is going to be forced to go to the other (useless) side of the universe in a week's time.

7:18 p.m.

I can't believe that after all the time it has taken to trap the SG, all the make-up I have had to buy, the trailing about, popping up unexpectedly when he was out anywhere... all the planning... all the dreaming – it's gone to waste. I finally get him to snog me (number six) and he says, "Let's see each other but keep it quiet for a bit." And at that moment, with classic poo timing, Mutti says, "We're off to New Zealand next week."

My eyes are all swollen up like mice eyes from crying. Even my nose is swollen. It's not small at the best of times, but now it looks like I've got three cheeks. Marvellous. Thank you, God.

9:00 p.m.

I'll never get over this.

9:10 p.m.

Time goes very slowly when you are suicidal.

I put sunglasses on to hide my tiny mincers. They are new ones that Mum bought me in a pathetic attempt to interest me in going to Kiwi-a-gogo land. They looked quite cool, actually. I looked a bit like one of those French actresses who smoke Gauloise and cry a lot in between snogging Gerard Depardieu. I tried a husky French accent in the mirror.

"And zen when I was, how you say? *Une teen-ager, mes parents, mes très, très horriblement parents*, take me to *Nouvelle Zelande*. Ahh *merde!*"

At which point I heard Mum coming up the stairs and had to leap into bed. She popped her head round the door and said, "Georgie... are you asleep?"

I didn't say anything. That would teach her.

As she left she said, "I wouldn't sleep in the sunglasses if I were you, they might get embedded in your head."

What kind of parenting was that? Mum's medical knowledge was about as good as Dad's DIY. And we had all seen his idea of a shed. Before it fell down on Uncle Eddie.

Eventually I was drifting off into a tragic snooze when I heard shouting coming from next door's garden. Mr and Mrs Next Door were out there, banging and shouting and throwing things about. Is this really the time for noisy gardening? They have no consideration for those who might want to sleep because they have tragedy in their life. I felt like opening the window and shouting, "Garden more quietly, you loons!"

But then I couldn't be bothered getting out of my snuggly bed of pain.

Police raid
Mucho excitemondo
12:10 a.m.

When the doorbell rang I shot out of bed and looked down the stairs. Mum had opened the door wearing a nightdress that you could quite easily see through! Even if you didn't want to. Which I didn't. She has no pride. There were a couple of policemen standing at the door. The bigger one was holding a sack up in front of him at arm's length and his trousers were shredded round the ankles.

"Is this your bloody cat?" he enquired, not very politely for a public servant.

Mum said, "Well, I... er."

I ran down the stairs and went to the door.

♡ 11

"Good evening, constable. This cat, is it about the size of a small Labrador?"

He said, "Yes."

I nodded encouragingly and went on. "And has it got tabby fur and a bit of its ear missing?"

PC Plod said, "Er... yes."

And I said, "No, it's not him then, sorry."

Which I thought was very funny indeed. The policeman didn't.

"This is a serious business, young lady."

Mum was doing her tutting thing again, and combining it with head shaking and basooma adjusting. Deeply unattractive. I thought the policeman might be distracted by her and say, "Go and put some clothes on, madam," but he didn't, he just kept going on at me.

"This thing has had your neighbours penned up in their greenhouse for an hour. They managed to dash into the house eventually but then it rounded up their poodles."

"Yes, he does that. He is half Scottish wildcat. He hears the call of the wilds sometimes and then he..."

"You should keep better control of it."

He went moaning on in a policemany way for hours

and hours. I said, as patiently as I could, although I had enough things to think about as it was, "Look, I'm being made to go to Whangamata by my parents. It is at the other, more useless, side of the universe. It is in New Zealand. Have you seen *Neighbours*? Is there nothing you can do for me?"

My mum gave me her worst look and said, "Don't start, Georgia, I'm not in the mood."

The policeman didn't seem "in the mood" either. He said, "This is a serious warning. You keep this thing under control otherwise we will be forced to take sterner measures."

Mum was hopeless as per usual. She started smiling and fiddling with her hair.

"I'm really sorry to have troubled you, inspector. Would you like to come in and have a nightcap or something?"

It was so EMBARRASSING. He probably thought we ran a brothel in our spare time. The "inspector" was all smiling and he said, "That's very kind of you, madam, but we have to get on. Protecting the public from vicious criminals, dangerous moggies, and so on."

I didn't say anything as I took the wiggling sack, I just looked ironically at his chewed trousers.

Mum went BERSERK about Angus. She said, "He'll have to go."

I said, "Oh yes, perfect, just take everything that I love and destroy it. Just think of your own self and make me go halfway round the universe and lose the only boy I love. You can't just leave Sex Gods, you know, they have to be kept under constant surveillance and..."

She had gone into her bedroom.

Angus strolled out of the bag and strutted around the kitchen looking for a snack. He was purring like two tanks. Libby wandered in all sleepy with her blankin'. Her night-time nappy was bulging round her knees. The last thing I needed was a poo explosion at this time of night so I said, "Go tell Mummy about your pooey nap-naps, Libby."

But she just said, "Shhh, bad boy," and went over to Angus. She kissed him on the nose and then sucked it before she dragged him off to bed.

I don't know why he lets her do anything she likes with him. He almost had my hand off the other day when I tried to take his plate away and he hadn't quite finished.

14

Monday July 19th
11:00 a.m.

I am feeling sheer desperadoes. It's a day and a half now since I snogged the Sex God. I think I have snog withdrawal. My lips keep puckering up.

I HAVE to find a way of not going to Kiwi-a-gogo land. I went on hunger-strike this morning. Well, apart from a Jammy Dodger.

2:00 p.m.

Phone rang.

Mum yelled up at me, "Gee, will you get that, love? I'm in the bath."

I yelled back, "You can wash the outside clean, but you can't wash the inside!"

She yelled again, "Georgia!!!"

Dragged myself up from my bed of pain and went all the way downstairs and picked up the phone.

"I said, "Hello, Heartbreak Hotel here," and all I could hear was just crackle, crackle, surf, swish, swish. So I shouted really loudly, "HELLO, HELLO, HELLO!!!!" and this faraway voice said, "Bloody hell!"

It was my father, or Vati as I call him. Phoning from New Zealand. He was, as usual, in a bad mood for no reason.

"Why did you shout down the phone? My ears are all ringing now."

I said, reasonably enough, "Because you didn't say anything."

"I did, I said hello."

"Well I didn't hear you."

"Well you can't have been listening properly."

"How can I not listen properly when I am answering the phone?"

"I don't know, but if anyone can manage it, you can."

Oh, play the old record again, it's always me that does things wrong. I said, "Mum's in the bath."

He said, "Just a minute, don't you want to know how I am?"

"Er, let me guess… funny moustache, bit bulky round the bottom department?"

"Don't be so bloody cheeky! Get your mum. I give up on you. I don't know what you learn at that school besides how to put on lipstick and be cheeky."

I put the phone down because he can grumble on like

that for centuries if you let him. I shouted, "Mutti, there is a man on the phone. He claims to be my dear vati but I don't think he is because he was quite surly with me."

Mum came out of the bathroom with her hair all wet and dripping and in just a bra and pants. She really has got the most gigantic basoomas, I'm surprised she doesn't topple over. Good Lord.

I said, "I am at a very impressionable age, you know."

She just gave me her worst look and grabbed the phone. As I went through the door I could hear her saying, "Hello, darling. What? I know. Oh I know. You needn't tell me that... I have her all the time. It's a nightmare."

That's nice talk, isn't it?

As I point out to anyone who will listen (i.e. no one), I didn't ask to be born. I am only here because she and Vati... urgh... anyway, I won't go down that road.

My room
2:10 p.m.
I could hear her rambling on to Dad, going, "Hmmm – well I know, Bob... I know... Uh huh... I KNOW... I know. Yes, I know..."

♡ 17

In the name of pantyhose, what are grown-ups like? I shouted down to her, "Break the news to him gently that I'm definitely not in a TRILLION years coming."

He must have heard me because even upstairs I could hear muffled shouting from down the other end of the phone. I wasn't amazed by the shouting as my vati is prone to violence. Once I poured aftershave into his lager and lime when he was out of the room. For a merry joke. But he didn't get the joke. When he stopped choking he went all ballisticisimus and shouted, "You complete IDIOT!!!" really loudly at me. It's the kind of thing that will cost me hundreds of pounds in therapy fees in later life. (Should I have a life, which I don't.)

2:30 p.m.
Playing sad songs in my bedroom, still in my jimjams.

Mutti came into my room and said, "Can I come in?"

I said, "No."

But that didn't put her off.

She came and sat on the edge of my bed and put her hand on my foot. I said, "Owww!!!"

She said, "Look, love, I know this is all a bit complicated, especially at your age, but this is a really big opportunity for us. Your dad thinks he has a real chance to make something of himself over in Whangamata."

I said, "what's wrong with the way he is now? Quite a few people like fat blokes with ridiculous moustaches. You do."

She came on all parenty then. "Georgia, don't think that rudeness is funny because it isn't."

"It can be."

"No it isn't."

"Well you laughed when Libby called Mr Next Door 'nice tosser'."

"Well Libby is only three and she thinks that tosser is like Bill or Dad or something. Can't you see this trip as an exciting adventure?"

"What, like when you are on your way to school and then suddenly you get run over by a bus and have to go to hospital, or something?"

"Yes, like when... NO!! Come on, Georgie, try to be a pal, just for me."

I didn't say anything.

"You know that your dad can't get a job here. What else is he supposed to do? He's only trying to look after us all."

After a bit she sighed and went out.

Life is *très merde* and double bum. Why doesn't Mutti understand I can't leave now? She can be ludicrously dim. It's not her that I get my intelligence from. It is certainly no thanks to her that I came top in... er... well anyway, it's nothing to do with her what I do. I am just the unfortunate recipient of some of her genes. The orang-utan eyebrow gene, for instance. She has to do a lot of plucking to keep her eyebrows apart and she has selfishly passed it on to me. Since I shaved mine off by mistake last term they seem to have gone even more haywire and akimbo. The shaving has encouraged them to grow about a metre a week. If I left them alone I'd be blind by October. Jas has got ordinary eyebrows, why can't I?

Also, while I am on the subject, the worst news of all is that I think I have inherited her breast genes. My basoomas are definitely growing. I am very worried that I may end up with huge breasts like hers. Everyone notices hers.

Once, when we were on the ferry to France, Dad said to Mum, "Don't stand too near to the edge, Connie, otherwise your chest might be declared a danger to shipping."

5:00 p.m.

I've just had a flash of whatsit!! It's so obvious, I am indeed a genius! Simple pimple. I'll just tell Mum that I'll stay behind and... LOOK AFTER THE HOUSE!! The house can't just be left empty for months because... er... squatters might come in and take it over. Anarchists who will paint everything black, including, probably, Mr and Mrs Next Door's poodles. They'll be begging for Angus to come back.

Excellent, brilliant fabulosa idea!! Mum will definitely see the sense of it.

I'll promise to be really mature and grown-up and responsible. I mainly want to stay in England because of the terrifically good education system. That is how I will sell it to Mutti.

"Mutti," I will say, "this is a crucial time in my schooldays. I think I may be picked for the hockey team."

Thank goodness I didn't bother Mum with my school report from last term. I saved her the trouble of reading it by signing it myself.

5:05 p.m.

You would think that Hawkeye could think of something more imaginative to write than, *Hopelessly childish attitude in class.* Just because she caught me doing my (excellent) impression of a lockjaw germ.

5:10 p.m.

I could have groovy parties that everyone would really want to come to. I'm going to make a list of all the people I will ask to the parties:

<u>First – Sex Gods</u>
Robbie... er, that's it.

<u>Second – the Ace Crew</u>
Rosie, Jools, Ellen and, I suppose, Jas if she pulls her pants up and makes a bit more effort with me. She has been a bit of a Slack Alice on the pal front since she got Tom.

<u>Third – close casuals</u>
Mabs, Sarah, Abbie, Phebes, Hattie, Bella... people I like for a laugh but wouldn't necessarily lend my mum's leather jacket to... then acquaintances and fanciable brothers.

5:20 p.m.

I may even allow crap dancers like Sven to come if they have pleasing or amusing personalities (and gifts).

5:23 p.m.

I tell you who I won't be asking – Nauseating P. Green, that's who. She is definitely banned. If I am made to sit next to her again next term I will definitely kill myself. Why is she so boring? She does it deliberately to annoy me. She breeds hamsters. What is the matter with her?

Who else will be on the exclusion list? Wet Lindsay, Robbie's ex. It would be cruel to invite her and let her see Robbie and me being so happy and snogging in front of her, etc. Also she would kill me and that would spoil the party atmosphere.

Who else? Oh, I know, Jackie and Alison, otherwise known as the Bummer Twins. They can't come because they are too common.

9:10 p.m.

Looking out of my window. I can see Mark, the boy with the biggest gob in the universe, going off to town with his mates. People are out there having fun. I hate that. I haven't

♥ 23

got any real friends – as soon as a boy comes along they just forget about me, it's pathetic.

I could never be that shallow.

I wonder if the Sex God is having second thoughts about me because of my nose?

9:15 p.m.
Jas phoned. Tearing herself away from Tom for a second. She said, "Have you told her you are not going, yet?"

"No, I try but she takes no notice. I told her that it is a very important time for me as I am fourteen and poised on the brink of womanhood."

"On the what?"

Jas can be like half girl, half turnip. I said, "Do you remember what our revered headmistress, Slim, said at the end of summer term? She said, 'Girls, you are poised on the brink of womanhood, which is why I want to see no more false freckles painted on noses. It is silly and it isn't funny or dignified.'"

"False freckles are funny."

"I know."

"Well why would Slim say they weren't?"

"Jas."

"What?"

"Shut up now."

9:30 p.m.

I've got Libby, her scuba-diving Barbie doll, which has arms like steel forks, and her Thomas the Tank Engine, all in my bed. It's like sleeping in a toy box only not so comfortable. Plus Libby has been making me play Eskimo kissing; it has made my nose really sore. I said, "Libby, that's enough Eskimo now," but she just said, "Kwigglkwoggleugug," which I suppose she thinks is Eskimo.

What is the matter with my life? Why is it so deeply unfab?

10:00 p.m.

Looking at the sky outside my window and all the stars. I thought of all the people in history and so on who have been sad and have asked God for help. I fell to my knees (which was a bit painful as I landed on a plate of jam sandwiches I had left by my bed). Through my tears I prayed, "Please, God, let the phone ring and let it be Robbie. I promise I will go to church all the time if he rings. Thank you."

Midnight

So much for Our Vati in Heaven. What on earth is the point of asking God for something if you don't get it?

Decided to buy a Buddha tomorrow.

1:00 a.m.

As time is short it might be all right to ask Buddha for something before I actually invest in a statue of him.

I don't really know how to speak to Buddha. I hope he understands English. I expect, like most deities, it's more a sort of reading your thoughts job.

1:30 a.m.

Because I haven't been a practising Buddhist for long (half an hour) I'll restrict my requests to the essentials.

Which are:

1. When I suggest to Mum that she leaves me behind to look after the house, she says, "Of course, my darling."
2. The SG rings.

1:35 a.m.

I'll just leave it at that. I won't go into the nose business (less of it and more sticky up) or breast reduction requests, otherwise I will be here all night and Buddha may think I am a cheeky new Buddhist and that I'm only believing to get things.

Tuesday July 20th
10:00 a.m.

My room... soon to be a shrine to Buddha. Unless God gets his act together. Birds tweeting like birds at a bird party. Lovely sunny day. For some. I can see the sunshine glancing off Mr Next Door's bald head. He's playing with his stupid yappy little squirt dogs. Just a minute, I've spotted Angus hanging about in the potting shed area. Uh-oh, he looks a bit on the peckish side, like he fancies a poodle sandwich. I'd better go waggle a sausage at him and thereby avert a police incident.

How in the name of Mr Next Door's gigantic shorts am I supposed to be a Buddhist with these constant interruptions? I bet the Dalai Lama hasn't got a cat. Or a dad in New Zealand. (I wonder if the Dalai Lama's father is called the Daddy Lama?... I amaze myself sometimes because even though my life is a facsimile of a sham I can still laugh and joke!!)

10:36 a.m.
What is the point? Mum just laughed when I told her about looking after the house and told me to go and pack.

Midday
Even though it is quite obvious I am really depressed and in bed Mum comes poking around being all efficient and acting as if life is not a tragedy of a sham (which it is). She made me get up and show her what I had packed for Whangamata. She went ballisticisimus. *"Men are from Mars, Women are from Venus*, eyelash curlers, two bikinis and a cardigan?!"

"Well I won't be going out anywhere as I don't like sheep and my heart is broken."

"But you might wear your bikini?"

"I've only packed that for health reasons."

"What health reasons?"

"Well, if I can't eat anything because of my heartache, the

sun's rays may keep me from getting rickets. We did it in biology."

"It's winter over there."

"Typical."

"You are being ridiculous."

That's when all the pain came raging out of me. "I'm being ridiculous!!??? I'm being ridiculous??? I'm not the one who is dragging someone off to the other side of the world for NO good reason!!"

She went all red. "No good reason?! It's to see your dad!"

"I rest my case."

"Georgia, you are being horrible!" And she stormed off.

I feel a bit like crying. It's not my fault if I am horrible. I am under pressure. Why can't Dad be here? Then I could be horrible to him without feeling so horrible. (And without having to go to the other side of the planet. Most teenagers only have to go into the sitting room to be horrible to their dads.)

It's not easy having an absent dad, that's what people don't realise. I am effectively (apart from my mum and grandparents and my crap cousin James, etc.) an orphan.

1:00 p.m.

Libby crept into my room carrying a saucer of milk really carefully. She was on her tippy toes and purring. I said, "You are nice, Libbs. Just put it down; Angus is out hunting."

She very slowly and on tippy toes brought the saucer over to me and put it on my desk. She put her little hands on my head and started stroking my hair. My eyes filled up with tears. I said, "If I can't be happy in my life I can try and see that you have a nice life, Libbs. I will give up all thoughts of happiness myself and be like your Buddhist nurse. For your sake I will wear flat shoes and those really horrible orange robes and..."

Then Libby started pushing my head quite roughly down towards the saucer of milk. "C'mon, Ginger, come on. Milky pops."

She'll make me sleep in a cat basket soon. Honestly, I think it's about time she started kindergarten and mixed with normal children.

It takes twenty-four hours to fly to New Zealand.

6:00 p.m.

Uncle Eddie roared up on his pre-war motorbike. He's come round to collect Angus. How can I live without the huge furry fool? How can he live without me? No one else knows his special little ways. Who else will know that he likes you to trail his sausages around on a string so that he can pounce on them from behind the curtains? Who else will know about mouse racing? Not Uncle Eddie, that's for sure. He truly does come from Planet Bonkers. He came in wearing his motorbike leathers, took off his helmet and said, "How're you diddling?"

What is the matter with him? Why Mum thinks anyone as bald and barmy as him could look after an animal I don't know. Anyway, it's irrelevant what anyone thinks as he will never in a zillion years catch Angus and get him in a basket.

6:30 p.m.

I don't think I could be more sad. We are going to be away for months. I will miss all my friends; I'll lose the SG. My hockey career will be in ruins. Everyone knows the Maoris don't play hockey. They play... er... anyway, we haven't done New Zealand in geoggers yet, so I don't know what they do. Who cares?

♥ 31

6:35 p.m.

Time ticking away. It's like waiting to be buried, I should think. Or being in RE.

Phoned Jas. I wanted to know if Tom had heard anything from his gorgeous older brother, the Sex God, but I didn't want to let Jas know that I wasn't interested in her life. So I asked her a few questions about her "boyfriend" first.

"Hi, Jas, how are you and Tom getting along?"

She went all girlish and giggly. "Well, do you know, we were just laughing so much because Tom said that he was in the shop the other day and—"

"Jas, did he mention anything, you know, interesting?"

"Oh yeah, loads."

There was a pause – she drives me INSANE!

I said, "Like what?"

"Well, he was thinking of suggesting that they start selling more dairy products in their shop, because—"

"No, no, Jas I said interesting – not really, really boring. Has he, for instance, mentioned his gorgey older brother?"

Jas was a bit huffy but she said, "Hang on a minute." Then I heard her shouting, "Tom! Have you spoken to Robbie?"

In the distance I heard Tom shouting, "No, he's gone away on a footie trip."

I said to Jas, "I know that."

Jas shouted again, "She knows that."

Tom shouted, "Who knows that?"

"Georgia."

Then I heard Jas's mum shouting from somewhere, "Why does Georgia want to know about Robbie? Isn't she off to New Zealand?"

Jas shouted, "Yes, she is. But she's desperate to see him before she goes."

I said to Jas urgently, "Jas, Jas, I wanted to find out when he's back, I didn't want to discuss it with your street."

Jas went all huffy. "I'm only trying to help."

"Well don't."

"Well I won't, then."

"Good."

There was a silence. "Jas?"

"What?"

"What are you doing?"

"I'm not helping."

I'm going to have to kill her.

"Ask Tom when Robbie is due back."

"Huh. I don't see why I should, but I will."

She shouted out again, "Tom, when is Robbie back?"

Jas's mum yelled, "I thought he was going out with Lindsay?"

Tom yelled back, "He was, but then Georgia and him got together instead."

Jas's mum said, "Well, Lindsay will be very upset."

This was UNBELIEVABLE.

Tom yelled back again, "Tell Georgia he's not back again until late Monday."

Next Monday! Next Monday. By that time I would be being bored half to death by Maoris. I tried to be brave so that I wouldn't upset Jas. "I know I can joke about it and everything, but I have fancied Robbie for so long. And it's not just because he is in The Stiff Dylans. You know that. It's a whole year since I started stalking him. It was so groovy when he kissed me, I thought I would go completely jelloid and start dribbling. Luckily I didn't. And I think he will forget about that chunk of my hair snapping off, don't you?"

There was this clanking noise and then Jas said, with her mouth full, "Hello? Hello? What were you saying? I just went and got myself a sandwich while Tom was shouting at you."

Qu'est ce que le point?

7:30 p.m.

I can't believe Jas. She is dead to me. Like in the *Bible*, when somebody goes off and becomes a prostitute or something. She is now the girl who has no name.

9:00 p.m.

Phone rang. I leaped downstairs.

It was Rosie, Ellen, Jools and She Who Has No Name (Jas) calling me from the phone box at the end of our road. Rosie said in a fake Chinese accent, "Bringey selfey to phone boxey."

I put on some mascara and lippy so that no one would know about my broken heart. Not that it made the slightest difference to Mutti and Uncle Eddie – they were too busy trying to trap Angus.

He's lurking on top of my wardrobe. I know he's got a few snacks with him because he dropped a piece of mackerel on my head when I passed. He'll be happy up there for hours. Serve them right if they can't find him. Catnappers!

♥ 35

I don't want to be rude to the afflicted but Uncle Eddie is bald in a way which is the baldest I have ever seen. He looks like a boiled egg in leather trousers. Once he came round and after he and Mum had had their usual vat of wine he fell asleep in the back garden face down. So I drew another face on the back of his head. Very, very funny indeed, especially as I did it in indelible pen. He got his own back, though, by turning up to a school dance on his pre-war motorbike and asking all my mates where I was because he was my new boyfriend.

Still, that is life for you... one minute you are snogging a Sex God and have got up to number six on the snogging scale without crashing teeth. The next minute you are made to go to the other side of the world and hand out with Kiwi-a-gogos. Whose idea of a great time is to sit in mud pools and eat toasted maggots. (This is very, very true as I have been reading a brochure about Kiwi-a-gogo land and it says it in there.) Oh pig's bum!! Or as our tiny French friends say, *Le gran* bum *de le* porker!!!

9:30 p.m.
When I got to the phone box the gang were all in there. They squeezed open the door and Jools said, "*Bonsoir, ma petite nincompoop.*"

Once I was in we were all squashed up like sardines at a fish party. Rosie managed to get a hand free and give me one of those photobooth photographs.

"We brought you a present to remember us by."

It was a picture of her, Jools, Ellen and Jas (She Who Has No Name), only they had their noses stuck back at the tip with Sellotape so that it made them look like pigs with hair.

On the back it said, GRUNTINGS from your mates. STY in touch. This is a PIGTURE to remember us by.

It made me a bit tearful, but I put on a brave face. "Cheers, thanks a lot. Goodnight."

We had to get out of the telephone box because Mark (the boy from up the road with the enormous gob who I went out with for a fortnight but dumped me because this other girl Ella let him "do things to her") came to use the phone. He just looked at us as we all struggled out. He really has got the biggest mouth I have ever seen. I was lucky to escape from snogging him with my face still in one piece.

BG (Big Gob) said, "All right?" in a way which meant, "All right, you lesbians?"

What do I care, though? My life is over anyway.

We all walked back to my house arm in arm. I wouldn't link up with Jas though because she has annoyed me. Uncle Eddie must have eventually got Angus into the cat basket because the gardening gloves he was wearing were lying in the driveway with the thumbs torn off.

We all hugged and cried. It was awful. I'd nearly got to the door when Jas sort of threw herself at me. She couldn't speak because she was crying so much and she said, "Georgia, nothing will be the same without you... I... I love you. I'm sorry I ate my sandwich."

Wednesday July 21st
Dawn — well, 10:00 a.m.

Phoned my dearest friend Jas who loves me. Huh.

Now that she thinks she has got a "proper" boyfriend she acts like she is one hundred and eighty.

"Look, Gee-gee, I can't talk really because I am on the dash to meet Tom. Dig you later, though. *Ciao* for now."

...*Ciao* for now? I wonder if she has finally snapped? Nobody really cares about me. No one wants you when you are in trouble; no one is interested when you are not the life and soul of the party. I may have to try to make it up with God again at this rate.

2:30 p.m.

I don't care what happens. I am not going to New Zealand. Not. Definitely. They will have to carry me on to the plane. Or give me knock-out drugs.

That is it. I am not going.

3:00 p.m.

I am not speaking to Mum but as she has gone out shopping (again) she probably hasn't noticed.

3:19 p.m.

Sitting by the phone and using telepathy to make it ring. I've read about it a lot – it's where you use your willpower to make something happen. In my head I was saying, "Ring, phone!" and "The phone will ring and it will be Robbie... by the time I count to ten."

3:21 p.m.

"OK, the phone will ring and it will be Robbie by the time I count to a hundred..."

3:30 p.m.

"...in French. By the time I count to one hundred in French the phone will ring and it will be SG." (God, or whoever it is that deals with willpower, will respect that I am making a bloody huge effort by counting in a foreign language.)

Everything really is sheer desperadoes and in tins. In two days' time I will be on the other side of the world and the Sex God will be on this side of the world. And, what is more, I will be a day ahead of him. And upside down.

3:39 p.m.

I've got an appalling headache now.

While we are on the subject of French, why in the name of Louise the Fourteenth did Madame Slack (honestly – that is her name) make us learn a song called *"Mon Merle a Perdu une Plume"*?

My blackbird has lost a feather. That will be a great boon and help if I ever get to go to Paris. I won't be able to get a sandwich for love nor money but I will be able to chat to *le* French about my blackbird's feathers. Not that I have got a blackbird and, if I did have one, believe me it wouldn't be just the one feather it would lose with Angus around. Not that he is around.

 40

I really miss him already. He is the best cat anyone ever had. I can still imagine his furry head snuggled up in my bed. Bits of feather round his mouth. The way he used to bring me little presents. A vole, or a bit of poodle ear or something.

3:41 p.m.
How do you say my blackbird has had its legs chewed off by my cat? *Mon merle a perdu les jambes...*

Phone rang
3:45 p.m.
Thank goodness, because I thought I was going to have to count up to a hundred in German and nobody wants that. (And besides, I can't.)

"It's me, Jas."

"Oh... What do YOU want?"

"I've just called to see how you are."

I said, "Dead actually, I died a few hours ago. Goodbye."

That will teach her. I'm not going to answer the phone if she rings back, either.

5:00 p.m.

She didn't ring back. Typical.

My room
In bed
10:30 p.m.

Mum and Libby came back in. When they popped their heads round my door I pretended to be asleep. Libby crept over quietly – well, her idea of creeping quietly, which is the loudest thing I have ever heard.

Mum whispered, "Give you big sister a kiss, Libbs, because she's upset."

Then I felt this wet thing sucking on the end of my nose. I shot up in bed. I said, "Does anyone else's sister kiss like that? Why is she so obsessed with my nose?"

11:15 p.m.

After the nose-sucking incident I am as awake as two awake things. Just gazing out of my bedroom window into the dark night. When you gaze at the stars it makes you feel really small. We have been discussing infinity in Physics: you know, how there is no end to the universe, and so on. Herr Kamyer said there might even be a parallel universe to the one we live on somewhere out there. There might be another Georgia Nicolson sitting in her bedroom, thinking, What on earth is the point?

11:17 p.m.
Another Georgia Nicolson who is being forced to leave a Sex God and all her mates (and this does not include Jas). To go to the other side of the world. Double *merde*.

11:29 p.m.
I've just had a horrible thought. If there is a parallel me, there will be a parallel Wet Lindsay. And a parallel Nauseating P. Green. And two pairs of Mr Next Door's shorts. Good grief.

Thursday July 22nd
Day before the last day of my life
Hunger protest
2:00 p.m.
Even though it is quite obvious even to the VERY dim that I am not eating, Mum hasn't noticed. She said, "Do you want some oven chips and beans?"

And I said, "I will never eat again."

She just said, "OK," and tucked in with Libbs.

I had to creep into the kitchen and finish off the chips she had left.

4:00 p.m.

In my room. Practising feeling lonely and friendless in preparation for the months ahead.

4:05 p.m.

I haven't heard from my so-called mates for days. Well, since this morning, anyway. I don't need to practise. I AM lonely and friendless.

4:10 p.m.

I went into the front room to watch TV. Libby was snoozing but woke up when I sat down. She stood up on her little fat legs and put her arms up to me.

"I love my Georgie, I lobe my Georgie."

She made it into a little song:

"Haha, I lobe my Georgie,

I love my little Girgie,

Gingie, Gingie.

Hahahaha. Ginger, I love Ginger... my Ginger."

In her tiny mad brain I am half cat, half sister. I picked her up and we snuggled down on the sofa together. At least I have someone who loves me in this family, even if she is bonkers.

Mum came in and said, "You look really sweet together. It only seems a little while ago that you were that size, Georgie. Dad and I used to take you to the park and you used to have a little hat with earflaps that were like cats' paws. You were such a sweet little girl."

Oh good Lord, here we go. It will be, "How did my little girl get so big...?"

Sure enough, Mum's eyes got all watery and she started stroking my hair (very annoying) and doing the "How did my little Georgie get so..." routine.

Fortunately (or unfortunately, depending on where you were sitting) Libby let off the smelliest, loudest fart known to humanity. It came out of her bum-oley with such force that she lifted off my knee – like a hovercraft. Even she looked surprised by what had come out of her.

I pushed her off my knee and leaped up. "Libby, that is disgusting!!!! I blame you, Mum, for the bean extravaganza.

It's not natural, the amount of stuff that comes out of such a little girl."

Phwoaar...

Grandad farted once when we were out in the street. Really loudly. When he looked around behind him there was a woman walking her dachshund dog. You know, those little sausage dog things. The woman heard Grandad's fart (who didn't?) and she said, "Well, really!!"

And Grandad said, "I'm terribly sorry, madam, I seem to have shot the legs off your dog." Which was possibly the last semi-sane thing he said. I'd still rather stay here with him than go to Kiwi-a-gogo.

I said to Mum, "Well, can I go and live with Grandad, then?"

And she said, "He lives in an old people's home."

And I said, "So?"

But she is so mad and unreasonable she wouldn't even discuss it.

11:30 p.m.

All my mates came and did a candlelit vigil underneath my bedroom window. Sven wore a paper hat. I don't know why.

Does it matter? It was just his Swedish way of saying goodbye. They all sang *"Mon Merle a Perdu une Plume"* as a tribute. Well, they sang the first verse before Mr and Mrs Next Door came and complained that they were frightening their dogs. Jas said, "I'm going to stay silently here all night."

But then Sven said, "Chips, now." And they all went off.

It was so sad.

Friday July 23rd
The day the world ends
Midday

Decided to have to be dragged out of bed by the police so that the world will know how I have been treated. I have tied myself to the bedhead with my dressing-gown sleeves. I can imagine the newspaper headlines: Promising hockey superstar teenager fights attempts to force her to Kiwi-a-gogo land. I've put on a hint of make-up just in case, for the photos.

12:10 p.m.

Mum surprised me by bursting into my room all flushed like a pancake.

"Guess what?!!!! We're not going to New Zealand because your dad is coming home!!!!!"

I said, "What?"

She was hugging me and didn't seem to notice I was like a rigid hamster in bed.

I was a bit dazed. "Vati, home, coming?"

Great news!!!!!!!!
1:00 p.m.

My dad has had his shoes blown off by a rogue bore!!!!! All this hot steam shot out of something he was fixing and he leaped off and broke his foot. Mum has put her foot down with a firm hand and said she will not take her children to a place where steam shoots out of the ground.

She said to me, "It's hard enough getting you to get out of bed as it is, I'm not giving you more excuses." Which is incredibly unfair, but I didn't say anything, because inside I was saying "Yessssss!!!!!!"

The only fly in the manger is that Vati is going to be coming home when his contract is finished. Still, if it is a choice of going to live in Kiwi-a-gogo land or having to put up with Vati snooping around my bedroom and telling me what it was like in the seventies, I suppose I will choose having the grumpy moustachioed one.

Mum is hideously happy. She won't stop hugging me. Which I think is on the hypocritical side but I didn't say anything. I just hugged her back and asked her quickly for a fiver. Which she gave me. Yesss!!!!

Beautiful English summer's day. Lovely, lovely drizzly rain!!! We don't have to go to Kiwi-a-gogo!!!

Thank you, God. I will always believe in you. I was only pretending to become a Buddhist.

3:00 p.m.
I put on some really loud music in my room and started to unpack my bikini. Lalalalala... fabbity fab fab. Marvy and double cool with knobs.

Uncle Eddie turned up with a bottle of champagne and Angus in a basket. I noticed Uncle Eddie had put a muzzle on him. What a week. Angus soon had it off and I could see him strolling around his domain. (The dustbins.) When I went downstairs Uncle Eddie had picked up Libby and was dancing around with her. She was singing, "Uncle Eggy, Uncle Eggy," which is quite funny when you think about it.

4:20 p.m.

My little room. I love you, my little room!!! Lalalalalalala. Fabbity fab fab. Ho-di-hum. Everything is so lovely: my little Reeves and Mortimer poster with them in the nuddy-pants, my little desk, my little bed... my little window overlooking next door's garden.

5:00 p.m.

Phoned the Ace Crew and they went mental. Just put the phone down when there was a ring on the doorbell. It was Mr Next Door. His glasses were on all sideways. He did not say, "I am so glad you are not going, Georgia." In fact, he didn't say anything but just handed over a sweeping brush and stomped off.

Attached to the bottom part of the brush was Angus. He dragged the brush into the kitchen. There was the sound of pots and pans and chairs crashing over. I called out, "Libbs, Angus is back."

11:00 p.m.

Before I went up to bed I looked into the kitchen. Libbs was feeding Angus cat food by hand. Aaahhh, this was more like it!! Back to normal.

Saturday July 24th
11:00 a.m.

Summer. Birds tweeting. Voles voleing. Poodles poodling. I notice that we have new neighbours across the road. I hope they are a bit more considerate than Mr and Mrs Mad who used to live there.

Oh, they've got a cat! It looks like one of those pedigree Burmese ones, all leaping around. In a sort of fenced enclosure. They are very expensive, pedigree Burmese cats. They are the Naomi Campbells of the cat world. Not that they do a lot of modelling. Too furry. And not tall enough. Although they would be really good on the catwalk!!! Hahahahaha. Lalalalala. I think I am a comedy genius. Now if only the SG would phone and say, "I'm coming round now, oh gorgeous one. I didn't realise how close I came to losing you. I am mesmerised by your beautosity." Life would be beyond fab and entering the marvy zone.

Midday

Met Jas and we went to the park. I've got a spot on my chin but I've made it look like a beauty spot with an eyebrow pencil. With my shades on I look a bit like an Italian person.

I think Jas was embarrassed about me not going to NZ after what she said. I am too considerate to mention it so I just said, "Do you really love me, Jas?"

She went all red.

As we strolled by the tennis courts we saw Melanie Griffiths sunbathing. I may have mentioned this before but she has got the largest breasts known to humanity. Some lads went by and went "Phwooar!". One of them pretended to be juggling. Sometimes I feel that boys will always remain a mystery to me. I've felt that particularly since BG from up the road rested his hand on my basooma for no particular reason. Mel saw us looking so I said, "Oh, hi Mel!" sincerely.

She said, "Hi!" but I don't think she meant it.

I said to Jas, "Where does she get her bras from? They must be made by those blokes who built the Forth Bridge, Ted and Mick Forth." I just made that up; I don't know what they were called.

We lay down on the grass to sunbathe and Jas said, "Do you think I should get a bra?"

I was thinking what I should wear when I saw Robbie again. I said, "Robbie hasn't phone yet, you know."

Jas was silent. I squinted round at her and she was sort of

wobbling her shoulders around. I said, "What in the name of pantyhose are you doing?"

She said, "I'm seeing if my basoomas wobble."

Jas can be spectacularly dim. I think that if I dressed Angus in her school uniform probably no one would notice for days. Unless they tried to take a snack away.

I said, "Do the pencil test. You put a pencil under a breast and if it falls out you are OK. If it stays there, sort of trapped by your basooma, you're not and you should get help and support in the bra department."

She was full-on, attention-wise, then. "Really?"

"Yeah. Sadly my mum can get a whole pencil case up there."

Jas was rummaging about. "I've got a pencil in my rucky, I'm going to try it."

"Jas, Tom hasn't said anything about Robbie, has he?"

As per usual Jas had gone off into the twilight world in her head. She was fiddling about with a pencil up her T-shirt. She said, "Hahahahaha, it fell out!!! I passed, I passed... you try it."

I wasn't interested. "Why would SG snog me and say 'see you later' if he didn't mean 'see you later'? Do you think he's worried about me being younger than him? Or do you think it's my nose?"

You might as well be talking to a duck. Jas was shoving the pencil at me. "Go on, go on... you're scared."

"Try it, then."

"No I'm not. I'm not frightened of a pencil."

"Oh for goodness' sake."

I grabbed the pencil from her and pulled up my top and put the pencil underneath my right basooma. Actually it stuck there, but I jiggled a bit. I said, "Yeah, it falls out."

Jas said, "You jiggled."

"I did not."

"You did. I saw you."

"I didn't. You're a mad biscuit."

"You did. Look, let me do it, I'll show you."

She grabbed the pencil and was trying to put it under my basooma when Jackie and Alison, the Bummer Twins, came round the corner of the tennis courts. Jackie removed the fag from her mouth long enough to say, "Well, well, well, our lezzo friends are out for an afternoon fondle."

Oh no, here we go again with the lesbian rumours. That will be something to look forward to next term.

Monday July 26th
2:00 p.m.

Phew, what a scorcher!!! Sun shining, birds tweeting. Mr and Mrs Next Door in their garden. They are wearing shorts – again. Mr Next Door's shorts really are gigantic in the bottom department. You'd think that out of courtesy to others he'd keep out of public view when he was wearing them. What if a very, very old person – even older than him – came along unexpectedly? And what if they weren't in peak medical condition? The sight of Mr Next Door in his shorts could bring on a dangerous spasm. Still, that is another example of the bottomless (oo-er!) selfishosity of so-called grown-ups for you.

Teatime
4:50 p.m.

Fabulous day... not. Grandad came round. Even he was wearing shorts. As I said to Mum, "There is really no need for that."

He is so bow-legged that Angus can walk in between his legs with a stick and Grandad doesn't even notice. Mind you he doesn't notice much as he lives in the twilight world of the elderly mad. After fiddling in his prehistoric shorts he gave me twenty pence and said, "There you are, don't spend it all at once." Then he laughed so much his false teeth shot out. He was wheezing away for so long I thought he'd choke to death and then I'd have to do the Heimlich manoeuvre. Miss Stamp (Sports Kommandant) made us learn it in First Aid. If someone swallows a boiled sweet or something and chokes, you grab them from behind and put your arms round below their breastbone. Then you squeeze them really hard until the sweet shoots out. Apparently some German bloke called Mr Heimlich made it up. Why Germans have to go round grabbing people innocently choking on sweets I don't know. But they do. That is the mystery of the German people.

8:00 p.m.
Well, that is it. No call from the SG. He must be back. I can't call him because I have pride. Well actually, I did phone him but there was no reply. I didn't leave a message. I don't understand boys. How could you do number six type snogging and then not call someone?

8:10 p.m.
Buddhism is the only way. I must meditate and be calm.

My room
8:20 p.m.

I found one of Mum's kaftans that she got when she went to India on the hippie trail. She has some very sad photos of her and Dad with hilarious haircuts in Katmandu. Dad looks like he has got a big nappy on. She gets the photos out when she is drunk, especially if you beg her not to.

I put on the kaftan and was listening to some dolphins on a meditation tape. It was called "Peaceful Universe". Squeak, squeak, squeak. On and on – it would go quiet for a bit and then squeak, squeak, squeak. If dolphins are so intelligent why don't they learn to speak properly? Instead of squeaking? It is fantastically irritating. I would turn it off but I am too depressed to get off the bed.

8:40 p.m.

Phone rings. Of course, everyone else is far too busy to answer it. So I'll tramp all the way downstairs and get it.

I yelled out, "Don't worry, Mum, I'll come all the way down and answer the phone which is probably for you. You try and get some rest!"

Mum shouted from the living room, "OK, thanks."

I picked up the receiver. "Yes?"

It was Robbie!!! Yes and treble fabuloso!! He's got such a lovely voice; quite deep – not quite as deep as Grandad's, but then he doesn't smoke forty cigarettes a minute. He said he'd been away.

I was thinking, I know you have, you great huge sexy hunk!!! My lips are stiff with puckering!!! But I didn't say that, I said, "Oh, have you?" which I thought was quite cool and alluring. Anyway, the short and short of it is that he's really, really glad that I didn't go to Kiwi-a-gogo and I'm going round to his place tomorrow!!! His parents have gone away.

Ooooooohhhhhh. I'm all shakey and nervous now. I'm like a cat on a hot tin roof. We did *Cat On a Hot Tin Roof* in English. There was no cat in it... or a tin roof... or... stop it, brain, stop it!!!!

8:45 p.m.
Phoned Jas.

"He called me!!"

"Who?"

It's like talking to a sock. "Jas. HE called me. HE – the one and only HE in the universe."

9:00 p.m.

Jas came round to discuss what I should wear. We went up to my room. Unfortunately I forgot to warn Jas about the hammock that Libby had made for her dolls. She'd made it out of one of Mum's commodious bras and tied it across the landing. Jas grazed her shins quite badly when she fell over. She was going, "Ow, ow!", but I can't be bothered with minor injuries just now.

She hobbled into my room and we looked through my wardrobe. I held things up and Jas went, "No. No. Maybe. No, too tarty. No, no... er... maybe."

I was trying on a suede mini and she said, "Erlack!! The front of your legs are quite hairy but the backs of your legs are all baldy."

I had a look. She was right!!! Time for operation smoothy legs. I grumbled to her as we went down to the bathroom. "What is the point of evolution? Why bother giving us hairy front legs and baldy back legs? When can that ever have been useful in our fight for survival?"

Jas said, "Perhaps it was to frighten things off."

I said, "Oh yeah, that will be it. Stone Age girl would have said, 'Here comes a big dinosaur chasing me from behind. It thinks I am a push-over because of my baldy legs, but wait till I turn round! I'll scare off the big lug with my terrifying hairy front legs.' That will be the explanation."

Jas wasn't interested in my scientosity because she was looking through the bathroom cabinet. "Your mum has got loads of anti-ageing creams, hasn't she?"

"I know. It's sad. Why doesn't she save all that money and put it towards some new spectacles or a hat? Or a decent bra that can contain her gigantic basoomas."

9:30 p.m.
Mum's hair remover worked a treat; my legs were smoothy smooth. I was tempted to use a bit on my eyebrows but I remembered the last time I had shaved them and they had taken two weeks to grow back.

Clothes-wise we decided on a turtle-necked crop top (implies that I am mature for my years, on the brink of womanhood, etc... but doesn't go as far as saying "I am desperate for a snog"). In the leg department it was the tight Capri trousers.

Jas said, "Tom is going away on work experience this term. I will be on my own for weeks. I'll really miss him. Do you know, he said the other day that he..."

60

In a caring way I said, "Go home now, Jas, I have to get my beauty sleep."

11:00 p.m.

In bed nice and early. I've barricaded my door so that Angus and Libby can't get in.

Midnight

I am SO nervous... What if I have forgotten how to snog? What if all my snogging lessons go out of my mind at the last minute and we bump teeth?

1:00 a.m.

Or I lose my grip altogether and go to the same side with my head as he is going, and knock him out? Heeeeelp!!!!

What if I have one of those laughing fits that you can't stop? You know, when you remember something... like for instance when Herr Kamyer took us on a school trip and when we arrived at the railway station he said, "Ach yes, here ve are!" and then opened the door on the wrong side of the train and fell out of the carriage.

Hahahahahahahaha... hahahahaa. You see, I'm doing it

♥ 61

now. I'm laughing by myself in the middle of the night in my room.

OhmyGodohmyGodohmyGod. Hahahahahahahahaha.

Tuesday July 27th
SG Day
Setting off to his house.
7:00 p.m.

It's taken most of the day to achieve my natural make-up look. Just a subtle touch to enhance my natural beauty(!). I wanted the just-tumbled-out-of-bed look, so I only used undercover concealer, foundation, hint of bronzer, eye pencil, eight layers of mascara, lip liner, lippy and lip-gloss, and I left it at that.

7:20 p.m.

Jas phoned to wish me luck. She said, "Tell me all about it when you get home. Remember what number you get up to on the snogging scale. Are you wearing a bra? I think it would be wise because you don't want to wobble all over the place."

I said, "Goodbye, Jas."

I'm not wearing a bra; I thought I would go free and akimbo. I just won't make any sudden movements.

Walking down Arundel Street
7:30 p.m.

Brrr, not quite as warm and bright as it was earlier. A bit overcast, actually, and... oh no... it's starting to rain! It's too far to go back home for an umby... it will probably stop in a minute.

7:40 p.m.

Outside Robbie's gate. It really is raining quite hard now. I'm wet through and really cold. I think my trousers have shrunk; they are hugging my bottom in a vice-like grip. I wonder if I look all right?

I'll nip into the telephone box opposite his house and check my mirror.

In the telephone box
7:45 p.m.

My trousers have shrunk so tight around my bottom that I can't bend my legs. This is hopeless. Brrr. Why is everything going wrong? I can't go to see the Sex God looking like this. I'll have to phone him up and say I'm ill.

7:50 p.m.

SG answered the phone, "Hello."

Swoon swoon.

I said, "Roggie, nit's ne, Neorgia."

"What's wrong with your voice?"

"Der nl'd gat a trrible cold nd Im nin bed."

"Do they have beds in telephone boxes?"

"Dnno."

"Georgia, I can see you through the window."

When I looked across at his house, he waved at me. Oh GODDDDDD!!!!!!

He said, "Come over."

What can I do, what can I do? My top is all wet. And there are two bumpy things in it. Great! It looks like I've got two peas down the front of my top. Typical, the only thing Mum has ever ironed for me and she has ironed it wrong.

As I walked up to the door I tried to flatten out the bumpy bits. But it wasn't my top sticking up... it was ME!!! My nipples!!!!! What were they doing?!!! Why were they sticking out? I hadn't told them to do that. How could I get them back in again? I'd have to cross my arms in a casual way and hope he didn't offer me a cup of coffee.

7:55 p.m.

The back door opened and there he was!! The Sex God had landed. I went even more jelloid. He was so gorgey... so... oooooh and er and yum yum and scrumbos and yummy scrumbos. His hair was all floppy, he had on dark jeans and a white T-shirt and you could see his shoulders (one on each side). He's got really, really dark blue eyes and long dark eyelashes and a big mouth, sort of soft looking. He's not a girlie boy though, he's definitely a boyie boy, which I think is handy in a boy myself.

Midnight

I love him, I love him. I love you, Robbie, oh yes I do. When I'm not near you I'm blue... What else rhymes with Robbie? Gobbie? Snoggie? Knobbie?

12:30 a.m.

I can't sleep, life is too brilliant. I may never sleep again.

It was such a fab night. We talked for a bit – well, I said, "My dad had his shoes blown off by a rogue bore," and he said, "Does anything normal ever happen to you?" Which I took as a compliment.

He played me a song on his guitar. I didn't really know what to do when he did that. I just sat on the sofa next to him with an attractive half-smile on my face and my arms crossed). It was quite a long song and by the end of it my cheeks ached like billio. In fact, I think I might have cheek strain. I tried to keep my nose sucked in at the same time; I didn't want it wandering across my face.

He told me that he is going to go to university to do music properly. I said, "I'm going to be a vet." I don't know why as I'm not. I didn't seem to be able to make anything come out of my mouth that had anything to do with my brain. He looked into my eyes and went quiet, and I went quiet and looked back at him. I tried not to blink. That seemed to go on for about a million years. In the end I had a sort of nervy spasm and went and looked at a photograph of a dog that was on a table. He probably thinks I am obsessed with animals as I am a trainee vet (not).

He came over and put his arm round my shoulder. I had an overwhelming urge to start doing Cossack dancing as a very funny joke, but just in time I remembered that boys don't like girls for jokes. Then he kissed me. I think he may be the best snogger in the universe. Although I have only snogged two other boys so far, and one of those was part boy part whelk, so I can't be entirely sure. SG does that varying pressure thing that Rosie says foreign boys do. You know, soft and then hard and then medium and then hard again. I could have quite literally snogged until the cows came home. And when they came home I would have shouted, "WHAT HAVE YOU COWS COME HOME FOR? CAN'T YOU SEE I'M SNOGGING, YOU STUPID HERBIVORES???"

I think I may be a bit feverish.

1:30 a.m.

I am going to be nice to everyone from now on. Even Wet Lindsay, Robbie's ex. I won't say to her, "Yesssssss!!!!" I will be grown-up and nice.

The only fly in the landscape is that when he walked me to my gate and said goodnight he tweaked my nose. And he said, "I'll see you later."

1:35 a.m.

What does that mean? Not the "see you later" bit, because no one knows what that means. I mean the tweaking the nose business.

1:40 a.m.

Does it mean, "Hey, you adorable cute thing," or does it mean, "Cor, what a size that conk is, I wonder if I can get all of it in one hand?"

Wednesday July 28th
3:35 p.m.

I am a Sex God's girlfriend. But I will not let it spoil my naturalness.

Phoned Jas: "Even when I have loads of interesting and glamorous friends I would still want to be friends with you. Because we are proper friends. We should never let boys come between us."

Jas said, "Tom is going to buy me one of those stick-on transfer tattoos. I'm going to put it on my bottom while he is away and not wash it off until he gets back."

"Jas, can you leave your bottom out of this? Please."

Friday July 30th
5:00 p.m.

Made my dear mutti and sister a meal today. Mashed potatoes and sausages. I thought Mum was going to cry.

10:00 p.m.

Early to bed, early to rise, makes a girl... er... anyway, it gets a girl out of the way of her mutti who had a nervy b. when she saw the state of the kitchen.

10:15 p.m.

Why do I always get the blame for every little thing? Is it really my fault that a couple of pans caught fire? I put them out.

Still, I refuse to be upset. I will remain calm beneath my egg and olive oil face mask.

Saturday July 31st
7:55 p.m.

Dreamy dreamy, smiley smiley.

However no phone calley. Never mindey.

Snogging Withdrawal

Sunday August 1st
8:00 a.m.
I've persuaded Jas to come to church with me to thank God for making Dad have his shoes blown off and also for giving me a Sex God as a plaything.

10:00 a.m.
When I got round to Jas's house she was sitting on her wall in the shortest skirt known to humanity. When I wear skirts like that my grandad says, "You can see what you had for your dinner." I don't know what on earth he is talking about but then neither does anyone else, except probably dogs.

Jas leaped off the wall. Her skirt was about four centimetres long.

I said, "Is it a long time since you went to church, Jas?" and she said, "It's OK, I'm wearing really big knickers."

Church
10:40 a.m.

Good grief. Now I know why I don't go to church much. It is not what is generally known as Fun City Arizona. I was forced to sing "All Things Bright and Beautiful" which is bad enough, but there was a further treat in store. The vicar, ("Call me Arnold") tries to be "modern". So to really get "with it" Call me Arnold had got some absolute saddos to play guitars as an accompaniment. One of the boys on guitar was called Norman and as if that is not cruel enough he had acne. And not just ordinary acne, he had acne of the entire head.

But as we left I remembered that I was supposed to be being grateful so I said, "Sorry about Spotty Norman, God, I will be nice to him next time I see him," (inwardly) and put a pound in the collection box.

Monday August 2nd
12:10 p.m.

Still no news from the SG. I've been going to bed really early to make the hours pass more quickly.

I tried snogging the back of my hand to stave off snogging withdrawal but it's no good.

3:30 p.m.

Cor phew... boiling again. The sun was shining like a great big fried egg. Jas and Jools and Ellen and me went sunbathing in the park. I took off my shades and got the shock of my life: in the sunshine my legs looked like Herr Kamyer's legs. They were all pale-looking. Not as hairy or German as his legs, obviously.

I said, "Ellen, why are your legs so brown?"

She said, "Oh, I used some of that Kool Tan stuff."

Maybe the SG noticed my Herr Kamyer legs? I must get some Kool Tan.

Tuesday August 3rd
10:30 p.m.

When Jas came round for us to practise hairstyles I made her let me kiss the back of her calf to see if she could feel any teeth. She leaped about, going, "Erlack, erlack, get off, get off, it feels disgusting, like a sort of sucky Spotty Norman." Which is not very reassuring.

She said Tom touched her basooma the other night. In revenge I said, "How would he know it wasn't your shoulder?" She honestly does think she is like Kate Moss. It is very, very sad.

Midnight

SG didn't touch my basooma. I wonder if that is bad? Mind you, I had my arms folded for a lot of the time because of the nipple emergency.

Wednesday August 4th
4:00 p.m.

Phoned Jas.

"I'm really worried now. It's been over a week. I wonder if it is my nose? Perhaps SG only likes little sticky-up noses like Wet Lindsay's?"

Jas said, "Maybe a headband would help. You should make more of your forehead and that would take the emphasis away from your nose."

"At least I've got a forehead, not like Wet Lindsay who has got a tiny little forehead. In fact, she is really just hair and then eyebrows. How could the SG go out with someone with no forehead?"

"She's got quite nice legs."

"What do you mean? Nice – not like mine? Shut up, Jas."

"OK, keep your hair on."

"Nauseating P. Green, on the other hand, has got the HUGEST forehead known to humanity. In fact, she is a walking forehead in a frock. I must get away from this forehead business, it's making me feel a bit mad."

4:30 p.m.

In the bathroom experimenting with a headband. Hmmm, headband seems to emphasise my nose. In fact, it's like wearing a big notice on my head that says, "Hey, everyone!!! Look at my incredibly big schnozzle!!"

4:40 p.m.

While I had been doing headband work I hadn't been paying much attention to Libbs. She had come into the bathroom and got up on the lavatory seat. Her hair was all sticking up like a mad earwig but she won't let you comb it. I said, "Libby, things will start nesting in it," and she said, "Aaahh nice." Then she started going, "Bzzz, bzzz, bzzy bzz, bzz," like a mad bee.

I was experimenting with sucking in my nose to see if it made it look any smaller when Mum came barging in. (Not bothering to knock or anything.) Anyway, she went even more bananas than usual. Libby had put all of the loo paper down her knickers because she wanted to be a bumble bee. I'd heard her buzzing but I didn't pay any attention. Mum was all red-faced.

"Georgia, all you think about is how you bloody look. The house could burn down around you before you would stop looking in that mirror."

I raised my eyebrows ironically. Talk about the pot calling the other pot a black kettle, er... well whatever. She really has got a volatile temper; she should go to anger management classes. I will suggest it to her. But not just now as she has got a brush in her hand.

4:50 p.m.
My violent, bad-tempered mother has gone out. Nothing in the fridge. Oh, I tell a lie, there is a half-eaten sausage. Yum yum.

♡ 75

4:55 p.m.

Grandad said that as you get older gravity pulls on your nose and makes it bigger and bigger.

5:00 p.m.

Why couldn't I come from a decent gene bank? Nice, well-formed parents, like Jas's mum and dad. Nice and compact, nothing too sticky-outy. Instead I get massive "danger to shippings" from Mum and a massive conk from my dad. If Robbie doesn't like me it is Vati's fault. If it is true about the gravity business then Dad will need a wheelbarrow to carry his nose around in soon. Good, serve him right for ruining my life.

7:00 p.m.

I'm so hot and restless. Oh Robbie, where are you? My nose feels tremendously heavy.

8:00 p.m.

I put on a really loud record and danced about to get rid of my excess snogosity.

8:05 p.m.

When I looked in the mirror I could see my basoomas bobbling about. Good grief and *sacré bleu*!! They look like they are doing their own dance!

In Mum's Vanity Fair it says that all the posh type ladies go to a special woman behind Harrod's to get their bras properly fitted.

8:15 p.m.

The Queen must go there, then. Apparently this woman who does the bras is such an expert that she can just look at someone and say what size bra they should have. No suggestion of pencil cases. I wish I could go to her.

8:30 p.m.

When the Queen goes, this woman must just look at her and yell to her assistant, "Get the Queen a bra in size forty-eight D." Or whatever size the Queen is.

9:00 p.m.

The Queen is about five foot high, so if she was a size sixty D that would make her like a five-foot ball.

9.30 p.m.

I wish I didn't have that in my head.

Midnight

Should I call him? Oh I don't know what to do. I don't know what to do.

Thursday August 5th
Still boiling
4:00 p.m.

Jools, Ellen, Rosie, Jas and me went to town to try on make-up in Boots and Miss Selfridge. I cheered up a bit, especially as we did this limping thing on the way home. You link up and all limp together. And you're not allowed to break arms no matter what happens. This tremendously old bloke got shirty with us because we accidentally stampeded his Labrador. After that we went into the park and sat on the swings for a rest. Rosie said, "Oh I fancy a fag."

I was shocked. I said, "I didn't know you smoked."

And she said, "It's just to relax."

Rosie put a cigarette in her mouth and got out her lighter. We were all looking. Unfortunately she must have set the flame too high because when she flicked it a flame shot up about twelve centimetres and set fire to her fringe. We beat it out but the hair was all singed and short. She went home with her hand over her fringe. After she had gone the rest of us swang backwards and forwards for a few minutes.

I said, "Rosie smokes quite a lot, doesn't she?"

And then we all got the helpless laughing. You know, that laughing that makes your tummy hurt and makes you cry and gulp and choke? And you've laughed for long enough and you want to stop but you can't. Then you do stop and you think it's all right but then someone starts again. I just couldn't stop. And that's when I saw HIM. The Sex God. With his mates from The Stiff Dylans. He looked like he was coming across to say hello. And you know when you really, really should stop laughing because otherwise it will be really bad and everyone will hate you? But you can't? Well I had that.

10:00 p.m.
Rang Robbie. His mum said he was at rehearsal. Still he likes a laugh himself, so it will be all right.

♡ 79

Midnight

On the other hand I wasn't by any means doing my attractive half-smiling when he saw me. I had a look at myself in the mirror doing proper, unadulterated laughing, the kind of laughing where you just let your nose and mouth go free and wild.

12:15 a.m.

That is it, my life is over; I must go to the ugly home immediately.

Friday August 6th

11:00 a.m.

A letter arrived for me. From Robbie. My hands were shaking when I opened it.

11:30 a.m.

Back in bed. I CANNOT believe my life. It is beyond pooiness. It has gone well beyond the Valley of the Poo and entered the Galaxy of *Merde*.

11:45 a.m.

I re-read the letter from Robbie again. It still says the same thing though.

> Dear Georgia,
>
> I have been thinking and thinking about this. And although I think you are great, and I really do like you, well, I saw you with your mates yesterday having a laugh and you seemed so young. The facts are that I am seventeen, nearly eighteen, and if anyone knew I was even thinking about going out with a fourteen-year-old I would never hear the end of it. Where would we go for our dates? Youth club or something? You see what I mean, don't you?
>
> I think it is best we stay away from each other for a year or so. You need to see someone more your own age. My brother has a really nice mate called Dave. He's a good laugh. You'd like him.
>
> I'm really sorry.
> Love Robbie xxxxxxxxx

Midday

On the phone to Jas. I was shaking with rage.

Jas said, "Well, erm... if he's a good laugh, maybe you should meet him."

"Jas, are you really saying that I should just stop liking one person and start liking another one, just like that? What if I said, 'Hey, Jas, forget about Tom, why not go out with Spotty Norman? He's got a really great shaped head underneath the acne'?"

Saturday August 7th
6:20 p.m.

I hate him. I hate him.

On the phone to Jas.

"How dare he find another boyfriend for me? I hate him!!!"

Sunday August 8th
3:50 p.m.

That is absolutely it for me now. He can't treat me like that. I have my pride. How dare he question my maturiosity?

On the phone to Jas. "Jas?"

"What?"

"You don't think I should just pop round to his house and sort of beg and plead, do you?"

Monday August 9th
11:40 a.m.

I will never get over this, never.

Mum says there are plenty more fish in the sea. Why is she so obsessed with fish? At a time like this! She doesn't care about my feelings anyway.

No one does.

Wednesday August 11th
2:49 p.m.

Took Angus for a long, moody walk. Part of me really hates the Sex God. Sadly it's only a little tiny part of me (near my knee), the rest of me really, really likes him!!!!

3:00 p.m.

Even my breasts like him. They want to break out of my T-shirt and yell, "I love you, I love you!!!"

3:32 p.m.

I hope I am not being driven to the brink of madness by grief. They say that some people never get over things, like whatshername, Kathy Thing. The one who wandered over the moors at night yelling, "Heathcliff, Heathcliff, it's me a-Kathy come home again." Was that Kathy Brontë, one of the Brontë sisters? Or was that Kate Bush? Anyway, whoever it was wandered off into the rain and died from heartbreak. That will be me. I feel a bit tired now. If I just lie down here in the grass I might never be found.

3:35 p.m.
Angus keeps tugging at his lead. It was murder getting it on him but at least it means he can't savage any small dogs that we see.

4:00 p.m.
Famous last words. Angus saw a Pekinese and dragged me to my feet and halfway across a field before I managed to get him under control. He's senselessly brave. There is something about small dogs that really irritates him.

4:30 p.m.
Angus can fetch sticks!!! I was just carrying a stick along, hitting things with it. Then my arm got tired so I flung it away. And Angus pounced on it and dragged it back!! Superdooper cat!!!

5:00 p.m.

I wonder if I could get him to carry a little flask of tea round his neck in case I fancied a cuppa when we were having our walk?

Friday August 13th
My bedroom
1:00 a.m.

Hot and stuffy. Big full moon. Sitting on the windowsill. (Me, not the moon.)

1:05 a.m.

I hate him.

1:06 a.m.

Oh I love him, I love him.

1:10 a.m.

I hate him, but he will not break me. I will make him regret the day he said, "I know a bloke called Dave. He's a good laugh."

She who laughs last laughs last.

2:00 a.m.

I am going to be a heartless babe magnet as revenge.

2:05 a.m.

Oh no, no, that's not what I mean. I don't want to be a babe magnet, that would mean I was a lesbian.

2:05 and 30 secs

Still, what is wrong with that? Each to their own, I say. After all, Mum must have kissed Dad (erlack).

2:06 a.m.

If anyone asked me to comment on sexuality, say in the *Mail on Sunday* or something, I would say that it is a matter of personal choice and nothing to do with nosey parkers. Or else I would say, "Don't ask me, I am on the rack of love."

Sunday August 15th
In bed
9:40 p.m.

In bed early, healing my broken heart in the "privacy" of my bedroom.

9:41 p.m.

How can I stop Libby hiding her pooey knickers in my bed?

Monday August 16th
9:00 a.m.

Up. Up at nine a.m. in the holidays. Nine a.m.!! This just proves how upset I am.

Mum hasn't even noticed, of course.

"Mum, shouldn't even you be able to potty-train Libby by now? At this rate she'll be a pensioner and still pooing all over the place. She'll never get a boyfriend... Still, that will make two of us."

Tuesday August 17th
8:30 a.m.

I think I've lost a lot of weight from my bottom. No one has noticed. Mum just wanders around in a dream. She has got a calendar up in the kitchen with the days marked off until Vati gets back and a heart drawn round the date. How sad is that at her age? I said, "Don't worry yourself about my breakfast, Mutti. I'll get it myself, you get on with your own very important life."

She was humming and slathering herself with creams and ignoring me. So I said even louder, "Something quite interesting happened last night; I slit my throat and my head fell off. Have you seen it anywhere?"

Mum called from the bathroom. "Has Libby got her shoes on?"

"I think Mr Next Door might be another transvestite like Vati."

She came out of the bathroom then. "Georgia, is it possible for you to help at all? Where is your sister?"

"Mum, have you noticed anything unusual about me? I am not happy... in fact, I am very unhappy."

"Why? Have you broken a nail?" And she laughed in a very unpleasant way. Then she called out, "Libbsy, where are you, pet? What are you doing?"

I could hear Libby's muffled voice from Mum's bedroom and a bit of miaowing. Libby called, "Nuffing."

Mum rushed in there, saying, "Oh God."

I heard bang bang, and Mum yelling, "Libby, that is Mummy's best lipstick!"

"It looks nice!!!!"

"No, it doesn't... Cats don't wear lipstick."

"Yes."

"No, they don't."

"Yes."

"Owww, don't kick Mummy."

"Bad Mummy!!!"

Hahahaha. She who laughs last laughs... er... the last.

Thursday August 19th
11:00 a.m.

Raining. In August. Typical. Squelching along on my way to meet Mrs Big Knickers, I was thinking... I could either give in and be a miserable, useless person, like Elvis Attwood, our barmy, sad old school caretaker. Or if I truly gave up I could be like Wet Lindsay. When Robbie dumped her she got all pale and even wetter than normal. She was like an anoraksick. (A person who is both very thin and wears tragic anoraks.) I just made that up as a joke. Even though I am very upset I can still think of a joke. I'll tell Jas when I see her. As I was saying, before I so rudely interrupted myself, I could be a sad old sadsack or I could gird my loins and be like in that song. The one where you have to search for the hero within yourself.

Jas was waiting for me at the bus stop. She said, "Why are you walking in that stiff way?"

"I'm girding my loins."

"Well, it looks painful, like you've got a stick up your bottom. You haven't, have you?"

"You really are sensationally mad, Jas. In olden days people would have thrown oranges at you."

As I said, I can sometimes surprise myself with my own wisdomosity. And humourosity. Even in adversosity.

Monday August 23rd
2:10 a.m.
In bed. Oh God, it's so boring being broken-hearted. I've spent so much time in bed I'll probably start growing a long white beard soon, like Rip van Thing.

2:15 a.m.
Or perhaps I could just grow my eyebrows and train them into a beard.

2:48 a.m.
I can't sleep. I've gone all feverish now. I'm going to creep downstairs and get Mum's *Men are from Mars* book and do some more research.

3:35 a.m.

God, it's too weird. Apparently boys might seem like they like you to be all interested in them, but really they want you to be like a glacier iceberg sort of girl. So you have to play hard to get. That's where I must have gone wrong. I have been too keen, I must do glacial.

Thursday August 26th
10:33 p.m.

Same bat time. Same bat place. Same scuba-diving Barbie digging me in the back.

According to the next bit in Mum's book, boys are like elastic bands. Good Lord!

It doesn't mean that boys are made of elastic, which is a plus because nobody wants a boyfriend made out of rubber. On the other hand, if they were made out of rubber you could save yourself a lot of time and effort and heartache by just rustling one up out of a car tyre. But that is not what the book means. Boys are different from girls. Girls like to be cosy all the time but boys don't. First of all they like to get all close to you like a coiled-up rubber band, but after a while they get fed up with being too coiled and need to stretch away to their full stretchiness. Then, after a bit of on-their-own stretchy, they ping back to be close to you.

Hmmm. So in conclusion on the boy front, you have to play hard to get (the glacier bit), and also let them be elastic bands. *Sacré bleu!* They don't want much, do they?

Friday August 27th
4:20 p.m.

Round at Jas's house. Been to town. I bought myself some new lippy to cheer myself up and Jas got a new hot air brush thing that gives you bouncability. She was making her hair all turn under at the ends.

As she was tonging away at her hair she said, "I looked for a bra but I can't get one small enough. In fact, I don't need one, I'm more like Kate Moss. You have to wear one though, don't you?... Because of the pencil-case test thing."

"Just pencil... the case was my mum."

"Yeah, but the pencil stuck, didn't it? You said that if it did you had to have help and support."

"I know what I said."

When Jas really annoys me (i.e. all of the time) I notice that her fringe is more fringey than normal, if you know what I mean.

Fringey went on, "I'm only saying – there's no need to have a nervy b."

Jas was really, really beginning to annoy me. A lot. All her things are really neatly put away which is the sign of a very dull person in my opinion. When Jas and I stalked Wet Lindsay and looked through her bedroom window all her things were very tidy as well. Jas even puts all her knickers in the same drawer.

Besides it being VERY dull to do that it would also be useless at my house as Libby mostly uses my knickers as hats for her dolls. Or Angus eats them.

To change the subject I said, In a really caring way, "When does Tom go off to work experience?"

Jas stopped hot brushing her hair then and looked all mournful. Hahahahaha. She said, "Next Saturday – it's going to be really horrible. Do you think he'll meet someone else in Birmingham?"

I looked wise and oracle-like and like I was really thinking (which I wasn't). I said, "Well, he's a young bloke and we all know what young blokes are like."

"Do we?"

I laughed bitterly.

She said, "Just because Robbie went off doesn't mean all boys do."

"It does... in Mum's book *Men are from Mars* it tells you all about it."

She was interested then and came and sat next to me. "What does it say in the book? Does it say Tom is going to go off with someone else?"

I said, "Yes it does, Jas. It says in the worldwide number one bestseller written by some bloke in America who has never met Tom, it says in Chapter Two, 'Tom Jennings definitely goes off with someone else when he goes to do work experience in Birmingham for a month.'"

She looked a bit miffed. "Well, what do you mean, then?"

I waited for a bit. Teach her to go on and on about my breasty problem and the fact that SG had left me.

"Can I try your new shiny lippy?"

She wasn't interested, it was all just me, me, me with her. She just went on about her problems.

"Anyway, Gee, what do you mean about this book? Isn't it American?"

"Yeah."

"Well it will be about American boys, then, won't it?"

"No, it's about boykind."

"Oh."

I paused. She looked all goggly and attentive, it was quite a nice feeling. Perhaps I might reconsider my career and think about becoming an Agony Aunt rather than a backing singer. Especially since I can't sing. But I know all about agony.

Jas was as agog as two gogs. She said, "Go on."

I explained, "Boys are like elastic bands."

"What?"

"Boys are like elastic bands."

"What?"

"Jas, if you keep saying 'what?' every time I say something we may be here for some centuries."

"Well, what do you mean 'like elastic bands'?"

"They like to be all close and then after a bit of being close they have to stretch and get far away... and you have to let them and then they spring back."

"What?"

"You're doing it again and it really annoys me. In fact, I will have to kill you now because I have a lot of untamed energy because of the Sex God. I'm going to have to give you a bit of a duffing up." And I shoved her.

She said, "Don't be silly and childish."

I said, "I'm not."

She got up and started making her hair have more bouncability with the air brush thing again. I waited until she had got it just right (in her opinion), then I hit her over the head with a pillow. She started to say, "Look, this is not funn–" but before she could finish I hit her over the head again with the pillow. And every time she tried to talk I did it again. She got all red-faced, which in Jas's case is very red indeed. It made me feel much better. Violence may be the answer to the world's problems. I may write to the Dalai Lama and suggest he tries my new approach.

My room
Midnight

I've got a plan. It involves the two "isities". They are "maturiosity" and "glaciosity". Firstly I have to prove to SG that I am very sophis and grown-up. Not a laughing hyena in a school uniform as he thought the last time he saw me. (This is the maturiosity bit.) Secondly I must be distant and alluring and play hard to get. (This is the glaciosity bit.)

The conclusion of these two parts is that SG comes springing back like an elastic band.

Saturday August 28th

2:10 p.m.

Phoned Jas.

I said, "I've worked out a plan."

She said, "I can't talk, Tom and I are going to choose my tattoo."

Huh. Typico.

Well, old huge knickers always puts her boyfriend first. Just as well I am so popular.

10:00 p.m.

In bed listening to a tape. Sadly it is "the Teddy Bears' Picnic". Libby has made me listen to it five times. If I try to turn it off she has a nervy spaz and growls at me.

I phoned up my "mates" earlier to go out, but they were all busy.

11:00 p.m.

I wonder if I had an emergency, like appendicitis or something, would my mates be too "busy" to come to the hospital?

11:30 p.m.

I have got a pain in my side. It might be a grumbling appendix.

11:32 p.m.

In blodge we learned that rabbits have got some sort of shrub growing in their appendix. How normal is that?

Sunday August 29th
6:30 p.m.

Mutti and Libbs have gone to visit the elderly mad. (Grandad.) Mum asked me if I would like to go, but I just looked at her with pity. Sadly she didn't get it and asked me again. I explained politely that I would rather put my head in a pair of Elvis Attwood's old trousers. She said I was a "horrid, bad-tempered spoiled brat". Fat chance I'm spoiled. I'm lucky if I get one square meal a week. I'm getting really, really thin. Apart from my nose. And basoomas.

8:00 p.m.

Ellen, Rosie and Jools came round and we sat on the wall, looking at boys. There are, it has to be said, a lot of fit-looking boys, but they haven't got that certain Sex God factor for me.

Mark (BG) went by with his girlfriend Ella. She is practically a midget. I thought he was taking a toddler for a walk. Rosie said, "So what happened with you and Robbie?"

I said, "he sent me a note and said that I should go out with some loser called Dave the Laugh."

Rosie said, "That's sort of dumping by proxy, isn't it?"

I said, "Are you supposed to be cheering me up?"

"But I thought you got to number six and everything."

"Yeah, but he said his parents would go ballisticisimus because I am so young. They'd think I was jail thing."

The Ace Crew were all full-on, attention-wise. Ellen even took her chewing gum out.

Jools said, "What is jail thing?"

I didn't really know actually but I improvised (lied). "Er... it's when you are underage and you go to... er... number eight with a boy."

Rosie said, "What, if you let a boy touch you above the waist you have to go to jail?"

I said patiently, "No, he has to go to jail."

Rosie said, "Well, that's it for Sven, then."

I said, "Fair enough." But I don't know what I am talking

♡ 99

about really. I'm all upset and confused and still have Herr Kamyer legs, even though it's the end of August.

Monday August 30th
1:43 p.m.

Borrowed Ellen's Kool Tan. Soon my Herr Kamyer legs will turn into sun-kissed boy magnets. Hmmm, smooth it on smoothy smooth and leave for an hour.

2:00 p.m.

If I move my bed and open the window I can sort of sunbathe on my bedroom floor. SG is going to find it damn difficult to resist the new tanned me.

4:05 p.m.

Woke up to orange Herr Kamyer legs and a huge red nose!!

5:00 p.m.

I've just scrubbed my legs off. They are not quite so orange but my nose looks like one of those red clown noses. Brilliant.

Operation elastic band

Wednesday September 1st
7:00 p.m.

It's boiling having to wear stockings in this weather, but better than being blinded every time I look down at my still orangish legs.

Eight days till we go back to Stalag 14. I'm going to put my foot down with a firm hand this term and make sure I don't have to sit next to Nauseating P. Green.

Mum has gone out to Uncle Eddie's with Libbs. He is teaching Mum salsa dancing – can you imagine? How very sad. The tremendously old can be very embarrassing. Imagine my mum salsa dancing with Uncle Eddie the human boiled egg.

In public.

Or private.

7:05 p.m.

Jas called. Tom has gone off to work experience and she wants to come round. I am a substitute boyfriend. Well she can think again if she thinks I am going to be constantly available when Tom goes off to work experience. I am not so cheap.

7:08 p.m.

I may make her give me some expensive present that I choose from Boots. Oh no, hang on, I've got a better idea.

7:30 p.m.

Jas moaning on about Tom.

I listened sympathetically and said, "Shut up, now, Jas."

Then she looked at me. "Why have you got pink panstick on your nose?"

I said, "Shut up, now, Jas."

7:42 p.m.

I made my famous French toast for Jas. (Beat an egg and put bread in it and then fry it. The French bit comes in when you are eating the toast and you have to speak with a French accent.) As we were munching through the toast I said, "Jas, *ma petite.*"

"*Quoi?*"

"I've got *le plan* to *impressez* the Sex God *avec* my maturiosity. It involves *vous.*"

She almost choked on her toast. "*Non.*"

"You will *aime* it."

"Oh *mon Dieu.*"

The first part of my plan was that we got dressed up to look as old as we could and get on a bus and get full fares. As an experiment. She was grumbling as she got made up but at least she was on the move.

8:30 p.m.

Ready. I must say I think we looked v. Sophis. We'd got loads more make-up on than we normally wear, and darker lipstick. And we wore all black. Black is very ageing, as I continually tell Mum so I can get her black T-shirt and leather trousers. I said to Jas, "We'd better get back before she gets home because I have borrowed her Gucci handbag. She specifically said she would kill me if I ever borrowed it.

She is very, very mean with her things, which is why I have to borrow them in secret."

As we walked down the street I had another idea. "Let's keep pretending we are French as well."

"Why?"

"Don't you mean *pourquoi*?"

"No, I mean why?"

"Just *parce que, ma petite* pal."

Midnight

Oui!!! Très, très bon!! Merveilleux!!!! It was *très, très bon plus les grandes knobs.*

The bus driver was like a sort of mobile version of Elvis Attwood, our school caretaker – i.e. very old, mad and bad-tempered, but sitting in a bus rather than a hut. I said to Mobile Elvis, "*Bonsoir, mon très* old *garçon. Mon amie et moi désire deux billets pour* Deansgate, *s'il vous plaît.*"

He understood we wanted to go to Deansgate but unluckily, like all very old mad people, thought he could be funny and witty. He gave us the tickets (full fare! Yesss!!! Result!!!!). I handed over the money and he said, "*Merci* buckets." Then he laughed himself senseless (easy enough as he was mad in the first place). I thought he would choke to death because he was laughing so much, but sadly he didn't.

What is the matter with people?

12:20 a.m.

Snug in my bed. Maybe I should leave school as I look so old.

2:30 a.m.

I could go off and have sophisticated adventures instead of hanging around with very young people.

12:35 a.m.

I could go to India and visit the Dalai Lama, or is it Gandhi who lives there? I don't know. We haven't done India in geoggers yet. All I know is what Mum tells me about it, and that is mostly, "Oh it was just so... you know... great." Anyway, even if we had done India in geoggers Mrs Franks is so bad at explaining things that I wouldn't know any more than I do now. She called concentration camps "contraception camps" while we were doing world affairs.

1:00 a.m.

Now on to part two of the plan. The glaciosity bit. I must look for an opportunity to show SG how stand-offish I can be.

Saturday September 4th

5:50 p.m.

Five days to Stalag 14 (school) and counting. I got my uniform out of the back of the wardrobe. Angus must have been using it as his lair by the look of it. I bunged it in the washing machine and hoped the bits of feather would come off.

I did cheer myself up a bit because I thought of something funny to do with my beret. Which we are forced to wear by the Oberführer (Miss "Hawkeye" Heaton).

6:00 p.m.

Phoned Rosie.

"I've thought of something really cool to do with the beret this term."

Rosie said, "I thought we were going to do the rolling it up into the sausage and pinning it under our hair at the back routine again?"

"Yeah I know, but what about this... what about if we use it as combination beret and lunchbox?"

Rosie said, "How do you mean?"

I had to explain, patiently. It is not easy being the leader of the gang. I sympathise with Richard Branson on this one, although I still see no reason for his ridiculous beard.

Anyway, I said, "Pop your sandwiches or crisps or whatever into the beret, then tie it on to your head with your scarf. *Voilà*, beret and lunchpack all in one."

"Hawkeye would go mad."

"Exactamondo, *ma petite amie.*'

Rosie said, "You are a genius." She is not wrong.

Sunday September 5th
5:10 p.m.

Au secours and *sacré bleu*!! Just walking to the park to meet the gang when I saw Call me Arnold, the vicar. I ducked down behind a car to hide until he had gone by. But the car was his car. When he got in he saw me crouching down. I had to pretend I was looking at a really interesting pebble.

God will know that I was hiding from his maidservant.

Still, I don't know how I could possibly be made to suffer more than I am already.

5:45 p.m.
Now I know. Cousin James is coming round tomorrow.

Midnight
If he gets all weird like he has done in the past and attempt to kiss me or anything, I may go mad.

Monday September 6th
10:00 p.m.
Cousin James asked me if I wanted to play strip poker. I was so embarrassed, I just said, "I don't know how to play poker," and he said, "Well, let's play strip snap, then."

I pretended I could hear the phone ringing. When he left, five million years later, I noticed there was something lurking under his nose. I thought it was a bogey at first, but sadly I now think it was a sort of moustache. Erlack!

Wednesday September 8th

10:00 p.m.

Mum came in my bedroom and asked if I wanted a wake-up call for Stalag 14 tomorrow. I said, "Oh, hello Mum, what are you doing in?"

She patted me on the head and said, "Goodnight, my sweet-natured little elf."

Nothing seems to bother her now that Vati is coming home. She might have put his moustache out of her mind but I haven't. In fact, to remind her I have drawn a moustache on the heart she put in the calendar.

10:30 p.m.

Washed my hair but couldn't be bothered drying it. I know if I sleep on it while it is damp I will wake up with the "stupid hedgehog" look. There will be bits sticking up all over the place, so I am sleeping with my pillow tucked under my neck and my head sort of drooping over the other side.

This is how Japanese Buddhist people sleep – it's probably whatsit... zen. They probably do it because it lets their chi flow free. Chi is energy that is in your body it says in my Buddhist book. Heaven knows I need as much energy as I can get for working out my plan for SG retrieval.

I think all the blood may have drained into my head from my shoulders.

11:00 p.m.

What happens if you get too much extra blood in your head? If you were meant to have two shoulders and a neck's worth of extra blood in your head you would have a bigger head, surely?

Or inflatable ears that could accommodate the extra blood and so on. Do Japanese have big ears?

Perhaps that is why Wet Lindsay's ears are so huge – because she's got Japanese ancestors. I wouldn't be surprised.

That would explain her tiny legs.

But not her big goggly eyes.

Thursday September 9th
8:00 a.m.

Woke up all snuggled down under the covers. I must have dropped asleep and forgotten about my zen position. My awake mind said, "Ha-so, I am a Japanese zen person ha-sleep with head h-over end of bed." But my English subconscious took over when I was asleep and said, "Snuggle down, you know you want to..."

Bathroom
8:10 a.m.
OhmyGodohmyGod... my hair looks like I've been electrocuted. No time to wash it. I'll have to gel it down.

8:30 a.m.
Pant pant, rush rush. Jas waiting for me.

She said, "Why do you look like Elvis Presley?"

As we ran up the hill towards school, we could see Hawkeye standing like a ferret by the gates. Oh here we go again... the beret patrol!!!! I hadn't got mine on. No time for the "sausage" or the "lunchpack". Only one thing for it. I fished the beret out of my bag and pulled it right down over my ears. You could only just see my eyes.

When we ran past Hawkeye she shook herself like something nasty had made a nest in her knickers.

"Two minutes to assembly; don't start the term with a detention."

Oh very caring. "Hello, Georgia, welcome back," would have been nice.

As we dashed to the cloakroom I said to Jas, "Imagine her having a boyfriend! Erlack, no no, I must pull my mind away from that otherwise I'll start imagining her snogging or something. Urgh!!!! Urgh! I've done it now: I've let it in my brain!!! Hawkeye getting up to number seven on the snogging scale. Putting her tongue in someone's mouth. Maybe Herr Kamyer in his lederhosen. Urghhhh. Erlack. Get out, get out!!!"

I ripped off my beret and coat and went into the main hall.

Rosie, Ellen, Jools and Mabs – otherwise known as the Ace Crew – were all there. I gave them our special Klingon salute. They looked at me like they had never seen me before. Had they forgotten all we had shared after so little time? I felt a hand on my shoulder. It was Hawkeye. What fresh hell? She looked down her big beaky nose at me and hissed, "Take this, make yourself presentable and get back here as quickly as you can, you stupid girl."

I looked down and saw that she had given me a comb. When I went into the loos I saw my hair had gone the shape of my pulled-down beret because of the superdooper hair gel.

Sacré bleu! I feel like *un* nincompoop.

9:00 a.m.

Took my usual place next to Rosie and Jas. Our revered headmistress "Slim" Simpson (so called because she weighs about a ton) lumbered on to the stage. I whispered to Rosie, "Crikey, she has got chins on her chins."

Slim bored us half to death by telling us what fabulous treats were ahead of us this term. Exams (yippee!); the challenge of modern languages and physics with Herr Kamyer (superdooper!!!); a school trip to the escarpments of the Lake District (oh marvy!!!)...

As she said each thing Rosie and I were clapping our hands together in delight until Hawkeye gave us the evil eye. Good grief.

Break
11:00 a.m.

Jools, Ellen, Mabs, Rosie, Jas and I met behind the tennis courts for a confab. Elvis Attwood, the grumpiest caretaker in the universe, shouted at us as we passed his hut, "I've got my eye on you lot. Don't come sneaking into my hut otherwise there will be trouble."

He's beyond bonkerdom. He came to a school dance and did some exhibition twisting on stage until his back went and he had to be taken to casualty. That's when we started calling him Elvis.

I waved and shouted back, "Greetings, oh mad one."

We were grumbling and moaning as we sat down. As usual in this fascist hell-hole we have been split up in class and not allowed to sit together. I have my "pal" Nauseating P. Green next to me. She wears those glasses that look like they have been made out of jam jars, which is very unfortunate. She's got really bulgy eyes anyway. Rosie said, "I think there must be a touch of the goldfish in her family genes."

As we ate our snacks you could see right up Jas's skirt. I said, "Jas, do you always wear those huge knickers? A small dog could creep up a knicker leg and you wouldn't know."

"Well I like to be comfy."

"They're not very sexy, are they?"

"You said you thought little knickers were stupid. Remember Lindsay's thongs?"

"Shut up, don't upset me. You know how visual I am.

Now not only have I got Hawkeye snogging Herr Kamyer in my brain, I've also got Wet Lindsay's thongs."

Ellen said, "Anything happening with you and Robbie?"

I explained about my glaciosity and maturiosity plan. They all nodded wisely. We are a very wise group. Full of wisdomosity. I am almost certainly wiser than God, who doesn't seem able to grant the simplest of requests. Which is why I have turned to Lord Buddha.

Rosie spoilt the moment of wisdomosity by saying through a mouthful of cheesy snacks. "What in the name of pantyhose are you talking about?"

4:45 p.m.
At the end of my glorious day today Elvis made me pick up a sweet wrapper in the corridor. All because I did my VERY funny impression of him doing the twist and then his back going. If he doesn't want people to make jokes at his expense he should stay indoors. He's a barmy old fascist. I bet he goes round dropping sweet papers on purpose.

5:05 p.m.
Jas phoned, all breathless and excited.

♥ 115

"I've got two letters from Tom."

I said, "He's only gone to Birmingham."

"I know, but... well... you know."

No, I don't know.

5:15 p.m.

Libby and Mum came home. Libby has had her first day at kindergarten which I think is a good thing as it will make her less mad.

5:16 p.m.

Wrong. Libby has made me something to wear at kindergarten. She was ramming it on my head. I said, "Steady on, Libby, be gentle with my head. What is it you have made?"

"It's nice!!!"

"Yes. I know. But what is it?"

She looked at me like I was a halfwit and put her face nose to nose with mine. She said really slowly, "For... egg!!!"

"For my head?"

She hit me. "No, no, no, bad boy... for your EGG!"

Mum came in.

116

"Look, Georgie, she's made you an egg cosy."

"Well why is she trying to put it on my head?"

"She must have got mixed up. Maybe she thinks the teacher said 'head cosy'." And Mum started laughing like a drain. Libby joined in while I just sat there.

7:00 p.m.

What is there to laugh at? I am on the rack of love. Life is a sham and a facsimile and a farce.

7:15 p.m.

But at least I have an egg cosy.

8:00 p.m.

I am soothing myself by pampering my mind and body. I am pampering my mind by reading (an article about mascara) and I am pampering my body by eating a LOT of chocolate.

9:00 p.m.

Now I feel worried, fat, but very well informed about mascara. Which is a plus.

Wednesday September 15th
Assembly
9:00 a.m.

Does Slim go to a special evening class on how to be boring? She was going on about tiny people with small heads or the poor or something. I don't know, who cares? Well obviously someone cares, and maybe I will care again one day, but at the moment all my caringness is used up on myself.

RE
10:00 a.m.

Despite my tragedy I did cheer up a bit in RE. Honestly. Miss Wilson lives in the land of the very mad. Where does she get her stockings from? It can't be a normal shop. It must be a circus shop. They are all thick and wrinkly like an elephant has been wearing them. Perhaps they are Slim's cast-offs?

Rosie sent me a note: Dear Gee, Ask Miss Wilson if God has a penis.

Even in my tragedy it made me laugh and Miss Wilson said, "Georgia, what is funny? Perhaps you could share the joke with us all."

"Er... well, I was just wondering if God had..."

Rosie looked at me in amazement.

Miss Wilson was encouraging me in my religious curiosity. "You were wondering if God had...?"

"Yes, if God had a... beardy thing?"

Miss Wilson unfortunately did not realise how very funny I was being. She went on and on about the fact that he wasn't really a bloke with a beard in the sky but more of a spiritual entity. She didn't need to tell me that there is no big bloke in the sky. I know that. I've tried often enough to speak to him and get stuff. Hopeless. That is why if she had bothered to ask me I would have told her that I have become a zen Buddhist.

1:15 p.m.

What is it with Elvis? Jas and me were innocently moaning by the back of the science block and he comes along. Ears flapping in the wind. Raving on and on.

"What are you two up to?"

I said, "Nothing."

"Don't give me nothing. I know you two. You've probably been messing about in my hut."

What is the matter with him? And why does he always

wear a flat hat? I wonder if his head is flat underneath it? Probably. As we walked away I said to Jas, "He's obsessed with us going in his hut. He's ALWAYS saying we go in his hut. He goes on and on about it, like a budgie. Why does he go on and on about it?"

Jas was walking along. I said, "Why? On and on and on about us going in his poxy hut. Why us? Why keep accusing us of going in his hut? Why?"

Jas said, "Because we go in his hut."

"So?"

5:00 p.m.

Jas's room at her house. Jas has just popped down to the kitchen to make me some nutritious snack (Pop-Tarts) to cheer me up. I'm just not interested in anything, though.

5:03 p.m.

God her room is tidy. It's pathetically tidy. All her cuddly toys are neatly lined up in size order on her bed. I'm going to mix them up for a hilarious laugh. Ho hum, pig's bum. She's even got a box with "letters" written on it. I wonder if she's got a drawer that says "enormous pants" on it. There are some letters in the box. Probably private ones. It says PRIVATE on the top of them. Probably private, then. Probably letters that Tom has written to Jas. Very personal and private, I'd better put them away.

5:16 p.m.
She calls him HUNKY!!!! This is hilariously crap!! Absolutemento pathetico!!! HUNKY!!! Tom!!! Hahahahahaha.

5:18 p.m.
He calls her Po!!! Like in the Teletubbies. Good grief, that is sad.

5:19 p.m.
Po, for heaven's sake.

5:20 p.m.
My lips are sealed vis-à-vis Hunky and Po.

5:21 p.m.
Even though it is very very funny I must never mention Hunky or Po.

5:23 p.m.

Jas comes back in. I say, "How is Hunky?"

My bedroom
7:00 p.m.

Jas is not speaking to me because I happened to find some personal letters of hers... She's so touchy."

10:30 p.m.

And unreasonable.

Thursday September 16th
8:20 a.m.

On the way to school. When I got to our usual meeting place Jas had already set off, walking really fast ahead of me. I yelled, "Hang on a minute, Po!!" But she ignored me.

Honestly, people really take themselves seriously when they have got a so-called boyfriend.

In a sort of a way it was very funny walking behind Jas. She walked really fast for about five minutes but she is not in tiptop physical condition. In fact, the only exercise she gets is lifting Pop-Tarts and putting them in her mouth.

Anyway, she got tired and had to slow down so then I could catch her up. I walked about half a metre behind her: it was annoying her quite a lot but she couldn't say anything as she is not speaking to me.

By the time I got to the school gates I was walking about ten centimetres behind her. Her beret was practically sticking up my nose.

She tried to escape me in assembly by standing next to Rosie but I squeezed in between them and looked at her with my face really near hers. She was all red and furious. Even her ears were red. Tee hee.

11:00 a.m.

Followed Jas into the loos. I went into the next cubicle to her and talked to her through the walls.

"Jas, I love you."

"What are you doing? You're being stupid!"

"No. YOU'RE being stupid, Po."

"It was really mean of you to read my private letters."

"They were only from Hunky."

"You shouldn't read people's private things."

"How would I know anything if I didn't?"

There was a bit of a silence from the other side of the wall. Then she said, "What do you mean?"

I went on reasonably, "I wouldn't even know you were called Po if I hadn't read the letters."

She was on the edge of bamboozlement. "Yeah, but that's not the point... I..."

"You shouldn't have secrets from your very best pal."

"YOU have secrets."

"I don't – I even told you about my sticky-out nipples."

"Well, Tom says they stuck out because it was cold."

I couldn't believe it. The bell went for the end of break and I heard Jas flush the loo and go out. I rushed out of my loo and set off down the corridor, following her. "You told Tom... about my sticky-out nipples???"

I couldn't believe it. My nipples had been made a public mockery of a sham... I was so incensed I barely noticed Wet Lindsay talking to some unlucky fourth former. Although I did notice that she looked like an owl in a school uniform.

I was hissing at Jas. "You discussed my nipples with Hunky... I can't believe it!!!"

Then from behind me I heard Wet Lindsay's voice,

"Georgia, your skirt is tucked up in your knickers... I don't think it sets a very good example to the younger girls."

Then she went off, sniggering in a pathetic sniggering owl sort of way.

5:00 p.m.

In the bath. That is it. I am on the warpath. I am now a loner. I have no friends. My so-called best friend only likes stupid Hunky and discusses my private body parts with him. And then he probably goes and discusses it with his older brother. And he and the SG have a good laugh.

5:15 p.m.

Angus is sitting on the side of the bath. He is drinking the water even though it has got bubble bath in it. His whiskers are all soapy.

5:20 p.m.

Now Libby has wandered in. Come in, everybody, why don't you? I'm only having a bath. Naked. I'm surprised Mr and Mrs Next Door don't pop in for a bit of a look.

I said to Libby, "Libby don't push Angus like that, he'll—"

5:21 p.m.
Angus is soaking and furious. When I fished him out of the bath he savaged my hand. Libby couldn't stop laughing. What a life.

6:00 p.m.
Jas phoned. I said, "What do you want, nipple discusser?"

She said, "Look, can't we call it quits? I won't mention the Hunky business again if you forget about the nip nips incident."

I didn't want to give in because I was in too bad a mood so I just went, "Huh."

But then I was all agog attention-wise because she said, "Tom phoned and told me The Stiff Dylans are doing a gig at the Crazy Coconut club a week Wednesday. AND WHAT'S MORE Dave the Laugh is going to be there. AND WHAT'S MORE my mum is staying at my aunt's in Manchester."

6:02 p.m.
Thinking.

6:05 p.m.
Thinking and eating cornflakes. Hmmm.

6:07 p.m.

Obviously this is it!!! This is my chance to implement the elastic band theory. I have to go to The Stiff Dylans gig and get off with Dave the Laugh. In front of the SG. This will serve the twofold purpose of maturiosity (being at a nightclub) and glaciosity (getting off with another boy). SG will be very jealous. He will want to come pinging back (the elastic band theory).

11:00 p.m.

I must start softening Mum up so that she will not be suspicious when I say I am staying at Jas's on Wednesday night.

Saturday September 18th
Morning
10:00 a.m.

Mum nearly dropped Libby when I said, "Do you want me to get anything for you while I am in town this afternoon?"

She said, "Sorry, love, I thought for a moment you offered to do something for me. What did you really say?"

Even though I was irritated by her I kept a lovely smile on my face. "Oh Mutti... as if I never do anything for you!"

She said suspiciously, "Why are you smiling like that? What have you got on that is mine? If you have borrowed my gold necklace I'll go mad."

I snapped then. "Look, what is the matter with you? How can I ever be a nice person if you are so suspicious all the time? What are you, a mother or a police dog? Do you want to do a body search before I go out? Honestly!!!"

Then I remembered my Operation Elastic Band just in the knickers of time. I said nicely, "I just thought you might want me to bring something back for you. I know how busy you are, that's all."

In the end I think I convinced her, which is a bit of a drag as now I've got to lumber home with waterproof panties for Libbs. Hey ho. What sacrifices I make for the SG. I've almost forgotten what he looks like.

10:05 a.m.
I've remembered what he looks like. Yum yum yum.

1:00 p.m.

Miss Selfridge changing room. I tried on a size twelve T-shirt and I couldn't get it on. Jas (very loudly) said, "I think your breasts are definitely getting bigger, you know."

This was in the packed communal changing room and everyone looked round.

I said, "Er... Jas... I think there is someone in Australia who might not have heard you properly."

Rosie and Ellen met us in Luigi's coffee bar. I told them about The Stiff Dylans gig and my plan vis-à-vis Dave the Laugh. Rosie was eating the foam from her coffee with a spoon and slurping. So was Ellen. It was stereo foam slurping. After ten years had gone by Rosie said, with the spoon in her mouth which was very unattractive but I didn't say... anyway, she said, "So you're going to the gig so that you can get off with Dave the Laugh and that will make the SG into an elastic band?"

How difficult can life be? Very, very difficult, that's how. I said patiently (well, at least without hitting her), "Yes, yes, thrice yes!!!"

More slurping. She was obviously thinking about my masterplan (or mistressplan actually, as I had thought of it and I am a girlie). Then she said, "Can I borrow your brown leather boots?"

4:00 p.m.

Lugged home Libby's waterproof nick-nacks. All quiet on the home front when I got in. Where was everyone?

9:30 p.m.

Early to bed, early to rise, makes a... whatsit.

10:00 p.m.

I may wear some false eyelashes for the gig. I must be careful though, last time I tried them the glue tube burst and I couldn't get my eyes apart for twenty minutes.

Tuesday September 21st

4:15 p.m.

Boring day apart from when Wet Lindsay got her bag caught on her foot and fell up the science-block stairs.

11:00 p.m.

Libby in bed with me. I don't know why she can't sleep the right way up, her feet keep poking me in the eye.

11:10 p.m.

I wonder what Dave the Laugh looks like?

Friday September 24th
Morning break
11:00 a.m.

Ellen told me that her brother and his mates go out on "cat patrol".

I said, "Do they really like cats, then?"

She said, "No, him and his mates are the cat patrol and they go out looking for birds... you know, chicks... girls."

Good Lord.

Lunchtime
12:30 p.m.

Ellen says that her brother also calls breasts "nunga-nungas".

I know I shouldn't have asked but somehow I just had to.

Ellen said, "Well, he says that if you get hold of a breast and pull it out and then let it go... it goes nunga-nunga-nunga!"

I may be forced to become either a celibate or a lesbian.

Afternoon break
2:30 p.m.

Me and Ellen were sitting in the loos with our feet up against the back of the doors, so that the Hitler Youth (prefects) wouldn't know we were in there and send us into the torrential rain. The Hitler Youth call it a "slight shower". They'd still say that if the First Years were being swept to their deaths by tidal waves. Or if Elvis's hut was bobbing along with a sail up, or... anyway, who cares what they say?

I said to Ellen through the cubicle wall, "Is your brother a bit on the mad side?"

I could hear her crunching her crisps. She thought about it. "No, he's quite a laugh, really. He calls going to the loo 'going to the piddly-diddly department'."

I could hear her through the wall, laughing and choking. I just sat there staring at the loo door. After a bit she controlled herself and said, "If he's going to the loo to do number twos he says, 'I'm just off to the poo-parlour division'." And she was off, wheezing and choking again. *Sacré bleu.* I am surrounded by *les idiots.*

3:30 p.m.

If it's cold, Ellen's hilarious brother says it is "nippy noodles".

4:15 p.m.

Walked home. Thinking about the difference between girls and boys. For instance, when girls walk home we put on lippy and make-up. We chat. Sometimes we pretend to be hunchbacks. But that is it. Perfectly normal behaviour. When the Foxwood boys come out they hit each other, trip one another up and stuff leaves or caps down each other's trousers. Ellen told me that sometimes her brother sets fire to his farts.

On the way to my house we passed through the park. There is a park Elvis. He is supposed to be the park keeper but mainly he prods at things with a pointy stick. Oh and his second job is to yell, "I can see you!" at innocent snoggers in bushes.

We hung around on the swings for a bit just to annoy Park Elvis. Rosie (who by the way, since the flaming fringe incident is an ex-smoker) said she had made it up with Sven her Swedish boyfriend. She fell out with him because he said to her parents, "Thank you for your daughter, she is, how you say? *Jah...* a great SNOG."

I said, "How can you tell he's sorry? No one can usually understand a word he says."

And she said, "He knitted me a nose warmer."

It's really not worth asking.

Ellen said, "What about Dave the Laugh?"

I said, "What about him?"

"Well, do you really fancy him?"

"I don't know. I don't know what he looks like."

"Well, what is the point, then?"

"Well, he's like... erm... a red herring. In my elastic band strategy."

They all looked at me. It was no use them all looking at me like I know what I am talking about. I'll be the last one to know what I am talking about, believe me.

4:30 p.m.

My so-called private bedroom.

Angus was in my bed. I suspect not alone. I daren't lift the cover in case it's like in that film where there was a chopped-off horse's head in the bed.

6:07 p.m.

Lying on the floor on cushion but at least Angus is nice and comfy. In Mum's *Cosmo* it says, "Buddhism is the new optimism."

Okey-doky. That's what I'm going to do. Be a cheery Buddhist. Om hahaha om.

Monday September 27th
Sports
2:50 p.m.

It's windy and rainy. Naturally these two facts mean that Miss Stamp our games mistress (who is definitely Hitler reincarnated in a gym skirt... she even has the little black moustache)... Anyway, these two facts mean that Adolfa has decided that the best thing we can do is... play hockey outside!!! I'd write to the newspapers to complain but I'll probably drown out on the hockey pitch.

In bed
9:30 p.m.

Brrr. If I have pneumonia and die and never get to number ten on the snogging scale I'll blame Adolfa. Just because she doesn't have a life. Even now I'm only just getting feeling back in my bottom.

10:30 p.m.
When Mum said goodnight I took my opportunity and said, casually, "Mum, can I go and stay round at Jas's on Wednesday night? Her mum says it's OK if it's OK with you. We're doing a science project together... I mean me and Jas not me and Jas's mother – that would be stupid."

(Shut up, shut up now. Leave it! Don't babble on, she'll get suspicious and you will say something really stupid.)

Mum said, "You don't usually do your homework, Gee. This is a bit of a change of heart."

"Hahahaha – yeah right... I..." (Careful, careful, don't say anything stupid.) "...I... thought I might be a scientist." (Too late, she's bound to rumble me now!)

"A scientist – not a backing singer, then?"

"No."

"Hmmm."

"So can I?"

"Oh yes, I suppose so. Night-night."

Result!!!!!! Yesssss!!!!

Wednesday September 29th
Operation Elastic Band
Kitchen
8:00 a.m.

I grabbed a piece of toast and mumbled, "I'm off now, see you tomorrow night."

Mum didn't even look up from trying to fasten Libby into her dungarees. Libby had her porridge bowl on her head. Mum said, "OK, love, bye. Kiss your sister bye-bye."

I said, "Pass," I had kissed Libby before when she had been eating porridge and I didn't want the experience again. I blew her a kiss. "Byeeeeee!"

Phew. Now then, quickly out of the door. Victory!!!!! I've packed all my clubwear and make-up and so on in my rucky. Here we go with Operation Elastic Band.

Just at the end of the path when Mum came out of the house, shouting, "Georgie, what do you mean, 'See you tomorrow night'?"

OhmyGodohmyGodohmyGod.

I laughed casually (sounding a bit like a casual hyena). "Oh I knew you would forget, I'm staying at Jas's tonight – remember?"

She looked blank.

Inwardly I was shouting, "LET ME GO!! SHUT UP, SHUT UP!! I MUST HAVE THE SEX GOD. LET ME GO. LET ME GO. YOU HAVE HAD YOUR LIFE!!!!" Outwardly I said, "Mum, I have to go, I'll be late – see you tomorrow."

Yessss!!! I am cool as *le* cucumber. Or possibly *le* ice cube.

3:50 p.m.
Last bell. Jas and I ran down the hill. Only five hours to get ready.

I said to Jas as we ran, "Mutti was really suspicious this morning when I reminded her I was staying at your house. It was like she didn't believe me. You know, like I am bound to be lying."

"You are lying."

"Oh picky, picky, Jas."

Jas's house
5:00 p.m.
A nourishing meal to set us up for the evening: oven chips, mayonnaise and two fruit Pop-Tarts (for essential vitamin C). In Jas's room we put on some groovy music and started

getting ready. Jas had a bit of a moony attack when she looked at Tom's photo by her bed. She started sighing and saying, "I just can't seem to get in the mood to go out."

I pointed at her with my mascara brush. "Jas, snap out of it, you know that Hunky would want you to go out. He phoned you up to tell you about it. He wouldn't want you moping about: he wouldn't want you to let your mates down by staying in. He wouldn't want to come home and find out that your mate had stabbed you with a mascara brush."

Jas was a bit huffy, but she got my nub. As she was putting her hair up she said, "What will you do with Dave the Laugh when you have got off with him?"

"How do you mean?"

I was stalling for time. I'd only really thought as far as getting my make-up on. The rest of it was a bit of a haze of a dream.

"Well, will you be... like his girlfriend then? Will you snog him?"

Luckily the phone rang. We both answered it. It was Rosie. She and Sven were calling from a phone box.

"We just rang to say we've made up this great new dance; it's called 'the phone box'."

She played a radio down the phone and in the background I could hear a lot of grunting and shuffling and Sven going, "Oh *jah*, Oh *jah*, hit it, lads!" or something in Swedish or whatever it is he speaks. Gibberish, normally. Not English, anyway. Then there was a bit of what sounded like tap-dancing. Rosie came back on the phone all breathless. "Brilliant, eh? See you in the next world... don't be late!" And she slammed the phone down.

9:15 p.m.
Left the house to catch the bus down town to the Crazy Coconut. I had so much make-up on I could hardly move my face, which is a plus really because it meant I wouldn't be tempted to go for full-on smiling. I was a vision in black leather. Prayed to God Mutti didn't go through her wardrobe before I could sneak things back in.

When the bus arrived and we got on I couldn't believe it. The driver was Mobile Elvis!! Sadly he remembered us and said *"Bonsoir"*. And charged us full fare.

Crazy Coconut
9:30 p.m.

Rosie and Sven turned up. Sven was wearing silver flares. Good Lord. When he saw us he started twisting his hips, saying, "*Jah*, groovy. Let's go, babies!!!!"

The whole queue was looking.

I said to Rosie, "Does Sven always have to be so Svenish?"

Then the van with The Stiff Dylans in it arrived. Robbie got out. Oh bum, all my glaciosity turned to jelliosity.

He saw us and said, "Hi."

I went, "Nung." (I don't know what "nung" means, it just came out.)

The queue started to move and he sort of looked at me for what seemed ages, then he said, "Don't get into any trouble."

I was so mad. How dare he tell me not to get into any trouble? Now he had said that I was going to get into LOADS of trouble just to show him.

I'd show him how much maturiosity I had. At least I would if I managed to get in past the bouncers without them saying I was under age. I said quietly to Rosie and Jas and Sven, "Be really cool."

That's when Sven lifted me up under one of his huge Swedish type arms and shouted at the bouncers, "*Gut* evening, I have the bird in the hand and one in the bushes, thank you!" and strode in.

I don't know whether they let us in because we looked mature or whether they were so amazed by Sven they didn't notice us.

Anyway, Operation Elastic Band was underway.

11:00 p.m.

Us girls went to the loos and did some emergency make-up repair work. It was quite dark and sort of red lightish in the loos. I was just thinking we looked like groovy chicks around town when the Bummer Twins walked in. I say walked but they waddled. Jackie was wearing a dress that was SO tight. Not a wise choice for a girl who is not small in the bottom department. She is so common. They were both smoking fags (*quelle surprise*). Jackie said, "Oh look, they must be having a sort of crèche here while the grown-ups are clubbing."

She went off into the loo. I could hear her weeing. It sounded like a carthorse. Alison was looking down her nose at us. I'm surprised she could see anything past the huge spot that was on it. She looked like she'd got two noses.

The club was amazing. It had loads of flights of stairs all leading down to a big dance floor, and a stage at one end. You had to go down the stairs from the loos to get to the dance floor. I hoped that no one could see up my skirt because I couldn't remember what knickers I had on. Jas would be all right with her biggest knickers known to humanity.

There were flashing lights and mirror balls and laser beams. The music was really loud and rocking. Rosie and Sven did their phone box dance. Sven was yelling "Whoop!" and "Hit it, lads!" They had loads of space to dance in because nobody wants to be flattened by a huge bloke in silver trousers.

Jas shouted in my earlug. "There's a gang of Tom's mates by the bar – can you see them? Over there. Dave the Laugh is probably one of them."

Jools said, "Yeah, but which one? There's ten of them to choose from."

I said, "Is anyone laughing?"

Jools looked at me. "Why?"

"Well, if he's called Dave the Laugh everyone will be laughing around him."

We looked across at the lads who were mostly looking around the room. Then I had another thought. "But what if he is called Dave the Laugh because HE laughs all the time?"

We looked again; now they were all laughing.

Jas for once in her life went all decisive and sensible (it was a bit scary, actually). She said, "I recognise one of them, he's called Rollo, he's been round to Tom's house. I could ask him who Dave the Laugh is."

I said, "Yeah, OK, but be really cool, Jas. Just find out which one is Dave the Laugh so we can look at him. But don't mention anything about anything."

Jas said, "I am not a fool, you know."

I didn't know that, actually.

Jas went over to the lads and I could see her going chat, chat, nod, nod, nod, wiggle, wiggle, wiggle, flickey fringe, flickey fringe... (Why does she do that? It is so annoying.)

I was acting really cool, doing a half-smile and sort of nodding along to the music. Sipping my drink, waving at people, even ones I didn't know. Then Jas came back. She was all breathless. She POINTED really obviously at a dark-haired boy in black combats. "That's him!"

Naturally he saw her pointing at him and he shrugged his

shoulders like he was asking a question. Jas then turned to me and POINTED again... AT ME, and nodded like one of those nodding dogs.

I couldn't believe it. It was unbelievable, that's why. My face was like a frozen fish finger. All rigid and pale. (But obviously not with breadcrumbs on it.)

I said out of the corner of my mouth, "Jas, I'm going to kill you. What in the name of your huge knickers have you said?"

Jas said huffily, "I just said, 'Who is Dave the Laugh?' and Rollo said, 'This is Dave the Laugh,' and Dave the Laugh said, 'Why?' and I just said, 'Because my mate Georgia really rates you'."

I was going to kill her and then eat her.

Out of the corner of my mouth – because Dave the Laugh was still looking – I said, "Jas! You told him I FANCIED him? I cannot believe it."

Jas said, "Well I think he's quite cute. If I didn't have Hunky I would..."

Just then SG walked by carrying his guitar. On his way to the stage to do the first set. He smiled as he passed. Even though in my heart I wanted to leap into his arms like a seal I ignored him. I looked through him as if he was just a floating guitar in midair.

Midnight

The Stiff Dylans were playing and I was dancing with Rosie and Sven and Jas. Jools and Ellen had gone off with some of Tom's mates. They were all quite fit-looking boys, actually, but... there is only one Sex God on the planet. SG looked sooooo cool; it's not fair that he is so good-looking. All the girls were looking at him and dancing in front of him. They had no style. Every time he came off stage there would be some girl talking to him. I tried not to look but I couldn't help it. What if he got off with someone in front of me? How could I bear it? There was a moment when our eyes met and he smiled. Ooohh, Blimey O'Reilly's trousers, he'd got everything... back, front, hair, teeth... I could feel my snogging muscles all puckering up but I thought NO! Think Elastic Band.

I made Jas go to the loos with me for a bit of a break from the tension. The Bummer Twins were still in there. I could hear them talking from one of the cubicles and a spiral of smoke coming under the loo door. Do they live in the lavatories? I said to Jas, "Perhaps the Bummer Twins have trouble in the poo-parlour department!!" and we both got the hysterical heebie-jeebies. I had to hit Jas on the back to

146

stop her choking to death. And we had to reapply mascara twice.

On our way back to the dance floor Dave the laugh stopped me!! He said, "Hi."

I said, "Oh hi." (Brilliant.) And I half-smiled, remembering to keep my nose sucked in.

He said, "Are you Georgia?"

1:OO a.m.
Dave the Laugh is actually nice-looking in a sub SG way... and er... quite a good laugh.

2:OO a.m.
Dave the Laugh has been dancing with me a lot. He's a cool dancer. He even did a bit of mad dancing with Sven. I don't think he expected Sven to pick him up and kiss him on both cheeks, but he took it well. We all left the club together. I saw SG looking over at us as he cleared up his gear. There was some drippy blonde hanging about wanting his autograph or something (on yeah! Emphasis on the something). Time for a display of maturiosity and glaciosity. Dave the L. said, "Georgia, are you walking to the night bus stop?"

♥ 147

I made sure that SG was looking then I laughed like a loon on loon tablets. "Hahahahaha, the night bus! You make me die, Dave, you're such a laugh!!!!"

Dave looked a bit on the amazed side. He probably didn't think the night bus was his biggest joke. Me and Jas and Dave walked along. When we got to the bus stop there was a bit of an awkward pause. Jas was standing really close by like a goosegog. How was my plan vis-à-vis getting Dave the L. to go out with me going to happen if she just hung about like a goosegog? I kept raising my eyebrows at her but she said, "Have you got something in your eye? Let's have a look."

As Mrs Big but Stupid Knickers was prodding about at my eye Dave's bus came. He gave me a peck on the cheek and said, "Well, this is my bus. It was a great night; maybe see you later." He looked me in the eyes for a second, winked and then got on the bus.

As Mrs Loonyknickers Goosegoghead (Jas) and I walked home I was all confused.

"Does Dave the Laugh like me or not? He winked at me – what does that mean? SG definitely noticed us leaving, didn't he? And he saw me really laughing at what Dave the Laugh was saying."

Jas said, "That's when I thought Dave the Laugh might have gone off you, because he said, 'Are you catching the night bus?' and you nearly split your tights in half laughing. Your face went all weird and your nose sort of spread all over your—"

"Jas."

"What?"

"Shut up."

"Well, I was just saying."

"Well don't."

"Well I won't, then."

"Well don't."

"I won't."

"Well don't."

There was a bit of welcome silence for a bit then Jas said, "I won't."

She is so INCREDIBLY annoying.

3:00 a.m.

And she takes up loads of room in bed. I had to make a sort of barrier out of her cuddly toys to put down the middle of the bed. To keep her on her own side.

What does Dave the Laugh mean, "See you later"?

♥ 149

3:30 a.m.

Do I want to see him later even if he does mean "See you later"?

4:00 a.m.

If the Sex God was really jealous he would ring me up tomorrow and try to get me back.

Or maybe he is not fully extended elastic band-wise.

Thursday September 30th

3:00 p.m.

I fell asleep in German. Herr Kamyer is a very soothing teacher. I drifted off when he started telling some story about Gretchen and a dove in a dovecote. (Don't even ask, as I have mentioned before, the Germans are a mystery to me since I learned about the Heimlich manoeuvre.)

4:30 p.m.

On the way home we practised our new grasp of the German language.

I said to Jas, "What is 'a dove in a dovecote' in the German type language?"

Jas said, "Er... *'ein Duff in ein Duffcot'*, I think."

"Ach gut... so... Jas... Du bist ein Duff in Duffcot nicht wahr?"

Jas said, *"Nein, ich nicht ein Duff in Duffcot."*

I said, *"Jah."*

Jas said, *"You have just said I am a dove in a dovecote."*

"You are."

"You're bonkers."

I think I might be hysterical.

4:45 p.m.

So tired when I got in that I thought I would just have a little snooze.

5:00 p.m.

"Ginger, ginger, me home!!!"

Oh Lord, it was my dearly beloved sister. I heard her clattering up the stairs. Then a bit of deep breathing, and bumping, "Here we are, Ginger."

Then she and Angus got in bed with me. And they weren't alone. There was scuba-diving Barbie and Charlie Horse. And something really cold and slimy.

I shot up in bed and looked down at her. "Libbs, what is that?"

She gave me her idea of a lovely smile, which in her case

is terrifying. She scrunches up her nose and sticks her teeth out. I don't know why she thinks that is natural. She said, "It's nice."

I looked under the covers. "What is? Oh God."

Mum called up, "Libbs, where has your jelly rabbit gone?"

Giganticus pantibus

Monday October 4th
9:30 a.m.

No news from either SG or Dave the so-called Laugh.

Geoggers
10:00 a.m.

Brrr. It's only October and it's like Greenland here. Well, apart from the ice floes and Eskimos and polar bears. It is, as Ellen's amusing brother would say, very "nippy noodles" today. I didn't mean ever to start saying things like that, but it is really catching. What's more, just because I said it all the gang is saying it. It's like brain measles. In geoggers Rosie put up her hand and said to Mrs Franks (who is not what you would call "fun"), "Mrs Franks, could I just pop to the piddly-diddly department, please?"

Mrs Franks said, really frostily, "What is the piddly-diddly department, Rosemary?"

And Rosie said, "Well it's not the poo-parlour division."

We all laughed like stuffed animals. Mrs Franks didn't. In fact she said, "Grow up, Rosemary Barnes."

She let Rosie go though, and started to explain something indescribably boring about the wheat belt. Behind her Rosie started lolloping out of the door like an orang-utan. She was trailing her arms on the floor. It made me laugh A LOT. But silently, as no one really wants to do two hours' detention.

Break
11:00 a.m.

They are a bunch of sadists here. We get forced to go out into sub-Antarctic conditions. Even Elvis Attwood won't come out of his hut and he is half human, half walrus. Meanwhile the so-called prefects and staff get to hang around in the warm. Wet Lindsay, the Owlie One, said to me, "If you wore skirts that were a bit longer you might not be so chilly."

I said to Jas, "Did you hear a sort of hooting noise, Jas?"

Me and Jas sheltered out of the icy winds behind a wall but we were still cold, so we had an idea. We thought we would button our two coats together to make a kind of big sleeping bag. We fastened the buttons of Jas's coat into the buttonholes of mine. Then we buttoned the buttons of my coat into Jas's buttonholes. With us in the middle. All nice and snug. It did make it very difficult to walk and unfortunately we had buttoned ourselves up a bit far away from our bags. Our bags with our nutritious snacks in them (Mars Bars and cheesy snacks). We tried synchronised shuffling to get to them but Jas tripped and we fell over. We were laughing, but not for long, because the Bummer Twins arrived.

Jackie looked down at us all tied together in our coats and said, "Look, Ali, the little girls are playing a little game. Let's join in."

And then they sat on us.

And they are not small girls.

Alison said, "Fancy a fag, Jackie?"

We heard them light up. We were just trapped there.

Then Jackie said, "Oooh look, someone has left some cheesy snacks for us. Fancy one, Ali?"

Me and Jas were the Bummer Twins' armchair.

My bedroom
5:30 p.m.

No phonecalls.

Mutti came in.

I said, "Oh come in, Mum, the door is only closed for privacy." I said it in a meaningful way but she didn't know what I meant. She was all pink.

"Dad phoned again; he sends his love, he's really looking forward to seeing you. He's got you a present."

I said, "Oh goodie, what is it? Sheepskin shorts?"

She started that tutting thing.

I don't think she has asked me one thing about myself for about four centuries. What is the point of procrastinating... no I don't mean that, what do I mean? Oh yeah... procreating... What is the point of having children if you are not going to take any notice of them? You might as well get a hamster and ignore that.

5:35 p.m.

Oh yippee.

This is my gorgeous life:

1. I haven't been kissed for a month; my snogging skills will be gone soon.

2. I have a HUGE nose that means I have to live for ever in the Ugly Home. Address:

> Georgia Nicolson
> Ugly Home,
> Ugly Kingdom,
> Ugly Universe.

3. My Red Herring plan has failed.
4. I am the Bummer Twins' armchair.

6:00 p.m.

Mum called up. "I'm just taking Libbs to the doctors'; she needs her ears cleaning out."

Oh please. Save me from that thought.

6:30 p.m.

Phone rang. If it's Po moaning on about Hunky I'll go BERSERK!!

6:45 p.m.

I'm seeing Dave in the swing park after school on Friday. He got my phone number from Tom through Jas! Good grief. The Red Herring has landed. I'm quite excited, I think.

Am I?

He said it would be "groovy" to see me again.

He also said he hoped it wouldn't be too nippy noodles in the park. He made me laugh.

I am still only using him as a red herring, though.

8:00 p.m.

Mum came back with Libby. I was busily trying to save myself from starving to death by eating cornflakes.

I said, "The doctor didn't find my fishnet tights in Libby's lugholes, did he?"

Mum seemed to be in even more of a coma than normal. She said, "I borrowed them for salsa dancing with Uncle Eddie."

Charming. I'll have to boil them before I wear them again.

Mum said, "They've got a new doctor at the surgery."

Silence.

"He's very good."

Silence.

"He was so nice to Libby – even when she shouted down his stethoscope."

What is she going on about?

"He looked a bit like George Clooney."

9:40 p.m.

When I went up to bed she kissed me and said, "You haven't had your tetanus injection renewed, have you?"

What is she talking about?

Tuesday October 5th
10:30 a.m.

Rosie said she might go across to Sweden land with Sven in the Chrimbo hols. I said, "Are you sure? You're only fourteen and you've got your whole life ahead of you. Are you sure you want to go to the other side of the world with Sven?"

She said, "What?"

I said, "Going to the other side of the world with Sven – is it a good idea?"

She said, "You don't know where Sweden is, do you?"

"Don't be stupid."

And she said, "Where is it, then?"

I looked at her. Honestly. As if I don't know where Sweden is. I said, "It's up at the top."

"Top of what?"

"The map."

And she went, "Hahahahahahahaha."

I think she must be a bit hysterical.

I may forgive her. Because so am I.

Maths

10:35 a.m.

Oh good grief, welcome back to the land of the crap. The Bummer Twins sent round a note: *Meet in the Fourth Year classroom as 12.30 today. Everyone comes, and that means you, Georgia Nicolson and your lesbian mates.*

I wrote a note to Jas and the others.

Dear Fab Gang,

This is it. Things have got sheer desperadoes. We have to put our feet down with firm hands. I for one am no longer prepared to be the Bummer Twins' armchair!!! Meet in the science block at 12.15. Or be square.

Gee-gee

xxxxxxxx

12:32 p.m.

Hiding from the Bummer Twins in the science-block loos. Jas, Jules, Rosie, Ellen, Patty, Sarah, Mabs and me... all in one cubicle. We have to keep our feet off the floor so that no one will know we are in here. It's hard to keep your balance when there are eight of you standing on one loo seat.

Alert, alert!!!! Two people came into the loos. I recognised their voices. It was Wet Lindsay and one of her mates, Dismal Sandra.

Wet Lindsay said, "Honestly, some of the younger girls are so dim. One of them came to see me and asked me if she could get pregnant from sitting on a boy's knee."

Jas mouthed at me, "Can you?" Which I thought was quite funny but I couldn't laugh otherwise we would end up quite literally down the pan.

I wanted to look over the top of the cubicle so that Owlie would know I had seen her in the loo. Seen her removing her thong from her bum-oley!!!

Then Owlie's weedy mate Dismal Sandra said, "What's happening with Robbie?"

I was full-on, attention-wise.

♥ 161

Wet Lindsay said, "Well he says he doesn't want to get serious because of college and the band and everything."

I nearly yelled out, "It's not that, Owlie, it is because he DOESN'T like you..."

Dismal Sandra said, "So what will you do, then?"

Lindsay said, "Oh, I've got my ways, I'll charm him back in the end. He's not seeing anyone else, he says. I expect he's still upset about us splitting up."

Oh yeah, in your dreams, Owlie.

Physics
1:30 p.m.

Herr Kamyer was twitching about in his sad suit. It's sort of tight round the neck and short round the ankles. Do normal people wear tartan socks? Anyway, he was adjusting his spectacles and saying, "So zen, girls, ve haf the interesting question about ze physical world. Ver question is (twitch twitch), vich comes first... ze chicken or ze eggs?"

No one knows what he is talking about so we just carried on writing notes to each other or making shopping lists. Ellen was actually painting her toenails. You would think that Herr Kamyer would notice that she had her head underneath the desk, but he didn't seem to.

He really does jerk around. He sort of blinks his eyes and screws up his nose and flings his head round all at once. Someone said it was because he has had malaria. Once when he was walking across the playground and it was icy he had such a spasm that he slipped and crashed into the bike shed. Elvis had to restack sixty bikes. He grumbled for about forty years. You would think Elvis would have more sympathy for the afflicted. As he is so afflicted himself.

Suddenly about ten girls started sneezing really violently. Really violently, like their heads were going to blow off. Their eyes were streaming and they were stumbling for the door. Jackie Bummer managed to say, "Oh we must be... ATISHOO... ATISHOO... allergic to something in the science lab, Herr Kamyer. ATISHOO!"

They all got sent home in the end.

I found out later what the Bummer Twins' meeting was about. They had made everyone at the meeting put bath crystals up their noses in the middle of physics, and that had brought on the sneezing attacks. All because the Bummers wanted to go to some club in Manchester, and needed to be home early.

Good Lord. Three days to my date with the Herring.

♡ 163

5:00 p.m.

Jas made me go home with her. She is planning a special celebration for when Tom gets home.

"It will be one year since we first met on the day he gets back!"

I just looked at her.

"And look!" Before I could stop her, she pulled up her skirt and pulled down her voluminous pants to show me her stupid heart tattoo. "I've been washing round it!"

She went on and on about what she was planning to do. Even though I found some matchsticks and put them over my eyelids so it looked like they were holding my eyes open. Eventually I said, "Look, why don't you do a nice vegetable display for him?"

Midnight

Honestly, Jas is so mad and touchy. And violent.

Wednesday October 6th

4:30 p.m.

After swimming today Miss Stamp came into the showers to make sure we all went in. She says we pretend to have a shower and that we are unhygienic. That is why she must supervise us. But really it is because she is a lesbian.

She watched a few of us go through (twirling her moustache). She shouted, "Come on, you silly ninnies, get in and get out!"

I dashed in in the nuddy-pants and was soaping myself like a maniac in order to get out quickly because Miss Stamp is a lesbian and might... well might... er... look at me. As if that wasn't bad enough I had to be on even more red alert because Nauseating P. Green lumbered into the shower next to me. What if she accidentally touched me? It's a sodding nightmare this place, like the Village of the Damned. If P. Green fell against me I would be smickled with Nauseatingness. She really is a most unfortunate shape. What on earth does she eat? All the pies, that is for sure. In fact, she has no shape. You can only tell which way up she is because of her glasses.

As I was getting dried I did feel a bit sorry for her because the Bummers had hidden her glasses while she was in the shower. She blundered around in the elephantine nuddy-pants, looking for them. The Bummers (who had managed to get out of games by "having the painters in" AGAIN! How

♡ 165

many periods can you have in a month?) were singing, "Nellie the elephant packed her bags and said goodbye to the circus." Then the bell went and the Bummers slouched off.

After they'd gone I gave P. Green her silly specs. She would have been in the shower rooms for the rest of her life otherwise. I hope she doesn't think that makes me her mate.

My bedroom
6:00 p.m.
No phonecall from SG. I wonder what Wet Lindsay means about using her charm on him? What kind of charm do owls have? Perhaps she will lay him an egg.

OhGodohGod. I'm getting the heebie-jeebies about my Red Herring extravaganza. How do I keep him as a herring without snogging him?

In *Bliss* in the letters page there's a letter from a girl called Sandy. She didn't really like a boy and was just using him to get off with someone else. Unfortunately the advice from Agony Jane was not "Carry on and good luck to you". The advice was "You are a really horrible girl, Sandy. You will never have a happy life, you cow." (Well, it didn't exactly say it in those words but that is what the gist and nub was.)

Decided to put the squeaking dolphins on and do some calming yoga. I used to be quite good at doing the sun salute last term until Miss Stamp surprised me in the gym with my bottom sticking up in the air.

Mmmmmm – much much better. All soothing and flowing. Lalalalala. Lift your arms up to worship the sun... breathe in... hhmmmmmm, then put your arms down to the floor like in "we are not worth" in football... aahhh, breathe out. Much calmer. Then swing to the right and swing to the left.

That's funny... if I turned to the right, then the left, a funny noise came out of me. Like a sort of wheezy noise. Could it be the dolphins? I didn't know they did wheezing.

Turned the tape off.

Now then, to the right, to the left. Oh no. Wheeze wheeze. If I went really fast from the right to the left I could hear wheeze wheeze wheeze. Which is not what you want.

It was really quite loud. Wheeze wheeze.

I'd probably caught TB from being made to do swimming in freezing conditions.

Mum came in with a cup of tea for me (without knocking, naturally) and caught me doing my wheezing movements. She said, "Are you dancing?" and I said, "No I'm not, I'm wheezing. I think I may have caught TB. It's not as if I'm in tiptop physical condition, with the kind of diet that we live on."

She said, "Don't be so silly, what is the matter?"

I didn't want her to listen to my wheezing but I had really freaked myself out. I let her listen. Side to side, wheeze wheeze.

She looked worried. (Probably thinking she would be chastised by the local press for child abuse and neglect.) She said, "Look, I think maybe we should pop up to the surgery and see George Cloon— er... the doctor. Get your coat."

Before I could protest she grabbed Libby and we were out of the door. As she started the car I said, "Look Mum, perhaps if I had a warm bath and you made me a nourishing stew..."

The next thing I knew I was in the doctors' waiting room. It was full of the elderly mad, all coughing. If I wasn't sick now I was soon going to be.

Libby got up on a table to do a little dance for everyone. It must have been something she had learned at kindergarten. It seemed to be sung to "Pop Goes the Weasel".

Libby sang (loudly and with a lot of actions), "Ha ha pag of trifle atishoo atishoo all fall down." The finale was her throwing up her dress and pulling down her panties.

Mum hadn't expected that bit. Who could? There was a lot of muttering from the very old. One woman said, "Disgusting!" which was a bit rich coming from someone wearing a balaclava.

Eventually we got to see the doc. Mum practically threw herself through the surgery door and I was left dragging Libby because she wanted to do an encore.

Mum said, "Oh, hello, it's us again!" in a really odd girlie voice. When I had got Libby's knickers back on I looked at the doctor. He was quite fit-looking actually, not at all the surly red-faced madman that normally treated us. There was a bit of the young George Clooney about this one.

He smiled (ummm) and said, "Yes, hello again, Connie. (Connie!) Hello, Libby." Libby gave him one of her very mad smiles.

Then he looked at me. I gave him my attractive half smile. (Curved lips but no teeth, nose snugly pulled in.)

He said, "And this must be Georgia. What can I do for you?"

Mum said, "Tell the doctor, Gee."

Reluctantly I said, "Well, when I do this..." (and I did the side to side thing), "...a wheezy noise comes out of me."

The doctor said, "Does it happen any other time?"

I said, "Er... no."

And he said, "Only when you go from side to side?"

And I said, "Yes."

And he said, "Well, I wouldn't go from side to side, then." And that was it.

Thanks a lot. All that money we (well, my parents) paid in taxes for his medical training not gone to waste, then!! He smiled at me, "When you move like that you force the air out of your lungs and it makes a sort of noise. That's all. They're just like bellows, really."

I felt like a fool. Two fools. It was Mum's fault for making me go. And she just hung around the doctor for AGES. Making conversation. Telling him she was learning salsa dancing. Did he like dancing? Etc. She kept saying, "Oh, I mustn't keep you," and then going on and on. It was only when the nurse knocked on the door and said one of the pensioners had fallen off their chair that Mum pulled herself together.

It was so embarrassing; Mum was practically dribbling.

She has zero pride. Now that my life was not in danger I noticed that even in the emergency of getting me to the doctor she had managed to squeeze herself into a tight top. You could see she was thrusting her "danger to shippings" at him. In a way, and I never thought I would say this, it will be quite a relief when Vati comes home.

In the car going home she said, "He's nice, isn't he?"

I said, "Mum, honestly, have a bit of dignity. You have made your life choice and the large Portly One is on his way home in a fortnight. It is not a good idea to risk your marriage, and also incidentally make yourself a laughing stock this late on in life."

She said, "Georgia, I really don't know what you are talking about."

She does though.

Do I have to worry about every bloody single thing round this place? When do I get a chance to be a selfish teenager? Jas's mum and dad have aprons and sheds, why do I have to have Mr and Mrs "We've Got Lives of Our Own" as parents?

The Bummer Twins have both got their knickers in a twist. They saw Nauseating P. Green coming out of a classroom, talking to Wet Lindsay. P. Green was probably telling her something about hamster feed. But the Bummers are saying she is a snitcher because they got done for knocking off school the other day. They call Nauseating P. Green "Snitcher the Elephant" now. They stole her *Hamsters Weekly*. I thought she was going to cry which would have been horrific.

Rosie sent me a note in Maths; it said, I am an equilateral triangle.

I wrote back and said, Does that mean all your angles are equal? and she wrote, I don't know, I'm a triangle.

I looked over at her and pushed my nose back like a pig. She did the same thing back. We could while away the hours much more amusingly if we could sit together.

I said that to Slim when she split us up last term. I said, "Miss Simpson, it is a well-known fact that if friends sit together they are encouraged to do more work." But she just shook in such a jelloid way I thought her chins would drop off.

She said, "The last time you two sat together, you set the locusts free in the Biology lab."

Oh honestly, not only has she got legs like an elephant, she has got a memory like one. How many times did we have to explain it was an accident? No one could have imagined they would eat Mr Attwood's spare overalls.

It is RE in a couple of hours so I will be able to have a decent chat to my mates instead of wasting time learning about stuff.

RE
1:30 p.m.

Rosie bunked off, she said she was going to the pictures with Sven. It must be nice to have a boyfriend, even if it was Sven. Oh well, ho hum, pig's bum. While Miss Wilson raved on and hitched up her sad tights I chatted to Jas. She wasn't officially speaking to me because of the veggie business, but I put my arm round her every time I went near her. In the end, to stop me and also to avoid more lezzie rumours, she forgave me (ish).

I said, "My vati is back on the nineteenth."

"Are you glad?"

"No, Jas, I said my vati is back on the nineteenth."

"I like my dad."

"Yes, but your dad is normal. He's got a shed. He does DIY. He fixed your bike. When my vati tried to fix my bike his hand got stuck in the spokes. We had to walk to casualty. I don't see why I had to go with him, everyone was calling out in the streets. And they weren't calling out 'What a brilliant dad you've got!'"

3:45 p.m.

I've managed not to think about meeting Dave all day. I am a bit nervous, though.

7:30 p.m.

In my bedroom. I've got my head under my pillow. This house is like a mental institution. In the front room Uncle Eddie and Mum are practising salsa. He turned up on his motorbike with a crate of wine. First of all he came snooping up to my room and opened my door (I don't know why we don't just take it off its hinges and leave it at that). I think he must have already had one crate of wine because he had a tennis racket he was pretending to play as a guitar and he said, "Georgia, this is a little song entitled, 'Get off the stove, Grandad, you're too old to ride the range'," then he laughed like King Loon and went off downstairs singing, "Agadoo doo dooo."

Honestly, what planet do these people live on? And why isn't it further away? Libby is in the airing cupboard with Angus. She says they are playing doctors and nurses.

11:00 p.m.

Does anyone care what happens to me?

I've got to meet Dave the L. tomorrow and somehow cover up the fact that I have a broken heart. I must be glittering and glamorous and brave.

I could hear Mum and Uncle Eddie giggling. I called down, "Mum... Libby is still in the airing cupboard if you were wondering, which I don't suppose you were as you are busy drinking and carrying on, and so on."

I wondered if I should confide in Uncle Eddie about Mum and George Clooney. Maybe he could have a word with her? Then I heard him coming upstairs again. He popped his very bald head round my door, the light glancing off it almost blinded me, and he said, "We can go and meet your dad on my motorbike if you like!!"

Yeah, in your dreams, oh mad bald one.

Friday October 8th
4:00 p.m.

The Fab Gang came round and we hung around in my room, listening to the Top 20. We were discussing Operation Red Herring. Well me and Mabs, Rosie, Jools and Ellen were, Jas wasn't there. Too busy waiting for her "boyfriend" to come home to worry about her very best pal in the world, who would never dream of putting boys first.

Ellen said, "OK, this is the plan. Say to the herring you have to be home by nine thirty because you are grounded for staying out too late."

I said, "Yes, that's good because it makes me seem sort of like dangerous and groovy but it also means I can get away if I need to. Good thinking, Batwoman."

Ellen went on, "And me and the rest of the gang will sort of be around the park any time things might be getting heavy."

I said, "Yeah. Because that is like double cool... almost with knobs. It means I have loads of mates that I just casually bump into at every whiff and woo AND it will stop any hanky panky in the snogging department."

Rosie said, "Exactamondo. Let's dance!"

And we did mad dancing to calm ourselves down.

7:00 p.m.

Met Dave the L. in the park. I went for casual glamour: leopard-skin top (fake, because otherwise Angus would have followed me thinking he'd made a new big mate) and jeans and leather jacket. It was a bit awkward at first. You know, like a first date. He is quite a good-looking bloke if you like red herrings. He said, "Hi, gorgeous," which I think is nice. I admire honesty.

He told me he wanted to be a stand-up comedian when he leaves school and I said, "You should have my life, that would give you lots of material."

He laughed. It was funny but I didn't feel nervous, not like with SG. I didn't say I wanted to be a vet or anything. I very nearly made sense.

As we walked along chatting our arms sort of brushed against each other a couple of times. I didn't mind and he's got a nice crinkly smile. But then he grabbed hold of my hand. Uh-oh. Hanky panky. Also he is slightly smaller than me and I had to do the bendy knee business so I could be more his height. I don't know what it is about boys these days but they seem on the small side. Or perhaps I am growing. Oh no. That might be it. I might only be half the size I am going to be. I might turn out to be a female Sven and that might be God's punishment for me turning Buddhist. Anyway, I lolloped along as best I could, trying not to be like an orang-utan. But, oh *sacré bleu* and *merde*, then Dave pulled me round to face him and took hold of my other hand. I had to lift up my shoulders so that I didn't have excess arm. I felt like that woman in *The Sound of Music*, you know, Julie Thing. Surely he wasn't going to start dancing round with me? Nooooo, he wasn't. He was going to kiss me!! Oh no, this wasn't in the Herring plan... Where were all my so-called mates???

As he looked at me and started to bring his face closer I said really quickly, "Have you noticed how when you go from side to side there is this sort of wheezing noise?"

But I only got to "Ha..." when he put his mouth on mine. I could have bitten through my tongue. I kept my eyes open because I thought that wouldn't be like a real kiss. But it made me go cross-eyed so I closed them. It was, in fact, quite a nice kiss. (But what do I know? I've only ever been with SG, a whelk boy and BG (Mark) who had such a huge gob that no experience with him can be counted normal. You've just got to be glad to escape without being eaten.)

My room
Thinking
11:00 p.m.

My so-called mates arrived at last. They gave us both a bit of a start, leaping out from behind a tree. Also if Rosie is thinking of taking up drama I would advise her against it. She said, "Oh hello, Georgia. It's YOU!!! What on EARTH are you doing here. I thought you were GROUNDED?" But she said it like somebody had hit her on the head with a mallet (which, incidentally, somebody should do).

11:30 p.m.

Hmmm. I am in a state of confusosity. I'd rate him as seven and a half as a kisser. Maybe even eight. He didn't do much varying pressure and his tongue work was a bit like a little snake. On the other hand he didn't do any sucking (like whelk boy) and there was no crashing of teeth. Or dribbling, which is never acceptable. He did nibble my lower lip a bit, which I must tell the gang about because it isn't on our list. It was quite nice. I might try doing it myself. When I retrap the SG.

Midnight

Also he didn't rest his hand on my basooma, which is a plus.

12:30 a.m.

Maybe he didn't rest his hand there because he thought he might never find it again? I wonder if my basoomas are still growing?

12:32 a.m.

Terrible news!! I can fit a pencil case underneath my basooma and it actually stays there for a second!!

I feel all hot and weird. Still, what else is new?

Saturday October 9th

11:50 a.m.

Angus is in love!!! Honestly. With Mr and Mrs Across the Road's Burmese pedigree cat Naomi. (I call her that, they call her Little-Brook-Running-up-a-Tree-With-a-Sausage-up-its-Bottom Sun Li the Third, or something foreign.) I saw Angus on their wall, giving Naomi a vole he'd killed. He was parading up and down sticking his bottom up in the air and waggling his tail about. Disgusting, really. Especially as he had a clinker hanging out of his bum-oley. Cats think that is attractive. So does Libbs.

Mr and Mrs Across the Road didn't seem too thrilled by his attentions. In fact, they threw stones at him. They are going to have to try a lot harder than that, he was brought up having bricks thrown at him. They should try a bazooka.

My room
2:30 p.m.

I must find some calm. I've got an instruction booklet on Buddhism from the library. Miss Wilson, who doubles as sad librarian, is beside herself with pleasure – she thinks I am taking religion seriously due to her excellent teaching. Sad really. She'll want me to go round for coffee at her house soon. I might go and ask her where she buys her tights. The book is called *Buddhism for the Stupid*. No, it's not really, but it should be.

Good grief. It's so boring. It's just all about world peace and so on, which is OK but you would think I could do that later. Once I was happy. And had got what I wanted.

4:00 p.m.

Jas turned up. She was really mopey like a cod.

"I got all ready for Tom to come home and then he called up from Birmingham and said he was going to stay on for a few more days. He says that he likes Birmingham and has got some great new mates."

I was thinking, Oh, good grief! As if I haven't got enough to worry about without having Hunky and Po in trouble. But I didn't say anything.

Jas moaned on: "He didn't used to like going out with mates, he used to like being with me."

I said wisely: "Remember he is a Jennings boy. He is the same as Robbie. Remember the elastic band thing, Jas... let him have his space. In fact, why don't you say you think you should have a break from each other for a bit? You know, to sort of find yourselves."

Jas said, "I know where he is, he is in Birmingham."

It's easier chatting to Angus. I kept on, though. "Don't be silly, Po! Anyway, I want to talk to you about Buddha. Do you know what Buddha says?"

"Didn't he say quite a lot?"

"Yes, but he said, 'When a crow finds a dying snake, it behaves as if it were an eagle. When I see myself as a victim I am hurt by trifling failures.'"

There was a silence and Jas started fiddling around with her fringe.

"Do you see?"

"Er... what has that got to do with Tom? He's not an eagle."

Honestly she is so dim. I explained, as patiently as I could, "It means, if you think your life is poo it will be."

"Well why didn't he say that?"

"Because a) he is Buddha and b) they do not have poo in Buddhaland."

5:30 p.m.

Phone rang. Mum yelled up, "Gee, it's for you... boyfriend."

Honestly, I could kill her. I went and answered the phone and sat down on a stool. It was Dave the Laugh. He said, "Hello, Gorge. I had a great time last night. I've just about recovered from meeting your mates. What are you up to?"

As I was chatting to him Libby came humming into the hall. She wanted to get up on to my knee.

I said, "Libbs, I'm on the phone, go find Angus to play with."

She gave me her frowniest look. "NO... UP!!! NOW!!!

183

BAD, BAD BOY." And she started spitting at me so I had to let her on my knee. Before I could stop her she was "talking" down the phone. "Hello, mister man. Grrrrrrr. Three bag pool, three bag pool."

Oh God. I struggled to get the phone off her and then she shouted, "Georgie has got a THERY big SPOT! Hahahahahaha."

I grabbed the phone back and put Libby on the floor. "Sorry about that, Dave, my little sister has... er... just learned to talk and, er she must have... er..."

Libby was singing, "Georgie's got a THERY big spot, lalalalala, THERY, THERY big spot... ON HER BOT... ON HER BOTTY."

6:00 p.m.
She's right, actually. How can you get spots on your bottom? I must have more vitamin C.

6:05 p.m.
Me and Jas chomping on bananas. Jas said, "Save the skins because they make really good face masks."

6:30 p.m.

As usual Jas is completely wrong. We washed off the banana on our faces; it felt disgusting.

I said, "I'm meeting Dave again tomorrow. He seems to really like me."

Jas was busy picking bits of banana out of her hair. "Does he? Why?"

"I don't know, he just does."

Bed
11:00 p.m.

Dave doesn't make my legs go jelloid and that is the point, isn't it? If a boy doesn't make you go jelloid you may as well be with your girlie mates... or boy mates that you are just mates with and no snogging involved.

11:30 p.m.

Oh, I don't know.

Midnight

Angus still on the wall looking down at Naomi the Burmese

sex kitten. She is rubbing herself against the wall, the little minx. I know what she feels like.

I wonder what the Sex God is doing now.

What shall I do about Dave?

1:00 a.m.

I really would truly prefer to put my head into a bag of eels than kiss Wet Lindsay.

1:15 a.m.

Sex God did take the bull by the nostrils and dump Wet Lindsay when he found true love (me). Even if he did then dump me.

1:30 a.m.

He was true to his feelings. Even though it upset Owlie he dumped her because it was the right thing to do (and it is always the right thing to do to dump Owlie).

Sunday October 10th
10:00 p.m.

Dave the L. turned up at my door earlier, wearing a false

moustache. He actually is quite a laugh. We went to the pictures and snogged again. He must be a bit surprised that my mates pop up every time we go anywhere. When Rosie put her head over the back of us in the pictures and said, "GEORGIA!!! HOW AMAZING!! What are you doing here?!!!" I thought he'd swallow his ice cream whole.

Monday October 11th
School
8:30 a.m.

I met Jas on the way to school. She was trailing her rucky along as we walked. I said, "Dave sent me a card today, it said, *Merry one week anniversary, gorgeous. Lots of love, D, kiss, kiss, kiss.*"

She didn't say anything. I said, "Jas, what are you doing?"

She was all pale, I noticed.

"I haven't heard from Tom and I tried to ring him and he was out."

"Ah yes, well."

"You said I should say, 'Have your own space, Tom'."

"Yes, well..."

"And now he's got loads of space."

"Ah yes."

"And so have I."

"Yes..."

"But I don't want it."

Oh good grief. I'm not going to be an agony aunt if all people do is moan on all the time.

Last bell
3:50 p.m.

Jas, Jools, Ellen, Rosie and me were lurking near the science block, hiding from the Gestapo (Hawkeye) who wants to ask me about the lunchbox beret idea. Everyone has been doing it. Slim told us not to be so silly; she said in assembly, "You are making a mockery of the school's good name in the community."

Anyway, we have taken her advice to heart and we are going to have a "blind day" instead. After last bell we went to the alleyway in between the Science block and main school, waiting for an opportunity to dash out of the gates when Hawkeye was not looking. We all had our lunchpack-berets on apart from old spoilsport knickers Jas.

Rosie said, "On the blind day next Wednesday the deal is we all shut our eyes for the whole morning and have to have minders that guide us around. From lesson to lesson."

I said, "Wait a minute, we have sports on Wednesday, it's hockey. That will be a laugh."

Jas said gloomily – she had been an unlaugh all day – "Hawkeye will stop us, with detention and so on."

Rosie said, "No, because we will explain that we are being sponsored and are doing it so that we will have a better understanding of the poorly-sighted."

That's when we saw something awful. The SG drove up to the school gates in his car and Wet Lindsay ran out and got in!

7:00 p.m.

In a way I feel free. If SG chooses Owlie over me then he is the loser. So be it. That is the Buddhist way. Omm. I will not be the crow finding the snake or whatever it found. Who cares? It's only a crow.

8:00 p.m.

I need a break from being a Buddhist for a minute. POOO!!! DOUBLE *MERDE*!!! Life really is a pooburger.

9:00 p.m.

Mum came in for a "chat".

"Dad's home in a week."

"Still time for a few serious medical complaints, then."

"What do you mean?"

"You and Doctor Clooney."

"Georgia, you're mad."

"Am I?"

"Look, all it is is that I think he's quite good-looking."

"Well that's because you are comparing him to Dad."

"Don't be rude."

"I'm not, I'm being factual."

"Anyway, you needn't worry, it's just innocent flirting."

"Yes it is for you but what if Doctor Clooney really likes you? And what about if he will be really upset if he finds out you are just toying with him? Like a toying person?"

She went off looking all worried. Good. That's two of us all worried and guilty. And confused.

9:30 p.m.

Dave phoned. He said, "I just called to say I really like you. Night-night."

Good grief.

I wonder if all heartless babe magnets feel guilty?

Tuesday October 12th
Hockey pitch
2:30 p.m.

Hockey match against boring old Hollingbury College. They really do think they are cool, but sadly they are about to find out that they are not.

I had a sneaky look in their changing room when I pretended to be fastening up my boots. It was a nightmare of thongs. I noticed Miss Stamp busily popping in and out, saying things like, "Don't mind me, I was just wondering if you had enough towels."

She was all red and keen. Running on the spot, and so on. Very alarming if you're not used to it. I noticed quite a few of the Hollingbury girls were rushing off into the loos when she came in. They were getting a bit jittery. So I used sporting tactics. I said, "Miss Stamp, I wonder if the

Hollingbury team would appreciate a bit of physio after the match. You know, if they had any little knocks or anything you could offer to... er... treat them yourself. Use those magic healing hands."

Adolfa was a bit suspicious. But she couldn't figure out my angle. I heard her go back into their changing room and say something about treatment. All of the Hollingbury girls shot out of the door and on to the pitch. Ah good, a nervous team, desperate not to get injured!! Result!!!

It's very nippy noodles. I've got three pairs of knickers on. I probably look like Nauseating P. Green from the back... or Slim. Still, better a fat bum than a numb bum. There is a little crowd supporting us, most of my mates actually. Although not Jas, she wasn't at school today. I hope she has not gone all weird because of Tom.

The slimiest wet weed who shall remain nameless (Lindsay) is captain of the team. Erlack... well I will not do anything that she says. In our pre-match talk she said, "So remember to watch me for instruction, and when you get into any kind of shooting position, watch for me to come and take on the shot."

Oh yeah, dream on, wet and weedy one. With a bit of

luck someone will knock her stick insect legs from under her. I am not saying I want her to be badly injured, just badly enough that she has to go away to a convalescent hospital somewhere (Mars) for a year or two. Thank you, Buddha. (You can see how I am not taking poo lying down.)

2:50 p.m.
Cracking match. I am playing a stormer, even if I say so myself. Zipping up and down the pitch, hitting the ball up to the forwards. Excellent passing!! I'm like David Beckham apart from the hockey stick and skirt and three pairs of huge knickers. Although who knows? Posh Spice may insist he wears sensible snug knickers in the winter time. She is a very caring person. But quite thin.

Half-time
No score
3:15 p.m.
Rosie, Ellen, Jools and Mabs are like cheerleaders. They have made up this song which goes, "One – two – three – four – go, Georgia, go!"

I said to them as I came off, "It doesn't rhyme," and Ellen said, "Well, it's too nippy noodles."

♡ 193

Brrr. She's right. I went into the loos to run my hands under the hot water tap. Oh no, the Bummer Twins had got Nauseating P. Green cornered in the changing rooms. She was blubbing. They didn't even look round when I came in. Jackie said, "So, Snitcher, what did you tell Lindsay about us knocking off school?"

Nauseating P. Green was trembling like a huge jelly elephant. "I... I... didn't say... anything..."

I thought I should shout at her, to help, "Tell them about your hamsters, P. Green, that will bore them to death and you can run off." But I looked at Jackie's big arms and thought I wouldn't bother.

As I was going out again the Bummers started shoving P. Green against the loo doors. Oh bum, bum.

Alison said, "We don't like snitchers... do we, Georgia?"

I said, "Oh, they're all right, I—"

Jackie shoved P. Green so hard that her glasses flew off. That did it. I could no longer be the Bummer Twins' armchair. I said, "Leave her alone now."

Jackie looked at me. "Oh yeah, big nose, what are you going to do about it?"

I said, "I'm going to appeal to your niceness."

She laughed and said, "Dream on, Ringo."

I said, "Yes, I thought that might not work, so this is plan two."

Actually there wasn't a plan two. I didn't know what I was doing. I was like a thing possessed. I leaped over to them and grabbed Jackie's fag packet out of her hand. Then I ran into the loos with it and held it over the toilet. I yelled, "Let her go or the fags get it!"

Jackie was truly worried then and had a sort of reflex action to save her packet of fags. Alison came towards me as well, leaving Nauseating P. Green trembling by herself. I shouted, "Run like the wind, P. Green!!!"

She picked up her glasses and just stood there, blinking like a porky rabbit caught in a car's headlights. Good grief! I tried to give her confidence. "Well, not like the wind, then, but shuffle off as fast as you can."

Eventually she went off and I was left to face the Bummers. I charged past them shouting, "Uurgghhhhgghhh!", that well-known Buddhist warrior chant. I chucked the fags out of the packet on to the floor. When I looked back as I dashed out of the door they were scrabbling around picking them up. I raced out on to the pitch for the second half to a big cheer from the

Ace Crew. I thought I may as well enjoy the game because the Bummers would be killing me immediately after it was over.

I noticed there were a few boys gathered at the opposite end of the pitch. One of them cheered when I ran on. Probably Foxwood lads. They sort of appeared any time there was the least hint of knicker flashing. Or nunga-nunga wobbling. I don't know how they knew, or had found out we were playing today. Probably Elvis Attwood got on the tom-toms in his hut and drummed out a message to let them know there was a match on. He was lurking around pretending to be busy, wheeling his wheelbarrow. There was never anything in it. Old Pervy Trousers. Anyway, let the lads look at my nunga-nungas if they wanted! Let my nostrils flare free. Let my waddly bottom waddle, what did I care??? I was going to be dead anyway when the Bummers got hold of me.

4:10 p.m.
Victory! Victory!!!!! We won one-nil.

It was a close match considering we were playing such a bunch of wets. One of their team blubbed when I accidentally hit her on the shin with my stick. I wonder if all the times I have been savaged by Angus have made me immune to pain? Anyway, it was a nil draw until the last few minutes. I raced up the wing and found myself in the opposition's penalty area. The Ace Crew were going, "Georgia Georgia!!" And then our so-called captain Wet Lindsay shouted from the left side, "Pass it to me, number eight!"

You know like in the movies when everything slows down and it's in slow motion? Well, I had that. I saw Owlie's face and her thin stupid legs and I thought, Hahahahahahaha! (Only really, really slowly.)

I kept the ball myself and raced for goal with it. I dribbled past one opposition player, then another. Tripped. Picked myself up, nipped the ball through someone's legs. The crowd were cheering me on. They were going BERSERK!! Then there was the goalkeeper. Good grief, she was a giant!!! But I feinted to one side of her and got past. Then there was just the open goal. I whacked the ball and scored!!!... just as Lindsay tackled me savagely from behind.

4:30 p.m.
Wet Lindsay tried to pretend that she had been "helping" me. Huh. Very likely... not.

Miss Stamp wanted Elvis to carry me to the sick bay but he said he had an old war wound and brought his wheelbarrow out on to the pitch. He said, "Get in. One of your mates will have to wheel it because I hurt my back serving this country."

Oh yeah. I said to Jools, "His back has probably seized up because he sits on his bottom all day."

Rosie wheeled me to the sick bay but I still couldn't walk even after the sadistic Adolfa Stamp had strapped up my ankle. While she was kneeling down in front of me bandaging it all my so-called mates were behind her doing pretend snogging. The Hollingbury girls didn't even bother to get changed, they just shook hands really quickly and got on their coach.

I hopped about a bit after I was strapped up but it was aggers. In the end Elvis said reluctantly that Rosie and Ellen and Jools could push me home in the wheelbarrow. Cheers, thanks a lot.

Elvis went grumbling back to his hut, saying, "Make sure you bring it back tomorrow... it's my own private equipment and shouldn't by rights be used for school business."

His own private wheelbarrow. How sad is that? Sensationally sad, that's how.

We set off, wheeling along. It wasn't very comfortable in

the barrow and there was the suggestion of something brownish in one of the corners. But I was being all brave and heroic as I was the heroine of the hockey universe. And attractively modest. For a genius.

When we got to the school gates Dave the Laugh was there!!! He had been one of the lads at the match!!! He has seen my gigantic bottom bobbling around on the pitch. Closely following my gigantic schnozzle, bobbling around. OhmyGodohmyGodohmyGod.

He was laughing like a loon as we squeaked up to him in Elvis's wheelbarrow. Then he got down on his knees and was salaaming and chanting "We are not worthy" to me.

He said to Rosie and Ellen and Jools, "Let me push the genius home." And as he pushed me along he sang that really crap song by that band that Dad thinks he looks like the drummer from – Queen. The song was "We are the Champions". The Fab Gang joined in really loudly. Everyone was looking as us as we went down the High Street. I don't suppose shoppers often saw anyone in a wheelbarrow. They probably had very narrow lives and travelled around by car. Or moped.

Dave the L. kissed me when he left me at my gate! In

front of everyone! And he said, "Bye-bye, beautiful. See you soon. Let me know how the ankle is. I'll bring you pressies."

When he'd gone the girls went, "Aaaahhh."

Ellen said, "He really is quite cool-looking. Has he done that nibbling thing again? I quite fancy the sound of that."

But he is just a herring. We must not forget this.

6:15 p.m.

Mum was quite literally ecstatic about my ankle. She just left me in the wheelbarrow outside the front door and got on the blower immediately. I could hear her talking to the doctors' receptionist.

"Yes, it really does seem quite bad. No, no, she really can't walk at all. Yes, well thank you."

Libby came trailing out with scuba-diving Barbie and got in the wheelbarrow with me. She gave me a big kiss. Don't get me wrong, I love my sister, but I wish she would wipe her nose occasionally. When she kisses me she leaves green snot all over my cheek.

Mum came outside and said, "The doctor will pop round after surgery, Gee. Will you just lend me your mascara? I've run out."

I said, "Huh, it's just one-way traffic in this house... if it was me, if the shoe was on the other boot, if I said, 'Mum, can I just borrow...'"

She wasn't listening. She called from indoors, "Hurry up, love, just get me it."

I yelled, "I can't walk, Mum! That is why the doctor is coming to see me. That's why I came home in a wheelbarrow."

"You don't have to walk, just hop out of the barrow and up the stairs and get the mascara."

Hop hop, agony agony, hop hop.

Why was I hopping around getting things for my mother who only wanted them so that she could make a fool of my father? (The answer to that question is I didn't want her poking around in my room. She might come across a few things that weren't strictly mine, things that in a word were – er – hers.)

I hopped into her bedroom and said, "It is pathetic and sad. You are trying to get off with a young doctor and my poor vati is coming home to a – a – facsimile of a sham!"

She just tutted and went on primping. She said, "The trouble with you is that trivial things are really serious to you, and stuff you should care about that is serious, you don't."

I said, hobbling off, "Oh very wise. Is that why you are

stuffing yourself into things that are quite clearly made for people a) smaller than you and b) several centuries younger than you?"

She threw the hairbrush at me. That's nice behaviour, isn't it? Attacking a cripple.

7:00 p.m.

Doctor Home-wrecker arrived. He strapped up my ankle again and gave me painkillers. I said, "I suppose that is my hockey career over. Do you think that perhaps I have weak ankles because of my diet?"

He laughed. He had a good laugh, actually.

Mum said, "Can I get you a coffee, John?"

John? John? Where did that come from?

Mum went off into the kitchen and I heard her say, "Take Angus out of the fridge, Libbs."

"He likes it."

"He's eaten all the butter."

"Teehhheeeeeheeee."

7:15 p.m.

I hobbled off to my room and played moody music really

loudly as a hint. It was ages before the door slammed. I looked out of my bedroom window. I could see John going off in his quite cool car.

7:45 p.m.

Lying on my bed of pain. Well, it would be if I could feel my ankle.

Mum popped her head round the door. She was all flushed. "How is the ankle?"

I said, "Fine if you like red-hot pokers being stabbed in you."

"That's my little soldier." She was humming.

Brilliant, a week before my dad gets back my mum starts a torrid affair with a doctor.

8:00 p.m.

Mind you, I would get tiptop medical priority.

8:30 p.m.

He might be able to get me a good deal on my nose job.

9:00 p.m.

I must get revenge on Wet Lindsay.

10:00 p.m.
I wonder how the Bummers will kill me?

10:10 p.m.
Why is the Herring so nice to me? What is wrong with him?

Wednesday October 13th
School
8:30 a.m.
Mum made me hobble to school. Unbelievable. She said a bad ankle didn't stop me learning things. I tried to explain to Mum that it would be just a question of hobbling in to be killed by the Bummer Twins, but she wasn't interested.

I made Jas wheel the wheelbarrow as I hopped along with a crutch. The Foxwood lads had a field day with us, shouting, "Where's your parrot?" and so on.

Jas had perked up enough to say, "I wonder how the Bummers will kill you?"

She sounded quite interested. She's only cheered up because Tom is coming home.

I managed to keep out of the Bummers' way for the

morning but eventually at lunchtime the fatal moment came. The Bummers cornered me in the loos. I tried to hobble off but they blocked the doorway. Here we go. Well at least death would solve the Dave the Laugh situation. Jackie just looked at me. She said, "Fancy a fag?"

What were they going to do, ritually set fire to me?

Jackie put a fag in my mouth and Alison lit it. Jackie said, "Cool," and Alison said, "Good call." And then they just went out.

What in the name of pantyhose did that mean? Why hadn't they duffed me up?

I hobbled over to the mirror to see what I looked like smoking. Quite cool, actually. I sucked my nose in. I definitely looked a bit Italian.

Out of the corner of my mouth I said, "*Ciao, bella.*"

But sadly smoke went up my nose and I had a coughing extravaganza.

I can't believe life. As I was having my coughing fit Lindsay walked in and booked me for smoking in the loos. I saw the Bummer Twins sniggering in the corridor.

Great. Stacking gym mats for the rest of the term. Elvis passed by and saw me hobbling and heaving mats around. He laughed.

4:00 p.m.

Left school limping along next to Jas. I think it's quite attractive if you like Long John Silver. I said to Jas, "You know, I think I am going to give up on boys altogether – tell Dave the Laugh it's over, forget the Sex God and just concentrate on lessons and so on. I might ask Herr Kamyer to give me extra tuition."

"He'd have a spasm to end all spasms if you did."

I said, "I think I might be over the Sex God anyway. When I saw him pick up Owlie in his car, that did it for me. Anyone who can go out with Wet Lindsay, with her stupid no forehead and sticky insect legs, and... er..."

"Goggly eyes?"

"Yeah, goggly eyes. Anyone who can do that has got something very wrong with them. You know, if he asked me out now I would say n–ung."

I meant to say "no" but that was when I saw him leaning against his car. The Sex God. Oh don't tell me he was waiting for gorgeous (not) Wet Lindsay. Pathetic. *Très* pathetic and *très très* sad.

I hobbled past him. He wasn't so very gorgey. Well actually, yes, he was. He was a Sex God. Really. He looked me straight in the eyes and I went completely jelloid. In fact, my other leg nearly gave way. He half-smiled and I remembered what it was like to be attached to his mouth. Somehow I kept hobbling. We'd got past him and I was feeling all shaky when he called after us, "Georgia, can I talk to you for a minute?"

OhmyGodohmyGod. Was this an elastic band moment? Jas was just goosegogging at my side. I said, "You walk on, Jas, I'll catch you up."

She said, "Oh it's OK, I'm not in any hurry. Anyway, you might fall over and lie for ages with no one to help you. Like a tortoise on its back or—"

I opened my eyes really wide at Jas and raised my eyebrows. After about forty years she got it and walked on.

Robbie said, "Look, I know I'm probably the last person you want to talk to, but... well... I'd just like to tell you something... I'm really, really sorry about what happened between us... I handled it really badly, I know. She, you know, Lindsay, just was like, so upset, and you were so young and I couldn't... I didn't know what else to do. I thought I'd be going away soon and that would just sort things out... but then I was at the match..."

God, was there anyone in the universe who hadn't seen my huge wobbly bottom and enormous conk bobbling around the hockey pitch?

SG was going on in his really sexy voice, "...and I saw how Lindsay deliberately hurt you... and I... I'm sorry. I've caused a lot of trouble and you're a really nice kid... Look, I'll..."

Then I heard, "Robbie!!"

Wet Lindsay was walking over towards where we were and I just couldn't handle any more. I hobbled off.

5:00 p.m.

OhGodohGodohGod. I love him, I love him.

He thinks I am a kid.

It's all a facsimile of a sham.

And in tins.

And pants.

And pingy pongos.

And *merde.*

He was at the match. He saw my giganticus pantibus.

But he still spoke to me.

Perhaps Jas is not as mad as she seems. Perhaps big knickers are boy magnets?

Oh I don't know.

Why does he still make me go jelloid?

6:00 p.m.

Dave the Laugh had left me a card at home which said, *One-legged girls are a push-over. Love Dave XXXXXX* And some chocolates. Oh GODDDDDDD!!!!

Saturday October 16th
11:00 a.m.

I am a horrible person. I have dumped Dave. I had to. It was really double poo. I thought he was going to cry. He turned up at my house with some flowers because of my injury. He is so sweet and it didn't seem fair to lead him on. I explained that he had only really been a red herring.

2:30 p.m.

Phoned Jas.

    "He said I was a user and, er... something else..."

    "Was it 'selfish'?"

    "No."

    "The crappest person in humanity?"

    "No."

    "Really horrible and like a wormey..."

    "Jas, shut up."

In bed
8:00 p.m.
Am I really horrible? Perhaps I am one of those people who don't really feel things properly, like Madonna.

10:00 p.m.
Personally I think I have shown great maturiosity and wisdomosity.

11:00 p.m.
Dave will some day thank me for this.

Midnight
Angus still on top of the wall across the road. Looking down at his beloved Naomi in her enclosure. He too is disappointed in love.

3:00 a.m.
Libby came in all sleepy. She said, "Move." And climbed in with the usual accoutrements – Barbie, Charlie Horse, etc. I've got about half a centimetre of bed. Marvellous. Bloody marvellous.

Monday October 18th
School
Break
2:15 p.m.

Well, at least life can't get any worse. Oh, I beg your pardon, yes it can. Raining again and cold and we have been forced outside by the Hitler Youth. I said to Wet Lindsay who was the prefect on duty, "It is against the Geneva Convention that we are forced outside in Arctic..." But she had locked the door and was sort of grinning through the window. She took off her cardigan as I was looking and wiped her forehead as if she was boiling. Oh *très amusant*, Owlie.

Jas and I wandered round to Elvis's hut to see if the old lunatic was in. If he wasn't we could sit in his hut for a bit and warm up. But oh no, there he was, reading his newspaper. Elvis had ear muffs on underneath his flat cap! Mrs Elvis must be very proud. I tapped on his little window so that I could say a friendly hello to him. But he couldn't hear because of the muffs.

I said to Jas, "As a hilarious joke I'll pretend to say something very urgent to him but I won't really be saying anything. I'll mime saying, 'Mr Attwood, my friend Jas is on fire!!!'"

So I went up to the hut door and I was mouthing, "Mr Attwood, my friend Jas is on fire!!!" and waving my arms wildly. In the end he took off his ear muffs, thinking that he couldn't hear me because of them. When he realised the joke he went ballisticisimus. He leaped up in a quite scary way for a one hundred and eighty-year-old man and came charging at us out of his hut. I hobbled off quite quickly. Unfortunately he didn't remember he had parked his personal wheelbarrow round the corner of his hut and did a spectacular comedy fall over it. I thought I would die laughing. Me and Jas went and bent over a wall at the back of the tennis courts.

I said to Jas, in between laughing and gasping for air. "Jas... Jas... he... he has got a flat head."

God it was funny. I had a real ache in my stomach from laughing too much.

French
3:00 p.m.
For a "treat" as it is Monday, Madame Slack taught us another French song. It was called "Sur le Pont D'Avignon". About some absolute saddos dancing about on a bridge. All I can say is that the French and me have a different idea of

having a cracking good time. Also, if I do go to French land, although I will be able to tell my new French mates that my blackbird has lost a feather, and be able to dance on bridges, I will not be able to get a filled baguette for love nor money.

At the end of the lesson Wet Lindsay came into the classroom in her role as Oberführer assistant. She smiled in a not attractive or friendly way and said, "Georgia Nicolson, report to Miss Simpson's office... NOW."

3:30 p.m.

Outside Slim's office. Oh dear. *Quelle dommage. Zut alors* and *sacré bleu* even. Now what? Unfortunately Wet Lindsay was my guard and as I looked at her I was reminded of her thongs lurking under her skirt. Going up her bum-oley. And it started me off again.

The jelloid one called me in. I was like a red-faced loon trying not to laugh. She said, "Georgia Nicolson, this is an unforgivable offence. This time you have gone too far. Berets worn like lunchpacks, noses stuck up with Selllotape, false freckles painted on noses, all these childish pranks I have put up with... Last term there was the skeleton in Mr Attwood's uniform, the locusts..."

213

Slim raved on and on, shaking like a gigantic jelly. "...I was hoping that you had grown up a bit. But to lure an elderly man, not in peak condition..." Blah blah blah.

It was useless my trying to explain. Mr Attwood has dislocated his shoulder and I am being held responsible. Fab. Anyway, the short and short of it is that I'm suspended for a week and Jas is on cloakroom duty. Slim said she was going to write a stiff note home to my parents telling them the circumstances. I helpfully offered to take the stiff note home myself but Slim insisted on posting it.

Hobbling home with Jas and the gang. I was a bit depressed. Again. I couldn't even be bothered putting my lunchpack-beret on.

I said to Jas, "Slim is so ludicrously suspicious! What she implied was that I would not take the note home and would pretend that I am not suspended!!"

Jas said, "Hmmm... What were you going to tell your mum after you had destroyed the note?"

"You're as bad as everyone else, Jas."

"I know, but just for interest's sake, what were you going to say?"

"I thought I might try the mysterious stomach bug. I haven't used it since last year's maths test."

4:00 p.m.

Home. Great. Life is great. Just perfectamondo. Suspended. Suspended just in time for Vati to come home and kill me. In love with a Sex God who calls me a kid. Called a heartless whatsit by Dave the Laugh. And the spot on my bum is like a boil. I wonder what Buddha would do now?

4:30 p.m.

Waiting for Mum to come home so I can break the brilliant news.

5:00 p.m.

Phoned Jas. Her mum answered.

I said, "Hello, can I speak to Jas?"

I heard her shouting to Jas, "Jas, it's Georgia on the phone."

And I heard Jas shout back, "Can you tell her I'll talk to her later. Tom's showing me a new computer game."

A new computer game? Are they all mad?

If I had called down and said that a boy was showing me a computer game my bedroom would have been full of parents within seconds!!

Unless that boy was my cousin James, in which case I would have been left up there for years, because my family doesn't seem to mind incest.

6:30 p.m.
Mutti went ballisticisimus about the suspension. Even though I explained how it was not my fault and how provoked I was by Elvis.

When she calmed down she said, "Don't you think you might have a bit of a stomach bug?"

I said, "Here we go. Look, Mum, this is no time to be visiting Doctor Gorgeous. We should be thinking about Vati."

She said, "I AM thinking of Vati. And do you know what I'm thinking? I'm thinking that he'll go mad if he comes back and the first thing he hears is that his first born has been suspended. Now, are you feeling a bit poorly?"

My room
8:30 p.m.

Mum "suggested" I went to bed early and thought about the important things in life for once. She's right. I will think about the important things in life. Here goes:

My hair... quite nice in a mousey sort of way. I still think that a blonde streak is a good idea, even after the slight accident I had last time I tried it. The bit that snapped off has grown back now, but I notice Mum has hidden all the toilet cleaners and Grandad's stuff that he puts his false teeth in when he stays. She really is like a police dog.

Anyway, where was I? Oh yes, eyes... Nice, I think, sort of a yellow colour. Jas said I've got cats' eyes.

Nose... Yes well, it doesn't get any smaller. It's the squashiness I don't like. It doesn't seem to have any bone in it. I still can't forget what Grandad said about noses, that as you get older they get bigger and bigger as gravity pulls on them.

8:35 p.m.

You can make a sort of nose sling out of a pair of knickers! Like a sort of anti-gravity device. You put a leg hole over each

♥ 217

ear and the middly bit supports your nose. It's quite comfy. I'm not saying that it looks very glamorous. I'm just saying it's comfy.

8:40 p.m.
It's not something I would wear outside of the privacy of my own bedroom.

8:45 p.m.
It's a good view from my windowsill. I can see Mr Next Door with his stupid poodles. He's all happy now that Angus has gone off poodle baiting in favour of the Burmese sex kitten.

8:46 p.m.
Oh hello, here comes BG, my ex, the breast fondler. At this rate he will be the one and only fondler. I will die unfondled. He must be coming home from football practice. I don't know how I could ever have thought about snogging him, he wears extremely tragic trousers. He is looking up at my window. He has seen me. He's stopped walking and is looking up at my window. Staring at me. Well, you know what they say – once a boy magnet always a boy magnet. I'm

just going to stare back in a really cool way. All right, Mr Big Gob, Mr Dumper. I might be the dumpee but you still can't take your eyes away from me though, can you??? I still fascinate him. He's just looking up at me. Just staring and staring.

Mesmerised by me.

8:50 p.m.
Oh my God! I am still wearing my nose hammock made out of knickers.

8:56 p.m.
Mark will tell all his mates.

8:57 p.m.
He will now call me a knicker-sniffer as well as a lesbian.

Midnight
Oh for heaven's sake! What now? Woken by loud shouting and swearing. Surely Dad is not home already? Looked through the window. It was Mr and Mrs Across the Road. They were hitting things in their garden, shouting and

shining torches. What on earth is the matter with them? This is no time for a disco inferno.

2:00 a.m.
Woke up fighting for breath from a dream about my nose getting bigger and bigger and my breasts getting bigger and bigger. And someone laughing and laughing at me. I couldn't seem to move anything except my head. Paralysis for being so horrid to Dave the Laugh. Libby was laughing like a loony. (Which of course she is.) She pulled my hair, "Look, bad boy!!! Aaahhh."

The weight was Angus curled up on my chest. Purring. I couldn't move, he weighs a ton. Big fat furry thing. I'm going to cut down on his rations. He's like a small horse.

Hang on a minute. He's not alone. He's got Naomi with him, curled up on top of him!!! Oh Blimey O'Reilley's trousers!

I managed to get them off me and they slunk off into the night – not before Angus had bitten my hand for my trouble. Naomi is a bit forward for a pedigree cat; she had her head practically up Angus's bottom as they went off.

I'll think about it in the morning. I mustn't do anything hasty. Like tell Mr and Mrs Across the Road.

Tuesday October 19th
8:45 a.m.

All hell broke loose. Mr and Mrs Across the Road came round "asking" about the Burmese sex kitten. Mr Across the Road had a spade and the words "Skinned and made into slippers" were mentioned. As she shut the door Mum said, "Honestly, Angus gets the blame for any bloody thing that goes on round here."

I said, "Yes... he's a scapewhatsit like me."

She said, "Shut up and get the balloons out."

Balloon city.
4:00 p.m.

The house is covered in balloons. I even made a banner for the gate, it says VELCOME HOME, VATI.

Libby has made something disgusting out of Playdough and bits of hair. She is wearing ALL of her dressing-up things: her Little Red Riding Hood outfit, fairy wings, deely boppers and, on top, her Pocahontas costume. She can hardly walk about.

No sign of Angus and Naomi. They will have made a love nest somewhere. Pray God my knickers are not involved in any way.

221

First of the loons arrive.
5:00 p.m.

Grandad almost broke my ribs; he's surprisingly strong
for someone who is two hundred and eight. He gave me a
sweet (!) and said, "Don't send your granny down the mines,
there's enough slack in her knickers!!"

What is he talking about? Mum gave him a sherry. Oh
good grief. That means he will take his false teeth out soon
and make them do a "hilarious" dance.

6:00 p.m.

Excitement mounts (not). Uncle Eddie and Vati turned up
on Uncle Eddie's pre-war motorbike. Vati leaped off the bike
in a way that might have caused serious injury to a man of
his years.

Mum and Dad practically ATE each other. Erlack!! How
can they do that? In public.

I think Dad was crying. It's hard to tell when someone is
as covered in facial hair as he is. He hugged me and went,
"Oh, Gee... I... oh, I've missed you! Have you missed me?"

I went, "Nnnyeah."

Then Mum gave me a look and I pretended my stomach

bug was quite bad. We'd "agreed" that we would do the stomach bug scenario early on, so as not to arouse suspicion tomorrow morning. I was beginning to feel quite ill, actually. It's weird having him back. At least Mum more or less ignores me. Vati tends to take an interest in, well, exam results and so on.

7:00 p.m.

More and more people arrived. The drive was full of cars and old drunks. Mum and Dad were holding hands. It is so sad to see that sort of thing in people who should know better. I wondered if I should tell Vati he was in a love triangle with George Clooney. But then I thought no, can't be bothered.

12:30 a.m.

What a nightmare! All the so-called grown-ups got drunk and started "letting their hair down". Well, those of them that had any.

Uncle Eddie was spectacularly drunk. He put one of Libby's rattles with a sucker bottom on his head, to look like a dalek. Libby laughed a lot. Uncle Eddie was going,

"Exterminate, exterminate," for about a million years. But then Libby wanted it back and Uncle Eddie couldn't get the sucker off his head. All the drunkards had to pull on it together, and when it eventually came off Uncle Eddie had a round purple mark about a metre wide on his forehead. Which actually was quite funny.

1:00 a.m.

I went down to tell them that some of us were trying to sleep, so could they turn down Abba's Golden Hits, please. I saw them "dancing". God it was so sad. Dad was swivelling his hips around and clapping his hands together like a seal. Also he kept yelling, "Hey you! Get off of my cloud!!" like a geriatric Mick Jagger, and as Mick Jagger is about a million years old you can imagine how old and ludicrous Dad looked. Very old and ludicrous, that's how.

Mum was all red and flushed – she was TWISTING with Mr Next Door and they both fell over into a heap.

Wednesday October 20th
12:30 p.m.

Up at the crack of midday.

Mum in the kitchen in her apron making breakfast for us all. Oh no, sorry, I was just imagining being part of a proper family where that sort of thing happens. In Nicolson land the M and D are still in bed, even Libby was in there with them. I tried to get her to come into bed with me last night but she hit me and said, "No, bad boy, I go with Big Uggy!" (That's what she calls Dad – Big Uggy.) Angus was somewhere with the sex kitten and I was just... alone in my room. In my bed of pain. Because my ankle still hurt, not that anyone cared. Very, very alone as usual.

As alone as a... er... an elk.

You never see elks largeing it up with other elks, do you? They are always on their own, just on a mountain. Alone.

Ah well, I decided to take a Buddhist viewpoint and just be happy that everyone else is happy...

12:45 p.m.

Doorbell rang.

I called down, "The doorbell to your home is ringing."

♥ 225

No reply from the drunks.

The doorbell rang again. It would be Mr and Mrs Across the Road wanting to search the house for Angus and the Burmese sex kitten.

Ring ring.

I yelled as I hobbled down to answer it. "Don't worry about the fact that I have a limp and a very serious stomach complaint that makes me too sick to go to school... I will get up and answer the door. You recover your strength from lifting glasses up to your mouths!"

Silence. Well, just a bit of snoring from Libby.

I opened the door.

It was the Sex God.

At my door.

Looking like a Sex God.

At my door.

The Sex God had landed at my door.

I was wearing my Teletubbies pyjamas.

He said, "Hi."

I said, "Hhhnnnnngggghhh."

1:00 p.m.

I got dressed as quickly as I could. The Sex God said he would meet me by the telephone box so we could go for a walk round Stanmer Park. I dithered for about five minutes about lippy. I mean, if there is going to be snogging, is it worth putting it on? But then, if you don't put it on, does it look like you are expecting to snog, and is that too much pressure for boys who might go springing off in an elastic band way again?

Ooohhhh, I could feel my brain turning to soup. I knew I'd say something so stupid to the SG that even I would know it was stupid. That's how stupid it would be.

I didn't take any chances with the nipple department. I wore a bra and a vest. Let them get out of that if they could.

I must be calm. Om. Om. OhmyGodohmyGodohmyGod. My tongue seemed too big for my mouth. Do tongues grow? That would be the final straw if I had a tongue that just lolled out of my mouth. Shut up, brain!

1:25 p.m.

There he was, leaning against the wall! He was just so cool. His hair was flopping down over one eye.

When he looked up I went completely jelloid. He said, "Hi, Georgia. Come here."

And I said, "My dad has grown a little beard and I thought I was going to be lonely as an elk."

What in the name of pantyhose was I talking about? I'd be the last to know as usual.

The SG HELD OUT HIS HAND... to me!!!! Something I had dreamed of. Do you know what I did? I shook it!!!

He really laughed then, and grabbed hold of my hand. We walked to the park. Holding hands. In public. Me and a Sex God. I honestly couldn't think of anything to say. Well I could, but it would only have made sense to dogs. Or my grandad.

In the park we sat down on the grass, even though it was a bit on the nippy noodles side. Unfortunately I did feel like going to the piddly-diddly department, but I didn't say.

He looked at me for what seemed like ages and ages, and then he kissed me. It was all surf crashing and my insides felt like they were being sucked out. Which you wouldn't think was very pleasant. But it was. He put his hand on my face and kissed me quite hard. I felt all breathless and hot. It was brilliant. We whizzed through the scoring system for snogging in record time. We got to number four (kiss lasting over three minutes without a break), had a quick breather and then went into five (open mouth kissing) and a hint of six (tongues). Yesss!!!! I had got to number six with the Sex God!!! Again!!!

Eventually we had a bit of a chat. Well, he chatted. I just couldn't seem to say anything normal. Every time I thought of something to say, it was something like, "Do you want to see my impression of a lockjaw germ?" or "Can I eat your shirt?"

He had his arm round my shoulder, which was good because then he got profile rather than full-frontal nose. He said, "I haven't been able to forget you. I've tried. I tried to be glad when you started seeing Dave. But it didn't work. I even wrote a song for you. Do you want to hear it?"

I managed to say "Yes" without putting on a stupid French accent or something. Then he sort of pulled me backwards on to him so that my head was resting on his lap. It was quite nice, but I could see up his nose a bit. Which I didn't mind, because he is a Sex God and I love him. It's not like looking up Cousin James's nose, which would make anyone immediately sick. But then I thought, if he looked down and saw me looking up his nostrils, he might think it was a bit rude. So I settled on closing my eyes and letting a half-smile play around my lips.

Then he started singing me the song he had written for me. There weren't many words – it was mostly, "And I really had to see her again." And then melodic humming and yeahing. Unfortunately he was sort of jiggling his knees for the rhythm so my head was bobbling about. I don't know how attractive that looked.

4:00 p.m.
The Sex God has left the arena. He wants us to be, like, official snogging partners after my fifteenth next month. He's going to tell his parents.

I am irresistible.

I am truly a BABE magnet.

Even in my Teletubbies jimjams.

Even without mascara on.

Life is fabbity fab fab!!!!

Yessssss!!!!!! And triple hahahahahaha-di-haha!!!!

5:00 p.m.
M and D eventually got up. I didn't care because I am in the Land of the Very Fab, in fact beyond the Valley of the Fab and into the Universe of Marvy.

Vati is in a hideously good mood. He keeps looking at things and going, "Aahh-h" and hugging me. I wish he would get back to normal. I wonder how long it will be before he drops this "happy family" nonsense and gets all parenty.

6:00 p.m.
An hour, that's how long.

I was on the phone when it started. Telling Jas about SG. I said to her, "Yeah, come round and I'll tell you all about it. It is so FAB. How long will you be? OK. Good. Yeah anyway, he just turned up in his car. He looked BRILLIANT – you know those black jeans he has got, the really cool ones with the raised seam that..."

Vati had gone into the kitchen to get a cup of tea. He came out, stirring it. Jas had just asked me what sort of jacket SG was wearing and I was beginning to tell her when Dad interrupted and said, "Georgia, if Jas is coming round why are you talking to her on the phone? Phones cost money, you know."

Oh, I wondered how long it would be before the fascist landed. I said to Jas, "Have to go, Jas, I may already have wasted two pence. See you soon."

7:20 p.m.

In my room, daydreaming about my wedding. Can you wear black as a bride? Dad came up and suggested we have a family "chat". I know what that means, it means they tell me what they are going to do and expect me to go along with it, and if I don't they call me a spoiled teenager and send me to my room.

But I don't care any more. I said to Dad politely, "Look, why don't we just skip the boring middle bit where I have to come all the way downstairs and you tell me what to do and I say no I don't want to and then you send me straight to my room. Why don't I just stay in my room?"

He said, "I don't know what you are talking about. Come into the front room. And what's wrong with your eyes? They look all bunged up, have you got a cold?"

"It's Vaseline, it makes your eyelashes longer."

He said, "Can't you stop messing about with yourself?"

As I went downstairs I was thinking he should try messing about with himself a bit more. He never had what you might call good dress sense but it's so much worse since he's been in Kiwi-a-gogo land. Today he's wearing tartan slacks which is a crime against humanity in anyone's language. Also he has clipped his beard so that it is just on the end of his chin. No side bits and no moustache, just a beard thing... on the end of his chin. When we went in the room Mum kissed him on the cheek and stroked his beard... How disgusting.

Anyway, I don't care because I am going out with a Sex God and life is fab. I said, "OK, I am sitting comfortably. Rave on, El Beardo."

El Beardo said, "Great news!!! I've been offered a cottage in Scotland, I thought we would all go there for a week together as a family. Spend some quality time there together. Mum and Libbs, Grandad, Uncle Eddie, we could even ask Cousin James if you'd like a bit of company your own age. What do you think?"

Sacré bloody *bleu*. *Merde* and poo!!! Is what I think.

Fortunately the doorbell rang and Mrs Huge Knickers and me scampered up to my room. My room, which as usual, was full. Libby was in my bed with scuba-diving Barbie, Charlie Horse, Angus and Naomi.

I said, "Go play downstairs with Daddy, Libbs."

But she just stood up on my bed and started dancing, singing, "Winnie Bag Pool, Winnie Bag Pool." She got to the bit where she takes off her panties, but I noticed they were suspiciously bulky, so I said, "Stop it, Libbs."

And she said, "Me let my legs grow."

"No, leave them on."

Too late. I thought Jas was going to faint. She doesn't have a clue what it's like to have a little sister. Me and Jas went off to the utility room for a bit of privacy. I was dying to tell her all about my snogging extravaganza, but she went raving on about Tom: "We went to the country."

Oh good Lord. Still I thought I'd better pretend to be interested otherwise I would never get to talk about myself. I said, "What for?"

"You know, to be on our own in nature."

"Why didn't you just go and sit in your room with some houseplants instead of tramping all the way to the country? You only snog there, anyway."

"No we don't."

"Oh yeah? What else do you do?"

"We looked at things."

"What things?"

"Flora and fauna and so on. Stuff we do in blodge. It was really interesting. Tom knows a lot of things. We found cuckoo spit and followed a badger trail."

I clapped my hands together and started skipping round the room. "Cuckoo spit!!! No!!! If only I could have come with you! Sadly there was a Sex God I had to snog."

Jas got all huffy and pink. It's hilarious when Jas gets miffed, and a reason in itself to make her irritated. She goes all red and pink apart from the tip of her nose which is white. Very funny, like a sort of pink panda in a short skirt and huge knickers.

She was all sulky, but then I put my arm round her. She said, "You can stop that."

I said, "I feel a bit sad though, because I'm so lucky and I can't help thinking about Dave the Laugh. He was a really nice bloke, and you know... er... a good laugh. It's sad that I have broken his heart."

Jas was poking around in Dad's fishing bag, which is not a good idea as he sometimes leaves maggots in there which turn into bluebottles. She said, "Oh, I meant to tell you. He's going out with Ellen. Tom and I are meeting them later at the pictures."

Midnight

Bloody *sacré bleu*. Dave the Laugh was supposed to really like me. How come he is going out with Ellen? How dare she go out with him? He is only just my ex.

1:00 a.m.

Still, I am going out with a Sex God. So I should be nice to everyone.

1:05 a.m.

Dave was a laugh, though. Even if he didn't make me go jelloid.

1:10 a.m.

I definitely go jelloid with the SG. Mmmmm, dreamy. But he doesn't make me laugh, he makes me stupid.

1:15 a.m.

I wonder if Dave the Laugh did that nibbling thing with Ellen?

1:20 a.m.

Looking through the window. Angus and Naomi are lurking

about on Mr and Mrs Next Door's garden wall. Angus is just dangling his paw down at the poodles. I hope there is not going to be group sex. (Whatever that is.)

1:25 a.m.
Perhaps I could have a jelloid boyfriend and an ordinary one for laughing with.

1:30 a.m.
Good grief! What in the name of pantyhose is going to happen next?!?

Georgia's Glossary

aggers · Agony. Like I said, no one has the time to say whole words, so aggers is short for agony. The unusually irritating among you might point out that aggers is actually longer than agony. My answer to that is – Haven't you got something else to do besides count letters?

billio · From the Australian outback. A billycan was something Aborigines boiled their goodies up in, or whatever it is they eat. Anyway, billio means boiling things up. Therefore, "my cheeks ached like billio" means... er... very achy. I don't know why we say it. It's a mystery, like many things. But that's the beauty of life.

Chrimbo hols · No one has the time to say long words, so Chrimbo is Christmas and hols is holidays. As in snog fest (snogging festival).

conk · Nose. This is very interesting historically. A very long time ago (1066) – even before my grandad was born – a bloke called William the Conqueror (French) came to England and shot our King Harold in the eye. Typical. And people wonder why we don't like the French much. Anyway, William had a big nose, and so to get our own back we called him William the Big Conk-erer. If you see what I mean. I hope you do because I am exhausting myself with my hilariosity and historiosity.

crèche · Kindergarten. Nursery. Playschool. Working muttis leave preschool children so they can "enjoy themselves" making things. A sort of day prison for toddlers.

dalek · In England we have this hilariously crap TV show called Dr Who where this bloke in a scarf goes time travelling. His archenemies are these senselessly violent creatures (no, not Angus surprisingly). They are called daleks. They're a form of robot. They have weird mechanical voices and a sort of gun sticking out of their head bits. They say, "Exterminate, exterminate!" Well, I told you it is crap.

DIY · Quite literally "Do It Yourself"! Rude when you think about it. Instead of getting someone competent to do things around the house (you know, like a trained electrician or a builder or a plumber), some vatis choose to do DIY. Always with disastrous results. For example, my bedroom ceiling has footprints in it because my vati decided he would go up on the roof and replace a few tiles. Hopeless.

duffing up · Duffing up is the female equivalent of beating up. It is not so violent and usually involves a lot of pushing with the occasional pinch.

geoggers · Geoggers is short for geography. Ditto blodge (biology) and lunck (lunch).

get off with · A romantic term. It means to use your womanly charms to entice a boy into a web of love. Oh, OK then – snogging.

gob · Gob is an attractive term for someone's mouth. For example, if you saw Mark (from up the road who has the biggest mouth known to womankind) you could yell politely, "Good Lord, Mark, don't open your gob, otherwise people may think you are a basking whale in trousers and throw a mackerel at you!" Or something else full of hilariosity.

goosegog · Gooseberry. I know you are looking all quizzical now. OK. If there are two people and they want to snog and you keep hanging about saying, "Do you fancy some chewing gum?" or "Have you seen my interesting new socks?" you are a gooseberry. Or for short a goosegog, i.e., someone who nobody wants around.

gorgey · Gorgeous. Like fabby (fabulous) and marvy (marvellous).

Jammy Dodger · Biscuit with jam in it. Very nutritious (ish).

jelly rabbit · Jelly made into a rabbit shape. Children like this sort of thing. You make some jelly and pour it into a rabbit-shaped mould. When it is set the child amuses itself by eating its bottom with a spoon. Or scooping out its eyes. Or, in Libby's case, by placing it in my bed.

knickers · Amercians (wrongly) call them panties. Knickers are a particular type of "panty" – huge and all encompassing. In the olden days (i.e., when Dad was born) all the ladies wore massive knickers that came to their knees. Many, many amusing songs were made up about knicker elastic breaking. This is because, as Slim, our headmistress, points out to anybody interested (i.e., no one), "In the old days people knew how to enjoy themselves with simple pleasures." Well, I have news for her. We modern people enjoy ourselves with knicker stories, too. We often laugh as we imagine how many homeless people she could house in hers.

jimjams · Pyjamas. Also pygmies or jammies.

lippy · Oh come on, you know what it is! Lipstick!! Honestly, what are you like?!

loo · Lavatory. In America they say "rest room", which is funny, as I never feel like having a rest when I go to the lavatory.

mincers · Cockney-type people in London use rhyming slang so that other (normal) people will not know what they are talking about. I don't know why – that is the beauty of the Cockneys. Mincers is short for mince pies, which rhymes with eyes. Get it?

Neighbours · A really crap daytime soap opera set in a suburb in Australia. Kylie Minogue was in it.

nub · The heart of the matter. You can also say gist and thrust. This is from the name for the centre of a wheel where the spokes come out. Or do I mean hub? Who cares. I feel a dance coming on.

nuddy-pants · Quite literally nude-coloured pants, and you know what nude-coloured pants are? They are no pants. So if you are in your nuddy-pants you are in your no pants, i.e., you are naked.

panstick · Stick of makeup that you use to cover up spots with. Or in my mutti's case to cover up the ravages of time and a careless attitude to skin care.

physio · A sort of massage. Short for physiotherapy. For instance, if you had a muscle that really, really hurt and that you wanted left alone, a cruel person (Miss Stamp) would insist on giving you a violent pummelling to make it better. Ha.

rate · To fancy someone. Like I fancy (or rate) the Sex God. And I certainly do fancy the SG, as anyone with the brains of an earwig (i.e., not Jas) would know by now. Phew – even writing about him in the glossary has made me go all jelloid. And stupidoid.

Reeves and Mortimer · Are a comedy double act. They are very mad indeed. But I like them.

rucky · A rucksack. Like a little kangaroo pouch you wear on your back to put things in. Backpack.

shirty · Flustered and twitchy and coming on all pompous.

Slack Alice · A Slack Alice is someone who is all stupid and nerdy. The sort of person who is always pulling their knickers up because they are too big (i.e., Jas).

umby · Umbrella. Also "brolly". Mary Poppins used to say "gamp" for umbrella. But what I say to that is – who cares?

wet · A drippy, useless, nerdy idiot. Lindsay.

whelks · A horrible shellfish thing that only the truly mad (like my grandad, for instance) eat. They are unbelievably slimy and mucuslike.

P.S.

Turn the page for a peek at my next book...

FABULOUSLY FUNNY BESTSELLER

'Knocked out by my nunga-nungas.'

You'll laugh your knickers off!

Louise Rennison

www.georgianicolson.com

Return of the loonleader

Thursday October 21st
1:00 p.m.

Looking out of my bedroom window, counting my unblessings. Raining. A lot. It's like living fully dressed in a pond.

And I am the prisoner of whatsit.

I have to stay in my room, pretending to have tummy lurgy, so that Dad will not know I am an ostracised leper banned from Stalag 14 (i.e. suspended from school). I'm not alone in my room, though, because my cat Angus is also under house arrest for his love romps with Naomi the Burmese sex kitten.

2:00 p.m.

They'll be doing PE now.

I never thought the day would come when I would long to hear Miss Stamp (Sports *Oberführer* and part-time lesbian) say, "Right, girls, into your PE knickers!"

But it has.

3:30 p.m.
All the Ace Gang will be thinking about the walk home from school.

Applying a touch of lippy. A hint of nail polish. Maybe even mascara because it is RE and Miss Wilson can't even control her tragic 70s hairdo let alone a class. Rosie said she was going to test Miss Wilson's sanity by giving herself a face mask in class and see if Miss Wilson has a nervy spaz.

Jas will be practising her pouting in case she bumps into Tom.

3:50 p.m.
How come Jas got off with cloakroom duty and I got banned? I am a whatsit... a scapethingy.

4:10 p.m.
Robbie the Sex God (MY NEW BOYFRIEND!!! Yesss and three times yesss!!!!!) will be going home from college now. Walking along in a Sex Goddy sort of way. A walking snogging machine.

4:30 p.m.
Mutti came in.

"Right, you can start making your startling recovery now, Georgia."

Oh cheers. Thanks a lot. Goodnight.

Just because Elvis Attwood, school caretaker from Planet of the Loons, tripped over his own wheelbarrow (when I told him Jas was on fire) I am banned from school.

Mutti rambled on, although she makes very little sense since Vati got home.

"It's your own fault, you antagonise him and now you are paying the price."

Yeah yeah, rave on.

4:45 p.m.
Phoned Jas.

"Jas."

"Oh, hi Gee."

"Why didn't you phone me?"

"You're phoning me. I would have got the engaged tone."

"Jas, please don't annoy me, I've only been speaking to you for two seconds."

"I'm not annoying you."

"Wrong."

"Well, I've only said about two words to you."

"That's enough."

Silence.

"Jas?"

Silence.

"Jas... what are you doing?"

"I'm not annoying you."

She drives me to the brink of madnosity. Still, I really needed to speak to her, so I went on. "It's really crap at home. I almost wish I hadn't been banned from school. How was Stalag 14? Any goss?"

"No, just the usual. Nauseating P. Green smashed a chair to smithereens and back."

"Really?! Was she fighting with it?"

"No, she was sitting on it having her lunch. It was the jumbo-sized Mars bar that did it. The Bummer Twins started singing "Who ate all the pies?" to her but Slim, our beloved headmistress, heard them and gave us a lecture about mocking the unfortunate."

"Were her chins going all jelloid?"

"Yeah. In fact it was Chin City."

"Fantastic. Are you all missing me? Did anyone talk about me or anything?"

"No, not really."

Charming. Jas has a lot of good qualities though, qualities you need in a bestest pal. Qualities like, for instance, going out with the brother of a Sex God. I said, "Has Hunky – I mean, Tom – mentioned anything that Robbie has said about me?"

"Erm... let me think."

Then there was this slurp slurp noise.

She was making slurping noises.

"Jas, what are you eating?"

"I'm sucking my pen top so I can think better."

Bloody *sacré bleu*, I have got *le idiot* for a pal. Forty-nine centuries of pen-sucking later she said, "No, he hasn't said anything."

7:00 p.m.
Why hasn't Robbie mentioned me? Hasn't he got snogging withdrawal?

8:00 p.m.
I can hear Vati singing "If I Ruled the World". Good Lord. I have only just recovered from a very bad bout of pretend lurgy. He has no consideration for others.

8:05 p.m.
The worsterosity of it is that the Loonleader (my vati) has returned from Kiwi-a-gogo land and I thought he would be there for ages. But sadly life was against me and he has returned. Not content with that he has insisted we all go to Och-aye land to "bond" on a family holiday.

But... na-na-na-na-na and who-gives-two-short-flying-pigs'-botties? because I live in Love Heaven.

Lalalalalalala.

I am the girlfriend of a Sex God!!!

Yesss!!! Result!!!!

Time Out
Paris

Penguin Books

PENGUIN BOOKS

Published by the Penguin Group
Penguin Books Ltd, 27 Wrights Lane, London W8 5TZ, England
Penguin Books USA Inc., 375 Hudson Street, New York, New York 10014, USA
Penguin Books Australia Ltd, Ringwood, Victoria, Australia
Penguin Books Canada Ltd, 10 Alcorn Avenue, Toronto, Ontario, Canada M4V 3B2
Penguin Books (NZ) Ltd, 182-190 Wairau Road, Auckland 10, New Zealand

Penguin Books Ltd, Registered Offices: Harmondsworth, Middlesex, England

First published 1989
First Penguin edition 1990
Second edition 1992
Third edition 1994
Fourth edition 1995
Fifth edition 1997
Sixth edition 1998
Seventh edition 1999
Eighth edition 2000
10 9 8 7 6 5 4 3 2 1

Reprographics by Quebecor Numeric, 37 av de la Marne, 92120 Montrouge. Printed and bound by Cayfosa-Quebecor, Ctra. de Caldes, Km 3 08130 Sta. Perpètua de Mogoda, Barcelona, Spain.